Poseidon's Wrath

Legend's Legacy #2

Amanda Witow

Prairie Owl Publishing

Cover images copyright to FreeImages.com/Marzena Osuchowicz, FreeImages.com/Shirley B, and FreeImages.com/Satoshi Tamura

Prairie Owl Publishing
2138 Wascana Greens, Regina, SK, S4V 2K9, Canada
contact@prairieowlpublishing.ca
www.prairieowlpublishing.ca

First Printing, 2018

ISBN 978-0-9952405-7-5

For my grandmothers, who were each
strong and wonderful in their own way

You will always be missed

Table of Contents

March 6, 1994

My darling children,

If you are reading this, then your mother and I are dead. Though the ouroboros hasn't marked anyone in our family for a few generations now, it seems like we never live very long. I hope your grandmother is raising you—she doesn't share our cursed blood, but she understands what it means. She can explain the mark to you, though I pray neither of you will be affected.

Our family has made many enemies over the years. If your mother and I are gone, then those vicious beasts and evil beings are to blame. Your mother believes one of the old gods is involved somehow. She says our family has too much bad luck to be a mere coincidence. I doubt any of them have survived to the modern age. But if there are any, you should search for those who owe our family a debt. Perhaps then you two will be able to finally break the curse on our family.

Jeremy, protect your sister. She will never be able to wield a sword or wrestle with monsters as you will. Keep her safe, but never underestimate what she can do. The women in our family are exceptionally capable.

Isabelle, keep your brother from being reckless. Even as toddlers, I can tell you will be the level-headed one. And my sweet girl, never be ashamed to ask for help. Your condition may prevent you from doing some things, but it doesn't have to define who you are.

I pray to the gods, old and new, that neither of you will be touched by this curse, or worse, marked by the ouroborous. But life, especially for those descended from the old gods, is never easy. It breaks my heart that I won't be there to help you.

Stay strong, my sweet children. We will be reunited in the afterlife.

Your loving father,
Vincent

Amanda Witow

Chapter One

A fierce sun burned down on an Ionian Sea as smooth and blue as the rarest of sapphires. The cloudless sky over Santa Maria di Leuca looked washed out and pale by comparison. Although the carefully laid cobblestone streets were hot enough Damien could feel the heat through his boots, a breeze blew across the water, a sharp reminder of the turning season.

Santa Maria di Leuca was a simple hamlet with a large church built high above the harbour. Droves of pilgrims clogged the streets. Locals and travelers alike wore a dizzying mix of styles and colours. Even their skin and hair seemed to cover the breadth of the rainbow. Which made Damien unremarkable as he strolled through the streets. Not even the black cloak around his shoulders, untouched by the dust and mud of his travels, and unmoving in the breeze, drew more than a passing glance.

He made his way toward the harbour and the sprawling inn sitting sentinel over it with light steps. Inside, a series of half-walls and archways broke the common room into sections. Several men sat in the area just beyond the door, a barmaid idly wiped down the bar, and another carried a tray laden with food and drink around a corner. No one paid him any mind. He paused only briefly before pressing deeper into the inn.

In a back section, tucked beside a wide set of stairs, he found his target.

A woman with long brown hair, half covered by a thick scarf, sat alone. Her haversack lay on the table next to the newly served food. Their eyes locked and she froze with her mug halfway to her mouth.

She hesitated before lowering the cup to the table. Her eyes flickered ever so briefly to the sword at his hip; his gaze strayed to the arquebus slung over the back of the chair beside her.

Damien forced his hand away from the hilt of his sword and smiled before approaching her table. She kicked a chair out for him. He caught and spun it so he could rest his arms across the back when he sat.

"Well now, this feels familiar," he said. He pulled his wide brimmed hat and cloak off, tossing them on the seat of an empty chair at the table.

Atalanta laughed. "We tried to kill one another last time—I almost drew my arquebus when you walked in."

"I'm a little surprised you didn't."

Her eyes widened and she pressed a hand to her chest. "You wound me, Damien. After all we've been through, you still don't trust me?"

"Mm." He grunted and waved for the barmaid. "Old habits die hard."

Atalanta's eyes narrowed for a moment before her face smoothed to a pleasant neutrality. "I suppose that's true."

Neither said anything else until after Damien ordered and the barmaid withdrew. In relative privacy once more, Atalanta withdrew a crumpled letter out of her bag. She smoothed it against the table before pushing it toward Damien. "What do you make of Calista's message?" she asked.

Damien briefly glanced at the letter before pulling his carefully folded copy from a pocket in his cloak. He unfolded it and placed it next to Atalanta's. Other than the salutation, they were identical. "It was certainly cryptic. Though after what happened to the previous Pythia, can you blame her?"

"I dislike being toyed with by priestesses and gods. I would have hoped Calista knew that."

"Letters can be read by anyone. A lot may have happened, but it has barely been a year since we met her. Do you honestly expect her to risk her life just because you want everything laid out for you?"

Atalanta squirmed in her chair, not meeting his gaze. "Fine," she grumbled. "I concede the point."

Damien gave her a small nod. He stood and switched his chair around when the barmaid approached with his food and drink. Atalanta let him eat in silence and he savoured every bite. There were enough chunks of vegetable and meat in the stew that there was very little broth left for the hard piece of bread which had come with it to sop up.

He leaned back in his chair with a satisfied sigh and waved a lazy hand to call a barmaid over. She was quick to respond. He ordered another round of drinks, but before he could retrieve the coins to cover it,

Atalanta pressed a small handful into the woman's hands.

"We'll also need two rooms for tonight," she said.

The barmaid nodded and gave them a bright smile as she tucked the coins into an apron pocket. She waited only a moment longer before leaving to fetch their drinks.

Damien's brows drew down and he studied his companion. Her clothes were just as dusty and mud-spattered as his own, but they were obviously new. No patches or stitched holes were visible, the leather was dyed a deep brown, and the scarf was a rich red.

"The last time I saw you, you barely had enough coin to make it back to Italy," he said, his voice soft and questioning.

"That was then." Atalanta took a noisy sip of the ale remaining in her tankard and then strained to see if the barmaid was returning with their drinks.

"I'm not comfortable receiving any benefit from...illegal means..." Damien's voice dropped to a whisper and he leaned forward.

Atalanta laughed. "Rest easy, hero. I earn my money fairly these days."

His eyes narrowed as he studied her. She still wouldn't meet his gaze. "And what exactly is it that you do?"

"None of your concern."

Damien's jaw clenched and he sucked in a sharp breath through his nose. When he opened his mouth to say something, Atalanta laughed and reached forward to pat his hand.

"I'm a personal guard for wealthy ladies in Tudela," she told him. "It isn't exciting work, most days. But it pays very well."

"That doesn't sound bad." He settled back in his chair, some of the tension draining from him.

"It isn't."

"Then why didn't you tell me about it when I first asked?"

Atalanta raised an eyebrow at him and he shifted uncomfortably, avoiding her gaze. She chuckled and asked, "We've exchanged, what is it now, two letters over the past year?"

"I believe so." Damien nodded.

"Sometimes it's hard to remember we aren't actually friends. Uneasy allies, of course, but we don't share everything with one another. Or are you wanting to tell me everything you've gotten up to this past year?" Atalanta asked, a smile quirking the corner of her lips up.

He ran a hand through his hair and shrugged a shoulder. "After Christmas in Rome, I had thought we might be more than just 'uneasy allies' to one another."

She tugged a chain out from under her vest, letting the gold and emerald ring on it dangle and spin. "I still think it's far too expensive. I may get paid well for my work, but not well enough to return the favour."

"The lock of hair you gave me means more than some trinket you might buy."

Atalanta snorted. "I can't believe you asked for that. It was the first time I'd ever taken a blade to my hair."

"All the more special then." Damien grinned.

"Hector was very amused I'd even agreed to it."

"How is your inamorato?"

She grimaced. "I told you before, he is only a friend."

"Given how much you talked about him last time we met, I thought you were only being modest. Or stubborn. Probably stubborn," he said with a lopsided grin.

"He is a very dear friend," she replied, crossing her arms over her chest. "Unlike some people I know, he is able to accept that I am uninterested in lovers, husbands, or any of that sort of thing."

"At least I don't have to worry about a jealous lover taking exception to my gift."

Atalanta snorted. "If I didn't know better, I would think *you* were trying to court me."

A tickle along Damien's neck made him roll his shoulders. He laughed, but it sounded false even to his own ears. "Can you imagine what our parents would say?"

"I expect they would start pulling me back into the Between to berate me for my errant ways."

"Have your dreams been safe, then?" he asked, a breathe of relief escaping for the safer topic of discussion.

Atalanta shrugged a shoulder. "If they wander, I have no memory of it. What of yours?"

"I never entered the Between in my dreams as fully as you did." He shook his head. "Though sometimes I have nightmares of that *daemon*. Nothing like when it actually stalked us, just normal dreams."

"Are you sure?" she asked, her voice sharp. "You didn't believe your dreams were wandering in the first place."

"Yes, I'm sure."

"How?"

Damien smiled a little at the snap in her voice. "I asked Calista."

"You've seen Calista since La Canea?" Atalanta asked, a flutter of sorrow crossing her face so quickly he wasn't sure if he imagined it or not.

"No. We exchange letters every few months. When the dreams first started, I asked for her advice."

"Oh."

He chuckled. "You almost seem disappointed. Did you want my dreams to be in danger again?"

"No, no. Nothing like that," Atalanta protested. "I just...I suppose I'm surprised you didn't mention it in one of your letters. Or in Rome."

"They're just regular dreams. There isn't actually anything to tell."

"I suppose..." Atalanta fell silent as the barmaid returned with their drinks.

"Your rooms are upstairs at the end of the hall, one on either side. And just so you know"—she gave them a knowing grin—"the only other guest for tonight is at the other end of the inn."

Atalanta's cheeks flushed. The barmaid gave them a wink before walking away and Atalanta buried her face in her hands.

"That was rude." Damien frowned at the retreating barmaid.

Atalanta's words were muffled by her hands and he had to ask her to repeat herself. "She thinks we're lovers trying to be discrete about our tryst."

Damien snorted. "What business of hers is it?"

Atalanta sighed, the flush draining from her cheeks. "I'm a woman, traveling alone, meeting a man at an inn. If we were a legitimate couple—or relatives—we would have arrived together. What else should she think?"

"I just meant, she should keep any such speculation to herself. I can't imagine many women dress in men's clothes to meet their lovers, so it's not like we've done anything to give anyone that impression. And even if we were, I doubt we'd appreciate her knowing smirks and winks."

"I expect she hopes we'll slip her a few extra coins to help make our affair easier."

Damien chuckled. "Then we can happily disappoint her."

Atalanta shook her head and muttered, "I can't wait for Calista to get here. People speculate less when she's with us."

Red light streaked through the open windows of the common room, bathing the evening crowds in a rosy glow. Atalanta slowly descended the stairs, letting the laughter and hum of people talking wash over her. She hadn't intended to fall asleep, but after the hearty meal and a couple of tankards of ale, Damien had suggested they wait in their rooms until the meeting time. She'd barely stretched out on her bed before she'd been asleep.

Three barmaids moved through the crowds like fish through water and for a moment Atalanta's heart squeezed. None of the women were blonde of any sort, and none had bells sewn into their skirts. Her momentary panic subsided and she smoothed her hands down her tunic before descending the rest of the way.

No one glanced up at her, and she craned her neck as she tried to spot Damien or Calista amongst the crowded tables. Even after weaving her way toward the door, she still hadn't spotted either companion. An annoyed huff escaped her. She forced her way toward the bar where the barmaids took turns filling tankards.

Atalanta gave them what she hoped was a friendly smile. "I'm looking for two people. A tall man with a black cloak, and a small woman with dark curls and a beautiful face."

The barmaids exchanged glances. One gave a dismissive sniff, gathered up several tankards, and, somehow, kept them all upright as she moved back into the press of people. Another shrugged and disappeared through a swinging door into what looked like a kitchen. The third pursed her lips and studied Atalanta.

"Can't say as I've seen anyone matching those descriptions. Though Dea mentioned a pair of lovers who rented rooms this afternoon. That fellow sounds like one of 'em, though the woman not so much."

Atalanta felt like her cheeks were on fire. "I was the woman at lunch, though we're not lovers."

The barmaid shrugged. "Ain't my place to judge, nor gossip. But as I said, I haven't seen either of those people tonight. You ain't the first to ask, though."

"What?"

The barmaid raised an eyebrow and tapped a finger against the bar. Atalanta stared at her, not understanding at first. She sighed and slid a coin over to the woman.

The barmaid snatched up the soldo and smiled. "A woman with dark skin and high cheekbones was asking after you and your friend. Said you might be looking for a pretty woman to be meeting you here tonight."

"Did she give you a name?"

The barmaid shook her head. "Paid for a private dining room and asked that you and your friend be shown to it when you came down. If you think she's the one you're looking for I can have my boy show you to the room."

"Yes, thank you."

The barmaid pushed open the door to the kitchen and shouted inside. A scrawny little boy scurried out; he'd barely appeared before the barmaid left to return to her duties. Atalanta gave him a warm smile, but he just stared at her with wide, solemn eyes.

His hands brushed against his pants, smearing grease more than anything, before he gestured for her to follow. He led her through the tables to a narrow door that opened into a hall with four doors along one side. The lanterns on the walls had yet to be lit and the dying light of the sun struggled through a grimy window at the far end.

The boy didn't seem bothered by the shadows clinging like spiderwebs to the walls as he led Atalanta to the last door. A quick knock was answered with a faint call to enter from the other side. The boy opened the door, nodded his head in an approximation of respect, and scurried back down the hall and out to the common room.

Atalanta pushed the door open wider and peered inside with a hand resting on the hilt of a dagger at her hip.

The room held a round table with cushion-covered stools tucked beneath its edge. A shelf along the inside wall held an assortment of bread, cheese, fruits, and dried meat. The outside wall had two narrow windows that had been opened to catch the last of the sunlight, as well as any breezes blowing off the harbour. A dark skinned woman with a broad face, thin lips, and a cinched waist carried a small bread trencher with food on it toward the table. She gave Atalanta a tight smile as she passed by, her eyes flicking briefly to the dagger still gripped in Atalanta's hand.

"Come, enjoy some food." She nodded toward the things laid out on the shelf before settling onto a seat at the table.

"I'm surprised to see you here, Hazina," Atalanta said. She stepped into the room and pushed the door closed behind her. "After Methoni, I thought our paths would never cross again."

Hazina bowed her head slightly. "Nor did I—but due to some complications, Calista asked that I attend this meeting in her stead."

Atalanta idly browsed the food, popping a small wedge of cheese into her mouth while she gathered a small collection savoury meats and honeyed fruit on a piece of bread. She settled onto a stool opposite Hazina and asked, "How long has Calista known she wouldn't be able to attend?"

Hazina made a wavering gesture with her hand. "She told me of this a few months ago."

Atalanta's mouth tightened. "So she lied in her letters when she said she would meet us here."

"Calista is no longer a priestess-in-training," Hazina said, her voice flat and eyes dark as she met Atalanta's gaze. "She has responsibilities beyond chaperoning you and your hunter. Responsibilities that keep her busy."

"Her letter to us said there is an issue of vital importance, to be dealt with as promptly as possible. I would think something like that would merit more than a misleading letter and a proxy," Atalanta countered.

Hazina's lips curled in a mockery of a smile. "From what I understand, this is not the sort of task where Calista would be particularly helpful. Which is yet another reason why she asked me to be here instead."

Before Atalanta could object, the door to the room opened again. The grubby little boy gestured Damien inside. His already large eyes widened further at the coin Damien pressed into his hand. His gaping mouth worked as the door was closed to shut him out.

Damien smiled warmly and settled onto a stool. "It is good to see you again, Hazina."

"And you, Damien."

Atalanta crossed her arms and spread a glare between both of them. "Am I the only one who actually expected Calista to grace us with her presence?"

"I expected our little priestess, but she is the new Pythia. It makes sense for her to send someone in her stead," Damien said, his eyes roving across the delicacies on the shelf.

Atalanta muttered to herself, but neither Hazina nor Damien paid her any mind. He rose and piled meat and cheese onto a large piece of bread before asking, "What task has Calista called us all together to take care of?"

"There are many disturbances across the Mediterranean. Strange storms, incursions of sirens, earthquakes, and other turmoil ravage the area. Few have connected all these together, though individually they are generally said to be the wrath of the Christ god on sinners," Hazina explained, her hands clasped together on top of the table.

"It sounds more like things Poseidon stirs up," Damien mused.

"Indeed. Poseidon, or someone wielding powers similar to his, has become very active of late. Calista has spent much time and energy trying to uncover the motivation behind these attacks on humanity by the god, but it is shrouded from her. She only knows that unless these actions are stopped, then before the year is out, hundreds of thousands will be dead. And twice that many every year after until no man can claim residence around the Mediterranean."

Atalanta blinked, her anger forgotten. "She can't expect us to kill a

11

god. Even a weakened god on the edge of the eternal sleep would be all but impossible to kill."

Damien settled back at the table with his food. "She didn't say 'kill Poseidon.' Simply stop him."

"Really? Can you think of another way to stop an angry god from wiping out humanity?" Atalanta snapped at him.

"Well...no..."

Atalanta turned her anger on Hazina. "I don't suppose Calista deigned to give us any ideas about how to stop this onslaught?"

For the first time that night, Hazina looked uneasy. "She had one vision she thought might be of use. It meant nothing to me, or her, though she insists it will make sense when it can be of use."

"Well that's wonderful," Atalanta said, the sarcasm dripping like molten lead. "Let's hear this useless bit of help then."

Hazina's mouth pinched, but she didn't argue. She cleared her throat and recited:

> *Where black sails fly, a northern son resides;*
> *Though exiled and cursed, do not spurn his hand.*
>
> *When broken and sore a rest will appear,*
> *Do not take the seed, else the world's rest will turn.*
>
> *Among stone fingers, where cormorants fly,*
> *The lonely leaf will lead you astray.*
>
> *Where the old man stalks through ruins,*
> *Do not fear injury, else worse will be your fate.*
>
> *The conquered's daughter must lead through shadows*
> *To avert the hand of he who watches vows.*
>
> *And last, where disaster and death awaits;*
> *Ignore the lost and distrust the kin.*

Silence filled the room, so thick it seemed to trap Hazina's words, hovering over their heads like a threat. Even the noise of the common room faded away. Damien finally broke the silence when he asked, "Any theories on the meaning?"

Hazina shook her head. "I'm afraid not. Calista thought black sails might refer to a pirate ship, but she has no idea who—or what—a 'northern son' might be. And all further speculation is as incomplete and unhelpful."

"It almost seems to get more obtuse the further into it you got," Atalanta said, her fingers drumming lightly on the table.

Hazina let a little sigh escape as she nodded. "Apparently that is common for prophecies which span any length of time. The further away something is, the less certain it is that the event will even occur. Prophetic visions see a possible future, and generally the most likely, but they are no guarantee something will happen."

"So, how do we even start this?" Damien asked.

"There is a place up the coast which has lost several members of the community to suspicious circumstances. Calista was able to see that we will discover something there, though not what. She believes going there will set us on the right path."

Atalanta growled softly, the sound vibrating in her chest. "It feels like walking into a trap."

"You think Calista is attempting to trick you?" Hazina asked, genuine surprise making her eyes wide.

"Not a trap laid by Calista, but one laid by the Fates. Not a verse of the prophecy had anything even remotely good about it. High costs to be paid, swift death and disaster. It all feels like some cruel joke."

"I cannot argue with your reasoning," Hazina said slowly. "But I do know Calista would not send you into potential danger without a very good reason."

"What Calista considers a good reason, and what I consider one are two very different things," Atalanta said dryly.

Chapter Two

Before dawn, when grey still mingled with pink in the sky, the trio of companions left Santa Maria di Leuca. The faint breeze blowing off the crystal waters filled Damien with an eagerness for the adventure ahead. He glanced behind him at Hazina and Atalanta—neither woman looked particularly happy.

Hazina wore a simple, two-layered dress with a wide belt that covered almost her entire abdomen. Her over-sized satchel was tied to the belt, though she kept a tight fist around the straps. He wondered if she had brought more than two gowns. If this quest proved to be anything like the last, she would be wearing tatters by the end.

A faint clinking punctuated every other step Hazina took. She shifted the satchel and the sound stopped. She blew out a breath and clenched a fist in her skirts so they didn't drag in the dirt. Atalanta smirked and gave her tunic a satisfied tug before lengthening her stride to draw even with Hazina.

Her voice was too low for Damien to hear, but she gestured to Hazina's satchel and then to her own bag. Hazina's lips pressed and she shook her head firmly. Atalanta shrugged and fell back a pace. Hazina's gaze seemed to dare Damien to say anything.

He slowed, letting Hazina catch up and pass him. Atalanta fell into step beside him without a word. Strands of hair had escaped her scarf and fluttered around her face in a mockery of the snake heads she kept hidden. Her eyes were bloodshot and, every couple of steps, she pressed her fist against her mouth to stifle a yawn. Damien gave her a bright smile, but she just glowered in return.

He shook his head and called to Hazina, "Where exactly are we going?"

Hazina paused and turned to face Damien and Atalanta. "There is a...collection of homes just outside the city of Otranto, about a day's walk up the road."

Damien frowned. "Why didn't we meet in Otranto then? It would have been simpler—"

"The people of Otranto are not trusting of outsiders," Hazina cut in. "It took eleven long months for the city to be freed from Mehmet the Conqueror's forces. Many people were murdered in that time."

"We're not outsiders. We—well, I'm Italian," he said.

Atalanta scoffed. "You think that will make them warmer? She just said it took almost a whole year for the *Italian* forces to come to their aid."

"There are constantly other battles to be fought against the Ottomans," Damien said defensively.

"Nevertheless, Calista and I did not think it wise to meet in Otranto," Hazina said, her voice crisp.

"So why are we going there now?" Atalanta asked.

"It seems to be central to the deaths and disappearances happening along the coast."

Atalanta's eyebrows shot up. "Deaths and disappearances?"

"Men have been…murdered. Mauled. While women have been taken," Hazina said, her mouth twisting like she'd bitten into something rotten. "Local authorities are calling it pirate attacks. Though some believe it to be petty attacks by the Turks."

Damien squinted out over the blue waters stretching away on their right. The gentle waves rippling toward the shore seemed peaceful and inviting, but a cool shiver down his spine said there were unseen dangers lurking just beyond sight. "How much of the coast has suffered?" he mused.

"All of it."

Atalanta coughed. "How much is 'all of it?'"

Hazina gestured at the shoreline. "Anywhere touching the sea has been affected in one way or another. If people realized how far it spread, they would not believe it to be the work of pirates."

"Do you know what it is then?" Damien asked.

"No."

Atalanta crossed her arms and glowered at Hazina. "It seems strange that Calista's vision, or prophecy, or advice, or whatever we're going to call it, starts with what sounded like pirates, yet you're sure it isn't."

"It might not be pirates, however it sounds," Damien pointed out.

"And Calista was able to see enough to know that whatever we find outside of Otranto will set our path, but it is not until we are already on our way that her prophecy starts."

Atalanta squeezed her eyes shut and pressed a hand to her temple. "This is so confusing. How does Calista know that? It sounds like her visions are vague, but this is a very specific sequence of events."

Hazina made a wavering gesture with her hand. "I studied a different form of magic, and am not inclined to reenter apprenticeship."

"You didn't ask?" Atalanta scoffed.

"I understand there are some mysteries which cannot be explained to a layman. And I understand some things must simply be taken on faith."

The look Hazina leveled at Atalanta should have hit like a slap across the face, but Atalanta just smirked back. Damien shook his head and muttered under his breath about troublesome snakes.

The three companions fell silent and resumed walking. They continued in silence that grew more tense the further they went. An occasional traveler headed back toward Santa Maria di Leuca passed them. None stopped to gossip, and most made a point of drawing as far from the trio as the road would allow.

Damien couldn't blame them. He found himself wishing he could pull away from the tension that seemed ready to drop and shatter into a million glistening fragments that would shred the flesh of any foolish enough to be nearby.

The sun was half below the horizon before Hazina led them off the main road. A small cluster of buildings huddled next to the sea. Ten houses. A small church, barely large enough to hold a dozen people, and what looked to be a communal barn. All of the buildings were freshly whitewashed and in good repair, but there was no one in sight.

"Looks like we'll be sleeping beneath the hedges tonight," Damien said.

Atalanta rolled her eyes. "You are surprisingly spoilt sometimes." She didn't wait for Hazina and Damien as she walked toward the church.

16

The ground sloped steeply and spiky grass grew in small patches. She was halfway down the incline before Damien and Hazina started their own descent. The grass crunched beneath their feet, breaking up the soft susurration of gravel shifting underfoot. Atalanta stopped in front of the church and waited for them to join her.

A cross made of dark wood marked the peak of the building, and the doors were carved with religious motifs. Though the whitewash looked recent, the carvings were weathered and many were indistinct. Even down amongst the buildings, no one was visible and none of the houses had lights in their windows.

Atalanta knocked on the church's door. Damien waited beside her while Hazina wandered around the side of the building. She had only been gone from sight for a moment before she called for them to join her.

Seven fresh graves lay on the far side of the church.

The oldest of them, with the rocky dirt almost indistinguishable from the unturned ground around it, was marked with a carved stone cross. Two others had carved wooden crosses sitting sentinel over the mounds. Then there were three graves marked only by two planks nailed together. The newest grave, with dark earth and the scent of salt and dirt still clinging to it, had no markings at all.

"Begone, demons!"

The shout and a burst of flames drove Damien, Hazina, and Atalanta back a step as a man ran toward them. He thrust a torch toward them with one hand and rattled a set of prayer beads in the other. Behind him, two more men hurried forward with torches in hand. Between the dying sunlight and the darting torch, the men's faces were lost in flickering shadows.

"Do we look like demons to you?" Hazina asked, drawing back another step.

One of the men swished his torch through the air and growled. "Demons can be winsome creatures as often as monsters from the darkest of nightmares."

Damien tracked the movement behind the torches as best he could, shifting to position himself between Hazina and the men. "Do I look like a winsome creature to you?"

"You could be here to tempt our women into witchcraft and unholy trysts," the third man shouted. His voice was higher and cracked on the last word.

Atalanta pursed her lips and eyed the torches with distaste. "Short of letting you set us on fire, how can we assure you that we aren't demons? Or demon-possessed?"

"Or in league with demons," Hazina hastily added.

The men paused in their torch waving and drew together. Though they kept their voices low, snatches of their conversation drifted to Atalanta, Hazina, and Damien.

"Throw them in the sea…"

"That wouldn't work. Our torments come from the sea."

"Bleed them…"

"Test of iron…"

Hazina shifted closer to the wall formed by Atalanta and Damien and whispered, "I do not like the sound of where this is going."

Damien shrugged and cast her a quick glance before returning his gaze to the still arguing men. "Any tests or assurances we might suggest will be met with suspicion. A demon wouldn't suggest a test it wasn't confident it could pass. It's best to wait and see what they're going to do."

"And, if it's unreasonable, we run as fast as we can away from here," Atalanta added.

"Enough conspiring!" One of the men growled and shoved his torch toward them again. "Into the church with you."

The three men herded them toward the church door and Atalanta asked, "Where is your priest?"

"Dead. Killed by you or your demon-kin." The man snarled and shoved his torch so far forward it hit Atalanta's arm.

She sucked in a sharp breath and flinched away, clamping a hand over her burnt sleeve.

The other two men opened the door and set their torches inside metal brackets on the walls. The light filled the small space with red and yellow flickering, revealing simple benches and a rough-hewn table meant to be the altar. A narrow white cloth beneath a small metal cross draped down to pool on the floor in front of the altar.

When the third man entered the temple he handed his torch to one of the others and pulled the door shut. He grunted and lifted a heavy wooden bar to slam it down over the door. His grin was wide and crazed when he turned back to stare at Damien, Hazina, and Atalanta.

Without the torches being waved about, the men were clearly visible, and obviously related. One of the men looked only a bit older than Damien and Atalanta, though grey had already started to thread its way through his brown hair. Another was barely a man at all, with the thin awkwardness of a fast-growing child. The final man, the one staring at them with a hateful hunger, had a heavy mix of grey in his hair and lines creasing his face so he looked like a bit of forgotten wood, weathered and dark.

"Sit," the oldest man snapped. "We'll test you one at a time."

He didn't wait for them to respond before grabbing Atalanta's burnt arm and dragging her toward the altar. A shove and kick at the back of her knees forced her to kneel before the white cloth and crucifix. Damien took a step forward before the middle man placed a restraining hand on his arm, though his brow was furrowed and mouth pinched.

The old man's angry mutterings almost covered the rising sound of hissing and Damien gritted his teeth. If Atalanta's snakes roused, there would be nothing they could do to convince the men they weren't demons.

A heavy thud and grunt pulled Damien out of his worry. The old man had slammed his prayer beads against Atalanta's chest, driving the tiny wooden crucifix into the hollow of her throat.

Atalanta jerked away and coughed. "That's going to leave a bruise. No need to be so rough."

The old man snarled and grabbed a handful of her hair, yanking her head back as he dragged her toward a basin of water set off to the side. She wrapped a hand around her loose hair and winced. Damien's fists clenched and unclenched over and over as he struggled to keep from interfering. The need to let the men assuage their fears battled with his desire to rip the old man away from Atalanta. When the man slammed Atalanta's head down into the basin, Damien let out a surprised shout.

"He's going to kill her!" Hazina shouted as Atalanta thrashed.

The old man pulled her head up for just long enough that everyone could hear her cough up a lungful of water before slamming her face back into the water.

"Stop this," Damien demanded, his voice bouncing off the walls of the church. The man who had been poised to hold him back leapt forward and grabbed the old man. The boy darted up to help and they dragged him away from Atalanta and the basin.

"Stop, father! This is too far!" the other man said. The old man just roared incoherently as he struggled against them. The old man's flailing fists landed with heavy thuds against the body and faces of the other two. The boy staggered back from a blow to his eye, but quickly leapt forward to hold him again.

Damien ran to Atalanta's side. She had barely been able to lift her head out of the water since being freed. He slid an arm around her as she coughed and spluttered. The oily water had soaked into her clothes and hair, but he lifted her to her feet anyway. She shot him a withering glare and tried to take a step on her own. Her legs buckled and she fell back against him. Her hair rustled as snakes tried to wind their way out of the confining scarf.

Damien made soothing noises and led Atalanta to one of the benches. He ran a gentle hand over her hair and tried not to wince when the snakes bit him. Hazina stepped forward and positioned herself between them and the three men still struggling with each other. She threw her shoulders back and held her head high as she stared down the old man's hatred.

"They took my daughter—your wife! And you're worried I might kill one of them?" the old man bellowed.

"It wasn't them, Grandfather," the young man said. Already his cheek and eye were darkening into a nasty bruise.

The old man roared. His arms stretched toward Damien, Hazina, and Atalanta as if he could rip them limb from limb. The other two forced him back until they had him pressed against the opposite wall. All three panted and sweat dripped from their brows, but still the feverish light in the old man's eyes shone as strong as ever.

"Do not presume to mete out divine justice, lest your soul be so tainted you will never know the graces of heaven," Hazina said, her voice ringing through the room.

For a moment longer, the old man glared at her, then he lowered his eyes. Though his jaw clenched and his face was red, he slumped against the wall. She nodded once and relaxed.

"Are you satisfied?" Damien demanded. He stood and glared at them over Hazina's head. "Or do you plan on torturing us until we're so beaten and tired we confess to a crime we didn't commit, just so you will kill us and end the torment?"

"Do you hear that, old man?" the middle-aged man asked. "What you're after isn't justice. It isn't even revenge. It is torture and murder."

"I'll avenge her death, even if you won't," the old man muttered, keeping his head down.

"They're just travelers, Grandfather. They know nothing of our troubles," the boy pleaded.

The old man didn't respond, but his shoulders fell. He slid down the wall and sat in a crumpled pile, face buried in his hands. The young man sat next to him and placed a hand on his knee as he whispered. A ragged sob tore from the old man.

Hazina cleared her throat. "We had heard pirates frequently attack here, and had thought to offer our assistance. Though it seems things are far worse than we were led to believe."

The other man ran a hand over his face and sighed. "We have asked for assistance numerous times. They tell us these attacks are the work of pirates. But pirates don't gnaw on the bodies of the dead. Or take a single person from a locked home and leave the others."

"Was it your priest who thought it the work of demons?" Hazina asked.

"Aye. He had his faith and the trappings of his position when he went to confront the sea demons. It should have protected him. Yet the morning after he went, we found him. Well…half of him." The middle-aged man shuddered and sat down abruptly on another bench.

"Do you know why the pirates, or demons, have attacked here so frequently? Seven graves, in what I expect has only been a month, is a steep price for such a small community to pay," Damien asked, relaxing only slightly. None of the men seemed likely to be a threat in the immediate future, though he worried the older man would make another attempt at a later time.

"Demons and witches must strike at the most righteous first, to weaken the resolve of humanity as a whole," the old man said, raising his head. His eyes were still tight and angry, but his voice was soft and weary.

The middle-aged man tsked. "Truthfully we do not know why these demons have struck so heavily against us. But the light will have left us and it will be true night soon—if it isn't already. You might stay in the church until the sun rises again. I recommend using the bar to keep out demons. Or anyone else intent on mischief."

The old man grumbled but didn't say anything else as he slowly pushed himself to his feet.

Damien inclined his head a little. "Thank you. I am Damien, this is my sister, Atalanta, and our dear friend, Hazina."

The ghost of a smile crossed the lips of the middle-aged man. "I am Cleon Pennas," he told them. "This is my son, Atelo, and my wife's father, Spiro Artino."

Atalanta leaned to the side to peer around Damien and Hazina at the three men. "Those are very Greek names for the Italian coast."

Atelo smiled shyly at her. "Our forefathers came from Greece. In fact, every family living here are descended from those that once lived there. Otranto was once the famous city Hydrus, you know."

"There is a familiarity among families descended from Greece that we do not find among other peoples," Cleon added.

The corners of Damien's mouth twitched downward and he turned to exchange a puzzled glance with Atalanta. Before either could say anything, Hazina said, "I do not mean to be rude, but it is late and we have had a...tiring day. May we continue our conversation in the morning?"

"Of course," Cleon answered immediately. He pushed himself to his feet and gestured for Spiro and Atelo to precede him out of the church. Spiro didn't move until Atelo took his arm. Once they had left and closed the door, a loud click made it obvious that Damien, Hazina, and Atalanta were being locked in. Damien moved to the door and replaced the wooden bar across it.

The peaceful quiet of the the church slowly returned and the three companions took a moment to soak it in. Without the need for a discussion, they each claimed a bench and made themselves as comfortable as they could in the sparse space. Sleep was surpassingly quick to claim them all.

Chapter Three

A sliver of light crept past the shuttered windows and filled the church with a dim, silvery glow. Atalanta pressed gentle fingers to her throat and winced at the tenderness where Spiro had slammed the crucifix. She pushed herself up and bit her lip to keep from groaning. Everything hurt. She wouldn't have thought the walk or the brief abuse from the previous night could be so hard on her body.

"I'm getting old," she muttered.

Her clothes were stiff, and cold, and clung to her clammy skin. She shivered and worked through a quick series of stretches before searching her haversack for fresh clothes. With clean leathers in hand, she moved as quickly as she could to change.

Neither Hazina nor Damien stirred by the time she finished. Atalanta slid a hand along the bench and moved toward a window. It took a moment of fumbling in the dim light before she was able to find the latch for the shutters and open the window.

Outside, the world was bathed in gold. Pale sand and stones looked like the surface of the sun itself while the gentle ripples of the water beyond could have been liquid metal. Even the grass and scrub were various shades of yellow and orange.

She breathed deeply, taking in the scent of dew and salt and copper-tainted peat. It was a peculiar combination, but not unpleasant. As she stood at the window breathing in the fresh air, the colours shifted. Gold faded away, burning the dew off the leaves, as the day prepared for a thick warmth, as if to make up for the chill reminder on the previous day's breeze.

Atalanta turned away from the window when she heard a grunt and rustle of clothing behind her. Both Hazina and Damien were getting up. He stretched and moved about the church to warm his muscles, much as she had. Hazina, meanwhile, sat on a bench and ran her fingers through the hundreds of braids in her hair, before twisting it up and pinning it back into place. Atalanta pulled dried meat and small, hard buns out of her bag and passed the food around.

They had barely started eating when the church door banged against the bar holding it closed. Whoever was on the other side paused and then rapped hesitantly on the wood. Damien, with a chunk of bread held between his teeth, lifted the bar aside and opened the door.

Atelo stood there. His face had been creased with worry, but melted into a smile as soon as he saw Damien. "Good morning. My father thought you would like to see where we found the bodies…" He trailed off as he glanced past Damien to see Atalanta and Hazina staring at him. "Uh… that is… if you're still willing to help us."

"Of course," Damien said around his mouthful. He swallowed and gestured for Atelo to enter. "We're almost finished, then we can go."

Atelo nodded and stepped inside, though he remained by the door as the three companions finished their simple meal. Atalanta could feel his eyes following their every movement, though whenever she glanced toward him he dropped his gaze and flushed. It made the hair on the back of her neck tingle, but she doubted he meant anything malicious by it.

Once they were finished, Atelo led them out amongst the small cluster of buildings. The sounds of people moving about and talking in hushed voices drifted from the homes. Only a few brave souls had ventured outside to watch as Atalanta, Hazina, and Damien followed Atelo toward the beach. Several of them made the sign of the cross when the small group passed by.

It didn't take long to reach the expanse of sand and small rocks behind the row of houses. Atelo stopped and glanced at them. If they hadn't been told about sinister things happening on the shore, it would have looked like any other.

"When was the last death?" Hazina asked, her eyes following the slight curve of the land. It stretched away in both directions for some distance before curving back and out of sight.

"Our priest was found three days ago. My mother went missing five days before that, and a boy I had grown up with was found four days before she was taken."

Atalanta shook her head. "I doubt we're going to find tracks or any other sign of the attackers after this many days."

"There never were any signs to see," Atelo said, gesturing at the shore around them. "The attackers must be very clever, or not of the mortal world."

"What can you show us, then?" Hazina asked. She lifted her skirts as she moved down the beach so they wouldn't drag in the sand or soak up the waves gently lapping at the shore. "Or did you simply wish to show us the sun rising?"

"Uh..." Atelo flushed and chewed on his lip. After a moment his eyes lit up. "We've found all the bodies in the same spot."

Atalanta coughed and cocked an eyebrow. "You didn't think that was the first thing you should show us?"

"I'm sorry," he said, his eyes widening and shoulders hunching. "I'll take you there now."

He didn't wait for a response before turning and almost running down the beach. Hazina blew out an annoyed breath and hiked her skirts higher before jogging after him. Atalanta and Damien fell into step behind her.

The young boy led them along the shore until only the church's steeple was visible. He stopped in front of a large rock propped against a smaller one. The flat top stretched out over the water, making a faux cliff as high as Damien's shoulder. Waves lapped directly against the bottom stone. The water beneath the rocks frothed with each pulse of the waves, yet rolled serenely up the sand on either side.

"Where..." Hazina paused to take a gulp of breath, "where exactly were the bodies found?"

Atelo panted a little and pointed to the small area between the bottom of the overhang and the waves. "The bodies have always been in the water—the waves keep them trapped there."

"Any sign that this is where they were killed? Or were the bodies tossed in the sea for the currents to carry here?" Damien asked.

"What sort of sign?" Atelo scratched behind an ear.

"Blood on the sand? Scuffs and grooves from where a person might have fought or been dragged?"

He shook his head. "No. But Grandfather says the current doesn't flow right to have carried the bodies here."

Damien nodded absently and stepped into the water. He crouched to look under the protruding rock. Water soaked into his clothes, but he didn't even seem to notice as he ran his fingers across dark striations on the stone. After a few moments he straightened and nodded to Atelo. "Thank you for bringing us here. We'll need to look around for a bit longer. You should wait for us at the church."

"O-oh...I shouldn't wait here until you finish?"

"No. We'll let you—and everyone else—know what we find, back at the church."

Atelo's shoulders slumped and he gave a lethargic nod of his head before trudging back the way they had come. He glanced over his shoulder frequently until he was out of sight.

Once he was far enough away that he wouldn't overhear, Damien chuckled. "I think he was hoping to spend the day with us."

Atalanta waved her hand through the air as if to dismiss the boy's presence and the topic of conversation. "Well he's gone now. So, tell us what you've found, Damien."

"There's blood on the rocks."

"Not surprising given that they told us the last body was half-gone," Hazina said. She walked to where the back of the rock rested against the sand and put a foot on the stone, as if to test its stability.

Damien shook his head and stepped out of the water, wringing the edge of his tunic out. "It was more than just blood from wounds rubbing against the rocks. Much more. It looked like blood had been sprayed across the underside—and more than once. The dead, and quite possibly the missing too, have to have been lured beneath the rock and had their throats slit."

"Or torn out," Atalanta added.

"It's certainly messy enough under there for it." Damien nodded.

Atalanta wrinkled her nose. "We're going to spend the night out here and hope we catch these beasts or people in the act, aren't we?"

Damien grinned. "Of course. Where's your sense of adventure?"

"Back in Placoleum, regretting I ever met you and Calista," she grumbled. Damien simply laughed.

Hazina looked down at them from the rocky overhang. She gestured away from the sea and said, "There is a line of brush up the beach which looks to have rocky ground rather than sand on the other side of them. It might prove to be a good vantage point."

Atalanta moved up to the brush and pushed past. Pebbles and stones mixed with sand to create a gritty surface, but the scrub wasn't so heavy she couldn't see through it when she crouched down. "I can see you from here, can you see me?" she called down to Damien and Hazina.

"I can see your scarf," Damien answered. "Though in the dark I suspect it won't stand out quite so much."

Hazina nodded. "Even from here you are hard to see."

"How quickly could we reach the shore though?" Damien asked.

Atalanta pushed off the ground and leapt over the line of scrub. The sloped sand slipped under her feet and she stumbled. She let the momentum pull her to the ground and turned the fall into a somersault that carried her back to her feet. It took seven more steps to reach Damien, though she skidded past him and into the shallows before she could stop.

"Not too long," she said, her breath panting a little as she tried to shake the sand out of her hair and clothes.

"First line of defense will need to be your arquebus then. I don't know how well we could fight if we're skidding around on the sand," Damien said, his eyes laughing at her.

Atalanta glared at him and moved out of the water, trying to ignore the sand rubbing between her clothes and skin.

"Since we last met, I have learnt how to throw knives," Hazina added, pushing her belt down to reveal a band of small knives around her stomach.

"Good." Atalanta smiled. "I can almost guarantee a kill with a shot, but it is a slow process to reload and fire again. You'll be much quicker."

Damien let out a dramatic sigh. "I suppose that leaves me to take the tumble down the beach and fight whomever we find hand-to-hand."

"Well if you don't want to use your over-sized sword, you could always hit them with your head. It's certainly hard enough," Atalanta said dryly.

Damien laughed and the three companions began the walk back to the church. They had only gone a few paces down the beach when Hazina paused and looked back at the rock with a frown.

"Is something wrong?" Damien asked.

"I am unsure," Hazina said. "There is a sense of… how do I say it in Italian… watching danger?"

Atalanta's eyes raked over the scrub, beach, and water. There was nothing out of place that she could see. A distant bird wheeled overhead and the sea whispered with each wave as the breeze toyed with the stiff scrub. "I'm not seeing anything," she said.

"It is not a presence here, but a sense of a mistake about to be made," Hazina tried to explain. She grunted and tugged at her skirts. "Even after years of speaking this language, I still am not always able to explain myself. Especially when it comes to things outside the mortal realm."

"Do you know what to do? To prevent this mistake?" Damien asked.

Hazina shook her head. "Unless I can know what the mistake is, I will not be able to prevent it. But I feel that if we leave now our surprise this night will be ruined."

"Ambush," Atalanta corrected softly. "Our ambush tonight."

"Yes, thank you."

The three companions stared at the scene before them, each trying to puzzle out what they were forgetting. After several long moments Atalanta let out an annoyed tsk. "Our footprints."

"What?" Damien's forehead crinkled.

"Look at the sand. If anyone were to come by this way they would be able to see exactly where we were looking."

Hazina snapped her fingers. "Of course. The people of Otranto are far too frightened to come wandering around out here."

Damien stared at the tracks in the sand. The trail leading to and from the rock was simple enough, but the sand between beach and scrub had been thoroughly churned up. "I'm not sure how we're to cover them all."

"Leave that to me," Hazina said. She opened her satchel and pulled out a small ceramic ball. It was slightly misshapen and had a small glob of wax on one end. Wavy grey lines were painted on the reddish-brown surface. The faint clinking of ceramics bumping together came from the satchel before Hazina closed it again.

She crouched down and scooped up a handful of sand. With the ball in one hand and the sand in the other, she straightened and took a step forward. Her voice whispered out as she spoke in an unfamiliar language. It flowed much smoother from her tongue than Italian did, sounding almost lyrical. On the last word, she crushed the ball in her hand and let the shards drop to the beach while the sand poured out of her other hand.

A wisp of smoke rose from the shards and danced into the air, turning and twisting until it took on an almost human form. The smoke-being was only a few inches tall and hovered at eye height for a moment. It gave a little bow and then darted away from them toward the rock.

Sand flowed and smoothed behind the smoke-being as if an invisible hand were brushing across it. A few swirls and loops later, the beach before them looked completely untouched. The being returned to Hazina and bowed again.

"That's amazing, Hazina," Damien exclaimed.

"It is…very difficult…to keep the spirit bound," Hazina said through gritted teeth. Sweat dripped down her brow and she wiped it away with an impatient hand.

Atalanta placed a hand on her shoulder. "I'll guide you so you can keep an eye on it. We'll need to cover our tracks for a little further."

Hazina gave a small nod and they slowly continued back to the hamlet. They were able to go almost twenty feet before Hazina stumbled and fell on her back. As soon as her line of sight broke from the smoke-being it dispersed into nothingness.

"Are you all right?" Damien asked, crouching beside her.

"Yes. Tired," she responded, using his help to sit back up.

"You did well—I think we've covered our tracks far enough to not raise any suspicion in our query," Atalanta said her eyes roving across the smooth sand between them and the distant stones.

"How did you summon and control that spirit?" Damien helped Hazina back to her feet and kept a hand nearby as she brushed herself off.

"I believe I told you I studied under the Queen Mothers before

Mashaka killed them and fled north. Part of the training was how to communicate with spirits," she explained. "Unfortunately my quest for revenge meant I never finished. It is unheard of for a girl to abandon her training. So even when I returned home with the happy news that the murderer had been vanquished, I was not welcomed back."

"I'm so sorry, Hazina." Atalanta laid a gentle hand on the dark-skinned woman's arm.

Hazina gave her a tight smile. "I would love to return home, but I am not surprised I was not welcome. Still, I know a little of the magic my people practiced. And I've learnt a little of other magics over the years as I hunted Mashaka. It is how I can summon small spirits and have them do my bidding."

"You look exhausted though," Damien pointed out.

"Tired, yes," she agreed. "A bit of a rest and some food will put me right well enough."

Atalanta pulled a bruised apple from her pack and gave it to Hazina. She took it with a grateful smile and ate while they finished walking back to the church. The silence was oddly comfortable and Atalanta wondered if that's how it felt to be quiet with friends rather than rivals.

A small group of people stood outside the church. Cleon and Spiro seemed to be the head of two factions. The people behind Spiro were all older, their faces well weathered and full of anger. Those behind Cleon ranged in age from a girl younger than Atelo, up to a bald old man. There were a few more behind Cleon, all of whom look more determined than angry.

"Look!" someone called out as Atalanta, Hazina, and Damien approached. "They're back!"

Several voices fought with one another as questions and accusations surged forth. Damien quieted the crowd with a gesture and sharp order. The group fidgeted beneath his gaze but remained silent while Hazina explained what they intended for the evening.

"It isn't safe to be outside after dusk," a pregnant woman said, her hands wrapped protectively around her swollen stomach.

"We have the means to protect ourselves," Damien assured her.

"If crosses and holy relics do not deter these demons, what good will steel be?" Atelo asked, his eyes wide and shoulders hunched.

31

"We are strangers to you, so you have no reason to trust us, but we are strong and capable," Atalanta said.

The crowd murmured but was silenced when Spiro spoke up. "You don't appear to be demons, though I can't think why else you would come here. Still, even if you get yourselves killed, it's good somebody is trying to do something."

"How could you say that, Grandfather Artino?" Atelo asked, aghast.

"Who are they to us, boy? Strangers. If they're here, then they're only good to send against the demons." Spiro turned a challenging glare on the three companions. "If you three disagree then you can leave. No one would be sad to see you go."

Cleon scoffed and shook his head. "You cantankerous old man. It would serve you right if they took offence and struck you down for such rudeness."

Spiro sniffed and cast a baleful glance around everyone assembled in front of the church. There were more disapproving looks than supportive ones. He grunted and turned on his heel to storm away. A few others drifted after him.

"We're sorry for causing a divide in your community," Damien offered, his voice soft.

Cleon scratched his neck. "The divide was caused by these attacks. We'll recover once things return to normal. If they ever can."

The remaining people talked briefly with Atalanta, Hazina, and Damien before they too withdrew. Cleon and Atelo wished them a restful day and luck in the evening before leaving the three companions at the church. Alone, they waited, rested, and discussed their strategy. They were unable to agree on much beyond where they would hide while they waited. Everything else depended on what would come out of the sea.

When the sun began to sink into the west, they left the church and made their way back to the rocks. It was a slow and tedious journey. Atalanta wistfully stared at the smooth sand in the dying light. It would have been so much easier to walk along the shore, rather than climbing through the scraggly brush, but Hazina had said she didn't have the energy to summon another spirit to hide their tracks.

They reached their destination just as the last sliver of sunlight faded from the sky. Without saying a word, they separated and found places to hide. Though Hazina knelt only five feet from Atalanta, she blended into the shadows as if she were born for it. Beyond her, Atalanta could just make out the the silhouette of Damien among the brush. The rock jutted over the water, hanging ominous and threatening, below them. Shadows clung to it like maggots to a corpse. Not even the rising moon and stars could banish them.

A breeze blew across the water, cutting through their clothes to steal the warmth of their bodies. Atalanta grimaced and tried to shift her weight from foot to foot without giving away her position. A hand pressed against her arm and she bit her tongue to keep from shrieking. The immediate panic receded once she realized it was simply Hazina—Atalanta hadn't even noticed her crawling through the scrub.

"There has not been a reliable gap between attacks," Hazina whispered, her teeth flashing in the dark. "I wonder if perhaps we may have to spend several nights here."

"The priest was attacked the first night he came out to…exorcise the sea, or whatever it was he thought he was doing," Atalanta whispered back.

"You think if we offer a bait these beings will take it, regardless of whether they are hungry or not?"

Atalanta frowned out at the still and silent sea. "Men have died, but women have gone missing. I'm not sure the women are being killed. And Atelo said it was the priest, his mother, then another man before that."

"You think they will want a woman next?" Hazina asked, her head bobbing a little.

"Possibly."

"I will tell Damien and then come out of hiding."

"Hazina, wait." Atalanta caught her arm and pulled her back. "Only the priest came to the beach. The others were taken from their homes."

"I had not thought of that. Do you think they will realize it is a trap if I walk along the beach?"

"Who knows. Depending on what we're dealing with, they might not care."

Hazina gave a decisive nod. "Then I will be our bait."

Atalanta huffed and shook her head. "It should be me that goes. I'm used to fighting my way out of corners."

"Perhaps. But in the darkness, and with your choice of attire, they might think you are just another man."

Before Atalanta could protest further, Hazina slipped away into the darkness. All she could do was curse under her breath and ease the arquebus from its holster while she waited. A few minutes later, Hazina stepped out of the brush. With her dark skin and dress, she almost looked like a shadow wandering the beach.

She had only gone a few steps before something pale broke the surface of the water near the rocks. Atalanta wasn't sure if Hazina saw it, but had no way to warn her without giving away the ambush. Hazina paced eight steps away from the stones and eight steps back.

The silent watcher disappeared beneath the water only to return a moment later with two others. From where she was crouched, Atalanta could only make out pale, hairless heads breaking the surface. She glanced toward Damien's hiding place, but could no longer see him in the dark.

Though she only took her eyes off the water for a moment, when she looked back, only one creature remained. It slowly crept forward. The white skin almost seemed to glow in the thin moonlight and it moved in halting movements until it reached the beach. There, it rolled onto its back and let out the piteous cry of a hungry baby.

Hazina's head whipped around at the sound and she stared at the creature lying on the ground. For a moment her body swayed as if in time to some unheard song. Then she let out a gasp and moved toward the creature. "You poor thing!"

"Hazina!" Atalanta shouted, shooting up from her hiding place.

The creature stopped crying and pushed itself up on a chubby little arm. Though it was roughly the shape and size of a baby, it was hairless, with wide, dark eyes, and no visible anatomy to mark it male or female. A whining mewl snaked its way from the creature to her, pressing into her head like a claw digging into the dirt. Atalanta cried out in pain. Her arquebus fell to the ground, and she pressed the heels of her hands to her head.

"Atalanta? What is wrong?" Hazina asked, her voice sluggish. She turned away from the creature, wobbling slightly.

It snarled and began to cry again. Almost instantly, Hazina froze. She turned back to the creature and took slow, jerking steps toward the water where it sat crying.

Damien burst from his hiding place and rushed toward Hazina with a shout. His arms wrapped around her waist and spun her away from the crying beast.

"No, you must let me help it," Hazina screamed, thrashing against him. "It needs a mother!"

Atalanta jumped the brush and stumbled down the beach. Hazina fought against Damien as if her life depended on it—scratching and clawing at his face while he tried not to hurt her. Atalanta grunted and slammed a fist into the side of Hazina's head. She went limp in Damien's arms, her eyes open but unfocused.

"We don't have time to play nice," Atalanta snarled. She grasped the hilts of her long daggers and drew them. "Grab, or kill, that creature before its friends return."

Damien nodded and carefully set Hazina down. Atalanta didn't wait before stalking toward the creature. It squealed and wriggled its way back into the water at her approach. As soon as it was half in the water again it let out a horrendous shriek. Both Atalanta and Damien winced and stumbled back from the noise. The creature rolled in the water and began to swim away from them.

"Oh no you don't." Atalanta snapped a hand back and then forward, sending one of her blades slicing through the air. Water sprayed up as the dagger buried itself in the creature's leg. The beast screamed, sounding truly human for the first time, as it flailed about.

Another pale head poked above the water and gasped in horror. This one was slightly larger, with a fuzz of white hair growing on its head. In one quick movement, it moved to the baby-like beast and snatched it out of the water. Though the second creature was the size of a young child it had a vaguely feminine curve to its body while still being as featureless as a statue. The older creature made burbling sounds and pulled the dagger from the baby's leg. It threw the blade back toward the beach and wrapped a pale hand around the wounded leg to staunch the flow of black blood.

"What the hell are these things?" Damien asked, stopping at the water's edge to stare at the strange girl-creature cooing to the injured baby.

"I don't know," Atalanta replied with a shake of her head. "But I think we should kill or capture one."

The creature hissed at them and drew back further into the water. Two more pale heads broke the surface of the water near her. One had the same white fuzz growing on its head. The other looked more human. Silvery hair hung to its shoulders and its eyes were too large for its face, but its body was starting to look genuinely female.

The second young one screeched and started forward with hands crooked into claws. The silver-haired one gasped and pulled the other back. "Sister, no! Do you not recognize them?"

Atlanta and Damien exchanged confused glances, but the silver-haired creature wasn't finished. "They are *anairetai*, sister. The ones we heard of. From Methoni."

The two fuzz-haired creatures gasped and shrank back. The one holding the crying baby dove beneath the surface and disappeared. The silver-haired creature shook her hair out of her face and leveled a glare at Atalanta and Damien full of enough hate to wither the skin off their bones. She turned to the other remaining creature and she said, "Fetch the brothers, sister. I will not let them follow you."

"Methoni?" Damien muttered, his gaze locked on the strange scene playing out before them.

Atalanta shook her head and fingered the hilt of her remaining dagger. "They have to be sirens."

"They're so small though," he protested. "And barely even look human."

"Water-inhabiting sisters, who are scared, of us, because of something that happened in Methoni? It's the only possibility."

Before either of them could muse further on the creature's words, the water burst up in a frothy spray as six black horses reared out of the surf. Their manes were tangled with seaweed and reeds and, even from the shore, the scent of rotten fish was strong. Four of the horses tossed their heads and raced toward them, cutting through the waves as if they weren't there. Each pounding step sent up a spray of water and echoed like distant thunder.

"Gods' balls," Atalanta spat as she backpedaled. She wouldn't want to face against a normal horse with only a dagger, let alone whatever was charging toward them, but her arquebus lay back in the brush.

Damien roared a wordless challenge, drew his sword, and planted his feet. The first horse thundered past him, angling for Atalanta, and he swung his sword through its neck.

The beast collapsed, black blood spraying everywhere as it writhed on the sand. The second horse was so close on the heels of the first it tripped over the dying beast and landed with a scream and the snapping crack of several bones breaking. The two remaining horses pulled up and approached more cautiously.

One circled the bloody mass of injured and dying horse on the beach as it headed toward Atalanta. The other reared and ran at Damien. His sword flashed in the moonlight and clanged against a hoof lashing out. Teeth and hooves reached for Damien's soft flesh and he stumbled back, trying to deflect the attacks with his sword.

Atalanta threw herself to the side, rolling and coming up in a crouch as the other horse tried to trample her. She scrambled further up the beach toward the brush but fell with a strangled gasp when a hoof glanced across her ribs. She forced herself to ignore the searing pain and rolled out of the way before hooves slammed down where she had been a moment ago.

"I wish I had a good lance," Damien ground out. He was forced back step after step. He tried to draw the horse toward where Atalanta continued to jump and roll out of the way of the other horse, but the one attacking him drove him toward where Hazina lay instead.

Atalanta had no breath to spare. She dove away from lashing hooves. A ragged scream ripped from her when her shoulder slammed into a rock buried beneath the sand. Pain shot through her arm followed by angry prickles and a creeping numbness.

The horse whinnied in triumph and slammed its front hooves down on her. Atalanta screamed herself hoarse as she forced herself to roll beneath the beast. She gasped and drove her dagger up into the exposed belly above her. A wash of black blood bubbled over her hand and arm, instantly soaking her clothes. The horse gave a very human-like scream and leapt away from her.

The horse attacking Damien screamed its rage as another of its fellows fell. It lowered its head and charged at Atalanta while she pushed herself up on unsteady feet. Damien's warning shout gave her only enough time to turn and see the horse bearing down on her before it slammed into her. All the air was forced from her lungs, but rather than being thrown back by the blow, she found herself stuck to the horse's shoulder as if a million grasping hands were holding her.

The horse spun and crashed toward the sea and she gulped in a panicked lungful of air. The air was forced from her once again when the cold water closed over their heads. She thrashed but every part of her that hit the horse became stuck fast until she couldn't move. It took her a moment to realize she hadn't taken in any water, even though the horse dove deeper and deeper.

A shiver rippled through the water around them and Damien's voice seemed to shout from a great distance, "I have one of yours, and you have one of mine! Return her to me and I won't cut small pieces off him until the sun rises."

A pale creature with short hair that floated around its head like a halo bobbed in front of Atalanta with an angry snarl on its face. Beneath the water and with the anger on its face, it looked truly alien. The dark eyes were burning pits of coals and the teeth were sharp and vicious. The creature burbled something and then the horse was racing toward the surface.

They broke through into the air and Atalanta found herself somehow astride the back of the horse that had captured her. She shook the water from her eyes and squinted toward the shore. Damien stood with his sword pressed against the throat of a moonlight pale man, his other hand gripped in black hair.

"You have already killed two of our brothers, injured another, and maimed a sister," the girl-creature called out, her voice snapping like a whip. Atalanta peered around to see the creature astride another horse on her left and a third horse bobbed in the water on her right. Oddly, the girl's hair was completely dry, while Atalanta's dripped down her back.

"You and yours have killed countless humans, here and elsewhere," Damien countered.

The creature glowered and raised its chin. "We must eat, as all other living creatures do."

Damien jerked the head of his captive back and the whimper carried across the water to where the horses floated. His voice was almost as angry as the creature's when he said, "You will no longer eat the humans here."

"Does that mean we can eat your friend?" the creature asked, its laughter high-pitched and hysterical. "After all, she isn't exactly human."

"I will only say this one more time"—he drove a knee into his captive's side, eliciting a scream of pure agony—"return my friend to me or you'll listen to him die as slow a death as I can manage."

The creature bit its lip and glanced at the horses in the water. It burbled something and the horse it was riding tossed its mane and whinnied. The other two horses nickered back and the creature nodded. Their exchange complete, it glared at Atalanta and shouted back, "We agree to your terms."

The horse Atalanta was still stuck to dived beneath the water. This time she was able to appreciate and marvel at the fact that she seemed able to breathe the water as easily as air. The horse dissolved beneath her and for a moment she floated freely in the water before strong arms wrapped around her. They burst from the sea, a muscled young man carrying her onto the shore. His shoulder dug into her stomach and she could only see his back as he slowly approached where she assumed Damien stood with his captive.

"Let her go," Damien growled.

The man holding her slid her down his front until she was standing on the sand. With an arm still around her waist, he ducked his head like he was going to kiss her. Atalanta swung a fist up and connected with his jaw. It wasn't a hard hit, but he pulled back and let her go.

The man rubbed his jaw and glanced up at Damien. "My brother?" he asked.

"I should kill you both."

"Damien," Atalanta said, turning to face him even though it made her skin crawl to have the horse-turned-man behind her. "You're better than that."

For a moment he stood there, his arm tensed to bury his sword's edge in his captive's throat. His gaze shifted to her and something in his face changed. He released the man and shoved him toward the sea. The uninjured man gathered up his brother and they quickly disappeared back beneath the water.

Atalanta groaned and moved away from the water's edge. With the fight over, she was acutely aware of how much her ribs and shoulder hurt and that she had sand in places sand was never meant to be. She glanced at Damien and shook her head. "It isn't like you to be so blood thirsty."

He threw his sword down against the sand and snarled. "I remember what they did to me in Methoni. I will never be someone's puppet again."

Chapter Four

Hazina leaned on Damien's arm for the long trudge back to the church. The world was bathed in washed out pink as the sun crawled into an overcast sky. Grey shadows turned the whitewashed buildings of the sea-side community into bizarre edifices to forgotten gods. None of them spoke, only the scuff-and-slide of their tired steps broke the silence. A wave of gold and orange torchlight spilt out of the church when a withered old woman opened the door and stepped out. For a moment the trio stood frozen in the light.

"They're back!" the woman shrieked, turning back into the church.

People swarmed to surround Hazina, Damien, and Atalanta. Their chatter and shouts shattering the silence of dawn. The chaotic jumble of questions dissolved into laughter. Hands reached out to slap their backs and pull them into hugs.

"Enough," a sharp voice rang out over the happy crowd.

Silence fell like an anvil. Spiro stepped out of the church, his dark glower splitting the crowd so no one stood between Hazina, Damien, Atalanta, and him. He stepped forward, his feet crunching loudly on the gravel.

"What, exactly, happened on the beach?"

Damien cleared his throat. Before he could speak, Hazina took a half step toward the grumpy old man. Her head ached, especially around the ear and jaw where Atalanta had struck her, but she still pulled herself up to her full height and met his glare.

"We found those responsible for the attacks. Two were killed and the others were driven off."

"And what of those who were taken, rather than killed?"

Hazina's teeth clenched for a moment. She took a deep breath and tried to infuse her voice with as much sympathy as she could. "We saw no sign of them."

Spiro snarled. "Then why didn't you capture any of the demons and demand our people back?"

Damien placed a hand on Hazina's shoulder and said, "We were a bit preoccupied with defending ourselves. They were savage fighters."

"Were they demons?" someone in the crowd asked.

"I cannot say," Hazina replied.

Spiro let out a mirthless bark of laughter. "No mortals could have been responsible for our troubles."

Hazina shook her head. "They very well may have been demons, but we are not versed in such matters. If you go to the rocks and the bodies have not been taken, you will see that they look like men."

"Well if they're not demons, then what would you call them?" Spiro challenged.

"Evil," Atalanta said, her voice flat. She returned his glare with an equal amount of loathing and pity. "And now dead."

Atelo stepped out of the crowd, his eyes bright and smile wide. "Whatever they are, you've saved us. You are all heroes."

Damien sighed and scrubbed at his face. "We only killed two. There were others."

"But you drove them off?" Atelo asked, his smile slipping at the edges.

"Aye. I hope they will leave your community alone now, but we can't make that promise. They could return in a fortnight, or a year, or even tomorrow," Damien explained.

Cleon stepped up beside his son and shot a warning look at Spiro. "It is enough. We know they can be killed now. They will not find us so easy a target should they dare to return."

Soft murmurs of agreement rippled through the crowd. Though Spiro looked like he wanted to argue, Cleon placed a hand on his arm and drew him away from Hazina, Damien, and Atalanta. The rest of the crowd slowly dispersed. Their exuberance was faded, but many still offered a congratulatory word or slap on the back before returning to their homes.

When only Atelo and the wrinkled woman who had first discovered their return remained, the young man gestured at the church. "Old Mother Nanos can help you with your injuries. When you're rested, we would be happy to share a meal before you leave. My father and I live at the house on the end."

"Thank you." Hazina nodded to him before stumbling inside the church.

Atalanta and Damien followed her and sank onto benches while the old woman walked to the altar where a series of small jars and a stack of bandages were waiting. Hazina helped her tend to the bruises that Atalanta and Damien both sported. Once they were cared for, she allowed the old woman to apply a cool compress to the side of her head.

The chilling herbs stung at first, but quickly leached away the pain. Hazina breathed a sigh of relief and gave the woman a grateful smile. "Thank you, Mother."

The old woman smiled, revealing several missing teeth. "You've avenged my son and his wife. It might not be as what Jesus taught us, but it is satisfying. I'll leave this ointment with you—I expect you three get into scrapes fairly often."

"Thank you again," Hazina said, accepting the small jar. It was ceramic with a wax-sealed wood lid and she wrapped it in spare bandages before placing it in her satchel.

Damien closed the door once the old woman had left the church and all three released a sigh of relief. Both Atalanta and Damien had removed their tunics so their wounds could be tended. He kept his gaze down while he paced the length of the church. Atalanta gave her simple undertunic a tug to settle it over her bandages before shaking out her tunic. She grimaced at the sand that fell to the floor.

"I feel as if I'll never be fully rid of all the sand in my clothes," she muttered.

"A bit of discomfort is good for the soul," Damien returned, taking a seat near the front of the church so he could face away from her. Atalanta stuck her tongue out at his back.

Hazina clucked her tongue and shook her head. "We should discuss what we will do next."

"You mean, are we going to leave the 'sisters' and their 'brothers' to their mischief?" Atalanta asked, her voice muffled as she pulled her tunic on.

Damien grunted. "I dislike the idea of leaving them to prey on innocents, even if the people here are safe. But it would be the work of several lifetimes to hunt them all down."

Hazina gave a thoughtful nod. "So we must focus on the task at hand."

Atalanta snorted. Damien twisted to look at her and almost fell off his bench when he tried to stop himself halfway through the movement. His eyes darted to Atalanta and then he relaxed and straightened. He cleared his throat and asked, "Is there something you'd like to add?"

"This is the task at hand," she said. "Calista set us to find out why Poseidon's realm is so active of late, and then stop it. Seems to me that hunting down the sirens—though perhaps only a few of them—would be a good way of going about that."

Hazina pursed her lips. "I do not know your mythos fully, but were the sirens not governed by Am…Amp…Amitree, or some such?"

"Amphitrite, yes." Atalanta nodded.

"Then would following them not lead back to her rather than Poseidon?"

Damien blew out an annoyed breath. "No, Atalanta's right. Amphitrite is Poseidon's wife. I can't imagine she would direct the sirens to prolonged attacks without his knowledge or consent."

The three companions fell into silent thought. The sound of people going about their day outside was a muted reminder of time passing, as was the slowly growing warmth inside. Eventually Hazina broke the silence and asked, "When you encountered the sirens in Methoni, they were well established in the city, yes?"

Atalanta nodded. "Seemed to be." Damien's mouth twisted but he didn't disagree.

"Then perhaps it would be easiest to follow the sirens back to their home from there. They may have even remained or returned to the city after you, Damien, and Calista departed last year."

A soft growl crawled its way out of Damien's throat. "I really hate those sea bitches."

Atalanta, Hazina, and Damien remained in the cluster of homes outside of Otranto until the following morning. That night, Atelo and Cleon happily hosted them and the evening meal turned into a small, but festive, celebration with all the locals. The sky in the morning was clogged with heavy clouds and a brisk wind cut through cloak and clothes alike. Atalanta hated the sharp bite of cold, but Hazina shivered every step of the way back to Santa Maria di Leuca.

"H-how much fa-fa-farther?" she stuttered.

Atalanta glanced over her shoulder and gave Hazina a sympathetic smile. This, more than any trouble with the language, was a reminder of how far away her home had been. Her face was tucked so far down into her cloak it was a wonder she didn't trip. "Not far now. Just think of the fire waiting for you at the inn. And there will be hot stew, maybe even some bread fresh from the oven."

Hazina's head bobbed in what might have been a nod or a particularly violent shiver. Damien was nowhere in sight, though Atalanta knew he would be following close on Hazina's heels. As soon as he wrapped his cloak of shadows around himself, he disappeared from view. Prickles raced up and down Atalanta's spine, beating out the chills, to have him so near and yet not visible.

She turned back around and continued the slog. The brightly painted buildings with warm lights flickering in their windows beckoned them onward. Though it felt like an eternity of icy shards of air piercing through them, they reached the edge of the hamlet in a reasonably short time. With buildings around them, the wind lost much of its driving force. It was a welcome respite. They hurried on to the inn, their faces stinging from the cold.

They tumbled into the inn, all but tripping over each other in their haste. A fire blazed in the hearth, beating back against the sharp wind that tried to follow them inside. The sudden warmth made Atalanta's hands and cheeks feel like they had been dipped into liquid fire. Several miserable looking people sat on stools clustered around the hearth. A few patrons shouted profanities at them until the door swung closed. Only one barmaid moved about the room, her hair braided and wrapped into a crown. She hurried amongst the tables, dropping off food and drink, before retreating to stand in the kitchen doorway.

Damien had dropped his cloak before he entered the inn and Atalanta nodded at Hazina before jerking her chin toward the fire. He nodded back and took Hazina by the elbow to guide her to the warmth. Atalanta pushed her cloak back and approached the bar. The barmaid gave her a wary once-over before stepping away from the little bit of warmth.

"Miserable day out, ain't it?" the barmaid said, a stiff smile on her face. "Bit early for the winter storms to start, but suppose it's good for business. What can I do for you fine folks this eve?"

"Two rooms, three hot meals, and some hot beverages," Atalanta said. She fished a small handful of coins out and placed them on the counter. The bronze glinted warmly in the firelight, but the silver gleamed.

"Oh aye"—the barmaid nodded, her eyes locked on the coins—"we have some goat's milk, freshly warmed. Will you be wanting a private room? Could get a nice fire going there for you in just a trice."

Atalanta glanced over at Hazina and Damien. He had forced another stool into the lopsided semi-circle around the hearth so Hazina could warm her hands. The other patrons shot them looks ranging from annoyance to anger—though nobody seemed inclined to start a fight. Not when that would mean being tossed back out into the cold.

"A private room. Yes."

The barmaid dimpled and scooped up the coins. "We'll get the room nice and toasty and let you know as soon as it's ready. Have a seat out here and I'll fetch those drinks for you while you wait."

Atalanta settled at a table near Hazina. Damien joined her, chafing his arms to warm them. "Not sure how much good this fire is doing her. If I tried to get her any closer I think everyone would riot."

"I got us a private room. They're building a fire there—that should help her warm up," Atalanta explained, voice low.

"Good, good."

True to the barmaid's word, she brought out three mugs before they had fully finished settling at the table. Curls of steam rose off the creamy white liquid. She placed two mugs on the table and pressed the third into Hazina's hands.

"Do you have spiced ale?" Damien asked the barmaid, his hands wrapped around the mug.

"Aye," she nodded. "And if you've the coin, we even have honeyed wine."

Atalanta let out a happy sigh. "Honeyed wine with our food would be wonderful."

The barmaid nodded. "The kitchen boy should have the fire in your room ready in just a moment. I'll bring the wine and food once you've settled there."

Atalanta helped Hazina up from the fire while Damien gathered their things. They met the wide-eyed kitchen boy at the door to the hall. He quickly stepped back and opened the first of the doors in the shadowy hallway. Rich orange light spilled out, curling warm fingers around them. Hazina stumbled inside and collapsed onto a stool already placed before the fire. Damien pressed a coin into the kitchen boy's hand.

Atalanta removed her cloak and settled onto the bench under the table. The crackling of the fire and warm milk in her stomach fogged her mind. She jerked back, startled to realize the barmaid was placing platters of food on the table. A quick glance at Damien told her he knew she had briefly fallen asleep. His small smirk made anger flare. When he met her gaze, his smile turned commiserating and her anger fizzled into confusion.

"The food is perfect for a day like this," the barmaid said. Steam rose from a bowl full of vegetables and meat. An earthy scent mingled with a hint of salt and smoke and tantalized Atalanta's stomach into a grumble.

"Hazina, come eat," Damien called. "It'll warm you faster than the fire."

The barmaid silently slipped out and closed the door behind her. Atalanta, Hazina, and Damien fell upon their bowls of stew. For the next long while the only noises came from the hearth and the sloshing in their bowls. When the bowls were empty, and the bottle of honeyed wine drained of its last drop, the three companions settled back with a mix of sighs and yawns.

Atalanta eyed Hazina and Damien through drooping eyelids and stifled a yawn with her fist. "I suppose it's back into the wind and down to the harbour to find passage to Methoni." She forced herself to straighten in her seat and wrap her cloak about her shoulders.

Neither Damien nor Hazina said anything. Atalanta frowned at them. "No 'we'll go with you,' or even a 'wait until morning?'"

Hazina's head drooped toward her chest while Damien simply

shrugged. "We shouldn't have spent an extra night with Cleon and his family. We need to book passage today—which you have so graciously volunteered for."

Atalanta snorted. She pushed herself up and slung her bag across her back. "The gods have saddled me with the world's least helpful companions," she grumbled. Damien only gave her a tired wave as she left the warmth behind.

Though the common room's fire burned as merrily as ever, it did little to stop the chill from seeping inside. She tugged her cloak tighter and tried to smooth the glower she could feel pinching her face before she stepped up to the bar. "I need to book passage for me and my friends. Would I find the captains on their boats, or at a dockside alehouse on a night like this?"

The barmaid ran her eyes over Atalanta and drummed her fingers against the bar. "Depends where you'll be wanting to head to. And how soon."

"Methoni—leaving in the morning, if at all possible."

The barmaid leaned an elbow on the bar, a frown tugging at her lips. "Not many willing to go out that direction nowadays. If you don't meet pirates, then there's always the damn Ottomans to worry about."

A shiver of worry threaded its way around Atalanta's throat. "We would only be in the city for a day—two at most. It is unfortunately imperative that we go."

The woman's head bobbed as she thought. "There may be one. He will go almost anywhere, for the right price. He's not afraid of pirates or armies."

Atalanta's lips quirked to one side. "I assume in addition to exorbitant fees, he isn't the most reputable."

The barmaid chuckled. "He's not what one could call a traditional trader, it's true. But you can find him at the most crowded alehouse along the docks. Ask for Captain Ganim."

Atalanta's eyebrows shot up. "A Turk?"

"His Da was, true. But he grew up right here in Santa Maria di Leuca. He's more Italian than many folks round these parts. More Christian than some too."

"Thank you." Atalanta slid a few clipped coins across the bar.

She had almost reached the inn's door when the barmaid called out. "Miss! Before you go asking about for Captain Ganim…"

"Yes?" Atalanta waited as the woman shifted from one foot to another, her gaze locked on the bar.

"He'll be the smallest man in the alehouse, most likely. Short with dark hair and dark skin." She glanced up and quickly added, "Not near as dark as your friend though. More like browned bread."

"Why are you telling me this?"

"If you go asking about for Captain Ganim a big brute of a man'll tell you he's the captain. That'll be Petrillo. First mate to Ganim. If you don't know who Ganim is, they'll clean your coffers out."

Atalanta nodded. "Thank you. Again."

She paused and glanced back toward the people huddled near the fire. One of them, a dark-haired man, glowered at her. The hate in his gaze hit her like a slap across the face and forced a feeling of guilt to twist in her stomach. A few coins, silver and a single one of gold, hit the bar. "Some warm food or drink for any cold souls who wander in tonight."

The woman's eyes widened and for a moment she just stared at the money. "You are a kind soul," she said, her hand darting out to snatch the coins up. "I'll fetch them some things straight away."

Atalanta smiled. The man who had been glaring at her was no longer around the fire. She wasn't sure where he might have gone to in the brief time she'd looked away, but her guilt was eased. She turned and walked out into the biting wind gnawing its way through the small town. She saw no one else on the streets as she scurried from one pool of torchlight to another until she reached the harbour. Three alehouses sat watching the ships swaying on the water. One was so crowded, people almost seemed to tumble out the door as they left.

She pressed her way into the crowd. Two young women and a young boy scampered among the sailors to deliver food and drink to the patrons. A pretty man with a pointed chin and golden hair sat on the bar, strumming an instrument as he crooned to the crowd.

The sailors glanced at Atalanta when she pushed her way past them. Some raised eyebrows, others returned to their drinks without a second glance, and still others called out rude remarks. She clenched her jaw and ignored the propositions, her eyes locked on the far corner of the space. She had spotted her quarry almost as soon as she walked in. A small man with brown skin and dark hair sitting next to a beast of a man.

Ganim glanced up from his tankard in surprise when she settled at his table. The brute, Petrillo, started to rise from his seat but settled back at a small gesture from his captain.

"Do I know you?" Ganim asked. His voice was soft and pleasant, with a surprisingly lyrical lilt. "Before you answer, you should know I almost never forget a face, and I'm quite certain I would remember a woman dressed in men's clothes."

Atalanta gave him a tight smile. "I have heard of you, though we have never met."

"Have you now? I can't say the same about you."

Atalanta laughed. "I would have been worried if you had heard of me. Only my friends, or those I'm about to kill, know who I am."

Petrillo glowered down at her, the muscles in his arm bulging. Ganim bared his teeth at her in a mockery of a smile. "Is that a threat?"

"The truth. But we aren't here to talk about me."

Ganim bit out a bark of laughter. "No, I suppose we aren't. You're here to engage my services."

"I need passage to Methoni."

He let out a low whistle and leaned back in his chair, running his eyes over her critically. "I didn't peg you as someone with a death wish when you first walked in, but I've been wrong before."

Atalanta shook her head. The blood pounding in her ears drowned out the raucous noise of the sailors drinking around them. She felt as if she were balancing on the edge of something, and tried to keep her voice light when she said, "The city hasn't been attacked yet."

"We all know it's coming."

"And I need to get in—and out—before that happens."

He crossed his arms and tapped a finger against his chin. "I may be able to help with that. But there is the matter of cost. Such a service wouldn't be some mere trifle."

"What are you asking?"

"First born child?"

Atalanta rolled her eyes and Ganim laughed.

"Not sure what I would do with a child anyway."

"My companions and I have coin. Name your price."

Ganim's gaze flickered around the crowded alehouse. "Companions? I see no one with you tonight."

She tossed her hair and tried to glare down the laughter in his eyes. "They are making inquiries elsewhere in case your reputation proves to be more than your mettle."

He chuckled. "You aren't a very good liar, my dear. But I find you oddly delightful. I will take you for two florins apiece. Bring your companions here at dawn. Petrillo will bring you to my darling."

"Your darling?"

"My ship, *the Lion*."

"We'll see you on the morrow," Atalanta said and pushed up from the table.

"Oh, one more thing, my dear," he said. Atalanta paused, half risen from her seat. He flashed her a wide grin. "Wear a dress as befits a proper Christian woman or you'll get no passage on *the Lion*."

Atalanta ground her teeth but nodded before diving back into the crowd and out into the cold. No matter how often she was forced to wear a dress to blend in, she had yet to like the feel of skirts smothering her legs. Still, she would wear a dress without complaint if it got them to Methoni.

Chapter Five

"Why is it always 'before dawn' with these people?" Damien grumbled. Though the streets were empty, the three companions hurried toward the docks.

A thin drizzle of rain pattered around them. It was just enough to soak into their cloaks and mute the smell of sea and town. Dark clouds shrouded the sky and stole any celestial light long before it could reach the ground. Despite the general gloom, birds determinedly chirped their morning songs. Every building they passed—home, store, or alehouse—was dark, with the doors closed and windows shuttered. The only light came from the occasional lantern hanging beneath an overhang to keep its flickering flame sheltered from the weather.

Atalanta's stride lengthened until she was almost running down the road. She had worn a dress that morning—a simple piece in drab blue, given shape more from a wide belt and the overskirt than by any skill in the cut. Despite being obviously angry about her clothing choice, she had refused to explain why she wore it. Damien shook his head and watched her run ahead with her skirts hiked up to her knees.

"Are we going to miss the boat? Is that why she is running?" Hazina asked.

"I'm not sure," he admitted. "But it looks like she's stopped in front of an alehouse up ahead."

Atalanta tugged on the door. She said something they were too far away to hear, and before Damien and Hazina could rejoin her, someone stepped out of the shadows. The stranger towered over her with broad shoulders that blotted out the light from a lantern a few doors farther on.

"Oi! Leave her alone," Damien shouted. The brute looked over Atalanta's head and grinned.

His skin was sun darkened and his brown hair cut so short his scalp was clearly visible. The man held up his hands, his smile flashing yellowed and crooked teeth. He took a step back when Damien's hand lowered to the hilt of his sword.

"Protective sort, ain't he?" the brute said, shifting his smile to Atalanta. His gaze traced over the modest curves her dress made visible. Damien's hand tightened on his sword.

"Petrillo, this is one of my companions. Damien, this is Petrillo—the first mate on the ship taking us to Methoni," Atalanta said, her hands rubbing down against the sides of her skirt as if to dry her hands.

Petrillo grunted, his gaze sliding past Damien to latch onto Hazina. "Quite the pair of pretty lasses for one man to take care of. Seems unfair."

Atalanta's back stiffened at his implication and fists clenched in her skirts. Damien kept himself from growling, though he couldn't force his hand to drop from the hilt of his sword. "My *sister*"—he paused to let the word hang in the air—"and our dear friend are able to keep themselves out of trouble well enough of their own. I only have to crack the skulls of particularly dim men."

Petrillo's eyes flashed with an anger that belied the grin still on his face. He gestured at Atalanta's body in a way that made Damien's teeth grind and said, "Captain will be glad you're not dressed like a boy anymore."

Even in the poor light, her cheeks visibly reddened. Petrillo laughed and gestured for them to follow him. He led them to a ship moored amidst several small fishing vessels. It towered over the smaller boats, with sleek lines and a freshly painted figurehead of a lion. A small, dark man stood on the deck, shouting an occasional order to men as disreputable looking as Petrillo. The hurried movements of the crew held a frantic edge to them and Damien wondered if they had wanted to set sail the previous day.

Petrillo whistled once and led Damien, Hazina, and Atalanta aboard the ship. The small man looked around and smiled at them as if they were cattle for the slaughter. "Welcome aboard *the Lion*. She may not be the fastest ship on the Mediterranean, but she is certainly the fiercest. I am Captain Ganim. You've already met Petrillo, and you don't need to know anyone else on my crew. We're casting off in just a moment. Petrillo will show you to your rooms and explain the rules of travel. Any disobedience will be met with swift, and final, punishment."

Before any of them could respond, Ganim stalked off toward a cluster of sailors fighting with a length of knotted rope and a small stack of crates waiting to be secured. His shout to cast off was echoed as several sailors repeated the call.

"You heard the Captain," Petrillo said. "Follow me and pay attention."

He gave them a brief tour that pointed out the galley and sailor's quarters below deck, and the ladder leading down to the hold—which he stressed was off limits. "You're free to roam this level, though I would recommend staying out of the sailors' rooms unless you're looking to play nug-a-nug."

"What kind of women do you take us for?" Atalanta demanded.

Petrillo waggled his eyebrows at her but didn't answer the question. He continued his tour by leading them to three tiny cabins. "Every morning, once the sun has fully risen, the captain leads all aboard in a prayer. We pray again after night has fallen. These are the only times it's permissible for you to be on deck, and short of grave illness, you have to attend if you wish to stay on board."

Damien glared at the other man. Petrillo was only a couple of inches taller, but significantly broader in the shoulders, and always stopped a little too close for good manners. "Any other requirements?" Damien asked through gritted teeth.

Petrillo smirked. "Not a requirement, but lock your doors. Our sailors can sometimes indulge a little too much. Would hate for any of them to mistake one of your rooms for their own."

The brute of a first mate turned and left before they could say anything. Damien growled softly. "Are you sure this was the only wreck that would take us?"

Atalanta plucked at her skirts and sighed. "No, I'm not sure. But most people are worried about the march of the Ottomans."

"Are they really a threat to us?" he asked.

Atalanta scoffed. "Have you been under a rock this past year? What of the raids on Sebenico? It's practically on our doorstep."

"Is that not simply the result of bored soldiers and mercenaries? I have heard that mercenaries raid communities on both sides of this conflict," Hazina pointed out.

Damien shook his head. "Venice is electing an envoy to smooth the tensions. I expect someone will be chosen soon, if they haven't been already, and then they'll travel to Istanbul. There have always been tensions between Venice and the Ottomans. I'm not really sure why everyone is getting so bothered this time."

"I hope you're right, but I expect there will be war within a year." Atalanta shook her head and opened the door to one of the small cabins.

It was a cramped space with two short bunks stacked against a wall, a narrow strip of floor between the beds and far wall, and three lockable drawers beneath the bunks.

Damien sighed. He doubted he would sleep well. The beds looked far too short for him, and narrow enough that his knees would hang over the edge if he didn't want his feet dangling. "Do they expect three people to share these cells?" he muttered.

"At least they are private rooms." Hazina gave his arm a sympathetic pat. "The boat I took to meet you in Santa Maria di Leuca had no such provisions. Passengers slept in bunks beside the sailors. If it had not been for the presence of two families making the same journey, I would not have felt safe enough to ever sleep."

Atalanta pulled open a drawer and shoved her bag inside. "It's the unfortunate nature of having to buy passage on ships meant to carry cargo. Perhaps someday there will be passenger ships leaving from most ports, with rooms large enough for a whole family."

Hazina laughed and switched places with Atalanta so she could put her possessions in a second drawer. "We may as well dream of ships which can take us from the shores of Italy to those of Greece in a single day."

"That would make our quest much more pleasant, wouldn't it?" Atalanta chuckled.

Damien leaned against the door frame and shook his head. "Why are you two sharing a room? There are three—we could each have our own."

The two women exchanged a look full of surprise. Hazina laughed self consciously and said, "I never even thought of it. I can move my things if that would make you more comfortable, Atalanta."

"No, no. I didn't think of it either," she said. "I just assumed we would share, like we do at inns."

Damien shrugged a shoulder and straightened. "Well if you two want to be cabin mates, then I won't stop you. I think you'll want the extra space by the time we reach Methoni though. What with being essentially confined to this level."

"Just because you aren't social enough to remain pleasant for an entire voyage..." Atalanta trailed off, her voice dripping with honey.

Anger clenched his stomach until he noticed the laughter in her eyes. He snorted, the fire ebbing as he turned away. It was a long, peculiar process to set aside his old hatred—and much more difficult to do when she was in front of him being a nuisance.

He claimed the middle room as his own and returned to Hazina and Atalanta with the rusted key to one of the drawers beneath his bunk tucked safely into a pocket. The two women were quietly discussing dresses. For a moment he was taken aback—neither struck him as vain. Then he realized what they were actually talking about.

"—it takes practice to run. Until you get used to it, a pair of hose beneath your skirts will prevent any embarrassment should the occasion arise when you need to hike them up," Hazina explained.

"And your belt?" Atalanta eyed Hazina's waist with a contemplative eye.

Hazina rapped her knuckles against her stomach. It sounded like a muffled knock on a door. "The knives are attached to a thin bit of wood, with the fabric of the belt to hide it all. A bit uncomfortable, true, but also protective."

"That's clever—but doesn't it make it hard to move about?"

"I do not notice it to be so, though I do not run and jump about as much as you do."

Damien cleared his throat.

"Did you want to join our discussion on dresses, hose and smocks?" Atalanta asked, her tone joking.

"A tempting offer. Perhaps another time. I thought we might like to take a walk around the confines of this deck."

Hazina nodded. "It would be good to get a better look at things without being hurried past everything of interest."

Damien, Hazina, and Atalanta had made their way to the galley when a scrawny boy with more dirt smeared across his face than his clothes approached. He shuffled toward them with his body twisted to the side, as if ready to flee. "Captain Ganim's about to do morning prayer," he spat out, already scampering away before his message was finished.

"Does anyone else think the sailors are acting strange?" Atalanta asked, her voice low.

Damien frowned and watched the few sailors near them climb the ladder-like stairs up to the main deck. He hadn't noticed anything out of the ordinary until she pointed it out. The sailors glanced toward them often, but always jerked their gazes away should they be caught looking. And more than the cabin boy scurried away whenever they approached.

"Perhaps they are of the mind it is bad luck to have women aboard," Hazina suggested.

Atalanta chuckled. "Well, in this case they might be right. We're hunting down Poseidon—or someone close to him. If that doesn't bring them bad luck, nothing will."

"Let's not tell them that, though," Damien said.

They followed the sailors up to the deck where men crowded around Ganim and Petrillo. The first mate stood taller than any of the sailors and the crowd rippled beneath his roving gaze. Almost every man flinched away from Petrillo's scrutiny. The small captain stood on a stack of crates so he was head and shoulders above even Petrillo.

Rain drizzled down on the crowd. From the look and smell of some of the sailors, the weather was likely the closest thing to a bath many of them had experienced in a month, or more. Only Ganim and Petrillo really looked as if they washed on a regular basis.

Ganim threw his head back and opened his arms at some unseen signal. His voice rang out over the gathered crowd and he recited, "Our father, which art in heaven, hallowed be thy name…"

The crew were quick to join the prayer. Some mumbled, most spoke, but a few looked almost as rapturous as the captain. When the prayer was complete, silence fell over the ship. It made the snapping of the sails and creaking of the wood seem ominously loud in comparison.

Ganim's gaze swept across the crowd, though his feverish eyes didn't seem to really be seeing the sailors before him. A wild grin split his face as he called out, "Oh Lord, open thou my lips."

The sailors responded, "And my mouth shall show forth thy praise."

Damien rocked on his heels, uncomfortable with the back-and-forth prayer around them. He knew enough to pass himself off as a fellow Christian in casual settings, but in the middle of a worship it would be painfully obvious he was not. Petrillo's dark gaze locked on them and Damien's stomach knotted with worry.

With the prayer finished, some of the sailors moved away. Atalanta took a step before Hazina grabbed her arm and shook her head. The sailors leaving were climbing into the rigging or taking up posts around the deck. The rest remained, watching Ganim. It took only a few moments for the ship to be tended once more. And then the captain began to sing.

"Oh come let us sing unto the Lord:
let us heartily rejoice in the strength of our salvation,

Let us come before his presence with thanksgiving:
and show ourself glad in him with Psalms…"

The remaining sailors joined in the song, and a soft echo suggested some of those above were singing as well. The men dispersed as soon as the song ended and Damien herded Hazina and Atalanta toward the hatch as quickly as he could. He hadn't liked the look on Petrillo's face during the psalm.

"Is something wrong?" Atalanta asked Hazina when they were safely below deck. Damien realized Hazina had been muttering beneath her breath since the song had stopped.

"That man is presumptuous and arrogant. I am not of his faith, but I have more respect for it than he does," she said. Her steps beat out a sharp staccato as she stalked down the narrow hall toward their cabins.

"What?" Atalanta hurried after her and linked her arm with Hazina's. Damien fell into step behind them with only a quick glance over his shoulder to ensure they weren't being followed.

Hazina's voice dropped so low Damien had to lean forward to hear her. "He takes the roll of a priest onto himself. I am fairly certain that is considered, what's the word? Blasphemous."

Atalanta glanced back at Damien, her eyes wide and worried. He could almost hear her thoughts, an echo of something she had said the last time they started on a quest together. *I do not want to anger any of the gods—new or old.*

"Are you sure?" she asked, turning her attention back to Hazina.

She nodded. "Their faith has several similarities to my own—many of the displaced have adopted it out of genuine belief, or fear of repercussions from those whose country we live in."

"But not you?"

Hazina hesitated a moment before shaking her head. "It seems a silly thing, but I feel as if I've lost so much of myself—through my own actions—that I don't want to lose this as well."

"Hazina…" Atalanta started then stopped. Hazina gave her a small smile and patted her arm.

They had almost reached their cabins when the ship rocked. All three of them slammed into a wall and were thrown against the other when the ship rocked again. Shouting and pounding feet drifted from the deck above. A crash and scream came from the hold below.

"What's going on?" Atalanta gasped. She and Hazina pulled apart to brace themselves in the hall as the ship continued to buck and pitch.

"Poseidon's Wrath?" Damien asked. He spread his stance for stability, but a particularly hard roll knocked him to the side so hard his head hit the wall. With a grumble, he braced with his arms like Hazina and Atalanta had done.

Hazina's eyes clenched shut and she bit off a groan as the ship heaved.

"I don't think so…Hazina, it might be better if you were in the room."

Slowly, with frequent pauses, Damien and Atalanta walked her the rest of the way to the cabins. Once she was safely inside, they wobbled their way back toward the stairs.

Sailors huddled on the floor and at the galley tables as they neared the hatch. Many muttered prayers and a few clutched rosaries in their white-knuckled fists. "What's going on up there?" Atalanta asked of no one in particular.

Damien pulled the nearest sailor to his feet and repeated the question. The man's eyes rolled as he shivered. "The sea is alive. God protect us!"

he moaned.

Damien snorted and let the sailor crumple back to the floor. Atalanta hiked her skirts up to her knees and scurried up the stairs before the sailor had even hit the deck. Damien followed her up.

The rain had increased from its gentle patter to an angry shower, but no wind buffeted the drops away. Each drop was like ice, lancing into Damien's cloak. Sailors darted about, fighting to lash things down and not be swept away while wave after wave rolled over the deck. Even Ganim fought to tame the ship alongside the sailors.

Damien couldn't see the shore through the windless storm, though he doubted they had sailed far enough from Santa Maria di Leuca to have naturally lost sight of Italy. Waves leapt from the otherwise still waters and dashed themselves against the sides of the ship. Sailors shouted curses and prayers with equal vigour.

"This isn't Poseidon's Wrath, but it sure as Hades is Poseidon's doing," Atalanta said.

Petrillo dropped down from low hanging rigging with a heavy thump. He straightened slowly, his height unfolding into a mountain of anger. "What do you two think you're doing?" he demanded.

Atalanta raised her chin. "We wanted to know what was happening. Your sailors below are doing nothing more than quivering and muttering prayers."

"Return to your quarters."

"What's happening? This isn't like any normal storm—"

Petrillo took a step forward, his face a blotchy red. The rain had left his clothes drenched and clinging to every twitching bulge of muscle. Atalanta shuffled a half-step back, bumping against Damien. He could feel the slightest of tremors running through her until he placed a gentle hand on her shoulder.

"You would do well to treat paying passengers with a bit of respect," Damien cautioned. "Perhaps such a storm is punishment for only paying lip service to the tenets of your faith."

Petrillo's face made his previous anger seem like a mere annoyance. If Ares were to materialize before them, Damien suspected the god would hesitate before challenging the anger of the first mate.

"Go. To. Your. Quarters."

Atalanta shook. It was a small flutter that Damien doubted he would have noticed if she hadn't been pressed against him. A small part of him wondered if she had ever been that frightened of him, but the part she would have derided as a hero rose up and quashed such feelings. She was afraid. Afraid of the brute in front of them.

He pushed Atalanta behind him and stared down Petrillo's inhuman anger. His heart beat harder and shoulders flexed, bracing for a punch from the first mate. Petrillo glowered, the anger slowly receding to more natural constraints. With the threat of a fight dying, Damien inclined his head and ushered Atalanta back down the stairs.

They were both soaked from their brief foray into the rain above. Damien pulled his cloak off and draped it over an arm as he followed Atalanta toward the cabins. She had scurried halfway there before her steps slowed and shoulders relaxed. He couldn't help but smile when she straightened and gave herself a shake.

"I think Poseidon knows where we are, and what we're trying to do," she said, glancing back at him only briefly. She locked her eyes on the cabin doors ahead and kept her back stiff while they walked.

"Likely a warning to leave him and his interest alone. We've seen his Wrath—this is nothing compared to that," he agreed.

"It'll make for a very long journey if it keeps up the whole way, though."

Damien grunted. "Now would be a great time to reveal some previously unknown ocean-controlling powers from your forefather."

She shot him a withering look. "No one in my family has ever gotten anything from Poseidon."

"Then he owes you," he reasoned.

Atalanta bit out a laugh. "What do you want me to do? Pray? Oh mighty Poseidon, forefather of my line, please stop tossing waves at us so we can come make you stop attacking people."

Damien snorted. "Maybe a less sarcastic—huh. The storms seems to have stopped." The absence of the rocking was so sudden it made him stumble. Even walking down the straight hallway felt odd.

They stared at each other for a moment. Atalanta laughed nervously. "Someone must have been listening."

"Calista did say we'd garnered the attention of several different gods. Can't think who else might have the power to calm the seas though," Damien said.

She shrugged and they wobbled their way back to the cabins. Atalanta pulled open the door to her room and then flinched. The sharp, sickly sweet smell of vomit greeted them. Damien clenched his teeth and took a step back.

"Wh-what happened?" Hazina asked. She held a dented chamberpot in her lap, though some of her sick-up had landed on the wall and floor.

"You poor thing," Atalanta said, an almost coo in her voice. She slipped into the room and wrapped an arm around her shoulders. "We should switch to the other cabin and let one of the sailors know this one needs to be cleaned."

"I do not want to be a bother," Hazina mumbled.

"Shh."

Damien took another step back, his stomach protesting the smell far more than it had even noticed the rocking of the ship. "I'll see if I can find a sailor who isn't an incoherent puddle."

He heard Atalanta briefly explain what had happened while he walked away. Her laugh and final words trailed after him. "Poseidon's threat has been delivered. Such a shame we're going to ignore it."

Over the next three days, the weather was beautifully fair. Clouds drifted lazily along the horizon, wispy and light, and the sun shone in defiance of the changing seasons. Hazina still felt sick though. She wobbled her way around the deck. Petrillo's glare was heavy on her the entire time. It felt like fire against her skin.

Ganim had decided she, Atalanta, and Damien should be allowed brief forays above deck. He claimed the sea air was fortifying. Petrillo had vehemently disagreed, but Ganim overruled him. So it went that twice a day, once between the morning and evening prayers, and once just before dusk, the three companions were allowed to take a quick walk around the deck and enjoy the open air.

The prayers themselves were shorter and less elaborate. None of the sailors commented on the change within Hazina's hearing. If it was

Ganim's usual way, or more respect after what could only have been divine anger, she didn't care. It felt right that they should only say simple prayers.

She paused midship and leaned on the railing to gaze over the sea. Pink and orange streaked across the sky as evening idly approached. Salt, wood, and tar had become the constant scent of their journey so the tantalizing hint of lemon perked her interest. Her eyes scanned the horizon.

"Do either of you know how to find your position at sea?" she asked.

"No," Atalanta answered. "Why?"

Damien squinted across the calm water. "After our last voyage I started studying how to orient oneself by the sky."

"And do you know where we are?" Hazina asked.

"Not a clue—I'm not very good at it."

"It has been three days and we can still see the coast of Italy. Does that seem right to you?" She gestured at the smudge of land on the edge of the horizon.

"No, it doesn't."

Atalanta grumbled. "I'm really starting to dislike this captain. If he's skirting the Italian coast, then he's either going to kill us or sell us. And he's made me wear a dress this entire time."

"I think your concerns may be a little off the mark," Damien said with a chuckle.

Atalanta gave him a flat look. "If I were to put my leathers back on in anticipation of trouble, then Ganim and his crew would know we know something is amiss."

Hazina nodded and sighed. She was starting to really hate boats. "If—"

"Captain says it's time to head below deck," one of the sailors interrupted their discussion. Like so many of the others, he kept his distance and ran off as soon as the message was delivered. It had seemed strange, if perhaps superstitious, to start, but now had an ominous undertone to it. Like a superstition about befriending the farm chicken to be eaten at the end of the week.

"Let us talk away from curious ears," Hazina suggested.

Hazina led the retreat below deck. Atalanta and Damien followed close behind, and the three made the trip back to their cabins in silence. Only now that Hazina was aware something was wrong did she realize there was always a sailor sitting in the door nearest to their rooms. He would see whenever they left and whenever they returned. She suspected there were others positioned in similar locations elsewhere to keep an eye on them.

She didn't remember if it had always been the same sailor, but the one sitting there as they passed was pretending to whittle. He had a piece of wood and a knife, but he was simply turning the block of wood into a smaller block of wood.

"We must be careful what we talk about," she whispered when they paused outside their doors. She nodded her head ever so slightly toward the non-whittling sailor. Atalanta's face tightened and she twitched as if she wanted to twist and stare. Damien leaned a shoulder against his door and crossed his arms, though even that wouldn't give him a clear line of sight.

"Do you think we're safe to talk in our rooms?" he asked.

Hazina smiled and nodded. "No. It will be easier to listen to our conversations when we are in a small space."

"So how are we to figure out what to do?" Atalanta asked. She crossed her arms and scowled.

"Tomorrow, during our walk," Hazina suggested. "I should be able to summon a small spirit to whip up the wind a bit. It should keep our conversation from curious ears."

"That sounds like a good idea," he said.

Atalanta nodded her agreement and the three companions separated into their rooms. Hazina tried to have simple conversations about inconsequential things, but Atalanta only answered with a few words when she didn't just grunt. After awhile, Hazina gave up and changed into her sleeping smock.

"What are you doing?" Atalanta asked.

"Getting ready to sleep."

"But—"

"It is time to sleep; I am tired and you are not a very good conversationalist this evening."

A flush spread across Atalanta's cheeks. "Uh, well. A bit on my mind, I suppose."

"Does that mean Damien?" Hazina asked with a chuckle and sat on the bottom bunk.

"What? No. Why would you think that?"

Hazina studied Atalanta in silence for a moment. Though Atalanta wore a dress, she hadn't bothered to do anything else more feminine. She still wore her hair wrapped in the scarf, she still stood and walked everywhere like she expected people to get out of her way, and she never gave false, flirtatious smiles. Yet Damien had treated her more like a lady each day. More like he treated Hazina.

"When we first met, you told me you and Damien had known each other for almost your entire lives," she said, not sure how to express the changes she had noticed.

"That's right," Atalanta nodded. She took a seat beside Hazina on the bed.

"But it was only last year that you both learnt to set aside your hatred."

Atalanta laughed. "Is there a question in all this?"

"Did you spend much time together after Methoni? When I last saw you two, it was an uneasy truce with perhaps the first sparks of respect. Now..." Hazina shrugged. Calista had warned her of the bickering and simmering hatred, yet she hadn't seen much evidence of it.

"Other than the rest of our journey with Calista, we've only spent about a week together over the past year."

"Did something happen? Calista said—"

Atalanta smiled. "I'm sure she said you would need to make sure we behaved and didn't try to kill each other."

"Not in so many words."

"We ran into each other completely by accident around the winter solstice—Christmas. I had been given a job to escort a lady to see relatives in Rome over the holidays, but wasn't required once in the city. Damien was... you know, I'm not sure why he was in the city."

"Did it not come up in conversation?" Hazina asked, tucking her feet up beneath her as she settled in.

"No, but then if you asked him, he wouldn't know why I was there either."

"If you two did not talk, then what happened while you were in Rome? Alone?" Hazina raised an eyebrow.

Atalanta snorted, though her cheeks were bright red. "We talked about our families, actually. For all that we were raised to hate each other, our parents were very similar. Strict and always pushing us harder. Never letting us rest during our training. I suppose we must have bonded over it."

"And?"

"And what?"

Hazina sighed. "You two are attractive and similar in so many regards. Unless one, or both, of you have a sweetheart elsewhere, I am a bit surprised nothing has come of it."

Atalanta rubbed her temples and sighed. "We did exchange gifts, and Hector was amused for some months afterward. He said they would have been sweetheart gifts between anyone else."

"Wait... who is Hector?"

"My friend and employer in Spain."

Hazina's brow pinched. "Is he...or, do you want him to be your sweetheart?"

Atalanta laughed. "Hector is the dearest friend I have ever know. If I had to marry, he would be my first choice. But... it's not something I want. And I doubt that will change in the near future."

"You are not going to be a young woman for much longer," Hazina pointed out. "If you have chosen Spain as your permanent home, people are going to notice that you remain unwed."

"So?"

"Unwed, wear men's clothing, and, I assume, live on your own?" When she nodded, Hazina continued, "You will be lucky if they only label you a trollop. They might decide you are a witch."

Atalanta wrinkled her nose. "I'm not hurting anyone. I'm not even stealing from them anymore."

"Give it some thought," Hazina advised. "Damien is quite similar and might make a good match, though it sounds as if this Hector may be just as suitable. If he is not already married."

Atalanta mumbled under her breath but still nodded. She rose and moved to her own bunk. Hazina blew out the small lamp in their room and climbed beneath her blankets. It seemed she had only closed her eyes when a shudder of the boat bounced her from the bed.

She groaned and pushed herself up, her cheek and knee stinging from the impact with the wall and floor.

"Hazina?" Atalanta asked, her voice thick with sleep. "Has something happened?"

"I am unsure."

She gave herself a shake and crept toward the door. She could hear shouting and running feet above them and out in the hallway beyond their cabin. Her hand had only just closed around the door handle when a deep boom broke the night and another shudder shook them.

Hazina pulled the door open and rushed through. She made it two steps before running into someone.

"Oof, careful there... Hazina?" Damien squinted down at her. In the darkness she could barely make out the outline of his face and shoulders, but the flickering lamplight was behind him.

Atalanta came up behind her, fingers pressing against her back before dropping away. "Do you know what's going on, Damien?" she asked.

"It sounded like cannon fire, but I'd expect more screaming if we were under attack."

A third boom split the night. Screams and splintering wood accompanied the rolling. The boat rocked so hard Hazina instinctively grabbed at Damien to keep from falling.

"Guess they hadn't hit us yet." Atalanta slipped past them and started down the hall, her skirt swishing in an eerie silence that followed the previous moment's chaos.

Hazina and Damien hurried after her. Sailors swarmed between the ladder and galley. Some rushed down into the hold, while others brought forth a surprisingly large supply of weapons. A variety of swords were thrown across the tables and benches. Some were long, others short. Most looked ill cared for with dark spots on the blades and peeling leather wrapped around the hilts. A few sailors fumbled with pistols that were as untrustworthy looking as the blades.

Damien overtook Atalanta and preceded her up the stairs. She barely paused before climbing up behind him. Hazina stopped just long enough to grab one of the blades off the table and wished she had thought to bring her throwing daggers. By the time she climbed to the deck, Atalanta and Damien were lost amongst the chaos.

A large chunk of the rail and some of the deck itself had been chewed up by a cannon ball. The metal projectile was buried in the wood, pinning the leg of a sailor who screamed and writhed while everyone else ran around him. Ganim, despite his lack of height, was easy to spot. He shouted at sailors, directing them to position cannons and return fire. She wasn't sure where they had been hidden before, but they were chained to the deck now.

She turned to stare at the ship attacking them. It looked like the sister of the one they were on. Tall masts stretched up to the sky with sails so dark they might have been made of the night sky. The figurehead on the other ship was serpentine, with teeth bared. It was painted so that, even in the sliver of moonlight bearing down on the battle, it gleamed.

Men ran about the other deck, shouting and loading cannons. They waved swords and clubs overhead, and maneuvered long planks of wood. For a moment Hazina didn't understand what they were doing. She jumped back when the first plank slammed down, bridging the distance between the two vessels. Hooks on the end of the planks bit into the deck to anchor them. The boards were still vibrating from the impact when the first sailor ran across.

Hazina swung with all her might and buried her borrowed blade into the attacker's stomach. He gaped at her and she planted her foot against his leg to yank the sword free. His gurgle was lost as he fell overboard. She didn't have time to feel sorry for his death as more men dashed across and forced her back into the press of defending sailors.

Cannon fire flashed back and forth between the ships. She flinched when a metal ball barreled through the sailors who had been fighting beside her a heartbeat before. One had been a sailor on *the Lion*, but the other had been an attacker. In the dark, it was almost impossible to tell friend from foe.

Hazina's blade was dull and clubbed men more often than cutting them. She had no idea how it had dug into that first man's stomach. It wasn't long before she abandoned the weapon all together. Her fists were quicker and almost as effective.

Blood and gore spread across the deck as men were cut down. She was vaguely aware she had received her fair share of injuries. She was acutely aware, however, of the fact that, if she paused for even a moment, someone would kill her. Briefly, she saw Atalanta and Damien fighting back-to-back before the roiling crowd swallowed them up from view again.

A red glow spread over the scene and smoke billowed across the deck. Someone screamed "Fire!" and the battle paused while the call was taken up by other sailors. Hazina spun in a circle, searching for the source of the flames. The smoke burned her eyes and throat. For a long moment, she thought *the Lion* was on fire. Relief flood through her when she realized it was the other ship.

Silence fell. The crackling roar of fire was the only thing to break the stillness as hungry flames climbed the masts and licked the sails. A shift in the wind blew the smoke away from *the Lion* and revealed the devastation of the other ship in all its glory. The men nearest the planks worked together to dig the hooks out of the wood and push the beams overboard before the fire could crawl across to them.

The glow faded in increments as the ship sank beneath the sea. The darkness that followed seemed so much deeper and more threatening than a normal night.

"Lions, to me!" Ganim shouted from somewhere to the aft of the boat.

"Vipers, attack!" a man near the midship shouted in return.

At once the fighting began anew. There was a desperate edge to it now. Hazina's fists were no longer enough to deter an attacker. A man with a club tackled her to the ground so hard the breath was knocked from her lungs. He raised the club overhead, but, before he could slam it down on her, an arm wrapped around his neck and dragged him off. She snatched up a pitted sword and scrambled to her feet.

"All right, Hazina?" Damien asked. He threw the limp body of the club wielder toward a cluster of men pressing toward them.

"Things are never dull around you two," she gasped.

Atalanta twirled through the sailors, almost like a dancer, as she thrust, parried, spun, and slashed. Her eyes glittered, though something dark was smeared across half of her face. "Been awhile since I've been in a good brawl."

A man stabbed at Damien with a dagger, the blade glancing across his hip. The sailor lost his grip on the small blade when Damien slammed his fist into the man's nose.

"I'd prefer one without sharp weapons to worry about." Damien grunted.

The three formed a small circle and beat back anyone who drew too close. It was both easier, and harder, than fighting alone. Atalanta and Damien seemed to have an easy rhythm with each other, even going so far as to switch places. Hazina struggled to fit into their dance. Slowly a ring of space opened around them as sailors stumbled into their enemies rather than draw near enough to be hit by the three companions.

"Enough! Lay down your weapons!"

Hazina wasn't sure where the voice had come from, though she knew it wasn't Ganim. The fighting around them ceased, though most of the sailors hesitated before letting their weapons drop. She rose on her tip toes and craned her neck to see who had called the fight to a halt.

A man jumped up on a box and was handed a lantern. He raised it high so the glow fell across his olive skin and high cheekbones. Dark hair fell in loose waves to his shoulders, though blood had matted it flat on one side.

"*The Lion* is claimed forfeit. All members of her crew may join me, or be thrown overboard. I have no tolerance for mutiny, and any found inciting such behavior will be bloodied for the sharks."

Faint grumbling rippled through the crowd, but no one protested. Once more, someone handed something up to the olive-skinned man. This time when he lifted it Hazina gasped. He held the head of Captain Ganim dangling by his hair. Though the dead man's jaw was slack, his eyes were open and seemed to glow with an inner, hellish light.

"I, Tamir Kattan, former captain of *the Viper,* claim *the Lion* as my own." He gazed out over the crowd with a solemn expression while his sailors cheered. He grinned and lobbed Ganim's head over the side of the boat. "All crew and passengers of *the Lion* are to line up. I'll speak with everyone and we'll see how many will litter the depths by morning."

His crew laughed. The sailors separated into Viper and Lion crews with an ease that seemed almost rehearsed. Hazina was sad to see how few of the defending sailors were still alive. Her eyes roved across the attackers and she realized there were barely more of them.

The line inched forward as sailors either joined in cleaning up the deck or were thrown overboard along with the dead from the fight. It didn't take long before the three companions stood before Kattan and another sailor. Captain Kattan wasn't a large man, though he wasn't small either. He lounged atop a box with an easy confidence that made him seem bigger than he was. The sailor next to him was as pale as any Italian woman of wealth might desire, though he was completely bald. He stood as tall as Damien with a broad jaw, cleft chin, and wide shoulders.

Kattan ran his eyes over them, lingering on Hazina. Her cheeks burned and she realized her simple sleep shift was slicked to her skin. Atalanta's dress hadn't fared much better, but she stared down the new captain with an anger that said she wasn't above clawing his eyes out if his gaze lingered.

"Crew and...ship trulls?"

Damien took a half step forward to place himself between Kattan's appraising gaze and Atalanta and Hazina. "Passengers."

The sailor standing beside Kattan laughed. "Truly?"

"Yes."

Kattan nodded. "From what I've heard, all three of you were fierce combatants. Not what I'd expect from simple passengers. Where was Ganim supposed to be taking you?"

"Methoni," Atalanta answered, leaning to the side so she could continue to glare at Kattan.

"Were you aware he wasn't taking you there?"

Hazina sighed. "We suspected, but had not yet decided what to do about it."

The bald sailor laughed again. "He was coming here to sell you. To us."

Atalanta glowered at the sailor. "Did you, or did Ganim, double-cross the other?"

Kattan leaned forward, propping his forearms on his knees. "He demanded more than the usual amount. Claimed you were worth twice what I normally pay. I disagreed. Though seeing you now, I suppose the old devil was probably right."

Damien growled and a faint hiss emanated from beneath Atalanta's scarf. The bald sailor's eyes locked on her, a peculiar expression clouding his features. Hazina placed a hand on her arm and squeezed gently. The hissing faded beneath the general sounds of men restoring the ship and the sailor's expression cleared, though he no longer grinned at them.

"What do you plan to do with us now?" Hazina asked.

Kattan scratched at a bit of dried blood on his chin. "I could take you as slaves, as had been the original intent. Or we could come to an arrangement."

"What sort of arrangement?" Damien asked, his fists clenched.

"You're a strong looking fellow. You can join the crew."

Damien's fists relaxed, though his shoulders were still tense. "What of my sister and her friend?"

"Sister, eh?" Kattan chuckled. "I can tell a lie when I hear it, but as you wish. Both women would be expected to provide companionship for the duration of the journey. To myself and the most loyal of my sailors."

"You will not touch them," Damien snarled at the same time Atalanta declared, "I'd wrestle a shark first."

Kattan jumped down from the box and stood before Damien. He stretched to his full height and the top of his head barely reached Damien's chin, yet he somehow towered over them. "You are on my ship now. I could slap all three of you in chains and sell you to whomever I please. And even the lowliest cabin boy would have his hour with your trulls. They would learn to beg for it."

It took both Atalanta and Hazina holding Damien back to keep him from attacking the captain. Hazina's arms burned. Atalanta couldn't have been trying very hard. She grunted. "It sounds as if… entertainment over coin…is what you want."

Damien twisted to stare at her with wide eyes and she stumbled from the sudden lack of resistance.

72

"Dancing and singing will not suffice," the captain warned.

Atalanta nodded thoughtfully. "I will fight any sailor willing to be humiliated. No weapons."

"Gladiatorial brawling?" Kattan grinned. If he had been at all worried about Damien striking him he didn't show it. "That might work. There would need to be something at stake, of course."

Atalanta sneered. "Of course. Any man who can best me can have me."

"No. Atalanta, you can't," Damien exclaimed. Both she and Kattan ignored him.

"Perhaps. Though that doesn't seem to be enough."

Her chin jerked up. "My freedom."

Damien moaned softly.

Kattan grinned wickedly and extended a hand. Atalanta shook it. He turned his grin on Hazina. "And what are you offering, Bellibone?"

"I can not fight like my companion, and my talents do not tend toward spectator sports," she said.

He tutted. "This was your suggestion. I will be disappointed if we have to pass you around after all."

Hazina's stomach fluttered. "I can best anyone at any game. Chess. Knucklebones. Alquerques. Even Hazard."

"There is always an element of chance to such things. I'm not sure how you expect that to entertain my men."

"I have certain drinks that are much more potent than whatever watered down ale remains in the galley."

Kattan's lips pursed. "What's to stop me from simply taking them from you?"

Hazina forced a smile on her face and prayed it didn't look as scared as she felt. "I did not realize you were familiar with brewing the sacred leaves from Yoruba. As you surely know, not long enough and there is no effect, too long and it can kill a man."

A flicker of worry ran across his eyes. "You're lying."

She shrugged. "I can bring you the leaves, but I ask you give me a bit more time to think of what else I might offer."

He studied her face, his brows knit, before giving a hesitant nod. "To ensure that your...leaves...are as potent as you suggest, you will brew a batch in the morning. If they prove to be satisfactory, then every man—winner or loser—who plays will receive a drink."

The flutter in her stomach increased to panicked flapping. "Then what is my cost of losing a game?"

Kattan's smile returned. "The same as your friend's. Any man who can beat you can have you, and should you lose a game your freedom will be forfeit."

"Agreed."

"I don't think this is a fair deal," Damien grumbled.

Kattan laughed. "I'm a pirate. If you ever think I'm giving you a fair deal, then you'll know you're about to be completely screwed over."

Chapter Six

A few hours later, though it felt like mere minutes, Damien woke to someone pounding on his door. He groaned and rolled out of bed. His muscles were sore from the prolonged fight and several cuts and scrapes stung when his bloodied shirt pulled away from where it had stuck. He grimaced. It would have been better to change, but he had been exhausted by the time Kattan allowed anyone to get rest.

He opened his door to see the bald sailor standing in front of Atalanta and Hazina's room. The sailor had somehow found time to wash up—there wasn't a drop of blood on him or his clothes. Damien's head felt like it were wrapped with linen and he just stared while he tried to piece together what the sailor would want with them so early in the day.

Atalanta yanked open her door and snarled. "What?"

"The captain wants to see you. All of you."

"Now?"

The sailor's lopsided smirk made Damien want to beat it off his face. "You could keep him waiting, if you want."

"Let us get dressed." Atalanta slammed the door in his face and Damien couldn't help but chuckle.

"She's a spicy one—is she like that when she's beneath you, as well?"

Damien's fist slammed into the sailor's face before he realized it. His knuckles throbbed. The sailor scowled and pressed a hand against his nose.

The sailor scowled at him. "If you ever hit me again, I'll string you up by your heels."

Hazina opened the door and stared at Damien and the sailor. Her lips tightened, but she didn't comment on the blood. She stepped out and Atalanta followed.

"Oh, no. You go back in there and change right now," the sailor said as soon as he saw Atalanta's vest and trousers.

She planted a hand on her hip and glared at him. "I assume we're being summoned because of the deal we made last night. I won't fight in skirts."

"Yes, you will."

She bared her teeth. "I'll not be disadvantaged by my clothing."

He shook his head, no trace of a smile on his face. "You'll fight in a dress or you'll fight naked. Captain Kattan wants a show, not a fair fight. And don't even think about wearing something beneath your skirts. If the sailors don't get at least one glimpse of your legs during a bout, you'll be lucky if all you have to do is fight another sailor naked."

She opened her mouth to argue but Hazina tugged her back toward the cabin. "We are already at a disadvantage. If we anger our captors they are likely to renege on all deals we have made with them." She shot a warning look at Damien before closing the cabin door.

"Your little priestess there has a good head on her shoulders."

"What? Hazina isn't a priestess."

"Oh?" The sailor's eyes widened and he pursed his lips in thought. "I was under the impression the only magic users in this part of the world were trained by some religion or another."

Damien's eyes darted to the empty hall stretching to the galley and stairs. Most doors were closed and the few open ones were dark inside, but that didn't mean they were away from prying ears.

The sailor smiled. It might have been genuine, but the blood smeared across his face made it more of a grimace. "You have nothing to fear from me—at least, not in this regard. I know a bit of magic myself, though nowhere near what my mother could do."

"Forgive me if I won't take the word of a pirate."

"Pirates have a code of honour. There are nine articles on *the Viper*, er... I suppose on *the Lion* now. Nine rules that apply to everyone on-board, from lowliest deckhand up to Captain Kattan himself."

Damien studied the sailor's face. There was no malice or deceit that he could see, but his throat clenched at the thought of trusting him. "So you say."

The sailor shook his head. "You're a member of the crew now. You'll learn soon enough, or you'll get tossed overboard."

Their conversation ended when Atalanta and Hazina stepped out of their cabin. Atalanta had changed into a simple gown and braided her hair, though she still kept the scarf wrapped around her head. Bandages with pinpricks of blood staining them were wrapped around Hazina's hands.

The sailor pulled a yellowed bit of cloth from behind his belt and wiped the blood off his face before smiling at Atalanta. "There now, don't you look lovely."

"Let's just get this over with," she said.

He shrugged and led the group up to the deck. In the early morning light the aftermath of the battle was fully visible. Rails, deck, and masts all bore scars from cannon balls and wild swings from swords and clubs. Although the bodies had been thrown into the ocean, the blood hadn't been scrubbed away, leaving the deck a strange mix of red, brown, and black over the honey-coloured wood.

Pounding from hammers and shouts filled the air as sailors scurried to and fro to repair the damage. Men climbed in the rigging to remove the sails. Damien nudged Hazina when she stopped to gawk at the black sails waiting to replace the torn ones being taken down.

Captain Kattan sat at a makeshift desk on the forecastle. Papers were bundled with string or tucked beneath bits of wood and chunks of broken iron to keep them from being blown away by the morning's gentle breeze.

"Eryx, you've brought me a pleasant distraction just when I needed it most," Captain Kattan said. He moved a small inkwell on top of the page he had been working on and leaned back in his chair.

"Aye, Captain."

Kattan ran his eyes over the three of them and nodded to himself. "As per our agreement last night, each of you will contribute to the crew for the duration of your stay with us. So long as your performances are satisfactory, you will be allowed to freely leave. When we reach Methoni."

Kattan's words set an itch burrowing behind Damien's navel. The captain looked like a cat after eating a bowl of cream.

"You, big one, will work as one of the sailors. Eryx is my first mate.

He will be the one to throw you overboard if you cause any problems. You will work under the boatswain—though I expect you'll be a simple swabbie, unless you've any aptitude for sailing.

"And you, pretty one, Eryx will escort you to the galley in a moment. You'll brew up a batch of your special drink and then one of the men will test it. If he dies, becomes ill, or is unaffected then I'll kill one of your friends. Slowly, and while you watch."

"We have names," Hazina said, her fists clenched at her sides.

"Aye, I'm sure you do. And if you survive for more than a week or two, I'm sure I'll learn them."

The itch in Damien's stomach turned into a fiery fist wrapped about his middle. "Weeks? When will you take us to Methoni?"

Captain Kattan shrugged. "We're doing quite well along this stretch, and there's fierce competition around Methoni. The Venetians want to keep it, the Ottomans want to take it, and pirates everywhere still remember when it was ours."

"How long must we play your stupid little game, then?" Atalanta asked, her braid twitching and rustling softly as agitated snakes struggled to free themselves.

"A few weeks at least. I'm unsure which side of the Mediterranean I want to winter on. But I'll know before a month is up. And to be fair, if I decide to stay along the Italian coast, I will let you off in some town."

"We need to be in Methoni within a week," Atalanta said, her voice almost raised to a shout.

Captain Kattan shrugged again. "You are free to try swimming there."

Damien's jaw ached from how tightly he had clenched his teeth. "You tricked us."

"I did no such thing. I made no promises to get you to your destination with all haste. In fact, I've been incredibly charitable given that I could fetch a nice stack of coins if I sold you three," Kattan pointed out.

"You—"

Kattan cut off Atalanta, "As I was saying, pretty one, if your drink is as good a diversion as you've implied, you will provide enough for every man who plays. Should you lose, the winner gets to have you for the night. Now, we do not normally allow for such extravagant gambling among the crew, but these are not normal events. You will play a game every other evening.

"On the other nights, my poplolly will have her fights. No weapons and no death. Same stakes. Though I will have someone check if we have anything more...enticing for you to wear. Your dresses are rather drab."

Atalanta snorted. "I thought I was to fight, not prance about in frippery."

"You will do both, and you will make it entertaining or I will consider it a loss," Kattan told her, his eyes dark and hungry.

"Is there anything else, sir?" Eryx asked. "Or should I escort them to their duties for the day?"

"No, that is all... Wait..." he called out as they turned to leave. "I will allow both women to rest tonight. Tomorrow, my bellibone will play. We want our poplolly to be properly rested for her first fight, after all."

Eryx inclined his head and led them back to the deck. He left Damien with a squirrelly looking man and escorted Atalanta and Hazina below deck. Damien worked until the sun half disappeared beyond the horizon. His arms and back burned from it all. The boatswain, called Bezio by the crew, tasked Damien with carrying the heaviest of supplies for the repairs and scrubbing the deck clean in between trips to and from the hold.

Damien collapsed onto a bench in the galley and let his head fall against the table. Men moved about as they ate, left for their beds, or up to the deck to sail *the Lion* through the night. Damien turned his head to the side and tried to focus on the conversation of the two sailors nearest him when he heard Hazina's name.

"—I've put my name in for the first night of gaming."

"You're a horrible gambler, Marino. You can't hope to win a night with her."

"I'm not so bothered about being the first to have her. But did you see what her drink did to that brute? What was his name? Petrillo. From the other crew."

"Kattan kept him alive? Wasn't he first mate to the other captain?"

"How am I supposed to know? He must have signed on to be crew under Kattan. Anyway, that Hazina woman banged around the galley making the strangest smelling thing I have ever smelt. Like mint, but sweet, and sort of burning."

"Who would want to drink something like that?"

"Just listen, Simon. So she made the drink and gives it to that brute. Of course, Eryx was there to make sure everyone behaved. Petrillo looked like he wanted to fight his way out of having to drink it, but he choked it down. At first he looked like he was going to be sick, then he got this strange smile on his face and started to laugh."

"What? Why?"

"I don't know. Hazina said people react differently to the tea, but they almost always find it relaxing and enjoyable."

"I don't trust it. That's why I'm going to spar with the other one—Lana, or something strange like that."

One of the sailors chortled. "She'll wipe the deck with your face."

"Will not. I've been training with Eryx."

"So you'll be able to take a punch or two, good for you."

Damien let his mind wander again as the sailors continued to bickered. A knot balled in his throat every time he thought about what Hazina and Atalanta were risking. Yet that wasn't the first such conversation he had heard about it. Most of the sailors seemed excited by the prospect—some were even interested in the novelty more than the possibility of forcing themselves on either of the women.

A bowl of soup sloshed when it was dropped in front of his face. Damien sat back in surprise and blinked uncomprehendingly at the bald sailor standing on the other side of the table.

"What do you want?" he demanded.

Eryx grinned and took a seat on the bench opposite. "You need to eat. Bezio worked you hard today, and he won't let up tomorrow. Would hate for you to faint and miss a single moment of the contests."

"I would gladly gut you and face the consequences if Hazina and Atalanta wouldn't also be punished."

Eryx laughed. "All three of you have such spirit. And I haven't smelt the kiss of magic in many years—makes me homesick."

Damien felt like his ears were burning. He glanced furtively around

80

them, but none of the other sailors appeared to have heard. He hissed when he turned back to Eryx. "Watch what you say. None of us want to be thrown overboard. Or worse."

"You don't need to worry."

"The other sailors might accept you—"

"No. I'm sorry, let me explain," Eryx interrupted. "I mentioned earlier that I knew some magic. It is very limited, I'll admit, but what it is good for is creating minor illusions. None of the sailors will realize we're talking about magic, or the preternatural, because it won't register on them. Though, if we do it too much, they'll be left with a sense of discomfort or unease."

"That…doesn't make sense, but sounds very useful," Damien said, some of his worry easing.

Eryx shrugged. "It's hard to explain to those who don't use magic themselves. But suffice it to say, the only people who will realize what we're talking about are those who already know of real magic."

"Why?"

"Well, I don't particularly want to be subjected to any of the horribly creative ways these people have to kill those they suspect of being witches."

Damien snorted. "No. I meant, why are you telling me this? Why do you seem like you want to help us?"

"Ooh. That."

Damien stared at Eryx, waiting for a response. After a long moment of silence, he asked, "Are you going to tell me."

"No. At least, not yet. It's nice to have a small taste of home, but I don't actually trust you."

Damien couldn't help but laugh. "You don't trust us? Really?"

"Aye, well, all I really know about you three is that you really want to get to Methoni for some reason," Eryx said and stood up. He paused and added, "Oh, and I know you and Atalanta have a complicated relationship. Protective yet antagonistic. Almost like you actually are siblings."

Damien was too tired to wonder about Eryx's parting remark. He slurped down the soup so quickly he didn't taste a single drop before stumbling his way back to his cabin. He fell on his bunk and was asleep before he could kick his boots off. A pounding on his door woke him far too soon.

"Wha'sit?" he slurred and yanked the door open.

A sailor with skin the colour of dark sand said something, but Damien was too busy trying to remember what the man's name was. After a moment of silence the sailor asked, "Are you all right?"

"Sorry, still half asleep."

"Bezio won't care. No one will."

"Then why are you here?"

The sailor rubbed a hand through black hair in need of a trim. "Eryx sent me to make sure you would be up. Said he didn't want you to miss a moment of Bezio's attention. Though if you were late you'd get a good thrashing. Would deserve it too. I would say the first mate was going soft, if he wouldn't knock my teeth out for it."

Damien grumbled a half-hearted thank you and tried not to stumble as he followed the sailor up to the deck. Bezio drove Damien until he started to daydream about snapping the squirrelly man in half and diving into the water to take his chances with the sharks there. He was taken aback when he was told to join the crowd gathered around Hazina and three men.

He didn't understand at first. The sun had started to dip behind the horizon and a board and pair of dice sat in the middle of the four players. Mismatched cups and small stacks of coloured tokens sat in front of the three sailors. Hazina held her tokens in her hand, letting them clink together while she studied her opponents.

Damien sank down onto a barrel. He watched in mute apprehension when Hazina took the dice and chose her main. Though he had passed many nights in taverns playing hazard, he found he couldn't follow as the dice circled between the players and tokens exchanged hands.

Eryx and Captain Kattan watched the game from the edge of the forecastle, cups of Hazina's brew in their hands. Damien wasn't sure if the grin on the captain's face was a good sign or not when the play whittled it down to only Hazina and one other sailor. Those watching laughed and commiserated with the poor luck of the two losers.

Damien vaguely wondered where Atalanta was. Eryx's words from the previous night taunted him. He shoved his worry over his old rival aside. He was just as concerned about Hazina as he was about Atalanta. He didn't treat them any differently. A grunt got tangled in his throat—that wasn't true and he knew it. He tried to tell himself that the only difference was due to the history between their families.

He had almost convinced himself when a cheer snapped his attention back to the game of chance. Hazina slumped forward, her shoulders shaking with laughter. Her opponent grinned and saluted her with his glass before joining the crowd. The sailors laughed and discussed the rolls of the game, but Damien paid them no mind. He pushed his way to Hazina's side.

"How are you?" he asked, crouching so he didn't have to speak loudly.

"Relieved that the game is over. Hazard is a risky game, but I think it provided a good show even for those not playing."

"And you won?"

Hazina's brow pinched. "I thought this was a common game here. Are you unfamiliar with it?"

"Ah, no, that is, I know it. I just…wasn't paying close attention. My mind was elsewhere," he admitted.

She nodded. "On Atalanta's fight tomorrow. Yes, I found myself worrying about it during the game as well."

"That could have been risky."

"If they had not been imbibing the steeped drink, then it would have been. I made them mild enough they should not see things of the spirit world, but even the best of the three struggled to make good calls."

Damien laughed. "Clever. I bet they don't even realize how much of a disadvantage it gives them."

Hazina smiled. "Exactly."

They retreated from the sailors still discussing the game and made their way to their rooms. Damien thought about asking Hazina where Atalanta was but pushed the desire aside. There wasn't anything he could do to help her prepare. It didn't stop his mind from buzzing until he fell asleep.

He woke just as groggy in the morning and half-stumbled his way through the tasks assigned by Bezio. By the time a space was cleared on the deck for Atalanta's fight, Damien felt as if his very bones were made of water.

Hazina stood beside him where he had collapsed onto a barrel. She kept a hand on his shoulder and squeezed when Atalanta's opponent stepped out of the crowd. He was built like an anvil—small but wide and incredibly solid looking. Atalanta stepped forward, a blue velvet cloak wrapped around her shoulders. Though her hair was still braided, someone had twined pearls into the plait, and her scarf was missing.

"Come now, poplolly, don't be modest," Captain Kattan called down at her.

She made a rude gesture and he laughed. Her eyes roved across the crowd until they settled on Damien and Hazina. The sad twist of her lips made Damien start to rise, but Hazina pressed him back down.

"She must face this alone," Hazina whispered.

"Gods help her," Damien murmured.

Atalanta threw the cloak back and let it fall to the deck. Her dress was a brilliant scarlet and laced so tightly she, somehow, appeared to have decidedly feminine curves. The sleeves were snug along her arms, but the skirts were quite full.

Several sailors whooped and her opponent grinned.

Her eyes narrowed. She grabbed fistfuls of skirt and squared off to him. At Kattan's call, she ran toward the sailor. His fist lashed out and she danced aside, turning to come along his flank. Yet she stepped on her skirts and stumbled.

The sailor's second punch landed squarely on her jaw. Blood and spit splattered against the deck and she reeled back. The crowd cheered. Damien felt a growl rumbling in his chest.

Atalanta shuffled back and threw an elbow that only grazed along her opponent's collar bone. The sailor grabbed her braid and yanked so hard she shrieked and fell to the floor. He cursed and dropped her hair almost instantly, pressing a bloody finger to his lips.

Hazina's grip on Damien's shoulders tightened almost painfully, but the fight continued.

The sailor was slow and unskilled, but Atalanta floundered in her skirts and restrictive gown. Orange and red sunlight bathed the deck as they circled each other. He stepped forward and jabbed at her head with a fist. She ducked beneath the strike, but he brought his other fist up to connect with her jaw. The crack echoed over the crowd, silencing everyone. Rather than crumpling, Atalanta lashed out and scraped her nails across his face.

He roared and stumbled back, blood dripping from four thin lines across his cheek. When he stepped forward and punched toward her face she sidestepped. Her skirts tore. She grabbed his wrist and placed a hand on his shoulder blade before slamming a knee into the outside of his thigh. His knee buckled but didn't give out.

Her snarl carried over the whistles and shouts of the crowd as she twisted the sailor's arm behind his back and drove a foot into the bend of his knee. His knees slammed into the deck and she dug her knee into his back, forcing him completely prone.

"Give up," she shouted.

The sailor roared and thrashed, pulling his free arm beneath him to try and rise. She shifted her grip ever so slightly, pulled, twisted, and dislocated his shoulder. The sailor's scream was met with gasps and laughter before the crowd broke into a smattering of applause and whistles.

Atalanta stumbled back, her chest heaving so hard it looked as if she were about to fall out of her dress.

Damien shoved himself to his feet and forced his way through the crowd with Hazina close on his heels. He caught Atalanta just before she fell in an exhausted and bloody mess.

"That was an entertaining fight," Kattan called over the crowd's noise. The sailors slowly fell silent. He nodded and added, "Hazina, see to my man's injuries before tending to your companion. She will have a day to rest before fighting again, but I need all my men in working form."

Hazina's jaw clenched but she nodded.

Damien scooped Atalanta into his arms and turned to go.

"One more thing," Kattan said. "In future fights, it would be advisable to not injure my sailors quite so much. Else we might need to renegotiate the terms of our deal."

Atalanta grasped Damien's shoulders so she could pull herself up enough to glare at Kattan. "I didn't kill him. That was the agreement."

"I didn't expect you to be so vicious, poplolly," he said.

"I'm not your poplolly, and I'm not some fainting damsel," she shot back.

Kattan laughed. "You've certainly proven that. I think your future opponents will be more ready for your tricks. What do you say, men?"

A loud cheer rose from the crowd in response. Damien ground his teeth and forced his way through the sailors. He didn't stop until he carried Atalanta all the way to her cabin. She winced when he placed her on the bottom bunk.

"I could have walked," she mumbled.

"Hush, you," he admonished and took a seat next to her.

She pulled away, then stopped when he grasped the end of her braid. With slow, careful movements, he unbound her braid. He closed his eyes and focused on the feel of her hair and the snakes mixed amongst the tresses. The snakes snapped and hissed as they came free. Damien hummed a half-remembered lullaby and ran a gentle finger across their heads. One-by-one, the snakes fell dormant until they sat in silence with a small pile of pearl hairpins on the bed between them.

He opened his eyes to see Atalanta rubbing the back of her hand across her eyes. She sniffled. "Thank you."

"You shouldn't have to be doing this."

"Can you think of another option?" she asked, turning to face him. Her eyes were red and her lip split, but no tears glistened on her cheeks.

Damien sighed. "I'm so tired I barely remember what we're even supposed to be doing."

She smiled, then winced. "We'll get to Methoni and deal with the real threat, we just need to convince Kattan to take us there right away. Even if it means I have to beat every single one of his sailors bloody."

"I wish I could help, or do it for you, or—"

"Your hero complex is showing again."

Damien smiled. "Atalanta."

"Fine, fine. The next time we're in a no-choice situation requiring somebody to get beaten repeatedly, then you can take the hit. I won't even argue."

He grunted, struggling to keep from laughing. "I suppose that's something at least."

Atalanta's breath hissed out when Hazina applied a stinging ointment to her arm. She was never quite sure how she got injured during her fights. As soon as the first punch was thrown, it became a blur of anger, blood, and pain. Sometimes she thought there was a second man, one made of shadows, who would trip or shove her, yet she was sure Damien or Hazina would object if that were true. It didn't stop the crawling itch between her shoulder blades every time she set foot on the deck.

"What was that?" Atalanta gave her head a shake and focused on Damien looming in the door to her cabin.

"The sailors are making very spirited wagers on this fight. You were vicious during your first, but you almost lost the second. They feel like they know what to expect from you now."

She tried not to flinch away from Hazina's fingers smearing ointment over her raw cheek. "I don't know how to fight in a dress—I'm not even sure what to expect from me."

"There. Now try not to rub it all off this time," Hazina said, wiping her greasy fingers on a rag.

"But that's the problem. Even though you won both times, it was far too close. You need to practice," Damien said.

Atalanta raised an eyebrow and tried to ignore the desire to rub a hand over her cheek. "You barely have enough energy to stagger back to your cabin most nights. You would be a useless sparring partner."

"Hazina?"

Hazina shook her head. "I am not a brawler. The best I could do is teach her how to run—which has yet to be a needed skill during these beatings."

"It would be better than nothing," Damien grumbled.

"I'll be fine," Atalanta told him. "Now get back to work before Bezio realizes you took a break."

He opened his mouth to argue then closed it when she glared at him. With an exasperated sigh, he turned and left.

"You do not need to be so difficult—he simply worries about you," Hazina said softly.

Atalanta snorted. "I don't need, or want, it. I am not some damsel to be rescued, or little sister to be protected."

"I do not think that is how he views you."

"Anything else would make things far too complicated, and I refuse to be a part of it."

Hazina laughed. "Whether you refuse or not—whether you even feel the same, or not—will likely have very little effect on his emotions."

"I'd never have this problem with Hector," Atalanta grumbled.

"Who is Hector?"

Atalanta looked up in surprise to see Eryx leaning in the door of the cabin, much the way Damien had before he left. The oily grin she had come to expect on his face was missing and for the first time she realized he wasn't staring at her and Hazina with the same hungry, contemplative look shared by the rest of the sailors.

"Did your mother not teach you it is impolite to enter a woman's room without invitation?" Hazina demanded. She shoved off the bed and stepped between Eryx and Atalanta as if her small frame could prevent him from doing as he wanted.

Eryx chuckled. "She taught me many things—but I haven't actually entered your room, and an open door is an invitation to passerbys. Has no one warned you to lock your door?"

"What do you want?" Atalanta asked, leaning to peek around Hazina.

"I've noticed you struggle with your dress each night and thought I might offer some assistance before tonight's bout."

"Damien has already suggested I practice fighting in the blasted skirts. I doubt it will make much difference."

Eryx's brow crinkled for a moment before smoothing into a grin. Atalanta wondered if he meant it to be a pleasant expression or if he realized it made him look like he was about to talk her out of her purse.

"No, practicing at this point would only tire you," he agreed. "What I had in mind were some…wardrobe modifications."

"The dress is already revealing enough, and it rips to reveal more during every fight, no matter how well we sew it back together," Hazina snapped.

"That's exactly the problem. The captain wants a show that tantalizes and entertains, so he's given you a dress that is probably a bit too small, and definitely not suited to being in a brawl. You, of course, want to maintain what little dignity you have left."

"Yes. We are all aware of this," Atalanta drolled.

"I think I know how make everyone happy—and make it easier for you to fight," Eryx continued.

Hazina asked why at the same time Atalanta demanded how.

"You might hide in your cabin between fights, but I think I like you three. You've got spirit. I'd hate to see it beaten out of you. As for your dress…"

Hazina and Atalanta instantly rejected the plan, simple as it was. Eryx calmly explained his reasoning until both women agreed it would make the fights easier without removing any of the salaciousness. Both of them were surprised when he folded himself to sit on the limited floorspace in the cabin and assist with the modifications.

"I'm still not sure why you're doing any of this," Atalanta said when they had finished.

Eryx shrugged and carefully unfolded himself so he could stand. "You remind me of home. All three of you, to some extent, but you specifically."

"Am I some sort of replacement for a sister you haven't seen in years?" Atalanta asked.

"No. My mother actually. She was full of fire, just like you."

Hazina tilted her head and studied him with a puzzled frown on her face. "If you miss your home and family, why do you not return?"

"I interfered in a sacred rite and was banished for it," Eryx explained, his eyes focused on some distant memory.

"That can be hard for a heart to bear," Hazina said, laying a soft hand on his arm. "I too am unable to return home."

He gave her a sad smile. "Surely a bellibone such as yourself could make a new home somewhere?"

"Perhaps someday. It is still fresh and I am unready to look for a replacement."

"Ah, there's your first mistake," Eryx said. "You will never be able to replace what you've lost. You can only start over and find happiness elsewhere. It won't fill the hole, but it will ease the pain."

"You haven't ever tried that, yourself?" Atalanta asked. "If you're so very homesick, why don't you make yourself a new home?"

"I tried, once. It ended in heartbreak."

"I am sorry to hear that." Hazina dipped her head.

He spread a grin on his face that didn't mask the pained look in his eyes. "Enough about that. The fight will be starting soon and Kattan will wonder where I am. I doubt he would appreciate the help I've provided."

"Thank you, Eryx," Atalanta called after him as he turned to leave. He gave a single wave before hurrying away.

Hazina closed the door and helped Atalanta into the modified gown. She sighed and stood back to study their efforts. "I dislike how revealing it is, but it should not hamper you near as much any longer."

"It does feel much easier to move," Atalanta agreed. She stretched and jumped, twisting and turning to test the gown. The bottom of the shortened skirts brushed against her knees, but didn't impede her. When it didn't rip or fall apart, she wrapped the velvet cloak around herself. "Time to prance for the crustaceans on the ship."

They made their way up to the deck where the sailors were already gathered. Off the starboard side she could clearly see the shore and what looked like a small town. Vessels of various sizes drifted on the calm sea, heading toward port as the sun sank. *The Lion* slowly crept closer to the shore as well, though not angled in the direction of the town. She had no idea where they were or what town it was they were drifting past, but also had no time to wonder further about such things.

The crowd of sailors cheered when she pushed through them. A scrawny man with a pinched face bounced from foot to foot, waiting for her. He had wrapped strips of fabric around his fists and his crooked nose attested to the fact that he knew what to do in a fistfight. When she stepped out of the crowd he grinned and pulled his shirt off. Though thin, his arms and chest were heavily corded with muscle.

The modifications to the dress felt foolish.

Atalanta's fingers trembled. She dropped her cloak and kept her eyes locked on her opponent. Stunned silence met her for the briefest of moments before the watching sailors whooped and whistled. Her cheeks burned and she forced herself to not tug at the knee-length skirt, or the shortened sleeves.

"Well, this is a welcome surprise," Kattan said, his voice ringing over the sailors. "Gives a bit more of a taste of what the winner will get to enjoy, eh boys?"

The sailors laughed and Atalanta's fists clenched. She could feel the snakes bound in her braid struggling to free themselves. She knew exactly how they felt. At least the headaches caused by keeping them bound up had receded to a dull, if constant, ache.

"Get on with it, then!"

Her opponent danced toward her, a lazy ease to his movements. She couldn't help but grin when she realized he still expected her to stumble around. Her grin widened when she darted in and slammed her fist into his face. The crunch of his cheek suggested she broke something, but he didn't make a sound.

His face was darkly furious though.

The sound of the crowd faded away. She and the scrawny sailor circled each other. Without the skirts to hamper her, she felt almost at ease as they traded punches. He landed three punches for every two of hers, and his certainly felt heavier than anything she could do. Yet all of her strikes hit his head, while his landed against ribs, arms, and back.

Blood streamed from his nose and his left eye was swollen shut from her first punch. A sharp jab to her ribs burned as if the sun had settled behind them. Before she could land another hit, he slammed a fist into her shoulder. Her right arm dropped and burning tingles raced up and down her arm. It hurt to lift, and she couldn't raise it all the way.

Each breath was a struggle and her strikes slowed until he was landing two strikes for every one of hers that connected. From the corner of her eye, she noticed Damien and Hazina at the front edge of the watching crowd. Their hands were entwined and a mix of fear and desperation was on their faces.

Atalanta grunted and planted her feet. Her opponent's fist slammed against her upper chest. Searing pain instantly flared through her right arm. She screamed when she tried to lift the arm back up. Even her shoulder sagged.

He jabbed toward her face with a victorious grin on his. She gritted her teeth and stepped to the side, her palm sliding along the outside of his arm. She slammed her elbow into his ribs, grabbed his arm and spun him a quarter turn, then drove her knee up as hard as she could. He recoiled, his arms dropping to cover his jewels as he retched. Atalanta buried her hands in his hair and pulled his head down at the same time she brought her knee back up.

He stumbled back a few steps before collapsing to the deck. His groaning whimper spread over the silent crowd while Atalanta swayed on her feet.

"Uh…" Kattan cleared his throat and tried again, "It would seem the poplolly has won again."

A smattering of applause met his statement. Murmurs rippled through the sailors. Atalanta focused on the captain's oddly neutral face. "I won? It's done?"

"Yes."

"Oh…good."

She collapsed to the deck, her body screaming at the abuse. She was vaguely aware of people shouting and moving around her, but her mind was a haze. It wasn't until someone tried to pick her up that she roused. Damien quickly put her back down on the deck when she cried out.

"What can I do?" he asked, his hands fluttering around her.

"Help me up… Not on that side!"

"Sorry, sorry, sorry," Damien muttered and moved to her left side, sliding her good arm around his shoulders. Her ribs ached when his hand pressed against them, but she gritted her teeth and scrambled back to her feet.

Eryx and Hazina stood between her and several angry looking sailors. Their words skipped and slid along her mind, their meanings disappearing into the ether. Even though she couldn't make the words sit still long enough to understand them, she knew they were angry about the outcome of the fight.

Damien tried to coax her to walk. Her feet wouldn't respond and he ended up dragging her more than anything.

"What about Hazina?" she asked, trying to twist to see what was happening. The movement made the world swing wildly around them. She squeezed her eyes shut and groaned.

"She'll be fine. Let's get you settled before you start worrying about anyone else," he told her.

Atalanta wasn't sure how, but the next thing she knew she was laying on the bunk in her cabin. Someone had removed her boots and covered her with a blanket. Gentle tugging on her hair made her twist, which elicited a hiss of pain.

"Calm, Atalanta. You're safe. Just rest," Damien cooed.

She closed her eyes and settled back against the bed. His fingers were soft as they undid her braid and soothed the snakes. She wondered what the snakes felt under his touch. Whatever it was, they fell dormant almost instantly.

He had almost finished when Hazina returned. Eryx followed close on her heels. They both stepped into the cabin and then shut the door, even though there wasn't anywhere near enough room for them all comfortably.

"So, what has Kattan decided?" Damien asked.

"Nothing yet," Eryx answered.

"Decided what?" Atalanta asked, struggling to sit up. "He said I won. He can't say I lost because I fell after!"

Damien pushed her shoulders down and Hazina squeezed in beside him to run cool fingers over her arms. Atalanta whimpered, unsure if her movement or their touch hurt more.

"You did win, but you are also clearly too injured to be able to fight again in two nights," Eryx explained.

A surge of panic flooded her and it was only by gritting her teeth and digging her nails into the bunk's straw filled pallet that she kept herself from trying to get up again. "I won't let him, or you, or anyone else, have me without a fight. I won't give up."

"Shh," Hazina soothed. "No one is saying that."

"Kattan wants to cancel your fights until you're better," Damien said.

"Oh…then what's the problem?"

Eryx sighed and ran a hand over his bald head. "While most of the sailors understand, there are several who are…disappointed. They feel this decision would rob them of the chance to claim you."

"But Kattan is the captain, and he said no, right?" Atalanta asked.

"He is the captain, but unlike on naval ships, pirate captains are voted. And they can be voted out if the crew are unhappy with them. It's why he hasn't said what his decision will be," Eryx replied.

"Oh…"

Damien growled softly. "Do you think it's likely he'll side with these savages?"

Eryx shrugged. "It's hard to say. There were only a few who complained when he suggested letting Atalanta heal, but the more they grumble about the unfairness of it, the more the other men might start to agree."

"We need to get off this cursed ship," Hazina declared.

"Easier said than done," Damien said, his voice rumbling so much it made Atalanta's skin vibrate where his hands still rested. "Kattan might recognize the need for Atalanta to rest, but as far as he's concerned, we still owe a debt of service."

"It's true," Eryx agreed. "He wouldn't let you off, no matter if you begged and offered all the jewels of Egypt itself. But who says we have to ask for his permission?"

"We?" Damien asked, his voice snapping like a whip. "You are not one of us. Go back to your pirates and leave us be."

His gaze shifted between the three companions. Damien glared, Hazina dropped her eyes, and Atalanta held his stare. She didn't agree with the extreme animosity in Damien's tone, but they didn't know Eryx. He had been helpful and somewhat friendly to them, but that didn't mean much.

Eryx cleared his throat. "I know you have no reason to trust me—"

"Absolutely none," Damien cut in.

The two men glowered at each other until Hazina sighed. "Children, play nice."

Damien opened his mouth to argue, but Eryx chuckled and said, "As you wish, bellibone."

"This is why we don't trust you"—Damien jabbed a finger at Eryx—"or your intentions. You're a pirate through and through."

"I wasn't always," he said softly. "I didn't intend to become one. I made some poor choices, and seeing you three has reminded me of who I am. I'm a son of the—"

"No one cares," Damien cut in again.

Atalanta frowned at him. "You're being ruder than necessary. And if he has a feasible plan for us to escape, I think we should hear him out."

Eryx inclined his head. "Thank you. We would steal a dinghy."

Hazina scoffed. "If we stole a dinghy and fled to the mainland, Kattan would be upon us before we even reached shore. And I doubt he would be in a charitable mood after we tried to flee."

Eryx shook his head. "We wouldn't head toward Italy."

"Heading anywhere else would be foolish," Damien pointed out.

"I can smell the sea in Atalanta's blood, surely she can do something to speed us along. Even if we go in the complete opposite direction expected, there's no other way for us to get far enough away that we wouldn't be spotted."

Damien snarled. "Your entire escape plan hinged on the belief that Atalanta has some sort of magic? You didn't think to check first?"

Eryx scowled in response. "Things have progressed rather quickly. I didn't realize an escape plan was needed until a little while ago."

"I have no powers and my forefather has never shown the least bit of interest in what happens to me," Atalanta explained before either man's voice grew any louder. A tiny part of her wondered what it would be like to have Poseidon recognize her as one of his descendants. She quickly, and ruthlessly, squashed the thought.

"I thought all half-gods had amazing abilities," Eryx said, his tone questioning.

"Maybe if we were half-gods, rather than being thousands of years distant from that blood," Damien said, his voice surprisingly thick with bitterness.

"What sort of intercession had you expected her to provide?" Hazina asked.

Eryx shrugged. "A magical wave to push the boat along? Perhaps dolphins or other sea life to tow us. This part of the world is home to the hippocampi, isn't it?"

"I cannot summon sea life to do my bidding, but I may be able to call on a water spirit to help," she offered.

Eryx's brows knit. "That's not how magic works. There are no such thing as elemental spirits."

"Perhaps not where you come from, but I have called on them before. They do not always answer me though," Hazina said, spreading her hands wide and gesturing.

"That's not...never mind. If you say you can 'summon a spirit' to help, then I think stealing a dinghy will be our best option," he said.

Damien grumbled about the room for fatal errors but had no other suggestions. Atalanta, Hazina, Damien, and Eryx quickly formed a plan to escape once the sun was fully gone from the sky. It didn't take long to lay out each person's tasks. With that done, Hazina shooed the men from the cabin and turned her attention to doing what she could for Atalanta's many injuries.

Hazina sighed. "I wish we could wait at least a day so you could have some time to recover."

Atalanta laughed, though it sent strange tingles through her ribs and arm. "I'm not sure even Asclepius himself could heal me enough that I wouldn't put everyone at risk. We will do what we have to and pray for the best."

"I did not realize you prayed to any gods."

"I don't, but these are desperate times. And last year certainly showed that there are plenty of them with an interest in Damien and I."

Hazina breathed a sigh of relief. "That is good. They will help us."

Atalanta started to shrug but stopped with a groan. "Maybe. I have no idea why they're interested. It could simply be boredom."

"That is less reassuring."

"There's only one I trust to not make a mess of things, but I doubt she could be of much help here. Ptokheia is a goddess of beggars,"

Atalanta explained.

"In this case, we are very much like beggars. Pray to her while I bind your ribs."

Chapter Seven

Hazina hugged the wall, teeth gritted and bag clutched to her chest, as she crept past the rooms where the sailors hung their hammocks. Atalanta followed, the soft sounds of her movements drowned out by the water lapping against the hull. Even with all of her various injuries, she was much quieter than Hazina. The air around them was cool and damp, the shadows tasting of sea and citrus. She wondered if Kattan had moved the ship closer to the shore after the fight, but pushed the thought aside.

She paused where the hallway turned. The stairs were to their left, but the galley was open to the hall and lay to the right. A single lamp flickered in the galley. There was no one immediately visible. Hazina sucked in a breath and shifted her bag so it rested against her back before scurrying up the stairs. She crouched and moved toward the ship's railing, her eyes scanning the dark deck for the sailors on duty.

Two men lounged on the quarterdeck, their soft conversation only a whisper louder than the creaking wood and sloshing sea. Another three on the forecastle leaned against the railing. Hazina frowned and swept her gaze from bow to stern and back. She wasn't sure, but she felt there should be more sailors.

Atalanta gave her shoulder a soft nudge and pointed up at the quarterdeck. Hazina nodded and crept toward the stairs. Their goal was to reach the dinghy lashed to the stern of the ship without being spotted, but she wasn't sure how they were to do that. They paused when they reached the bottom of the stairs. The sailors were no longer visible to them, but snippets of their conversation wafted on the fragrant breeze.

"—not sure I agree... Captain Kattan has our best interests in mind."

"Don't be soft. You saw what she did to Simon...her right now—"

A cold anger simmered in the pit of Hazina's stomach. The sailors were polite to her from the start—even though they competed for the same prize as those who fought Atalanta—but every single one had been savagely delighted at the idea of beating, and then having their way with, Atalanta. A small voice in her heart said it was because even those who lost during the games of chance were given something of some value. Mostly she seethed that the men couldn't, or wouldn't, recognize the extreme toll the fights were taking on her friend.

Her fingers slipped beneath her belt and closed around one of the throwing daggers hidden there. She was just about to start a slow crawl up the stairs when a shout from behind them made her freeze.

"Paolo, Gian, come here," Eryx called. The men on the quarterdeck moved to the railing and peered down at him.

Hazina and Atalanta flattened themselves against the wall beneath the railing. Even in the shadows, they would be easy to see if the sailors came down to the deck. Fear snaked its way through her stomach to coil around her heart—was Eryx going to betray them? This hadn't been part of the plan.

"What is it?" one of the sailors above them asked.

"I need help down below and didn't want to wake anyone. Come with me," Eryx instructed.

The sailors hesitated for a moment before one of them replied, "I'll help, but Captain Kattan would have our hides if we left the wheel unattended."

Eryx nodded. "Fair enough. We shouldn't be too long, then you two can laze about trading gossip undisturbed."

The sailors chuckled and one descended the stairs. He didn't look to the side, and disappeared down the ladder with Eryx. Hazina blew out a small breath. She had expected Eryx to betray them right up to the moment he disappeared below deck. A little worm of guilt pricked at her conscience. Despite being a member of Kattan's crew, he had been surprisingly helpful. She couldn't decide if it was enough for her to give him any amount of trust.

Atalanta tapped her shoulder and nodded once before slipping up the stairs as silently as a shadow. The gentle sound of wind and waves tugging at the ship and sails almost hid the soft thud of a body being lowered to the floor. Hazina crawled up the stairs and peered toward where Atalanta crouched over a prone body. It was too dark to tell at that distance whether the man was dead or not, and Hazina decided she didn't want to know, one way or another.

Atalanta moved away from the body in an awkward crawl that still managed to be almost perfectly silent. She gave a single nod and Hazina moved to the winch holding the dinghy secure. A quick cut with one of her daggers sliced through the ropes.

The small craft bumped against the larger vessel and Hazina winced at the dull noise. She glanced over her shoulder and bit her lip to keep from shouting when she saw two men climbing the stairs. Her heart stuttered in relief when she recognized Eryx's broad shoulders and Damien's prowling gait.

Atalanta leaned against her and whispered, "How does the boat look?"

"It is almost free. Though if I cut any more of these ropes I think it will drop," Hazina whispered back.

"Get in, then. Hopefully, Eryx knows how to lower it without the assistance of someone on deck."

Hazina climbed in and turned to help Atalanta. She stood with a hand extended to her for a moment before Atalanta accepted the help. A hiss of pain was the only sign her injuries impeded her in any way.

Once Atalanta was settled, Hazina braced against the ship as best she could to keep the dinghy from swaying and bumping it while they waited for Damien and Eryx to join them. The boat banged despite her best efforts when the men climbed in.

"Everything all right?" one of the sailors from the forecastle called.

"Yes, just tripped," Eryx called back.

Faint laughter met his answer. He pulled on a winch and slowly lowered the dinghy. Atalanta pulled a pair of oars free from where they had been tucked beneath the bench. Damien nestled Atalanta's sack between his feet and then took one of the oars. Eryx took the other once they were free of the ship and together the two men propelled them through the darkness.

The edge of the sky lightened to grey before they were free of the hulking shadow cast by *the Lion*. "Now would be a good time to do whatever it was you were planning on doing," Eryx told Hazina.

She nodded, though she doubted he could see it in the dark. Tucked into the final band of the knife sheaths across her stomach was a small ceramic ball. It was too dark to see what colour or symbol had been painted on it, which was why she had put it there rather than leaving it in her bag.

Hazina pressed the ball to her lips and prayed it would work. She scooped water into her hand, dropped the ball into her palm, and then crushed it, letting the water and liquid inside the ball pour back into the sea while she whispered an incantation beneath her breath.

For a moment nothing happened other than her heart pounding so hard against her ribs she felt sure one of them would crack. A faint splash heralded a tiny, silvery figure rising from the water. It twirled once, water flaring out around its waist like a skirt.

"Help us get away," she whispered to the being. "Help us be far from this spot before the sun rises."

The figure disappeared back beneath the water and then a roll of water rose behind the dinghy and carried it forward. The speed at which the spirit pushed them on made a breeze which snapped past them with chill fingers. Hazina was vaguely aware of Atalanta saying something, but she was too focused on keeping the spirit under her control to truly hear the words. Every moment they sped away from the pirate ship, she could feel the spirit draining her energy.

She knew it wouldn't be long before she had no energy left to give and the little spirit abandoned them.

Eryx's hands were blistered and sore from rowing. He dipped his hands into the water and winced at the bite of the salt. Blood had smeared, dried, and flaked off Damien's oar, but he didn't complain. Eryx admired his stubbornness.

Hazina lay curled against Eryx's legs and, even deep asleep, her exhaustion tugged at him. He silently berated himself for letting her overexert herself. It would be days before she would have the strength to use magic again.

Atalanta wasn't in much better shape. Red fading into dark purple, and sickly yellow at the edges, ringed her left eye. Scrapes marched over each other, from temple to jaw, on the right side of her face. Those injuries at least had the look of starting to heal. The unnaturally vibrant red bruising across her shoulder, chest, and neck almost hid the bulge along her collarbone. Her arm was in a sling, and though her other injuries were hidden beneath her tunic, her pain was like a rancid lemon pressing at his senses.

His eyes met Damien's and there was a surge of protectiveness from him. Eryx gave a weary nod. Neither of them were willing to pass the oars to either woman. No matter how blistered or bloody their hands were.

The Lion was nowhere to be seen. There was no land, or birds, either. Only open sea all around them. The only navigating they could do with the sun high overhead was to head East. Eryx was uncomfortably aware of the fact that they had no idea how far they had come, or how far they still had to go.

"You two need to rest," Atalanta said. Damien's jaw clenched so hard Eryx was surprised he didn't crack a tooth. Atalanta held up a hand and smiled. "I promise I won't try and row—at least, not until my shoulder is stronger. But you two are going to exhaust yourselves to the point of passing out like Hazina. That won't get us to safety any faster than if you take a break."

"It would be nice to drink and eat something," Damien begrudgingly admitted.

"Not too much though," Eryx cautioned. "We don't know how many days we have to spend in this dinghy."

"How long, at most, do you think it might take us to reach Methoni?" Damien asked, leaning his elbows against his knees.

Eryx pursed his lips. "Well, an average ship can make it in four days if they don't run into any trouble. I expect we're going half that speed—at best. But we won't be able to do a whole day of it, so…twenty days, give or take."

Atalanta sighed. "We're all going to be uncomfortably familiar with each other by the end of this."

"Once Hazina has recovered, we might be able to cut some of that time off," Eryx suggested. "And if she knows how, we can each give her a bit of our own energy so it isn't quite so taxing."

"Would that work? It seemed as if you two are familiar with different types of magic," Damien pointed out. He pulled Atalanta's sack out and retrieved a loaf of bread, wedge of cheese, and flask. Eryx was intensely curious about the magical bag, but Damien had refused to say anything more than that it was Atalanta's while they escaped the ship. He pushed aside his questions. There would be plenty of time, while they floated across the sea, for Eryx's curiosity to be sated.

Damien broke the food into four portions and distributed a piece to each of them, even waking Hazina to eat her share. They ate in silence while the sun beat down on them. The gentle waves of the sea pushed them around while they each sank into exhausted silence.

When the simple meal was finished, Eryx brushed his crumbs into the sea and asked, "Hazina, where did you learn magic?"

She stifled a yawn with her first. "I was chosen as a young girl by the Queen Mothers to learn. I had only started such training when the were killed by a corrupted vodunisi. Rather than remaining in my village, I dedicated myself to hunting her down. I practiced what little I had learnt, and was taught other tricks from some of the people I encountered along the way."

"Ahh."

"Ah?" Hazina's brows shot up.

"Magic has the same rules regardless of where you come from, but you talk about it as if it were something entirely different," he said. "Which makes sense if you had only really begun your formal training, before having to figure it out on your own."

Hazina's eyes dropped to her lap and her hands plucked at her skirts. "I did what I could."

"It's nothing to be ashamed of," Eryx reassured her. "In fact, it's quite impressive. Very few people would be able to take what little you had been taught and figure out enough to still be able to work magic. Despite what some think, magic requires study and is not simply an innate ability."

"I, uh...Thank you?" Hazina stammered.

Damien squinted up at the sun and sighed. "I think we need to get back to rowing. Though I'm not sure what we'll do when the sun falls."

"I can try to summon a spirit again, though I do no know for how long I could keep them here," Hazina offered.

Atalanta shook her head. "You're already exhausted. I'm sure there must be some consequences if you repeatedly tire yourself out like this."

"I do not see what other options we have. Without an anchor or somewhere to tie the dinghy, we will be at the mercy of the sea whenever we rest," Hazina said.

"Sailors have been dealing with the sea's mercy and anger since the first person decided floating a bit of wood on water was a good means of travel. Our lack of shelter from the sun and weather is more concerning," Eryx pointed out.

"Regardless, it's a little late to turn back now," Atalanta said. "We'll have to make do."

"Perhaps your goddess would help us?" she suggested, her voice soft and weary.

Atalanta shrugged her uninjured shoulder. "I can try. Though this really feels the sort of thing to pray to Poseidon for, rather than Ptokheia."

"Are you sure he won't receive your prayers?" Eryx asked. He had never had a particularly strong ability to sense the magic in someone's blood, but hers fairly sang with the strength of the sea.

Atalanta laughed. Despite the weariness, and hint of bitterness, it was bright and refreshingly pure. "We are on our way to put an end to Poseidon's rampage across the Mediterranean. I doubt he'd lend us any aid."

"What?"

She grinned and threw her left hand out, as if reaching toward the horizon. "Oh, mighty forefather, hear my prayer! Help us reach Methoni quickly, so we can come find you, and make you stop being such a god-sized bastard."

Hazina smiled weakly and Damien laughed. He knew they were amused at his expense, but he wasn't able to keep the grin off his face. "Alright," Eryx said, holding up his hands in surrender. "No divine intervention. We'll figure something else out."

Eryx and Damien turned their attention back to rowing. Though both women wanted them to rest, they kept at it for the remainder of the day. The further they went, the slower their strokes became, until they were both slumped and too tired to row further. The sun was a fiery disk of red dancing above the horizon, as if reveling in the burnt skin that crisped across Eryx's face and arms. Even Atalanta and Damien, who were shades of brown to begin with, had a definite tinge of red to their skin.

"We…we can't go further…not today," Damien panted.

"Rest. It won't make that much difference if we stop here or once the sun has sunk further," Atalanta said. "And tomorrow you'll let me row for at least part of the day."

Damien grunted, though whether it was in agreement or resignation was unclear. He pulled his oar in and tucked it beneath the benches. Eryx followed suit. They both shifted in a futile attempt to find a more comfortable position. No matter how they sat, the benches pressed against back or hip, and most positions ended with their legs tangled together. Damien's discomfort at the forced intimacy stole any delight Eryx might have normally felt in such a position with a handsome man.

Hazina trailed her fingers in the water, her gaze wandering across the open sea. She sat up so suddenly the boat rocked. "What is that?" she asked, pointing to the south east.

Eryx, Atalanta and Damien turned to stare where she indicated. A dark mound broke the sea, though it was barely higher than the gentle waves that rippled the surface.

"It could be land," Atalanta suggested, shading her eyes. "We could have a proper rest tonight."

Eryx shook his head. "I've never heard of a scrap of land like that out here."

"We've been to an unknown island before. Didn't stop it from being there," Damien said.

Atalanta pulled Eryx's oar up and awkwardly dipped it into the water. "It isn't far. We can make it before the sun sinks."

"You can't row one-handed," Eryx protested.

"Watch me."

Atalanta and Damien pushed on. The closer they drew to the outcrop, the more Eryx was sure it wasn't an island. Large plates of rock stacked edge to edge formed a small dome. Each piece was streaked with greens and blues amongst the predominant brown. It wasn't large—only twice as wide as he was tall—and no lichens or other plant life grew on it. Though a small pile of perfectly round, white stones were clustered near the peak.

The dinghy bumped into rock before they reached the visible edge. Damien probed beneath them with his oar and then stepped out of the boat. "Whatever this is, it extends some distance beneath the water."

Eryx stepped out as well, and together they pulled the boat up onto the rock. Hazina and Atalanta were quick to jump out on the dry surface. The two women carried the bags to the peak of the dome and settled down next to the white stones. Damien trudged over to them and all but collapsed. He put his own pack beneath his head and covered himself with his cloak. Hazina followed suit and soon they were both fast asleep.

Eryx took a seat next to Atalanta and frowned at their surroundings. "This isn't some naturally occurring spit of rock."

"It's free of people and things that want to kill us," she pointed out. "And we won't have to try and sleep curled up on top of one another in the dinghy."

He shook his head. "I have a bad feeling about this."

Atalanta patted his arm. "Try to get some rest. We have long days ahead of us, and will probably not see any other land until we reach Methoni." She curled up on the ground and closed her eyes.

"I don't think this is land either," Eryx muttered.

"Just go to sleep," Atalanta grumbled at him.

He sighed and lay down. The first stars blinked at him as they crept out of the darkening sky. For a moment it seemed as if the stars spun around each other. He gave his head a shake and they stopped moving. Though his mind wanted to puzzle over the stars, his body was too exhausted. He fell asleep as the island they were on rose further from the water and slowly rotated.

Chapter Eight

The pink blush of dawn traced delicate fingers over the world, but where they grazed against Hazina's closed eyelids, they became spears of pain. She threw an arm over her eyes and groaned. Her head throbbed, back ached, and every inch of skin that had been exposed to the sun felt aflame. While Atalanta, Damien, and Eryx all reddened beneath the sun, her skin had remained the same dark brown as always. The lack of change clearly didn't mean the sun hadn't burnt her.

Hazina sat up slowly before daring to open her eyes. Though the light still made her head hurt, the sky itself was soothing, with gentle swirls of pink and purple through the softest of blues. She breathed in deeply and let out a long sigh. There was a calm to the morning that she felt was much needed.

Atalanta lay to Hazina's left, curled and half laying on her stomach, with her injured arm cradled against her chest. Damien snorted in his sleep. He was stretched out on his side, with his cloak thrown over his body. At some point in the night, he had kicked the fabric off his legs, though it still covered his head. A little apart from everyone else, Eryx lay on his back with his hands tucked behind his head. If it weren't for his slightly open mouth and soft, nasally snore, Hazina would have thought he was merely pretending to be asleep.

Other than the spreading dawn, there was nothing to have roused her. She was certainly tired enough to sleep for a week without waking. Hazina grunted and climbed to her feet. Her eyes scanned over their surroundings and her heart squeezed.

The island was significantly bigger.

Though the dinghy was still only a few paces away from where they had slept, there were several paces of rock beyond it. The pile of round, white rocks in the centre of the outcrop almost seemed to glisten. They taunted her with a familiarity she couldn't pin down. Toward the east, a narrow strip of sea separated the bit of land they were resting on from a smaller spit of rock. Out past the second rock, the sea stretched away to a dark smudge on the horizon.

Hazina squinted. The unevenness along the horizon looked like land, but she was certain there hadn't been any in sight when they stopped. She tried to recall what she knew of the storm that almost destroyed the ship Atalanta, Damien, and Calista took the previous year. The dark smudge on the horizon didn't look like the clouds described to her. She crouched beside Atalanta and gave her a shake.

Atalanta jerked away from Hazina's touch with a startled gasp. Her eyes snapped open and she stared blankly for a moment before sitting up with a shuddering breath. She cleared her throat and scrubbed a hand against her eyes. "Wha-is-it?" she mumbled.

"The rock is bigger. And appears to have moved."

Atalanta froze. "What?"

Hazina gestured around them. Atalanta pushed herself to her feet and turned in a slow circle. She hadn't turned more than a fraction before her head started to shake. "What in Hades is going on?"

"I do not know. But what do you make of that?" Hazina asked, directing Atalanta's attention to the smudge on the horizon. It seemed a little thicker than before, but she wasn't sure if she was imagining it. "I do not think it is the Poseidon's Wrath storm you and Calista have told me about."

Atalanta nodded. "You're right. It's not. It really looks like land to me."

"Should we wake the others?"

Atalanta gave an absent nod. She crossed to Damien and prodded him in the ribs with her toe. "Wake up, Hero."

Damien swatted at her foot and rolled over. She kicked him harder.

"Stop kicking me," he grumbled and sat up.

"I didn't kick you, I nudged you. With my foot," Atalanta said, her voice prim. "It may have been harder than absolutely necessary."

He snorted. "I'd forgotten how annoying you can be."

"We have more important things to worry about, at the moment," Hazina interjected. She chewed her lip and studied Atalanta and Damien.

This was the first genuine bickering she had witnessed since meeting them in Santa Maria di Leuca. She hoped it was simply due to their fatigue and assorted injuries, rather than a breakdown in their truce.

"Can't you people let a body sleep?" Eryx asked, his eyes still shut.

"We have a problem," Hazina said.

Eryx grumbled. "Of course you do. Couldn't go one day without getting into trouble, could you?"

"Careful there, pirate," Damien warned. "You are partly to blame for all current and future trouble."

"I didn't make you get on a ship with a captain as seedy as Ganim," he shot back.

Atalanta rubbed tenderly at her swollen collarbone. "He came recommended from a barmaid."

"Oh, aye. I'm sure he did. He wasn't adverse to tossing florins around, and would readily tumble unhappy wives into his bed."

Damien glowered at Eryx. "You can't expect us to believe you haven't done the same."

"Believe it or not, I am very selective about who I take as a lover," Eryx said.

"You—"

"Enough!" Hazina cut Damien off. "This is a real problem, that needs to be addressed now."

"What's the issue?" Damien asked.

Atalanta gestured at their surroundings. "The island grew, and seems to have moved."

"What?" Eryx's eyes widened and he scrambled to his feet.

Damien shook his head. "That's not possible." His mouth twisted in resigned disappointment as he took in their surroundings.

"Possible or not, that's the pot we're in," Atalanta said. She turned to Eryx and asked, "Any ideas?"

"A few—" he started, but was cut off by a loud scoff from Damien.

"How can we trust anything he says?" Damien demanded.

Hazina frowned at him. She'd had similar thoughts during their escape from *the Lion*, but that was then. From the angry red of his skin, to the blisters on his hands, there was nothing about him to make her doubt his intentions any longer. Her gaze shifted between the two men, wondering if something had happened below deck before their escape. Anything she could think of to justify Damien's mistrust, would be serious enough he should have told them about it. She was about to ask when she saw Damien shift, ever so slightly, to stand between Atalanta and Eryx. She closed her mouth with a sigh. Jealousy was an unreasonable beast.

She shook her head. "Eryx has earned enough of our trust through his help in escaping Kattan's crew. Surely this can wait for another time?"

"We don't know why he helped us," Damien argued. "He betrayed his friends and crew, abandoned the ship he was *first mate* on. It isn't like he was some lowly, mistreated deckhand who wanted escape just as much as we did. By all appearances, he was living well. And now? Now, he's on some mystery island with people he doesn't really know. What, about any of that, makes you think we can trust him?"

"I'm standing right here," Eryx grumbled.

Damien glowered. "You claim you're homesick and we, somehow, remind you of home. That is the least believable excuse I've ever heard of."

Eryx's jaw clenched and his eyes flashed. "You want me to lay out all my secrets for you? What about all of your secrets, hm? Off to kill Poseidon? That seems like a dangerous task for you, let alone for the poor souls you rope into helping you. Poseidon is not known for his forgiving nature. What will he do to the sailors of *the Lion?*"

"They're all pirates. They deserve whatever comes to them."

"They have families!" Eryx thundered. "You have no idea why any of them turned to a life of piracy. Or why they remain. Who are you to judge them?"

Hazina's heart pounded and she quickly stepped between Damien and Eryx. The anger snapping between them was enough to frighten her, but she threw her shoulders back and gave each of them a stern frown. "This is not the time, nor the place."

"Hazina's right," Atalanta said. She placed a hand on Damien's arm and his shoulders drooped. She turned to Eryx and gave him a smile. "But to ease the tension, perhaps you can tell us why you're helping us."

Eryx dropped his eyes and shrugged. "It's not a short tale—and without it all, I doubt knowing my reasons would satisfy him."

Atalanta and Hazina shared a frustrated look. The smudge of land on the horizon was drawing ever closer, which meant the island, if it even was an island, was still moving. Atalanta cleared her throat and shook her head. "Tell us the minimum you think we'd need to understand,"—she squeezed Damien's arm and gave him a heavy frown—"and then we'll focus on what's actually important."

Damien snorted, but nodded his acceptance.

Eryx scrubbed his hands over his face. "Fair enough. I am not a mortal, though I am also not a god. At least, not how you think of them. My people have been called various things, though the name I am most comfortable with is *aos sí*. We live far from here, in realms built beneath sacred hills. There are very few of us left. The elders were temperamental and prone to arguments. Those who remain either care little for mortals, or try to fill the roles long left vacant by the elders. My mother is one such; she is a *bean sidhe*—one with the power to foretell death and grant boons to daring mortals. My siblings and I cared little for the mortals. We spent our days hunting and causing mischief."

"Not much has changed then," Damien muttered.

Eryx continued as if he hadn't heard him. "The short of it is, I came across a pair of mortals who shared perhaps the purest form of love I have ever encountered. I was drawn to them, as I hadn't been drawn to any other mortals before. For months, I lived along the edges of their tiny farm. They were respectful of the *aos sí*, and, despite having very little themselves, always left out offerings. In time, I came to view them as friends. At least, until the man returned home with the news that a *bean sidhe* had foretold his death."

"Oh, no," Hazina gasped.

He nodded heavily. "They cried and lamented the years they would lose, but never turned to me to help. They knew I was there, but were unwilling to risk the wrath of the *aos sí* to escape their fate. I, however, was not willing to see their beautiful life torn apart. I went in search of the *bean sidhe*. I should have known I would find my mother.

"She knew why I had come. She told me she was proud of me for giving up the petty tricks I used to play, but that it was time to return home and find a proper role. I tried to bargain with her. I promised to fulfill any role, any responsibility, if she would spare the farmer. My mother was disappointed. 'How many times have you watched mortals come to me, beg me to change their fate?' she asked. 'How many times have they laid gifts of precious metals and more precious baubles of sentimental value at my feet? Have I ever spared a person marked for death?'

"I didn't answer. I couldn't. She had never spared anyone, and never would. She was not some *leanan sidhe* to take what the mortals offered in exchange for a brief, shining moment. She was a Washer-at-the-Ford."

Atalanta glanced pointedly to the shoreline. "Is there much more to this story?"

Eryx's lips twisted and he shook his head. "I'll make this quick. I thought I knew better than my mother, and attempted to spare the farmer's life. It worked. Sort of. My interference trapped the farmer's soul in a body that knew it was supposed to be dead. He had no pulse, no breath, no vitality. My mother explained, for the first time, that the *aos si* are not from this world. We have great powers, and can guide mortal souls, but we do not decide the fates of mortals, and so cannot change them. For my meddling, I was banished, on the condition that I can only return once I discover how to undo the farmer's curse. I've spent years searching, and had long ago given up that I would ever find a cure."

"What does that have to do with us?" Damien asked. Much the anger and tension had drained from him, but his gaze still held a hint of suspicion.

"I realized during your first confrontation with Kattan that you were not mere mortals, and some sense, or inkling, has been whispering ever since that the key to returning home lies with you," he explained, then shrugged and gave them a lopsided smile. "Of course, I might simply be so desperate I am fooling myself."

Silence fell over them as they each took in his story. After a moment, Damien asked, "Your home is very far away then?" When Eryx nodded, he asked, "Why do you have a Greek name?"

Atalanta coughed and shot him an incredulous look. "You can't just ask someone that."

"I want to know what his real name is," Damien insisted.

Eryx chuckled. "A lover gave me this name, and it's what I've gone by for over a hundred years."

"Are you now satisfied, Damien?" Hazina asked.

He nodded grudgingly.

"Then we need to figure out what is going on with this island," she said.

"I'm not so sure it is an island," Eryx said.

"What else could it be?" Atalanta asked. She stamped a foot against the ground. "It seems solid enough."

"There are several possibilities, none of which are good. We should leave as soon as we're able," he cautioned.

Damien frowned at the pile of stones. "What are those, though? They're stacked far too deliberately to have ended up here by chance."

Hazina shook her head. "I do not like this. We should follow Eryx's advice, and leave."

Damien ignored her and walked over to the pile. He picked up one of the stones and turned it over in his hands. "These are heavier than they look," he said, eyes locked on the smooth surface. "There's something about them that seems familiar."

Atalanta slung her bag over her good shoulder. "Take it with us, if you want."

"Or not," Eryx put in. "I doubt taking it will lead to anything good."

Damien shook the rock and a soft sloshing came from within. He looked up with wide eyes. "I think they're eggs."

"Of what? They are a foot across!" Hazina exclaimed.

The rock beneath them shook, rising up higher out of the water. All four of them stumbled, and Damien dropped the white stone on the ground. Cracks spread out across its surface, and a golden liquid seeped from within. The island rocked, tilting back, and a whining groan emanated from it. A sharp tremor ran through the ground, knocking them to their knees. The pile of stone-eggs tumbled over one another and across the surface, catching in the grooves of the stacked plates. None of them cracked, but they wobbled in their dubious little nests. As suddenly as it had risen up, the island began to sink. Sea water rushed to swallow it back up, catching at the bottom of their dinghy and pulling it out to sea.

Eryx jumped to his feet and ran to the boat, rolling with the movement as another tremor shook them all. "Everyone into the dinghy. Now!" he shouted.

Atalanta, Hazina, and Damien were quick to gather up their things and run to join him. They splashed through waist deep water which was rising quickly. Eryx grabbed Atalanta around the waist and lifted her in, while Damien did the same for Hazina. Both men clambered in after, bringing a wash of sea water with them.

"We need to get away from here, quickly," Eryx said, pulling up the oars and shoving one into Damien's hands.

They only made it two strokes before the island rushed up. Rock slammed into the bottom of the boat, before the water rolling off could carry them away. The force of the blow knocked Hazina face first into a puddle in the bottom of the dinghy.

"Gods above," Damien gasped.

Hazina struggled to right herself and turned to see only a small rock bobbing at the surface a short distance away. Two large, black eyes over a narrow nose and bill blinked at them. The bill twitched ever so slightly.

"Is that a turtle?" Atalanta spluttered.

"Since when are there turtles as large as *the Lion*?" Damien asked.

"It's an aspidochelone," Eryx said. "And you broke one of its eggs."

Damien shook his head. "A what?"

Before Eryx could answer, the creature erupted next to them. The dinghy spun wildly in conflicting currents. Water rolled over the edges, further drenching the four companions. Eryx used his oar to fight against the buffeting sea. It did little to stop the tossing and spinning.

The beast snapped at them. Its beak sliced easily through the wood, leaving a deep gouge. Water rushed through the break. The lip of the boat sank dangerously close to the level of the sea. Atalanta grabbed Damien's pack and shoved it into the hole. Water seeped around the edges of the bag, but the boat stopped it's noticeable descent..

"That isn't going to last very long," Eryx shouted, his knuckles white around his oar. "Oiled leather can only hold up to water for so long."

Hazina scooped furiously at the water filling the bottom of the boat.

Her hands could only provide a momentary delay of the inevitable and she knew it. She grabbed Atalanta's bag, opened it, and held it beneath the water. The bag drank up every drop.

"I was not sure that would work," Hazina panted.

Atalanta nodded. "Wet clothes are worth not drowning."

"Brace yourselves," Damien called. He dropped his oar and drew his sword, turning to face the rising swell that heralded the creature surfacing again.

The giant turtle made a groaning whistle. Its massive flipper sailed past them and Damien lashed out with his sword. The blade bit so deeply it was almost torn from his grasp when the flipper smashed down. Water sloshed over the sides of the dinghy and blood spread through the sea all around them. A piercing shriek ripped the air and the turtle thrashed before disappearing below the surface.

"We need to get out of here before it comes back," Atalanta said, her back pressed against Damien's pack to keep it tightly wedged in the hole.

Hazina snatched up Damien's discarded oar and rowed in time with Eryx. The dinghy shot forward beneath their desperate strokes. The turtle shrieked at their retreat when it breached. For a moment, they four companions feared it would pursue them, but then it turned and swam in the opposite direction. Waves rocked the boat, pushing them further away.

"Unless we find land soon, we aren't going to be able to keep this damnable thing afloat," Eryx said. His muscles bulged and strained with each stroke and it was all Hazina could do to match his pace.

"Look," Damien said, pointing to the horizon.

Hazina paused and looked over her shoulder. What had been unidentifiable smudges before were now the distinct peaks and dips of trees and hills. A stretch off to the right even looked suspiciously like buildings.

Eryx let out a low whistle. "Well, I'll be…if the boat doesn't fall apart first, we'll reach Methoni before midday."

Chapter Nine

The sun cast long shadows as it sank behind the buildings and walls of Methoni. Few people remained on the streets at such a late hour. A pair of guards walked at a brisk pace down a narrow road lined with houses, turned at the smithy and continued their patrol. One had limp curls beneath a wide-brimmed helmet and wore a padded tunic that was so stiff his movements appeared exaggerated. The other carried a metal tipped club, had a conical helmet, and wore a tunic with plates of metal carefully sewn down the front.

"I hate night patrol," the guard in ill-fitting armour grumbled. "I could have been in bed with Susanna with a belly warm from stew and ale."

"Twas to be a Susanna night then, eh Nichola?" the other guard chuckled. "What happened to Catalina? Or old Bice?"

Nichola grinned. "I still see them from time to time, but Susanna is a better cook. You should know that, Giradus, you're the one who told me of her."

"If you're not careful, she'll trap you and then you'll be married to an old bawd," Giradus warned.

"Is that why you married someone so shrill even the fisherwomen wince when she goes to the market?"

Giradus growled. "Careful, boy. That's my wife you're talking about."

"I'll marry when I'm old. If I live to be old...damn Ottomans." Nichola spat and shook his head. "Why do we even have to patrol the streets? If the Ottomans have made it past the walls, then we've already lost."

"It makes people feel safer to know there are guards walking the streets, as well as patrolling the walls."

Nichola snorted. "We're just two caitiffs wandering around for half the night."

"Oi! Mind who you're calling a caitiff," Giradus snapped. "I'd man the walls if they'd have me. Just because you'd piss yourself if you saw a firefly in the brush—"

"No need to get nasty!" Nichola held up his hands in defeat. "I'm not a fighter, and neither are you. But with everyone worked up about the Ottomans, a man can be run from his home if he doesn't support the defence in some way."

"So why are you complaining about doing just that?"

"I'd prefer to do my part while the sun is in the sky so I can sleep in a warm bed and not worry that it's been warmed by another man."

Giradus snorted. "You don't earn enough to buy even old Bice's sole affections."

"Aye, but I don't want to be reminded of it every time we dance."

Nichola and Giradus walked on in silence until they completed the loop of four streets that made up their patrol. They paused at an intersection and waited for another pair of guards to join them.

"Ho there, is that Jacobo? Aren't you too young to be off your mother's apron strings?" Giradus called when the other guards came into view.

"And you're too old to eat meat," a gangly youth retorted.

His companion chuckled. "How fares the night?"

"Dull, as ever," Nichola complained.

The other man's eyebrows shot up. "What would you do, Nichola, if you found a Turk hiding in the shadows between the Bear and Harrow and de Piro's? Besides pissing yourself, that is."

"Ha ha, very amusing Michiel," Nichola muttered.

"Your patrol goes past the docks, does it not?" Giradus asked.

"Aye," Jacobo replied.

"Any news?"

Michiel shook his head. "Nothing of interest."

"That's not true. There were those travelers this afternoon. All the dock-hands are talking about them," Jacobo put in.

"That's just gossip," Michiel said. "I wouldn't wager a false penny on it being true."

"Sounds like a good story to tell, regardless," Nichola pointed out.

Jacobo grinned. "It is. Four people docked in a broken dinghy—claimed a turtle had wrecked their ship."

Nichola laughed. "What coxcombs."

The morning sun lit the common room by the time Atalanta clomped down the stairs of the Wilting Marmayd inn. Narrow windows overlooked the Methoni harbour and, although people bustled past the inn, the common room was empty except for Hazina, Damien, and Eryx. She tugged her scarf straight and joined them at a table with platters of food already on it.

The conversation at the table paused while Atalanta settled onto a stool and snatched up one of the small rolls of bread. Hazina's lips were pressed tight, Damien was glowering, and Eryx wore an ingratiating smile. Atalanta took a bite of the roll, studied her silent companions while she chewed, then asked, "What news?"

Hazina blew out sharply. "Rumours are spreading of the fools bested by a turtle—I still cannot believe you told anyone!"

Eryx shrugged and scooped up a bit of egg with a chunk of bread. He popped it in his mouth and gave Hazina a closed mouth smile. Her eyes narrowed at him.

"They'll have thought he was joking," Damien offered, though his glower didn't lessen.

Atalanta pressed the back of her arm against her mouth to stifle a yawn. "Does it matter?"

Hazina worried at a roll of bread until it was nothing but tiny crumbs. "I am surprised we were not thrown in the stocks for being drunkards, spies, or idiots."

"I'm sure they suspect we might be spies," Eryx said. "They'll suspect every outsider of working for the Ottomans. Of course, a group bested by a turtle is no threat to anyone."

Hazina snorted. "You had no way of knowing how they would react."

Eryx smiled, his eyes sad. "You do not trust me, even after everything we've been through."

"You were the cause for a lot of our troubles," Damien pointed out.

"Aye, I suppose. Can we begin anew?" he asked. "We have reached Methoni—it is a new chapter in your adventure, and I humbly ask to accompany you from here on out."

Hazina spluttered and Atalanta laughed until a bit of food got caught in her throat. She coughed raggedly and slurped down some of the weak ale from a tankard, uncaring that it might have belonged to one of her companions.

Damien's mouth twisted with distaste. "If we said no, would you leave?"

"I...Perhaps. I would hate to abandon my bellibone so soon. Especially when you three seem to have a penchant for finding trouble."

"That is unfortunately true," Damien said.

Hazina cleared her throat. "Neither of us are your bellibone. It is rude to assume we would accept such familiarity now that we do not have to."

"Who said I was talking about either of you?" Eryx quipped.

Damien's face purpled and his fists clenched. Atalanta chuckled. Eryx laughed and Hazina gave an uneasy smile. After a moment, Damien relaxed and the tension faded away.

"I am sorry for causing offence," Eryx offered, inclining his head to Hazina.

She blinked several times and leaned back in her seat. "Ah... it is forgiven."

"At least you were a bellibone rather than poplolly," Atalanta pointed out. "But then I suppose I can't blame a bunch of sailors for not calling me the pretty one."

"I disagree—you were very comely in the dress Kattan made you wear," Eryx teased.

Atalanta wrinkled her nose, ignoring the returning glower on Damien's face. "It was so indecent, I think it would have made Damien look like a comely lass."

Eryx laughed and shot a grin at Damien. "Aye, it may have. Though I think his eyes almost fell out of his head when he saw the skirts cut short."

Atalanta squirmed in her seat, her stomach twisting. The thought of Damien gawking at her like the sailors made the memory significantly worse. She forced a grin on her face and tried to keep her voice light. "It certainly would have been a shock to see a woman so brazenly bare."

"Perhaps this is a conversation best saved for another time," Hazina cut in. "There is still much for us to do."

"Yes. You three are set on killing Poseidon, then?" Eryx asked.

"We won't kill him unless we have to," Atalanta said.

"You are naive if you think you can reason with an angry god. A mere mortal? In the olden days, you would have been struck down for the hubris of even thinking it." Eryx shook his head.

"How is that worse? Killing a god, no matter how old or belligerent, is not something to be taken lightly," she countered.

"Oh, it's not worse," Eryx agreed. "You are all likely going to die by attempting it."

"So go find a brothel to crawl into. We don't need your assistance," Damien said.

"Will we not?" Hazina asked softly. "Atalanta is right that our task is not something to be taken lightly. Having an immortal to assist us could be the difference between success and failure."

Damien muttered beneath his breath but offered no other objections.

"We encountered sirens and strange, shape changing horse-men outside of Otranto," Atalanta explained. "Damien and I, along with another friend, encountered sirens in Methoni a year ago. Which is why we felt returning here would be our best course of action if we are to track the sirens back to Poseidon."

"Were the horses black, with seaweed tangled in their manes?" Eryx asked, straightening in his seat.

"Do you know what they are?" Hazina countered.

"They may be kelpies. I have no idea what they would be doing in the Mediterranean though."

"Are they kin of yours?" Damien asked

Eryx wobbled a hand side-to-side. "They are related to the *aos si*, but I never spent much time in their company. Too savage for my siblings and I."

"Perhaps you should see if you can find any rumours of kelpies, while the rest of us search for word of the sirens," Atalanta suggested.

"If the kelpies are migrating this far, then there may be more than Poseidon to contend with. They would never recognize the authority of a god."

"You think one of your kin may be working with Poseidon to stir up trouble?" Damien asked, his brows climbing his forehead.

"It is a possibility we should be prepared for." Eryx nodded. "I will wander the docks and see what I can learn."

Hazina offered to search for medicine women and other potential magic users who could have been aware of the sirens, while Damien said he would talk to the guards.

"Let's meet back here for the evening meal. Hopefully that will be enough time for one of us to discover something," Atalanta said.

They parted ways and Atalanta wandered up the street toward the centre of the city. People moved quickly along the road, rarely stopping. No one browsed the shops and stalls. The homes overlooking the street had all their windows shuttered and from the wind-blown debris cluttering the balconies it looked as if they hadn't been opened for some time.

Atalanta passed a man declaring the imminent end of the world. A small group clustered around the doomsayer, listening fearfully to his exhortation on how to ready their souls for the day of judgment. She snorted in disgust when a small child gave the man a worn coin in exchange for a blessing. One of the men in the group eyed her suspiciously, but let her pass by without comment.

Guards were frequent sights, patrolling the streets. Most had old or ill-fitting armour, and no two wore the same type of weapon at their hip. The people of Methoni would nod to the passing guards and scurry out of their way.

Around a curve in the road, a curtain of dark hair with streaks of red and orange in it hung over the railing of a balcony. The young woman sunbathing her hair flinched at every loud noise, making the curtain of hair dance and writhe. A withered old woman stepped onto the balcony and shouted at the young woman. They had a quick argument before the young woman was bustled inside and the doors to the balcony were slammed shut.

Buildings and shops became more familiar the further Atalanta wandered until she recognized the grubby windows of the inn they had stayed at the previous year. The iron arm above the door held no sign with the inn's name. She hesitated and stared at the forlorn looking building.

"Watch it," a man snarled when he bumped into her. He gave her a disapproving frown before continuing down the road.

Atalanta stepped up to the door of the inn and pulled. The door didn't budge. She cupped her hands against the grimy glass and tried to peer inside. It was too dark beyond and the windows too obstructed for her to see anything.

"That there's been closed for almost a year now," a woman said, stepping out of the flow of the crowd.

"I was here a year…and a half ago—it had seemed to be doing fine. What happened?" Atalanta asked.

The woman clicked her tongue and shook her head. "Nasty business that. Some sisters used to sing here every couple of nights. Then around about a year ago, they were attacked in this very inn. One of the girls was even killed."

"Really? Did they ever catch who did it?" she asked, a tremor running through her.

"Unfortunately not. Something had been put in the food or drink—not a single person there could remember what happened. The cook was blamed, of course, though he swore up and down he had nothing to do with it."

"Of course," Atalanta agreed, her stomach settling. She laughed nervously. "What else could it have been?"

The woman grinned a little and leaned in. "Some whispered of magic and demons. Not that right minded folks, such as ourselves, believe in that sort of nonsense."

"Aye…" Atalanta tried not to shift away from the woman, but an itch along her neck was an insistent reminder of her guilt in the death of the siren. "Do—do you know what happened after that?"

"Oh, well the sisters refused to play at the Pilgrim and Candle. Can't fault them for that. Eventually they stopped playing anywhere. Haven't been seen for several months now. Petrus fell ill shortly after, and some took it as a sign of guilt. After all, even if he wasn't the one to kill the poor woman, he's guilty of not keeping them safe."

"Is that why he closed the inn?"

"Suppose so. Locals stopped coming around, and he's so far from the harbour he hardly saw any travelers," the woman explained.

"Do you know where Petrus, or the sisters, are?"

The woman squinted at Atalanta and pursed her lips. "Why?"

"I…would like to offer my condolences."

The woman's gaze swept over Atalanta. She was acutely aware of her bruised face and other injuries on top of the men's clothing she favoured. The woman's lips pinched. "Petrus and Lippa have gone through enough. They don't need gawkers bothering them morning, night and noon. Off with you, now!"

Atalanta moved on from the inn and, when she glanced back, the woman was still watching her. She turned down a street and wandered until she felt confident she wasn't being watched any longer. With the information the woman had given her, she asked around about the sirens and innkeeper.

Every person gave her a little more to the puzzle. The sun was high overhead when she found herself talking to a woman who appeared to personally know the innkeeper and his wife.

"I did not realize Lippa had a sister," the woman said, eyeing Atalanta distrustfully.

Atalanta smiled and tried to project a sense of relaxed calm. "I haven't seen her in several years."

"And you chose now to come visit?" the woman asked, her eyebrows lifting.

"There is so much talk of the Ottomans coming here that I've come to see if she and Petrus will leave Methoni."

"Hmm…"

"But I didn't realize they had shut the inn down. Now I am unsure of how to find her before I must leave again," Atalanta continued.

"I will take you," the woman said begrudgingly.

"Oh, bless you!"

The woman grunted and gestured for Atalanta to follow. She led her through the streets to a small dead end near the outer wall of the city. The homes clustered there were all tall and narrow with an air of shabbiness to them. Most needed a fresh coat of whitewash. The woman led her to one indistinguishable from the those on either side of it.

"Thank you, your help is much appreciated," Atalanta said.

"Hmpf." The woman sniffed loudly and marched up to the door. She rapped loudly and eyed Atalanta with a smug grin while they waited.

For a moment, the house was absolutely silent. Then gentle sounds of someone moving inside heralded the door being opened. A young woman stared out at them, her face gaunt and hair lank.

"Yes?" she asked, her eyes skipping over Atalanta and the other woman as if she couldn't bear to look at them for too long.

"Blessings on you, Lippa. Have you been taking the herbs like I told you?"

"I've tried, Madame de Salis, but they make my stomach feel terribly upset."

Madame de Salis clicked her tongue and shook her head. "Lippa, you will never recover your nerves if you do not take the herbs every day," she admonished.

Lippa's lips tightened briefly and a fire flashed in her eyes. She locked gazes with the other woman. The fire disappeared just as quickly and her face sagged back into tired blankness. With a perfectly neutral voice, she asked, "Is there something I can help you with, Madame de Salis?"

"This woman claims to be your sister."

Lippa's brows scrunched and her gaze slid past de Salis to latch on to Atalanta. The fire flickered in the depths of her eyes and Atalanta wondered if they would let her slink off, or if they would call the guards on her. She gaped when Lippa's eyes widened and she said, "Oh, of course! Gilia! It's been so long, and you've been hurt. I didn't recognize you for a moment."

Atalanta smoothed the surprise off her face as best she could when Madame de Salis spun to gape at her. Beneath Lippa's direct gaze, a twitch of recognition taunted Atalanta.

"I'm sorry I wasn't here for you when things went so badly at the Pilgrim and Candle."

Madame de Salis's breath hissed out and she swiveled back to Lippa. She almost appeared more upset by Lippa's calm.

"You're here now. Thank you for brining my sister, Madame de Salis. I will see you in a few days for fresh herbs," Lippa said. She gestured for Atalanta to enter the house.

Atalanta slipped past a fuming Madame de Salis. Lippa closed the door on her and then led Atalanta down a narrow hallway to a tightly coiled staircase. She stopped with a foot on the first step and studied Atalanta.

"You were there when the singer was killed. When you and your friends disappeared after I wondered…"

A tongue of fear slid up Atalanta's spine. "We hadn't heard someone was killed before we left," she said, hoping the woman couldn't hear the half truth in her words.

"Mm. Follow me." She climbed the stairs without waiting for a response.

The second floor was a single room with a wide, derelict bed taking up much of the space. Mismatched dressers, a stool, tarnished mirror, and table with a missing leg replaced by a broken chair filled the rest of the room.

Lippa kicked the stool toward her before settling on the edge of the bed as regally as a queen. "Petrus, dear, we have a guest," she called out.

Groans and grumbling accompanied a form shifting beneath the blankets piled atop the bed. Atalanta jumped when a head poked up to gaze about with wild eyes. The pupils were so large they had almost swallowed the entire iris and his cheeks had the loose look of someone who had lost a significant amount of weight in a very short time. He frowned at Atalanta before glancing at Lippa and whining incoherently.

"Yes, dear. Why don't you go make yourself some of Madame de Salis's tea? That's it," she cooed and he fumbled his way out of the bed.

He wore several layers of clothes, all too big for him, and all in need of repair. He didn't even glance at Atalanta before scurrying to the stairs. He clomped down so heavily it shook the floor.

"Now we may talk freely."

"Uh…" Atalanta stared around the room before settling down on the stool. "I feel at a disadvantage."

Lippa flashed her teeth in what might have been a smile. "I recognize you. You stayed at the Pilgrim and Candle with a handsome young man and a lovely woman and then disappeared after the singer was killed. Convenient timing. And now you've sought me out?"

Atalanta tugged at her scarf and cleared her throat. "I am actually looking for the other singers, and was hoping you might know more about them."

Lippa froze before shooting to her feet, her face a twisted mask of hate as she screamed, "Those women ruined my life! They stole my husband's soul and made us unwelcome in our own community!"

"I—"

"If I could, I would wring their necks myself! I only let you in because I thought you had killed the other one. If you are another one of their blind sympathizers I'll rip your eyes from your head."

"I'm not a sympathizer!" Atalanta cut in.

Lippa's chest heaved and she sank back to sit on the edge of the bed, her hands trembling. Her breath gradually slowed and the feral glaze fell from her eyes. Atalanta waited until her breathing was relaxed before saying, "I am looking for the singers because they are part of a family that has been kidnapping people on the other side of the Mediterranean."

"I knew it. I knew they were no good." Lippa's grin was hungry as she nodded.

"What do you know about them?" Atalanta asked.

"I… It's a difficult story. So much happened. So much could have been God's punishment, but so much could have been their witchcraft," Lippa murmured.

"Start at the beginning. Wherever you think that may be."

Lippa drew a shuddering breath and nodded. "Petrus was…he was

126

not a good man. I lost three babies because he would hit me so hard. It is a husband's right to discipline his wife, and he always said if I were a more devout Christian then Christ would have protected my unborn children."

"What—"

Lippa continued as if she hadn't heard Atalanta, "Then one day he stopped hitting me. I thought Christ had finally answered my prayers. This was two years ago, and I was so happy. I didn't want to see the signs. But women whisper when they know a husband is warming a bed without his wife in it.

"I wasn't sure which of those women he was sleeping with. He looked at them, all of them, with such desire…I grew jealous. I prayed to have such sinful feelings purged from me, but it only grew. One night I followed him…" Lippa trailed off, her eyes clenched and hands buried in the blankets as her shoulders trembled.

"Do you need a moment?" Atalanta asked, half-rising from the stool. She was unsure of what to do—if they had been better acquainted she might have offered the other woman a hug, but they were strangers sharing a deeply intimate conversation.

Lippa shook her head. "I'm sorry. The house had several men waiting inside. I thought perhaps the sisters were running a brothel instead of simply tempting married men away from their wives. But then I saw them…feed…"

"Feed?" Atalanta's eyebrows shot up.

"They stripped the men of their clothes and bit them."

"What?" Atalanta blinked, taken aback by the bluntness of Lippa's description.

"The women must have been witches for none of the men reacted as each was bitten. I am unsure what they took from the men, but when they had their fill they instructed them to dress and leave. Out in the street, it was as if the men were sobering up from a heavy night of drinking. Many expressed confusion about how they had gotten there. Some laughed and said the strange nights were becoming a habit.

"I followed Petrus home. He didn't notice me until we entered our house. For a moment, his old anger surfaced and I thought he was going to hit me again. Then his anger just…disappeared. He smiled and asked

127

how long I had been waiting."

"Did you tell anyone what you had seen?" Atalanta asked.

Lippa's lip curled. "I mentioned it to Luchinus—Petrus's brother. He smacked me and said I shouldn't be nosing into my husband's private life. He indicated he knew of the affair. I tried to explain that Petrus wasn't having relations with the sisters, but Luchinus thought I was suffering from hysteria. I didn't want to be sent away, so I stopped talking about it.

"But I watched and waited. Then you showed up and killed one. The others never returned to the Pilgrim and Candle."

"Why is your husband ill?" Atalanta asked.

Lippa shrugged. "Every man I saw that night has fared similarly. If he hasn't died outright. It is as if their minds and bodies have withered."

"Do you know where the women went?"

"Home."

Atalanta stifled a sigh. "Where is that?"

Lippa shrugged again. "I do not know where they came from or where they went. All I know is that they had told some people they were going home. But they never booked passage on a ship, as far as I know."

"Couldn't they have left by land?" Atalanta suggested.

"I...I don't know. I don't think so." Lippa frowned, her gaze unfocused. Atalanta wondered if the woman's mind had broken.

"Well, thank you for your time," Atalanta said. She smiled politely and rose from the stool.

Lippa's eyes widened and she fluttered her hands. "No, no, no. You don't believe me. You have to believe me. I need you to hunt those bitches down and rip their throats out for what they've done to me!"

Atalanta gaped at the woman.

"I don't know where they live, but I heard them talking about their home. You have traveled to many places, have you not? Maybe you will know what they were talking about."

Atalanta sighed and gestured for Lippa to continue. The other woman brightened.

"They talked about feeding scraps to cormorants outside of a cave," she said. "The birds nest on stone fingers, whatever that means."

"Are you sure?" Atalanta asked sharply.

Lippa nodded fervently. "Yes, yes. Stone fingers."

"Anything else?"

Lippa chewed her bottom lip as she thought. "Uh... I'm not sure what it means, or if I heard them correctly, but I think they said something about the odd leaf being the key."

"That doesn't make any sense." Atalanta frowned.

"It's all I know, I'm sorry," Lippa said. "They might also come from a wealthy family. I heard them talking about their father's hall and how they missed their cousins. Even if they're daughters of a lord, will you kill them? Will you do that for me?"

Atalanta stared down at the rapturous face of Lippa. Her heart ached at the pain the other woman must have experienced to break her mind in such a way. She forced a smile on her face and lied, "I will avenge you, Lippa."

The sun had begun its slow slide into the sea by the time Damien was ready to head back to the Wilting Marmayd. He hadn't discovered much from talking to several guards. Most remembered the death of the siren, though with no body, and the surviving sisters leaving Methoni, not much had ever come of it. The guards were much more interested in talking about the fools bested by a turtle.

People scurried by as he meandered through the streets. It was an odd sensation to be so far removed from the worries and fears gripping Methoni. He knew the Ottomans were expected to attack any day, and yet, it felt like a nebulous thing to him. He and his companions would be gone before the city could be besieged. It felt like such a certainty he didn't even question his assumption.

Vendors called out in last, desperate attempts to sell their wares. Many of them wore patched clothes and had pinched cheeks. None of the people scurrying home even paused to glance at the items on display.

A flash of red caught Damien's eye. He turned to see a woman with a red scarf tied around her hair ducking down an alley. She was gone too quickly for him to make out anything more, but the tightening in his gut whispered *Atalanta*.

Damien turned into the alley. It was a narrow passage that cut off the fading sunlight within two paces of entering. He placed a hand on the rough brick to his left and followed it deeper. Some sense of danger stopped him from calling out. He paused and drew his sword before continuing on.

After twenty paces the alley split into two paths. The sounds of the city were distant and muffled, and only his footsteps rustling through light debris stirred the shadows. Atalanta, or whomever he had mistaken for her, was either too distant or too quiet for him to hear. Damien squinted down each branch.

The path to the right widened slightly, but continued on in darkness. The path to the left had a faint, flickering light beckoning at the end. He couldn't imagine any reputable business or home being accessible by such dark and narrow alleys. Would Atalanta have sought out such a place? Part of him said she was a thief and a vagrant, but another part said she was a kind-hearted woman.

He turned toward the light. Damien almost convinced himself that he chose it simply because he was tired of the dark. It took longer than he expected to reach, and when he did he was surprised to see a wide courtyard lined with stalls and doors. A collection of shacks clustered in the middle of the open space, leaning on one another like drunks stumbling out of a tavern. Somehow, the sky above was pure black.

People in drab clothes moved about the space, speaking quietly to one another. Damien sheathed his sword and stepped further into the courtyard. Even travel-stained and torn in places, his clothes were nicer than those worn by anyone else in the space. He felt more self-conscious there than he had being the only unworried person out on the main roads.

People stared as he wove through the crowd. Some drew back, but no one said anything to him. His eyes roved over the sea of people, searching for the flash of red which had led him there in the first place. All the colours were muted. Beiges, greys, dusty blue, dulled green, and faded yellow greeted him at every turn. Not so much as a flicker of red.

Damien was about to give up when a commotion caught his attention. A man reached across his wares and yanked on the wrist of a woman, pulling her so hard she banged into the wooden slats of his stall. Their voices were soft, but the anger in his, and fear in hers, carried farther than their words.

The woman shook her head and tried to pull away. The man snarled and drew a notched dagger. He waved it at her and she flinched back. None of the people around them did or said anything. Most averted their eyes and hurried past.

The dagger flashed and the woman cried out—it was the first non-hushed sound since Damien stumbled upon the strange courtyard. People flinched back, staring at the man and woman. Their expressions ranged from disapproval to anger. Damien expected someone to say something, but the crowd watched in silence. The man whispered angrily to the crying woman.

"Enough," Damien said, pushing his way through to the stall. Though he hadn't raised his voice, it seemed loud and echoing compared to the whispers all around them.

The man looked up, his eyes wide and startled before his face fell into an angry grimace. "Stay out of it, mortal." The words had a lyrical lilt to them, almost as if the man were singing, but they fell on Damien's ears like shards of glass.

Damien hesitated. The man's eyes were dark—they might even have been black. He wore a dusty brown, velvet tunic, the nap worn and threadbare. His ears were oddly shaped, and teeth needle-like. The scent of dry leaves and dust clung to him. The woman, on the other hand, wore a simple gown in rough-spun cotton with a thin belt around her waist the only thing giving it any shape. She had an elongated face, vaguely reminiscent of a marmot, and smelled faintly of jasmine and salt.

The woman's cheek was gashed and bleeding freely.

"You have no right to cut this woman," Damien said, stepping right up to the stall and lowering his voice.

"I have every right," the man snarled. "She is a beggar and a thief!"

"So turn her over to the guard. It is not your place to mete out justice."

The man laughed. It gurgled in his throat and dribbled down his chin. "You know nothing of our ways, mortal. Justice is dealt by those with the strength to enforce it."

The woman trembled, her nose twitching and teeth chattering. "P-please, Manoli. I did not take anything."

"Perhaps not this time, Nonna, but you will," Manoli said, waving the bloodied dagger toward her again.

"You can't punish someone for something they might do," Damien protested.

Manoli scoffed. "I can do whatever I please. I am the strongest one in this court."

Anger burned in Damien's throat. He didn't know if the man was some strange god, or a being like Eryx. Either way, he likely had magic or other tricks. But the woman's frightened crying spurred him on. He grabbed Manoli's wrist and squeezed until the man's hand spasmed and the dagger clattered to the stall's counter. "I think you might not be the strongest one anymore," Damien said.

"Are you challenging me? Me? The great Manoli of Hesperos?"

"No, sir, you mustn't!" Nonna cried. "He will kill you—or worse!"

"He can try," Damien said.

Manoli grinned and called out, his voice ringing all across the courtyard, "A challenge has been issued."

Gasps, whispers, and nervous laughter rippled through the crowd. A sense of hungry expectation fell over the space and Damien knew they were hungry for him. For his pain and his failure. Though the hair along his neck prickled, he didn't look around. He didn't need to look to know there were no other mortals.

Nonna moaned and sagged, only the stall and Manoli's hand still wrapped around her wrist keeping her up. "You mustn't fight," she pleaded. "Please. It is not worth the risk. Beg for Manoli's forgiveness and you might be able to walk out of here before everyone you know is dead."

Damien shook his head. "I cannot ignore those with power hurting those without."

Manoli released Nonna's wrist and pulled his own free from Damien's grip. "Enough talk. The challenge has been issued and accepted. We will fight...to the death."

Manoli turned and gestured for Damien to follow. He had no choice but to trail behind the man. Manoli led him to a door indistinguishable from all the other doors set into the walls of the courtyard. It was made of a dark wood with a silver handle. Manoli rapped twice on the door and it swung silently inward.

A sea of rippling grass lay before them. The sky was peppered with stars and a heavy moon hovered overhead, bathing everything in silvery light. The scent of rain mingled with some unidentifiable, but unmistakably, earthy fragrance.

"Am I in the Between again?" Damien wondered aloud.

Manoli's eyes widened slightly. "What does a mortal in these magicless days know of the Between?"

He grunted. "Enough. This doesn't feel like it though."

"It's not."

"Are you going to tell me what this place is?" Damien asked.

Manoli smiled like a cat watching a mouse. "No."

Manoli walked through the door and out into the sea of grass. Damien followed, and behind him trailed Nonna and a throng of other people. The people spread out into a ring around Damien and Manoli without a sound. Not even the swaying grasses made any noise.

"The rules are simple," Manoli said. His voice was soft, but it carried clearly. "To win by any means, and the winner is the sole survivor. This is your last chance to withdraw your challenge and accept a punishment instead of death."

Damien glowered. "It's also your last chance to back down with dignity."

Manoli laughed. It echoed strangely. And still none of the watching people made any sound. Damien's skin crawled and he eyed their audience with unease.

While his attention was elsewhere, Manoli closed the distance between them and lashed out with another dagger. This one shimmered like oil beneath the moonlight. Where the blade touched grass, the spears shriveled and blackened. Damien stumbled back from the attack just in time. The blade only sliced through his tunic.

He ducked under a swing of the oily blade and rushed at Manoli. His shoulder hit right where the ribs ended. The blow sent Manoli crashing to the ground and left him gasping for air. Damien drew his sword and swung at his prone opponent.

Manoli rolled away and the blade bit into soft earth. Damien freed his sword and turned to face him, only to find himself facing against six seemingly identical men. Each wielded an oily blade and wore a smug grin.

The slightest ripple in the grass made Damien flinch to the left. Another of the men sliced through the space he had been occupying only a moment before. Damien took a quick glance around and swore. There were a total of ten men. He wasn't sure if it were magic, or if Manoli had nine identical brothers who'd decided to join the fight. Either way, he was outnumbered.

"Gods give me strength," he muttered and closed with the nearest Manoli.

His sword bit into the man's side and the man flickered once before disappearing in a shower of silver dust. The sudden shift between resistance and no resistance against the blade made Damien stumble. Another of the Manolis tripped over him and fell, exploding into a cloud of silver dust from the impact.

Damien shoved himself up and took a quick inventory of his opponents. Three were to his left, two right ahead, and two to his right, leaving one unaccounted for and, presumably, sneaking up behind him. He roared and charged toward the trio.

The middle Manoli grinned and danced back while the other two swung their blades at him. The one on the right was felled before his dagger could reach Damien's skin, but the one on the left connected. It left a trail of fire across his ribs. Damien brought his elbow up sharply and slammed it into the attacker's nose. That Manoli burst, covering Damien in a cloying fall of the silvery dust.

While he coughed and wiped at his eyes, the middle Manoli and two others closed with him. The first slash of a blade bit into his arm, a grinding sound of blade against bone reaching his awareness before the searing agony set his nerves aflame. He hardly felt the next two lacerations in comparison.

Damien lashed out blindly. The flat of his sword struck one of the Manolis and he pulled back to make a quick jab. The point skidded along the side of the Manoli's thigh, but this one didn't disappear into a cloud of silver dust. Damien received another wound as he lunged forward and knocked the injured man to the ground.

It was too awkward to use his sword in such close proximity, so he let it drop to the ground. He wrapped a hand around the front of the man's throat and leaned all of his weight down. Something gave beneath his hand and the man disappeared into silver dust.

Damien stumbled to his feet and spun, glaring at the other Manolis circling him. He had taken out three or four already—the pain was making it hard to focus and he wasn't sure. He counted five remaining, but he had a vague thought that there was one missing.

"Gods I don't want to die," he muttered through gritted teeth.

Nonna's voice seemed to whisper in his ear, "Give up. Apologize to Manoli and you will live to see another day."

Damien shook his head. Even if it was only his fears of dying and not actually Nonna telling him to give up, he knew he couldn't. He had spent the last year trying to discover what it meant, what it truly meant, to be descended from gods and heroes. His whole life he had thought it meant hunting down Atalanta and her family and killing them before they could harm innocents—or so the reasoning went. He knew that wasn't the right path anymore.

A year spent seeking had resulted in no answers. No gods, old or new, answered his prayers. No texts held guidance. Not even Calista could help. She'd merely told him he needed to find his own definition of being a hero.

Pain stabbed through his leg, bringing him out of his delirium tinged musing. He stumbled back a step, regained his balance, then launched himself at the attacker. This Manoli had braced for the impact and they didn't tumble back to the ground. Damien grunted and threw his knee up. It missed the man's groin, but slammed into his stomach. Damien threw a punch into the side of the man's head so hard his hand went numb. The Manoli fell, turning to silver dust before he hit the ground.

This. This was what it meant to be a hero he decided. To fight, even a losing fight, to protect those who couldn't protect themselves. He briefly wondered if Atalanta would miss him when he didn't return, but couldn't linger on the thought because the remaining Manolis swarmed him.

Four of them jumped on him, dragging him to the ground. They'd abandoned their knives in favour of kicks and punches. Instinctively, he curled into a ball, arms wrapped around his head. The savage blows were like small bursts of agony.

Blindly, he kicked out and connected with one of the attackers. It didn't feel like a solid blow, but it caused enough of a respite that Damien was able to roll to his knees. His hand brushed against his discarded blade. The shallow cut from pressing against the edge was barely noticeable given all his other injuries.

He grabbed the blade as the hits began again. He gritted his teeth and straightened, spinning on his knees and sweeping his sword in a wide arc. Each body he hit burst into a shower of dust, stealing some of his momentum before disintegrating.

The world seemed to swing and tilt wildly and he fell to his side. Fire and searing pain coursed through his body. He knew the cut on his arm was bad—it was still bleeding and it hurt to move his fingers—and suspected that some of the others were serious as well. Even his eyes wouldn't focus clearly. Was there one or two Manolis approaching him with a satisfied smirk? There was a fleeting thought that if Manoli killed him, at least he wouldn't hurt anymore.

Damien gritted his teeth and shoved off the ground. He swayed once he was standing, but he didn't fall down again. Manoli strolled right up to him, easily side stepping Damien's weak punches. Damien hardly felt it when the blade slid between his ribs.

"You put up a good fight," Manoli said.

Damien snarled. "I'm not done yet."

Before Manoli could react, Damien wrapped his hands around the side of his face and squeezed. Manoli screamed as Damien's thumbs dug into his eyes and fingers compressed his skull. It was a slow and gruesome death and Manoli flailed, scratching and clawing to free himself, until his body dissolved into silver dust.

Damien groaned and dropped to his knees. It hurt to breathe, to move, to even think. His hands wrapped around the dagger still buried in his side and he wondered if it would be a quicker death to twist or to simply remove the knife and bleed out.

Cool hands brushed across his forehead and he struggled to focus on the woman standing in front of him. He thought it was Nonna, but she looked different somehow. More human. "You are dying, Damien Perseid."

He laughed, though it turned into an excruciating cough. Blood flecked over his lips and he wiped the back of a hand across his mouth. "Everyone has to die eventually. Not everyone gets to say they died fighting for what was right."

"Is that what you wish? To have a hero's death?"

He blinked at her. The question seemed heavy, though he wasn't sure why. "I don't want to die, but I can't say I regret the choices that led me here."

Nonna smiled and cupped his cheek. "You have defeated Manoli. Hesperos is yours by blood right—what would you do with it?"

"I don't want it. I just didn't want that bastard to keep hurting you," Damien muttered. He was starting to feel a cool numbness crawling its way up his body. It was a relief from the pain, but he knew it meant he was getting closer to death. He found it hard to be worried.

"Are you renouncing your claim on this place?"

"Yes. Are you going to keep bothering me with questions until I die?"

Nonna smiled, her eyes sparkling with laughter. "I only have one more. Will you pledge yourself to me, become my champion, and work to bring balance back into the world?"

"I...what? Who are you?" he asked. The world had started tilting again and he was finding it hard to focus on her.

"I am the forgotten goddess, and goddess of the forgotten; I am the shadows, and the protector of those who live in shadow. You can find me in the heart of every person who feels alone, abandoned, and hopeless. I am Ptokheia."

"I met you...in...Syracuse," Damien mumbled. A fleeting memory of a beggar taunted and shamed him. He hadn't been very kind to her.

"Yes," Ptokheia said. "You have met me elsewhere since then. You and Atalanta are very important."

Damien laughed, uncaring that it sounded delirious. "You should ask Atalanta to be your champion. She believes in you."

Ptokheia's lips tightened so briefly Damien wasn't sure if he saw it correctly. "Be that as it may, she is sworn to others—and not the one in front of me now."

Her words didn't make sense to him, but he dutifully nodded anyway.

"This is your final chance, Damien Perseid. Will you swear yourself to me?" she asked.

"Yes."

Ptokheia nodded as if she hadn't expected anything else. She pulled the knife from his side and then gently pressed her lips to his forehead. A wash of cold rushed through him. Pins and needles exploded all over his body and he felt a rush of energy. He wanted to run, jump, climb, be active. It was as if a bolt of lightning were coursing through his veins.

"What did you do to me?" he asked, rising to his feet.

"I made you whole again."

"How? Isn't that the domain of Apollo or Asclepius?"

Ptokheia grimaced. "Apollo is a puffed up dandy and his son is complacent. Asclepius's daughters, however, aligned themselves with me a very long time ago. It's through their power that I healed you."

Damien stretched and twisted. There was no pain, though he suspected he might not feel so hale once the rush of the healing wore off. The cut on the back of his forearm was puckered into a thick scar, not fully healed, but almost. "Thank you, my lady."

She inclined her head to him. "So long as you act on my behalf in the mortal realm, I will offer you what protection and assistance I can."

"How can I do that? What is it you want?" he asked. Already the lightning was fading and a weariness was replacing it.

"I want to restore this world's balance. Too long have my kin taken advantage of the powers to be had here. Their greed is poisoning the world."

"Uh…" Damien glanced around. The silent crowd had dispersed while he spoke with Ptokheia and they were alone in the moonlight grassland. "I hope you aren't wanting me to hunt gods."

"In a way—though not as you used to hunt Atalanta," she said. "The gods need to sleep so that the world can heal itself. They all will succumb eventually, but by then it might be too late. You can hurry them along."

Damien shook his head. "My lady, there are hundreds of gods, all across the world—it would be the work of several lifetimes to find them all. And I doubt it will be an easy thing to make them sleep."

Ptokheia laughed. It held the pure delight of children playing beneath the sun, the warmth of a proud parent, and the joy of someone being given new hope. "You need only worry about the gods who have made their homes around the Mediterranean. I have champions elsewhere in the world to deal with other godly families."

"How—"

"Keep going as you currently are. Your path will lead you to the worst of my kin," she forestalled him. "Take this symbol of my favour. It will offer guidance when you need it most."

Damien took the bronze brooch she held out to him. It was shaped like a quail, bordered by an olive branch grasped in its claws and a sheaf of wheat clutched in its beak. Tiny flecks of yellow glass decorated the wings, and a piece of blue glass marked the bird's eye. The eye seemed to glow beneath the moonlight.

When Damien looked back up, Ptokheia was gone. He turned and made his way to the doorway. It stood unsupported in the middle of the plain, with grassland stretching out all around it. The courtyard visible through the doorway was unsettling. It shouldn't be possible, but there it was. He wondered if Hazina or Eryx would be able to explain it—though he hadn't understood when Calista tried to explain the Between to him the previous year.

He was much more aware of how not-quite-human the people in the courtyard looked. He wasn't sure why he hadn't noticed it the first time he passed through. It seemed glaringly obvious to him now. And each and every one of them drew back when he passed.

Damien was grateful to be able to make his way back to the alley he'd followed to the courtyard. It was just as dark as before, but he felt no fear or worry as he left the dim light behind. The trip back to the streets of Methoni was much quicker than the journey away. He didn't know if it was a trick of his memory, or magic. He didn't really care either way.

The stalls and stores of Methoni were a welcome sight. The streets were tinted red from the disappearing sun and very few people were out. He slipped the quail brooch into his belt pouch and lengthened his stride as he made his way back to the Wilting Marmayd. His stomach rumbled and muscles ached—the idea of warm food and a soft bed spurred him.

The common room was full by the time he arrived. Sailors and dock workers seemed to make up the majority of the patrons. Atalanta and Hazina were surprisingly hard to find amongst the rowdy crowd. The two women were leaning close to each other, speaking softly when he settled onto an empty stool at their table.

Hazina jumped in surprise, her mouth hanging open for a moment before she gave him a wide smile.

Atalanta merely raised an eyebrow. "We were beginning to think we'd need to mount a rescue."

"I nearly needed one."

Atalanta blinked at him. Her eyes roved over him and her mouth pinched. "What happened?"

Damien briefly explained his adventure to the two women. Neither said anything for a long while after he had finished. He took the opportunity to flag down a barmaid and order food and drink.

"Are you sure you are in good health?" Hazina asked. "Do you trust that this goddess truly healed you?"

He nodded. "I'm very tired, and I ache like I've been training all day, but I wouldn't be alive right now if it weren't for her."

Atalanta reached out and ran her fingers along the frayed edges of his sleeve. Damien flinched when she touched the new scar beneath. She pulled her hand back and tsked. "For how clean a cut it looks to have been, that is a nasty scar. Rivals anything I've ever given you."

He laughed, though it sounded oddly strangled to his ear. He cleared his throat and said, "I think you still win for sheer number."

Her lips twitched toward a smile and she shrugged. "Might not stay that way if you keep getting into trouble—after all, I won't be adding to your collection anymore."

"Did you discover anything from talking to the guards?" Hazina asked.

He shook his head. "Nothing useful. Speaking of…where'd our pirate get to?"

"Eryx met some smugglers and is hopeful they might know more than they said," Hazina explained. "He has chosen to go carousing with them."

"Unless he has some *aos si* ability to not wake up hungover, I expect we'll be here for another day then?" Damien asked.

Atalanta shrugged. "Possibly. I would like to try to verify some of the information I learnt today anyway, so we need to stay at least half a day more."

"And you, Hazina? Did you learn anything?" he asked.

"Unfortunately not. People are very afraid right now. I could not get anyone to speak with me," she said, her voice pleasantly neutral, but her fists clenched.

"Besides, you're going to need a day to wash and patch your clothes," Atalanta pointed out. "You look like you've just returned from killing someone."

"I have just returned from killing someone."

Atalanta laughed and Hazina shifted uncomfortably, her eyes quickly scanning the nearby patrons. No one looked toward them, and the noise was such that it was hard to make out anything being said even at the table next to them.

Atalanta patted his arm and grinned. "I'm glad you're not so uptight. It makes it much easier to like you."

Damien sucked in a sharp breath of air. He was suddenly very aware of the fact that she wore one of his mother's rings on a chain around her neck. Though he couldn't see it, he knew the ring would rest between her...he yanked his thoughts away as if he'd been scalded. His cheeks felt like they were about to burst into flame and he glanced away.

"I...I'm very tired. I think I'll retire early tonight," he said.

Atalanta frowned. "Your food hasn't arrived yet—don't you want to eat first?"

His stomach growled, but it was no match for the warring emotions constricting his chest. "I'm not actually hungry," he lied.

"You need to eat to get your strength up," Hazina said, her gaze shifting between him and Atalanta. A knowing smile crept across her lips.

Before he could come up with an excuse, the barmaid arrived with his food. He tossed her a couple of coins without even looking at them and hurriedly ate. The fragrant stew was like sand in his mouth, but he forced himself to swallow. Between Atalanta's obvious confusion, and the sympathy on Hazina's face, Damien wished he were anywhere else but there.

"There. Now I've eaten. I'll see you two in the morning," he said, pushing away from the table.

"Oh…sleep well then," Atalanta said.

He hurried away, though not before he heard Atalanta ask, "What was that all about?" His feet betrayed him and he froze, straining to hear Hazina's soft reply.

"I warned you his feelings for you were not merely that of companions."

Atalanta snorted. "I've done nothing to encourage him. I don't see why he'd think of me any differently."

"The heart's desires are—" Hazina started, but Atalanta cut her off.

"We are not having this discussion again. He can pine all he wants, so long as it doesn't put any of us at risk. It won't change the way I feel."

Damien continued walking, not wanting to hear any more. His legs felt like they were encased in lead and the tightness in his chest had nothing to do with his injuries. It felt as if Manoli's blade were buried between his ribs again. He barely noticed finding his room and kicking off his boots. The pillows vaguely smelled of juniper when he slumped onto them.

The pain was being edged out by an old anger in the pit of his stomach. He rolled over and winced when something stabbed into his hip. He pulled the quail brooch out of his pocket and held it up so the coloured flecks of glass caught the last bit of light creeping through the window.

Both pain and anger were brushed away by the memory of cool fingers on his face. In the emptiness, he could admit he cared very deeply for his former rival. He worried when she was hurt, thought of her whenever something out of the ordinary happened, and wanted to always keep her safe. And he knew she wouldn't want him to feel any of that. They were practically family though. He'd earned the right to worry and care.

His thoughts didn't help settle the confusion of his emotions, but they soothed the hurt and he drifted off to sleep, dreaming of princesses to be rescued and annoying little brothers.

Chapter Ten

Two days later, Hazina bit her lip and surveyed the ship before them. It seemed sturdy enough, though without any obvious holes or rotten wood she really had no way of knowing. The name, *le Droit Margerie*, was faded and peeling, and the scent of pitch and tar clogged her nose, making it hard to breath. Men moved about the deck while Damien and Eryx conferred with the captain.

"Are we sure this is the only way to reach the island?" she whispered to Atalanta.

Atalanta shrugged her uninjured shoulder and grimaced when it made her bag shift. "Damien said no captain would take us, so Eryx found a seaworthy boat for sale. The captain still doesn't want to take us, but it's Damien's tub now."

"Yes, but could he not have found a vessel in better repair?"

"I doubt the bank would accept the guarantee for anything more expensive. Not only could Damien have lied about what money he has back in Italy, but it must be risky for them to retrieve it—given the tensions with the Ottomans," Atalanta pointed out.

"Are you two going to stand on the docks, staring, all day?" Eryx called down to them. The other sailors looked like children compared to him. Every last one of them was scrawny and dirty.

"I heard Eryx hired vagrants to be the sailors," Atalanta confided.

Hazina couldn't help but feel the men were one step away from becoming brigands. She tried to keep her voice light when she asked, "Where did you hear that?"

Atalanta grinned, though her eyes flashed with fire. "One of the guards suggested I see if Eryx would hire me."

"Oh, Atalanta, I am sorry—"

"Not surprising. I look like a beggar," she cut in. "The bronzed mirror in our room made it hard to tell what colour my face is, but the scratches and bruises are still very obvious."

"You...do look disreputable," Hazina said.

Atalanta laughed. "Aye, well, I'll fit right in with the crew on Damien's raft."

Hazina linked her arm through Atalanta's good one and they climbed aboard. The sailors paid them no mind, but two small children stared at them with wide eyes. The pair were almost as dirty as the sailors and had bare feet peeking from beneath their gowns. One had golden curls and the other had black hair that frizzed more than curled. Hazina wasn't sure if the pair were related or not, but their unwavering gaze made her uneasy.

Atalanta smiled at the children. "Hello there. Are your parents sailors on *le Droit Margerie?*"

"No," Eryx said, coming up on Atalanta's other side. "Damien agreed to take two families to Santa Maria di Leuca. I'm not sure why."

"Are they the only children? Where are their parents?" Atalanta asked.

Eryx shrugged. "There are three other children, and I believe their mothers are below deck. Only one of the families has a father sailing with us. I think he's helping secure cargo."

"It will be nice to have other women on the ship," Hazina said.

"Aye, well, there are no private rooms, so I expect they'll be just as glad to have you two aboard," Eryx said. He gave them a smile before moving off to berate some of the sailors.

Hazina eyed the small children warily. "Should you two not be below deck with your mothers?"

The children didn't say anything but scurried away. Hazina started to call out, to warn them about getting in the way of the sailors, but let them go. The men could tell the children off themselves, if they became a bother.

"Do you not like children?" Atalanta asked, her voice soft and head cocked to the side.

Hazina rolled her shoulders. "It is not that I dislike them, but...I find the little ones to be, how to put this...more trouble than they are

145

worth?"

Atalanta laughed. "I'm sure most are. Still, they have redeeming qualities."

"Like what?" Hazina muttered.

Damien joined them before Atalanta could respond. His smile was strained and dark circles beneath his eyes said he hadn't slept well for several nights. He fiddled with a quail brooch pinned to his cloak. "The captain has finally agreed to take us to the cormorant island."

"Is that what we've decided to call it?" Atalanta asked.

"It's better than 'Siren's Lair' or 'Poseidon's Island.' Certainly less likely to get us arrested," he pointed out.

"Damien, why did you take on passengers? And passengers with small children, no less," Hazina asked.

He glanced over his shoulder at the two children watching the sailors work. "The families are scared to remain in Methoni. Helping them costs me nothing."

"Costs you food and space," Atalanta countered.

Damien smiled and shrugged. "Nothing I can't afford."

Atalanta grunted and eyed him distrustfully. "Right, well, I'm going to go below deck and see what the sleeping arrangements are going to be like. Are you coming with, Hazina?"

"No, I would like to remain here for the time being."

Atalanta gave her a small nod before heading to the hatch and ladder leading below deck. Damien pursed his lips and said, "I'd offer to help her down the ladder, but I'm certain she would hit me."

"She doesn't like to feel helpless," Hazina said.

Atalanta awkwardly started down the ladder, only to slip and fall. The faint thunk of her hitting the bottom was followed by a soft expletive.

"She would say I'm being too much of a hero, trying to rescue any 'damsel-in-distress' around me," Damien said.

Hazina studied him. His voice was pleasantly neutral and a small smile curved the corner of his lips up, but his eyes were tight. Almost as if he were in pain. "I do not know how wanting to save others is something to be ashamed of."

He laughed and ran a hand through his hair. "It's not. She thinks I don't know how to tell when someone actually needs rescuing, rather than being inconvenienced by circumstances."

"Do other people—other damsels-in-distress—tell you the same thing?" she asked.

"No. Though it's rare for me to be in a position to rescue people."

Hazina snorted. "That is nonsense. You stepped in to rescue that goddess-in-disguise, and you have rescued these families from their fears, if not the Ottomans. You do such things without even thinking. It is only Atalanta's stubbornness which makes you realize your natural inclination."

Damien gaped at her for a moment. He gave himself a shake and smiled. "I…never thought of it like that. Thank you."

She nodded. "You are a good man, Damien. Do not let Atalanta, or anyone else, make you doubt that."

His gaze dropped and he rocked back on his heels. "Thank you, again. I should see if Eryx needs help with the sailors, though."

"Go on then. I do not need a chaperone," Hazina said, making a shooing gesture at him. He chuckled and left.

It didn't take much longer for the ship to set sail. Hazina watched the red roofs of Methoni slip away from them. A morose cloud of gloom stole over her. If things went according to plan, this would be the last leg of their journey before finding Poseidon. Their quest was almost over. It felt as if they had been traveling for many months, but also that they had only just started.

Atalanta and Damien would return to their lives, but what would she do? She briefly thought about studying with Calista before pushing the idea aside. She was too old to become an apprentice. There were still many places in the world to see, though she didn't like traveling alone. Perhaps she could ask Eryx to accompany her—he had certainly done his fair share of travel over the course of his long life.

Eryx glanced up and met her gaze, a slow smile spreading over his face. Hazina spun and hurried to the hatch, heart pounding in her throat. She climbed down the ladder and breathed a sigh of relief when the cool shadows of the hold wrapped around her.

"Who are you?" a small voice asked.

Hazina turned and met the inquisitive gaze of a young boy. He almost reached her collarbone and stood with his shoulders thrown back and chin raised. His face was streaked with dirt, as were his sleeves, and his hair swirled in strange patterns from the water still dripping from it.

"My name is Hazina," she answered. "Who are you?"

"I'm Corradin. My papa is a sailor."

"Oh? I did not think any of the sailors on this ship—"

"Not on this ship," Corradin interrupted. "My papa is a sailor on a big merchant ship. It's been years since I saw him. Mama says we won't see him, but I'm going to become a sailor and look for him and tell him how much we miss him and make him come home to Mama, and Gilia, and Dea, and me."

"I…wish you luck," Hazina said, uncertain what response the boy wanted. He gave her a wide smile and scampered up the ladder and on to the deck.

Hazina squinted in the gloom and wove her way through a maze of stacked barrels and crates to where a small lantern flickered. Atalanta sat on the floor, a rag doll in her good hand, while two dark-skinned children watched her with wide eyes and wider smiles. An older child worked on some mending, but kept glancing up as Atalanta told a story with the doll. A blonde-haired woman lay blankets on the ground, tugging and rearranging the make-shift beds over and over again.

"Did you need help?" Hazina asked the woman, keeping her voice low.

The woman looked up, her eyes ringed by dark circles and lines spread across her face making her look old and weary. "No. I should leave the beds be, but…I worry we will not make it to Italy." The woman glanced at the blanket clutched in her hands and scoffed. She dropped it and shook her head. "This does nothing to help."

"I have medicinal teas," Hazina told her. "It might help ease your worries for a time."

The woman shook her head. "I cannot pay."

"That is all right, I require no payment," she assured her.

The woman ran her eyes over Hazina. She sniffed and crossed her arms. "I'm not sure what your aim is, but you should be ashamed for praying on folks as what are down on their luck."

"I merely wished to help," Hazina protested.

The woman sniffed again and stalked away. Hazina could only watch and wonder why her offer of help had been so rudely rebuffed.

Atalanta handed the rag doll to one of the children and ruffled the hair of both of them before joining Hazina. "Is everything all right?" she whispered.

"Yes."

"You look worried, and that woman seemed angry when she left. Are you sure?" Atalanta pressed.

Hazina nodded and Atalanta didn't question her further. They left the children and small nook amongst the crates and searched out another place to store their things. The crates formed a warren of paths and niches, many of which already contained the personal belongings of the sailors.

"We almost need a map," Atalanta quipped.

"The dead-end corridor we passed is as good a place as any to claim," Hazina said.

Atalanta grimaced, shrugged, and then nodded. She followed Hazina back to the short corridor ending in a wall of boxes. It was a little more than a pace wide, and two paces deep. Not spacious, but more than enough room for the two of them.

"Where are Damien and Eryx going to sleep?" Atalanta asked.

"Will they not sleep with the sailors?"

Atalanta shrugged. "I suppose they could."

Hazina couldn't help smiling. "Did you want one of them, specifically, to sleep nearby?"

Atalanta glowered. "You know I don't. I just thought that, as we're still on a quest, they might want to sleep by us."

"Mm."

"Don't give me that look. I've told you I have no interest in that sort of thing."

"Might you develop an interest?" Hazina asked.

Atalanta shrugged. "I haven't yet. I know I would like to have a family—though I can't bear the idea of passing my curse on to another generation—and I know men expect certain things of their wives, but...That aspect is something I would rather not partake in."

"I have heard it can be quite pleasant," Hazina offered.

Atalanta laughed. "It doesn't interest me. Perhaps I'll find a man uninterested in women, and we'll take in orphans. That's the only way I can see myself settling down with someone."

Hazina shook her head. She wasn't fond of children, but she did envy women who had married and made a home. Whether her desire stemmed from her homesickness, or from a deeper wish to have a lasting connection with someone, she wasn't sure. The idea of having a home and a husband to return to was as sweet as spun sugar. And as nebulous. She thought her parents had been happy together—though she barely remembered them anymore. Her fleeting memories were all she had to base her abstract wish on, but they were good memories. She wanted that for herself.

For two days, Hazina tried to avoid the children and their parents. It was an impossible endeavour on such a small ship. Every time she went up on deck, Corradin would appear and take up a spot next to her. She hoped he would grow bored and leave if she didn't speak to him, but he never did. Staying below deck meant she had to listen to the shrieking laughter and petty squabbling of the other children though.

The sun was setting on their third day at sea before Hazina spoke to the boy. "Do you not wish to play with the other children?"

Corradin looked up at her with wide eyes and a delighted smile. "Mama says your a witch."

Hazina wanted to protest the accusation, but it wouldn't change what anyone believed. Instead, she asked, "Why would you spend all your time in my company then?"

Corradin looked down and scuffed his toe on the deck. "I thought maybe I could buy a charm, or a spell, or something witchy, to help me find my papa. I don't have any money, but I'm strong and a good worker. I could...uh, clean your broom, or carry things for you."

He looked so hopeful that Hazina's heart twisted. She crouched so she was eye-to-eye with him and tried to give him her most sympathetic smile. "If I were a witch, and I am not saying I am, but if I were, I would not be able to help you. I am very sorry."

Corradin pouted and crossed his arms. "I bet you'd help me if I had coin."

"No. There are different types of magic in the world and, if I had magic, I would not have anything that could help you," she explained.

"Is your friend who dresses like a man a witch too?" he asked, his excitement returning. "Does she have the right kind of magic?"

Hazina shook her head. "Atalanta cannot make magic. And I would advise you not to seek out witches in the future. They can be dangerous to your health and soul."

Corradin bit his lip and took a step back. She straightened and sighed. Better for the boy to be frightened of her, than always hanging at her side. She waited for him to leave. When he didn't, she frowned and asked, "Why are you still here?"

"You're nicer to me than the sailors, and the other children like to play baby games. They don't ever want to play pirates and soldiers," he said.

"Do you not want to do something? All we have done is stand and watch the waves for two days. You must be bored."

Corradin shrugged. "I just pretend we're trying to escape pirates, or racing away from a storm. It's not as fun when it's only me pretending though. Did you want to pretend with me?"

"No," Hazina said. The hope died so suddenly in his eyes that she was quick to add, "I am not very good at pretending. I could teach you a bit about the herbs and medicines I have."

"Really?" he exclaimed, bouncing on the balls of his feet. "You'd teach me to be a witch?"

"It is not witchcraft. It is medicine. A science," she admonished.

"Can I pretend it's witchcraft?" he asked.

Hazina sighed. "I doubt I could stop you."

She led Corradin below deck to the nook she and Atalanta had claimed as their own. He happily settled on the floor where she indicated and watched in fascination as she laid out a basic collection of six herbs. Despite Corradin's perpetual questions about magic, he was a good student. Hazina was a little sad to see him go when his mother called for him.

"Can you teach me more tomorrow?" he asked.

"Yes."

He gave her a huge smile and took off through the maze of boxes. She smiled to herself and put away the herbs. For a child, he wasn't too much of a bother. Teaching him would certainly make the journey less dull.

The ship jerked and Hazina was thrown on her face. She pressed a hand to her nose and stumbled to her feet. A second jolt was accompanied by wood groaning. She eyed the hull warily and then turned and ran to the ladder. She passed the children and their mothers huddled together, whispering fearful prayers. There wasn't anything she could do or say to allay their fears, so she hurried up the ladder.

Sailors ran about, bumping into each other as they tried to follow the captain's shouted orders. Two were struggling to maneouver an over-sized contraption reminiscent of a crossbow to the edge of the ship. Eryx and Damien stood at the bow of the ship, arguing, while Atalanta had her arquebus out, tracking something in the water below.

Hazina ran to join them. "What"—she paused to catch her breath—"is happening?"

The ship rocked and Atalanta fired. A piercing squeal split the air, followed by thrashing in the water.

"Hippocampi," Damien said, his jaw clenched.

Eryx sneered. "They weren't bothering us until she fired at them."

"They're Poseidon's creatures," Atalanta said, reloading her arquebus. "They weren't going to let us any closer to the island without a fight anyway. I just took took a preemptive shot."

Hazina squinted toward the horizon. A smudge of land was just visible. If they had to try and outrun sea creatures, there was no way they would be able to make it. She stepped up to the edge and peered down into the water. Strange beasts circled the ship. They had the front half of a horse, and the back half of a dolphin. Their colouring ranged from slate grey to an off-white. The creatures seemed wary, darting toward them and then veering off at the last second.

"Well you've certainly started the fight now," Eryx said.

The hippocampi swarmed forward as a group. Atalanta fired and hit one, but the others still slammed into the ship with their hooves. Wood snapped and shouting came from below deck. The herd circled away and back. They might lose one every charge, but they would keep coming until the ship was nothing more than driftwood and bloated bodies.

Hazina didn't have any of her prepared ceramic balls with her. She had no way to summon spirits. Except…except Eryx said magic didn't work the way she had always thought. She took a deep breath and closed her eyes, reaching for the feeling she got whenever she normally worked magic. She could feel it flickering inside her. It was distant and seemed to be swathed in layers of gauze she had to fight her way through.

She grasped the magic and the flickering turned into a raging fire, burning through her veins. She opened her eyes and gasped. Currents of colours swirled all around them. Instinctively, she knew each colour represented a different natural force. The currents seemed unaffected by the sailors, but they curled and rippled around Atalanta, Damien, and Eryx. Hazina squinted through the swirling colours and studied the hippocampi for a moment.

With her eyes open to the magic in the world, she could differentiate pods within the overall swarm. Each pod was led by a specific hippocampi. The pod leaders seemed to draw the currents into themselves and release an intricate web that lay over each member of their group.

Staring at the webs, it seemed so easy to reach out and tear them. Pain seared up Hazina's arm and she cried out. She was vaguely aware of someone supporting her—Eryx, she thought—but all of her focus was on the currents of magic. Touching the webs had been like grabbing a sword fresh from the forge.

Hazina took a deep breath and reached toward the free flowing currents. These were like silk beneath her fingers. She curled her fingers, tugging on the currents, and smiled to see lightning lance down from a clear sky. It didn't strike any of the hippocampi, but they still shied away from their charge.

She threw her arms out and brought them down, gathering currents to her. A mix of the blue and yellow made lightning, and a mix of red and green made the water around *le Droit Margerie* roil like stock in a soup pot. She could feel the magic draining her energy, but with so many currents in her hands, waiting to be used, it was hard to remember why that would matter.

Hazina mixed several currents together and threw the tangled ball at the centre of the swarm. Water exploded in a burst that drenched everyone on deck and sent dozens of hippocampi flying through the air. The remaining creatures fled and she let the gathered currents slide through her fingers back to their original paths. The moment she let go, exhaustion gripped her. She would have fallen if it weren't for Eryx still holding her.

"You foolish woman," he whispered. "You almost killed yourself handling that much magic."

"The ship is safe now?" she asked, her voice a whisper only because she had no energy to make it louder.

"The ship is. You not so much."

Hazina struggled to straighten and look around. Atalanta and Damien stood facing away from them, blocking her view. "What do you mean?" she asked.

"That was a very spectacular display of magic. Far beyond what my simple illusion can mask. The sailors and passengers aren't very happy having you on board any more," Eryx explained.

"We are almost to the island—we can worry about their discomfort with me after we have stopped Poseidon," Hazina said as forcefully as she could muster. It was a bit too much effort and she lapsed unconscious.

"The woman is a witch," a sailor shouted, pointing a crooked finger.

"She drove away the monsters," a scruffy-haired boy protested. Eryx thought he might have been the one who followed Hazina around, but wasn't sure.

One of the women gasped and pulled the boy to her. The boy struggled, but she held him against her hip. Her fear was thick and cloying, and so strong it was distinctive amongst everyone else's emotions.

"The witch must be cast into the sea, before God smites us all," another sailor shouted. Several others murmured their agreement.

Atalanta gripped her arquebus and glared at the frightened people. "You should be praising her for saving your worthless hides, rather than plotting her murder."

Eryx gathered Hazina into his arms and stood. Several of the sailors shrank back.

"Sir,"—the captain took a half step forward and looked up at Damien with pleading eyes—"we are all proper God-fearing Christians, here. Surely you must see that having a witch aboard *le Droit Margerie* is akin to spitting in Christ's face!"

Damien shook his head. "You say she is a witch, but all I saw was her performing a miracle. What else would you call driving off such demons?"

A thread of doubt raced through the cluster of sailors. Eryx felt it catch on several of them, while the rest shrugged it off. He stepped up beside Atalanta and Damien, meeting the eyes of those who hadn't let the doubt settle. "If it had been Damien, or myself, who called lightning and fire from the sky to drive the beasts back, you would be proclaiming us to be blessed by God. Instead, it was Hazina, and you call her a witch."

The sailors shifted. Their fear was mixed heavily with confusion now. The woman was the only one to not have any doubts.

Her face twisted with disgust. "If she were truly blessed by God, then why—"

A loud crash interrupted her, and the boat pitched so hard to the side that only the captain was able to keep his feet.

"Lord have mercy," a sailor cried, clinging to the ship's rail and pointing a shaky finger at something in the water off the port side.

A large head, with dark eyes over a pointed beak was staring at the ship.

Eryx's heart leapt into his throat and he set Hazina down as gently as he could before springing back to his feet. He shouted orders and rushed to the helm. Half the sailors jumped to follow his instructions, while the rest stood frozen and numb.

The aspidochelone dove at them. Wood splintered and the ship rocked violently, before settling back with a definite list. Eryx grunted and fought to guide the ship away. He jerked his chin toward the unmoving sailors and shouted, "Damien, drag some men below deck to stop up the holes this blasted turtle is making!"

Damien grabbed two men by their shirts and shoved them toward the hatch. They stumbled down the ladder while he grabbed two more. Those men who hadn't been shaken from their daze were sent tumbling when the aspidochelone rammed them from the stern. Eryx shouted at them, and Atalanta scurried around the deck, shaking men and slapping those who didn't jump to help.

"God is punishing us," the woman wailed, huddled in the middle of the deck with her son trapped in her arms.

"If that's so, it's because you wanted to throw an innocent woman overboard," Atalanta said, her voice snapping like a whip.

The woman sobbed loudly.

Atalanta ran to the aft of the ship and braced herself for the turtle's next attack. The ship pitched and she fired her arquebus. The creature shrieked in pain, it's fins flailing so violently in the water that waves washed over the deck.

"Hit it again," Eryx shouted. "Maybe it'll give up."

She grunted and focused on reloading the weapon. They were getting close to the little island. Eryx didn't let himself worry about whether there would be any protection from sea creature attacks—he simply focused on reaching it. He couldn't tell anymore where his own desperation ended and that of the sailors began.

The turtle screeched and hit them so hard the ship leapt forward. The starboard bow crashed into the rocky edge of the island. Atalanta fired again. The aspidochelone's pained scream was both heart-wrenching and satisfying.

Eryx panted, and turned to look over the aft rail. There was little to do for the ship, now that they were scuttled against the island. The giant turtle was nowhere to be seen, though slicks of blood floated on the surface of the water. A testament to Atalanta's aim.

She raised her arquebus and held it steady, her gaze tracking over the still waters.

"Do you think we drove it off?" he asked.

"Gods, I hope so," she replied.

After a few more minutes with no sign of the aspidochelone, they both relaxed.

"Is the monster gone?" the captain asked.

"Aye, for now," Eryx said.

"God be praised!"

The joyful cry was picked up by the other sailors on deck. Laughter and tears flowed freely from them all. The noise of it brought Damien and the sailors he'd grabbed back up. He joined Eryx and Atalanta, wringing out the bottom edge of his tunic.

"Well we've made it to the island. Do you think we can trust them to fix the ship while we deal with Poseidon?" he asked.

Eryx ran a hand over his head. "I think they can fix *le Droit Margerie*, but I don't think we can trust them to wait once she's seaworthy again."

Atalanta sighed and nodded. "Then we best get going, if we want to make it back before they leave."

They dispersed to gather their things. None of the sailors, women, or children were sad to see them leave. Eryx stood on the island and eyed the damaged ship. It would take several days to make rudimentary repairs. He hoped the captain was cautious enough to want to do more than the minimum.

He shifted his hold on Hazina so her head lay against his shoulder instead of bouncing freely with each step, and turned to follow Atalanta and Damien toward a pair of rock spires. The jutting stones leaned against each other with a matted tangle of twigs, mud, and other detritus draped over the top edge. Three cormorants sat in the large nest, watching them approach with dark eyes. When they stepped down a short slope, two of the birds launched from the nest. Their barking cries drummed against Eryx's ears.

"Stupid birds," Atalanta muttered.

One of the circling cormorants dove at them. Atalanta and Damien both ducked, but Eryx wasn't able to dip quick enough to avoid the bird's talons. The shallow cuts on the back of his head burned. He bit out an oath and asked, "Can't you shoot them?"

"They're sacred to Poseidon—" Atalanta started, but Eryx cut her off.

"So? You shot at the hippocampi without hesitation! They pull his chariot, don't they? What makes these stupid birds any more special?"

The circling cormorants shrieked in triumph and the one still in the nest puffed its chest and spread its wings.

"There are creatures that are associated with a god, and then there are creatures that are sacred to a god," Atalanta said, giving him a look that implied he should have already known the answer. "Bad things happen to people who harm sacred animals."

"Despite being here to kill Poseidon, I get the feeling we shouldn't hurt the dumb birds," Damien said begrudgingly.

Eryx ran his eyes over him. The coloured glass in Damien's brooch glowed faintly. He could feel a presence at the edge of his awareness. Someone or something was there. He shook his head. "Then what do you suggest? I don't feel like being clawed up by some birds today."

Damien squeezed his eyes shut and gripped his brooch. "Ptokheia," he whispered. "Help us."

A soft breeze blew against them and the circling cormorants trilled quizzically. Sweat beaded on Damien's brow. The birds settled back on their nest and turned their attention to the ship they'd left behind.

"What did you do?" Atalanta asked.

Damien wiped sweat from his brow and blew out a breath. "I...don't know. But I'm exhausted."

"You let someone channel magic through you," Eryx said, rolling his shoulders in discomfort. He could still feel the presence, but no matter how hard he strained, he couldn't do more than sense them at the edge of awareness.

"I didn't realize how tiring that would be."

Atalanta quirked an eyebrow. "Did you think Hazina weak for feeling tired after using magic?"

"No, of course not. But it wasn't my magic. It was Ptokheia's."

Eryx squinted at Damien. The quail brooch looked perfectly ordinary again, and the vague presence was starting to fade. "We should move on before this spell disappears."

Atalanta nodded and led the group forward into a small cave. Rancid meat assailed them, setting all three coughing. Hazina stirred in Eryx's arm, groaning and turning so her face pressed against his shoulder. He held her closer and tried to focus on the faint scent of soap emanating from her hair.

Atalanta rummaged in her bag for a moment before pulling out a battered lantern. She quickly lit it and held it aloft. Flickering orange light filled the space, revealing dark smears on the rock. Bones with scraps of rotting flesh clinging to them littered the floor. A carved capstone filled the far end of the tiny cave. "This is disgusting," she choked out. "It wasn't like this the last time we were here."

"Are you sure this is how get get in?" Eryx asked.

"You don't just put a capstone against a wall," Atalanta reasoned. "This has to be the entrance."

Damien shook his head. "Logically, the stone should simply be blocking the sea from coming in, but…everything related to the gods always seems to be much more complicated than it needs to be."

"That's what happens when beings from another world try to make this one their home," Eryx said softly.

Atalanta frowned at him but simply said, "The quicker we can get the capstone open, the sooner we'll be away from this."

Damien held out a hand and Atalanta passed him the lantern. He held it up high and peered at the carvings on the stone while she ran her hands lightly across the surface. Eryx crowded behind them, studying the waves, birds, horses, leaves, and mythical creatures flowing around the stone in no apparent pattern.

"That woman in Methoni said something about the key being the leaf that doesn't belong, right?" Ery asked.

Atalanta nodded absently. "Yes."

"Then that has to be it," Eryx said, shifting Hazina so he could point to the symbol that had caught his eye. "There are no others like it."

"Do we just press it?" Damien asked. Without waiting for a response, he reached out and pressed the carving. The leaf sank with a grating groan and puff of dust. He jerked his hand back and Atalanta leaned in to look at the leaf.

"That wasn't the right one," she said, her voice tight and a spike of fear cutting through the smell of rot.

159

Eryx gaped. "What? It was the odd one out—"

His words were cut off when a slab of stone slammed down over the cave's entrance. Eryx, Atalanta, and Damien stared at each other in mute surprise. A moment later, water gurgled up from some unseen spot on the floor. It was cold and continuous. It only took a moment for the entire floor to be covered. The water crept higher, lifting the bones with it as it passed their ankles.

"Right. Wrong leaf," Eryx conceded.

"It was one of a kind," Damien protested.

Atalanta shook her head. "It was an ash leaf—one of Poseidon's sacred leaves." She ran her hands over the capstone, skimming along the other carvings. Already the bottom of the stone was obscured by the rising water.

"What are you doing?" Damien asked, his knuckles white on the lantern's ring.

"Looking for the right leaf."

"What good will that do?"

"I'll let you know when I find it," she snapped back.

Damien opened his mouth to say something, then closed it with a click. He shoved the lantern at Eryx. "We need to get out of here."

Eryx eyed the stone blocking the exit dubiously. "I doubt it will be easy to escape this trap."

Damien grunted. He slid his hands along the edges of the stone, crouching to dip his hands beneath the water. He strained to lift the rock, but it didn't budge. The water was almost to his shoulder when he abandoned the attempt. He snarled and threw his shoulder against the stone.

"Perhaps if we worked together?" Eryx suggested.

Damien shook his head, a hand cradling his shoulder. "We'd break ourselves before making a dent in it."

Eryx glanced at Atalanta. She was still crouched, running her hands over the stone. The water was at her chin and her mouth was pressed in a tight line. He gave Hazina a gentle shake. "Come now, bellibone, we need you to get us out of here."

Hazina gave no indication she'd heard him.

"Aha!"

There was a snick of stone and Atalanta stood up, smiling triumphantly. Nothing happened. Her smile faltered as the water climbed up to their chests. Distant rumbling shook the cave and sloshed the water against their faces. All at once, the capstone fell away into darkness. The water rushed out with such force it swept their feet out from under them. Shattering glass and a hiss of steam accompanied the descent of total darkness.

"Th-that's what g-good it'll d-do," Atalanta said, her teeth chattering.

"We have no light now," Damien pointed out.

She snorted. "Always have to find the negative in any situation. Can't even say 'thank you' when I save you."

"You still haven't saved me yet."

Eryx shook his head and carefully climbed back to his feet. It had been a small miracle that he'd kept his hold on Hazina and hadn't landed on her when the water knocked him down. "You two bicker over the strangest things."

A whisper of air caressed his skin. It was cool and made his damp clothes feel all the colder. Hazina shivered in his arms and he held her tighter. He grimaced and slid his feet along the ground. Wet boots were possibly the worst kind of mundane misfortune. His foot hit the edge of the capstone and light flared around them.

It took a moment for his eyes to adjust to the light emanating from swirling shells half buried in the rough rock walls of a tunnel. Despite the unfinished look of the walls, they curved in to a pointed arch overhead. It gave the narrow passage an airy feel. The light was as bright and pure as an afternoon sun on a cloudless day, but as cold as the water they had almost drowned in.

Eryx glanced back at Atalanta and Damien and grinned. "I'm almost surprised you didn't take advantage of the darkness to sneak a kiss or two."

"What? Why would you think that?" Atalanta demanded.

"Truly? Has the thought never occurred to you?"

Damien winced and Atalanta glowered. Eryx shook his head.

"We are not now—nor will we ever be—lovers," she said, her words sharp and glare sharper. She shoved past him and stalked down the tunnel before he could say anything else.

Damien slowly followed. His voice was soft and dejected, almost a whisper, when he said, "Technically, we are blood enemies."

Eryx tried to give him a commiserating smile. "I think she does love you," he offered. "Just perhaps not in the way you—"

"Don't," Damien cut him off. "I know she doesn't love me. I am...resigning myself to it."

"Some women like to be...convinced," Eryx mused. "They want a man to fight to earn their affection."

Damien chuckled. "Not Atalanta."

"Are you sure?"

Damien breathed out, his eyes locked on her retreating form. "She is...straightforward. And honest. If she had any interest in me convincing her, as you put it, she wouldn't be so frustrated by people insinuating we are more than allies."

"You are more than allies, though," Eryx pointed out.

"All right, more than friends, then."

The two men followed behind Atalanta. Her pace had slowed, allowing them to slowly close the gap. Eryx dropped his voice and asked, "Is it possible she is frustrated because she doesn't think you feel that way about her?"

Hope flared in Damien's eyes and was swallowed by resignation. "No. I know her. I will not embarrass myself, nor disrespect her, by pressing."

Eryx nodded. "You are a good man, Damien. I am certain you will find a feisty young woman to love."

He laughed. "Aye, well, we have to survive Poseidon first."

"Will you two hens stop gossiping and look at this," Atalanta called to them.

They hurried forward to join her where the hallway abruptly ended at a balcony. A delicate, curved rail of glittering pearl was all that separated them from a massive drop down onto brightly coloured rooftops. A small city sprawled before them. Roads cut channels through buildings capped in yellow, blue, green, and purple. They were so eye-catching it took a moment for them to notice the dripping stalactites that were almost eye-level with the balcony.

"Do you think it's abandoned?" Atalanta asked.

Damien's eyes fluttered shut. "It's too quiet to be inhabited. In a city this size, there's never true silence."

Eryx eyed the buildings distrustfully. "Why would it have been abandoned?"

The three stared out over the city. A breeze carried the smell of salt, dust, and rotten wood to them. None of the buildings looked decrepit. They glittered and gleamed beneath the strange light emitted by the shells. Not a single shutter or roof tile was out of place. But the smell of decay was too strong. Eryx strained to detect an illusion. He thought he caught the flicker of one. If it was truly an illusion, and not some other magic, than it blanketed the entire city. He couldn't imagine who could posses enough power to cast such a spell.

"Well, we have to find a way down and across," Atalanta said, breaking everyone's reverie.

"What makes you so sure?" Damien asked.

She cocked an eyebrow and gave him a skeptical look. "There's a hall of some sort on the far side, and nowhere else to go."

Eryx pulled his gaze from the colourful buildings and found the place she was pointing to. A tall doorway, at least three storeys high, stood at the far end of the cavern. Reddish-gold light poured from the opening. Against the bright houses it was, it was unremarkable. The distance made it hard to tell for sure, but it appeared as if there were a plaza separating the hall from the rest of the city.

"Ah." Damien nodded. "Well then, how do you propose we get down?"

"Attach a rope to the banister and climb."

Eryx frowned. "I don't like the look of this material." It was exquisitely beautiful, the pearlescent sheen making the thin rails seem ever more delicate. There was an almost translucent quality to them.

Atalanta turned away from the railing and kicked back. Her foot slammed into one of the rails and bounced off. The only damage was a bit of mud transferred from her shoe to the rail. "Seems solid enough." She dug in her bag and pulled out a coiled length of rope with a triumphant smile. It only took a moment for her to tie a quick knot and give it a tug.

"Your shoulder is still injured," Damien pointed out. "Climbing a rope isn't going to be good for it."

She grunted. "Unless there are invisible stairs, I don't think we have much choice."

"Your goddess healed you, didn't she?" Eryx asked Damien. "Could you heal Atalanta?"

Damien ran a hand through his hair. "I could ask, I suppose. The healing she gave me didn't fix everything, and left me exhausted."

"Still better than climbing with a broken clavicle."

Atalanta grumbled, but pulled her tunic collar to the side to expose the discoloured and swollen bump marring her shoulder. Damien hesitated for a moment, then placed a hand over her injury. He closed his eyes, clenched his jaw, and rested his other hand on the quail brooch. Eryx felt a presence brush by, and then it was gone. Damien opened his eyes and pulled his hand back so he could see Atalanta's shoulder. The discolouration was gone, though a small bump remained.

"How does it feel?" he asked, his voice soft.

Atalanta rolled her shoulder and grinned. "It's stiff, but it doesn't hurt any more. I'm a little annoyed we didn't think to do this sooner."

"One more problem, though," Eryx said.

Atalanta snorted. "Of course. What is it now?"

"Hazina is still out of it. How do we get her down?"

Atalanta muttered some inventive curses under her breath and kicked the banister again. A sharp snap made them all freeze. Atalanta bent to examine the railing she'd hit.

"We definitely can't climb down now," Eryx said. "It's clearly not strong enough."

"Calm down," Atalanta said. She ran her hands over the railings, her eyes closed.

"If she has a second rope, I'm sure we could figure out how to get

Hazina down safely," Damien offered.

Eryx shook his head. "That won't do any good if—"

"Ah! No need," Atalanta cut in. She twisted a rail and pushed. A three foot section of the banister swung out. Spiraling steps shimmered into view, each of the same pearlescent material and floating unsupported in the air.

"That doesn't look any safer," Damien grumbled.

"Well you have three choices. Take the rope down, use the stairs, or stay here and die of old age," Atalanta told him, an impatient snap to her voice.

"Stairs it is," Eryx said with forced cheerfulness.

He slowly and carefully took the stairs. Between Hazina in his arms and the strange material of the steps, he couldn't see where he was putting his feet. He felt with each foot before committing his weight. By the time they reached the ground, his legs burned. He set her down, propped up against a building whose roof sloped to the ground in a curl reminiscent of a wave, and sank down beside her.

"Mm?" Hazina mumbled, shifting and blinking at their surroundings.

"How are you feeling?" he asked.

"…water?"

Atalanta crouched beside Hazina and pulled a flask from her bag. She passed it to Hazina and let her drink as much as she wanted.

"Where are we?" Hazina asked.

"Underground, practically on Poseidon's doorstep," Damien answered.

"Oh…good, I suppose."

Eryx nodded. "You're still in no condition to go far. I think we should find somewhere to rest."

"Aye," Damien agreed. He went to the nearest door and tried the latch. It depressed easily, but the door didn't open. He tried three other doors, all with the same result.

"Looks like we'll need to break in," Atalanta said.

Damien grunted. He pressed a latch and threw his weight against a door. The door swung in as if it hadn't been stuck only a moment before. The entire cavern flickered like a mirage before dissolving. Where the houses had been colourful and fanciful before, only bleached and rough edges remained. Most buildings were missing at least some of their facade. A few sagged so badly they appeared to have fallen atop their neighbours in a drunken heap. The smell of decay intensified and the light seemed sickly and grey.

"I think I speak for everyone when I say, I already hate this place," Damien muttered.

Damien stalked ahead of everyone else, his eyes scanning the shadows and holes left by the derelict buildings. Atalanta supported Hazina, and Eryx took up the rear. Though the city appeared abandoned, Damien didn't want to rest anywhere with gaping holes or other easy points of ingress. Just in case.

The road they were on wound through the city. It crossed other paths and split into separate streets. Everything curled and twisted. There were no straight lines. It made it hard to track how far they had come, but, for the moment, Damien wasn't concerned with that.

After an hour of exploration, they found a suitable building. It had been at least two stories tall, but all that remained was the mostly in-tact main floor. The rubble of the upper floors clogged the staircase, and the one window was easy to block with larger pieces of debris. The only feature remaining inside was a stone fireplace.

Eryx set about getting the fire started while Atalanta retrieved thin, straw-filled mattresses from her bottomless bag. Hazina rested on a broken piece of pale stone, watching everyone with tired eyes. Damien secured the rubble against the window and door as best he could before settling on the mattress Atalanta pointed him to.

"The chimney is damaged," Eryx said, sitting back from the little flame he had started. "We should put the fire out before we sleep, else the house might fill with smoke." Already tendrils of smoke curled out of the fireplace to swirl against the ceiling.

Damien nodded. "We shouldn't leave it going too long anyway. We don't know if the city is truly abandoned. A smoking chimney is like waving a flag at anyone who might be looking."

Atalanta set a small pot of water next to the flames before handing out dried food and a few withered pieces of fruit. "The bag might have no end, but it doesn't preserve things," she said apologetically.

Everyone sat in silence, lethargically nibbling on the food. Hazina threw a small handful of herbs into the water once it was heated. She set the pot of tea to the side to cool a bit while everyone set up their beds. Damien was hard pressed to not make a snide remark when Atalanta handed Eryx two blankets and a small roll of her clothes to use as a pillow. Of course the pirate wasn't prepared.

Hazina's tea had a delicate smell, reminiscent of flowers after a rain, and even less flavour. Damien drank a single cup before settling down to sleep. Atalanta and Hazina both drank two cups and fell asleep as soon as they lay down. Eryx sipped at his cup and settled next to the fire, watching the small flames die down to coals.

The crackling and popping in the hearth seemed unnaturally loud against the utter stillness outside of the ruined dwelling. Where there might have been creaking and settling, or a wind against the shutters, or even the whisper soft sound of other people breathing, in a normal home, here there were only the sounds their small group made. Damien couldn't stop himself from holding his breath and straining to catch some distant sound. Something, anything, to banish the feeling that they were camped out on death's doorstep.

"What's bothering you?" Eryx asked. His voice was soft, but it came so suddenly that Damien jumped.

"I, uh…" Damien rolled onto his side and met his gaze. In the fading light from the embers, Eryx looked as otherworldly as he claimed to be. "There's a sense of, I don't know, doom?"

Eryx nodded. "Places abandoned by the living tend to get like that."

"So it's nothing to worry about?"

"I never said that."

Damien remembered Eryx telling them he was the child of a death spirit. He slowly sat up, stalling to gather his thoughts. "I have never believed your reasons for helping us. You told us your mother would mark people for death. Are…are any of us—"

"Stop," Eryx cut him off. "You would know if you were marked. You would have been told. Of course that doesn't mean you will all survive. You do not have to be marked to die."

"That's reassuring," Damien muttered.

"Whether you believe me or not, I have told you the truth."

Damien grunted. He settled back down to his bed and stared up at the ceiling. "I cannot shake the feeling that we're not all going to survive this," he admitted after a minute of silence.

"It is a possibility, but I've come to know you all in the short time we've been together. You're resourceful and surprisingly hard to kill. I think you are simply nervous, what with being so close to facing Poseidon," Eryx suggested.

"Perhaps."

"You could try praying to your goddess. She has already proven to be a valuable, albeit absent, ally."

Damien grimaced. He couldn't deny the help Ptokheia had given them, first with the birds, and then by healing Atalanta's injury. Yet he hadn't prayed to any of the gods since he was a small child. His father maintained the gods were dead, asleep, or no longer interested in the affairs of mortals. Damien now knew that wasn't true. Still, he hadn't thought he would ever go back to the old ways. He wasn't even sure he remembered the proper way to pray.

He closed his eyes and closed a hand around the quail brooch. It was strangely warm. He knew he should make an offering of some sort, but Ptokheia was the goddess of beggars. She was probably used to not receiving burnt offerings. Damien promised himself and the goddess he would give her a proper offering once everything was over. All he had for the time being was his gratitude. He breathed deeply and cast his thoughts out, unsure if Ptokheia would hear them. The silent litany of thanks was met with a warmth settling over his limbs. It didn't negate his worry and fear, but it made them more bearable.

Eryx killed the embers and settled into his bed. It only took a moment for his breathing to deepen and Damien realized he was the last one awake. The warmth in his limbs called him toward sleep. He wanted to sleep. He was tired, his clothes were still damp in places, and the wounds Ptokheia had healed held dull aches. Even a few hours of sleep would be a blessed void from discomfort and worry. It eluded him.

He threw his blankets back with an annoyed huff. The room wasn't completely dark. Some of the grey light filtered through cracks in the walls, door, and barricaded window. It was enough to make out Hazina, Atalanta, and Eryx. They were darker shadows amongst the darkness, but he could see them. Hazina lay curled, with her arms pillowed beneath her head and one foot thrust out from beneath the blankets. Eryx was sprawled on his back, one arm over his chest and the other flung out toward the women. Atalanta lay on her stomach, her blanket twisted and tangled around her legs.

Damien bent and brushed hair off Atalanta's face. A quick flick of a snake's tongue brushed his hand and he froze. It was too dark to see the snakes individually, and he didn't think they could harm anyone Atalanta herself wasn't also focused on, but a shot of fear ran through him. When he didn't feel any more tongue flicks or other touch from the snakes he withdrew his hand. It had been a foolish gesture to make. She didn't care about him in that way. He knew it. He also knew she never would.

He stood and moved to the barricaded window. The cracks were too small to see out of, but he pretended to study the street outside. The silence wasn't so oppressive if he focused on the sleeping breaths of his companions. He was almost ready to return to bed when the silence outside was broken by quick skittering taps. Like tiny claws against stone.

Damien grabbed one of the pieces making up the barricade, ready to tear it off to see what was out there, but something made him pause. The skittering disappeared back into the silence and was replaced with velvety footfalls. The soft thumps could only be made by something light on its feet, but also very large. An image of a lion as tall as he was rose in his mind. Looking at what was out there could give away their hiding spot.

The soft footsteps were replaced by slapping feet hitting the stone street. A child's laugh echoed off the buildings.

Damien shivered and backed away from the window. Whoever, or whatever, was out there didn't seem to know where they were, so it could wait until everyone was rested. He tried to tell himself it was the sensible thing to do, but the sounds of things walking through the abandoned streets mocked him as he pulled his blankets around his shoulders.

The child's laughter followed him into a fitful sleep full of unseen monsters and hidden danger. He woke to the sound of Hazina and Atalanta talking softly. It seemed to have only been a minute since he closed his eyes, but a small fire burned in the hearth and a bubbling pot sat next to it.

"Morning—or whatever time of day it is," Atalanta said, giving him a small smile.

"Morning," he mumbled back.

She frowned. "What's wrong?"

"Nothing."

Hazina coughed and pointedly concentrated on the pot by the fire.

Atalanta's lips pinched and she shook her head. "You are exceptionally dour this morning."

"I am not!"

Eryx chuckled, giving the first sign that he was awake. "If you pout any farther your lip will flop past your chin."

Damien sat up and spread a glare at all of them. "I'm not pouting. Apologies that I'm not singing to birds and furry woodland creatures. It's been a long journey, I'm tired, and am not looking forward to what we still have to face."

"Kelpies?" Hazina offered.

"Sirens?" Eryx chipped in.

"Poseidon, himself?" Atalanta added.

"I hate you all."

Atalanta laughed, long and hard. Her eyes sparkled and her grin was infectious. First Hazina, and then Eryx, joined in the laughter. After a moment, even Damien found himself laughing.

With some of the tension eased, Hazina served up small bowls of a strange smelling porridge. There was a hint of cinnamon, but also something bitter that bit at the nose. "Eat," she instructed. "I fear we have a long day ahead of us. This will help."

It tasted as strange as it smelt. Damien choked it down with almost no coughing. His eyes watered and tongue felt numb. "What was it?"

"A herb to give us more energy. You should start feeling the effect in a few minutes," she explained.

Atalanta collected the empty bowls and rinsed them out before tossing them back into her bag. "There are plenty of times we could've used an energy burst. Why is this the first you've mentioned it?"

Hazina rubbed an ear and wouldn't meet Atalanta's gaze. "There are side effects."

"What kind of side effects?" Eryx asked.

"It is hard to say for sure. None of you have a tolerance for this herb, but…Dizziness, nausea, agitation, and a racing heart are common among those who take too much."

"You didn't think to ask if we wanted it first?" Damien demanded. He wasn't sure if it was the herb she had given them, or the worry about the side effects that were making his limbs feel like tiny bolts of lightning were racing through them.

Hazina raised her chin and met each of their eyes in turn. "I believed—believe—that in our current situation the benefit outweighed the risk. Do you disagree?"

"We'll see how everyone feels in an hour or two," Damien said.

"No. You do not get to decide the risk was worth it or not after the outcome has been decided. If I had asked if you wanted to take the herb, would you have declined?" she challenged.

Atalanta straighted her scarf and sighed. "No. I think we all would have agreed. It still would have been nice to be asked, though."

Hazina inclined her head. "I will remember for next time."

The four companions washed the porridge down with some stale bread and a weak tea before packing up their things. It didn't take long before they all had their bags settled and the only sign they'd been in the house were the new ashes in the hearth and the barricades over door and window.

"Before we venture out, you should know that I heard…things…moving about the streets during the night," Damien told the others.

"You didn't think to wake us?" Atalanta asked in surprise.

"Whatever was out there didn't know where we were."

Eryx frowned and asked, "What did it sound like?"

He rolled his shoulders and struggled to meet their eyes. "Giant insects, lions, and deranged children."

Atalanta laughed. "It sounds like you were dreaming."

He glowered at her. "I was awake, and I know what I heard."

"Exhaustion can play tricks on the mind," Hazina pointed out. "Combined with the pressures of our quest…it is unsurprising you heard strange things in the night."

He clenched his jaw and fought to keep from arguing further. Their explanations all made sense, and he wanted them to be true, but he knew the sounds, and whatever made them, were real. Instead, he mock bowed to the others and said, "Then let's leave this place and stick a sword or two in old fish-beard."

Chapter Eleven

The derelict buildings both muffled and reflected the sound of their footsteps. Each footfall was sucked away, only to be thrown back a short time later, amplified so it sounded as if an army were bearing down on them. Atalanta tried to ignore the noise, but it drilled into her skull and rattled around until it seemed to throb in time with her heartbeat.

She didn't know specifically what time of day it was, but she knew it could only be a few hours past midday, at most. The bouncing, seemingly endless, energy from Hazina's herb was fading. It left a dull ache behind. Atalanta wanted to curl up and sleep for a week.

Homes, shops, even a smithy, stood in silent reproach of their advance toward the far side of the cavern. If it hadn't been for the balcony at their backs, there would be no way to tell direction. They didn't even know if the other side was where they needed to go. It was a thought Atalanta pushed aside. They would figure it out when they got there. For now, they simply followed the meandering streets in the most direct manner they could.

The echoes of their footsteps somehow became even louder when they came to a broad intersection. The buildings standing guard at the corners must have once been stately things. Chunks of marble facade still clung to the rotting wood, and one of the buildings was broken open enough to see the warped remains of a sweeping staircase. Twenty men could have easily stretched out fingertip-to-fingertip from one side of the street to the other.

A fountain stood directly in the centre of the intersection. It was surprisingly simple given the former elegance of the sentinel buildings. A spire of pale grey stone rose in twisted swirls from the wide basin. It wasn't clear if it were meant to be waves, or simply hurt the eyes of onlookers.

Eryx, Damien, and Hazina didn't even glance at it as they trudged past.

Atalanta paused and peered into the dry basin. "Hold for a moment," she called out, raising her voice to overcome the pounding echoes.

Silence fell over them like a weighted net.

"What?" Hazina's voice was faint, but in the utter stillness it was more than loud enough.

Damien's shoulders hunched and he took a couple steps back toward the fountain and Atalanta. Nothing happened. No echo beat back at them.

Eryx grunted. "My head hurts too much to care why the noise stopped. I'm just grateful it did."

"What was it you wanted to stop for?" Damien asked, his eyes raking over the buildings and hand clenched around his sword hilt.

"There's an inscription in the bottom of the fountain," Atalanta explained. She leaned over, resting her hands on the wide edge as she squinted down at the faded letters. "Am—amf…ἀμφὶ Ποσειδάωτα, μέγαν θεόν? What does that—"

A rush of cold water splashed down on her head. She pulled back, coughing and brushing damp hair from her face.

Water cascaded over the stone spire, jumping off the twists and slopes of the stone. Atalanta gave her head a shake and sent water droplets flying.

"Careful," Damien grumbled. "Not all of us like being wet."

Atalanta gave him a flat look before making an exaggerated show of shaking herself off over the fountain's basin. She wrung her hair out. One of her snakes took exception to being squeezed and nipped her hand. A warning bite more than anything, but blood welled on her skin.

She dipped her hands in the basin to rinse the blood off. It spread through the water like a pink cloud and she frowned. It had been pinpricks. There shouldn't have been enough to turn a teacup pink, let alone the fountain's basin. The force of the falling water buffeted the pink to the edge of the fountain, but a thin tendril swirled its way to brush against the spire.

A groaning sigh trembled from the fountain and the spire twisted to the side, folding over on itself to form a rough oval. The water no longer cascaded into the basin, but fell as a sheet, creating an almost perfectly smooth surface inside the oval.

Atalanta leaned forward. Her face was reflected back for only a moment. A ripple shivered across the surface and when it settled there was the face of a sleeping man inside. His brown hair spread across a pillow, creating a dark halo beneath his head. Faint lines etched his forehead and around his eyes, while a curling beard hid his neck and upper chest. With heavy brows and an aquiline nose, he seemed familiar, though she couldn't figure out why. She was sure she'd never actually seen him before.

"Do you know who that is?" she asked, glancing over her shoulder at her companions.

"I only see your reflection in the water," Hazina said.

Atalanta turned back to the fountain. The man's face was still framed in the oval. It tugged at a memory, though one that slipped through her fingers like a fish when she tried to grasp it.

She knelt on the edge of the basin and reached her hand forward to touch the water holding the image. Her fingers broke the surface of the water and the basin disappeared. She threw her arms out to catch herself as she fell, but there was nowhere to go. She was standing in a featureless room.

No doors or windows broke the lines of the walls. The only thing there was a stone sarcophagus. The man from the fountain was carved into the lid so expertly it took her a moment to realize it was a carving and not a real person.

"Who are you?"

Atalanta spun at the sound of the deep voice. It rumbled like waves crashing against rocks and she knew that whomever the man standing before her was, he wasn't mortal.

He was taller than her and his eyes were a stormy grey. The colour that so many of the women in her family possessed. Her stomach sank.

"Poseidon." The word dripped from her lips almost against her will.

"Yes. Now who are you?" he repeated.

"No one of importance," she said, taking a step away from him.

He frowned, though it seemed more puzzled than angry. "It has been…a very long time since I have seen anyone. You must be of some importance to find me here."

She took another step back and shook her head.

His frown deepened and his gaze focused on her face. Quicker than she could follow, he closed the distance between them and grabbed her chin. She winced from the pressure of his fingers, but he didn't seem to notice as he tilted her face from side to side.

"You're a daughter of mine, or…a descendant at any rate. You smell too much like a mortal to be a recent descendant."

Atalanta pulled herself from his grasp and made a mocking bow. "It is a pleasure to have met you, but you've never shown the slightest interest in my branch of your family. At least, not once you forced yourself on the mother of my line."

His brows drew down for a moment before understanding took hold. "The priestess's daughters, yes?"

"I'm surprised you remember," Atalanta admitted, eying him warily.

He nodded, his gaze dropping to the sarcophagus carved with his image. "Did you know she prayed to me every night once she realized she was with child? Every night I heard her beg for me to protect a child she had never wanted, a reminder of everything she had lost."

"She was kind like that. Not that it ever did any good."

Poseidon grimaced, tracing circles on the stone carving with his hand. "There was, unfortunately, a matter of politics preventing any formal acknowledgment of your lineage. I regret I did not protest more, but it was a period when Amphitrite was especially volatile regarding my children born to other women."

"Seems to me the obvious solution to such a problem would be to stop bedding other women," Atalanta pointed out.

He chuckled softly. "I suppose you're right. But we're many years too late for that."

"If you're feeling guilty about abandoning my family, perhaps you'd consider stopping the storms, earthquakes, and siren attacks all around the Mediterranean? I'd call us even and you could go back to ignoring me in peace."

Poseidon frowned. "I've been asleep for almost half a century now. I can't be causing such destruction."

"What? Then how am I talking to you?"

He gestured at the featureless walls. "Welcome to the prison that is the eternal sleep. I don't know if all the gods are aware while they're trapped inside their own minds, but it is a particularly cruel form of punishment."

Atalanta sighed. "Did I fall into the Between again?"

"Not as such. This is similar to the World-Between-Worlds, but, as far as I can tell, it is not actually connected to that place. If it were, I would eventually be able to find a crack and escape. I'm unsure of how you came to be here, but I suspect it has something to do with being my descendant."

Atalanta nodded a little. "If you're trapped here, then who's been causing all the troubles out there?"

"I can think of no one who would have the means that also hates mortals enough to devastate them in such a way."

"I assume it will be another god, and one unlikely to agree to cease hostilities. Any idea how we might defeat them?" she asked.

"Find my trident. Only a true descendant can properly wield its powers."

Atalanta snorted. "I'm not even a recognized descendant."

He took a step toward her and cupped her chin much more gently this time. "I recognize you as my daughter, Atalanta," he said before placing a kiss on her forehead.

She fell backward as if the kiss had slammed a wall against her and landed on broken stones. The tinkling sound of water died and she groaned. Hazina was instantly at her side, helping her to sit up.

"Are you all right? What happened to you?" Hazina asked. "You touched the water and then fell backward as if you had been struck."

"I think I spoke with Poseidon," she groaned, her fingers probing across her forehead. She felt no physical sign of the kiss he had placed there, but a tingling warmth marked it nonetheless.

"What? Does he know we're here to stop him?" Damien asked, his eyes skimming the gaping windows and broken rooftops around them.

Atalanta shook her head. "I don't think he's behind the attacks and disasters. He said he's been sleeping for half a century. He told me to find—"

Laughter, high and sparkling, bounced off the buildings. As suddenly as it started, it stopped. Atalanta climbed to her feet and Eryx, Damien, and Hazina drew nearer. They stood back-to-back in a tight cluster, watching the ruined buildings apprehensively.

Far down the road, a small form stepped into the street. It looked like a young boy with dusky skin and no hair. A simple tunic was belted at his waist and fell to his knees. In one hand he held a staff of dark wood almost twice as tall as he was. Bands of gold and silver chased each other up the staff to a pointed crystal on the tip that shimmered with a soft internal light.

"Who in Hades is that?" Damien asked.

Atalanta tapped her elbow against his rib and called out to the boy, "Hello, there. We're passing through and mean no harm to you or any others who live here."

Laughter filled the streets again, and when the boy spoke his voice seemed to come from all around them. "You have very nice manners, Daughter of the Sea, but the Son of the Storm does not remember—or respect the old ways. And who have you brought to this sacred place, hm? An Untrained Spirit Whisperer and an Exiled Son of Northern Fate? Strange companions, Daughter."

Atalanta winced at his words. She could see Damien's grimace from the corner of her eye. "I—we—have come to—" she started.

"I know why you are here, Daughter. I would like to help you, but there are rules," he cut her off.

"What rules, guardian?" she asked.

He spread a hand wide in a gesture of helplessness. "I am bound to this place to prevent the passage of outsiders unless they can best me in a game."

"What type of game?" Hazina asked.

"You must capture, and hold, me for the space of one hundred heartbeats," he said. "For every form you can hold, I will answer one question. Should I escape, every heartbeat missed will be taken from your flesh."

Hazina leaned close to Atalanta and whispered, "Surely we can find another way. This game of his sounds too risky."

The boy tutted. "I can hear your whispers. It will do you no good to try and scheme. This is the only way to where you must go."

"Can only one person help in your capture?" Eryx asked.

"Ooh!" The boy jumped in excitement, a delighted grin splitting his face. "Yes, this might make for a more interesting game. As there are four of you, four times must I be captured before reaching the Hall of Light. This cannot change. For every time I am not caught, one life will be forfeit. But any of you may catch any of the forms. If one loses their hold, another may take over to complete the hundred heartbeats. And at the end, the debt owed will be paid by the individual, or individuals, of your choosing."

"What is the…debt, for not holding you for the whole hundred heartbeats?" Damien asked.

"One year for every heartbeat missed."

"How—" Eryx started, but the boy cut him off.

"No more questions. The game will start now."

He turned and fled down the street, his laughter bouncing off the buildings around them. Atalanta stared after him for a moment. Damien growled and pounded down the road, followed by Hazina and Eryx. Atalanta quickly fell into step with them. They rounded a curve in the street, but the tunic-clad boy was nowhere to be seen. Instead a large ram with gold and silver bands along its horns sprang forward. It leapt from road to roof and back again.

"He's a shape changer. This is going to be a painful game," Damien huffed.

The ram bound to a roof and down onto the street on the other side of the building. Though his gilded horns were occasionally visible above the broken rooftops, he remained effectively out of sight.

Atalanta drew one of her daggers, her lungs burning. "Just catch him and hold on tight. We need to split up if we're to catch him."

"In pairs," Eryx replied. "I've seen tricksters like these before. Being alone is a good way to die before the game is over."

"Pair then." Damien nodded. "Hazina?"

She nodded and they split off at the next intersection. Atalanta and

Eryx took the next cross street and ran as hard as they could down it. Their footsteps didn't echo as they ran, but the sharp click of hooves against stone surrounded them, giving no hint to where he was in relation to them.

A glow to their right grew stronger as they wound back and forth through the streets. Atalanta skidded to a stop, her sides heaving as she tried to catch her breath. Eryx stopped so effortlessly that, if it hadn't been for the sweat on his forehead and panting breath, she might have thought the chase was not a challenge for him. She pointed toward the glow.

"Wha—?"

Atalanta pressed her free hand to his mouth and shook her head. She didn't want the guardian to hear her plan. Eryx frowned and looked where she pointed. It took a moment, then understanding dawned on his face. He gave her a short nod and they changed their direction. The glow—what must be the Hall of Light—became their new target.

Twice the ram bounded across their path, but they didn't slow or change their direction. They broke from the last line of houses into a wide plaza before sweeping stairs. Colourful tiles created a design of waves and sea creatures frolicking across the plaza, but the gold-veined marble steps led to a hall filled with shifting gold and red light.

They had little time to admire the beauty of the plaza before the ram slid to a stop behind them. Its sides heaved as it pawed the ground, and tossed its head. It snorted and darted forward. Eryx and Atalanta didn't back up, instead they shifted only to keep themselves between the ram and the stairs. It dashed to the side when it was an arm's length away, but Atalanta and Eryx were ready for it.

Eryx threw himself in front of the animal, tangling his arms in the creature's horns, while Atalanta dove across its back. The ram reared up and up, stretching as the fur fell away and scales rippled across its skin. Eryx lost his grip on the beast's now-hornless head and slammed to the ground just as Damien and Hazina ran into the plaza.

Atalanta squeaked in surprise and wrapped her arms around its neck. Her dagger clattered to the tiles below and she dug her nails under the edges of the scales for better purchase. The massive snake swayed and shook. Her body flopped about, bouncing against its back. But she clung to it. The snake bent forward and she wrapped her legs as best she could to keep from flipping head over heels and tumbling to the ground.

Before the snake touched the ground, it changed into a large animal with fur once more. Claws reached around to swipe at her as she pressed herself flat against the back of the brown bear. It snorted and twisted, reaching its claws further back. This time, it caught her side and a wash of warm blood dampened her shirt and matted its fur.

She was vaguely aware of Damien, Eryx, and Hazina shouting and moving around them, but her focus had narrowed to the desire, the need, to keep her hold on the beast beneath her. Six more times it changed shape. Some were big and violent, thrashing about to dislodged her. Others were small and quick, almost slipping from her grip when there was suddenly less bulk to hold on to. But she never let it get away from her.

Atalanta blinked in surprise when she found herself in the embrace of a young man. His skin was dusky and he wore the same style tunic as the boy had. Being almost nose-to-nose with him, she noticed his eyes were a swirling, shifting blue. They changed from so dark they were almost black to so pale they might as well have been white, and everything in between.

"That was a good catch, Daughter of the Sea," he said, his smile warm and friendly. His arms were around her waist, just as hers were around his neck, and his staff pressed along her spine.

"We won?"

He nodded. "This round."

As soon as he confirmed it, she dropped her hold on him and pulled out of his grip. His features clouded for a moment, but disappeared back into the smile so quickly she wasn't sure if she had imagined it.

He tapped her side with his staff and the pointed crystal flared with a red light as heat seared across her skin. She pressed a hand to her side and was surprised to feel unbroken flesh beneath her fingers. Her tunic was still torn and bloody from the bear's claws, but she didn't even have a scar to mark where he had struck her.

"We shall see if you can do so well again." He tapped his staff twice on the ground and suddenly all five of them were standing beneath the balcony.

"Who, or what, are you?" Hazina asked, reaching out a hand to the nearest building to steady herself.

The young man bowed to her. "I have had many names from many different people, but you may call me Nereus." He didn't wait for any response before changing into a large rabbit and bounding away. He disappeared around the first corner and laughter filled the air around them.

Damien growled and ran after the rabbit, skidding as he turned to take the corner where it had disappeared from view.

"We won't be able to catch a rabbit by following its trail," Eryx said.

Hazina nodded. "I am exhausted from the first chase. I will make my way directly to the landing if you two wish to try and cut Nereus off."

Atalanta nodded. The soft patter of the rabbit's feet against the stones didn't seem to echo and surround them like the ram's hoof-beats had. The slap of Damien's feet overlaid and drowned it out frequently, but she thought she could make out the rough direction of the creature.

Atalanta and Eryx set off at a quick trot, pausing every so often to listen. They didn't bother trying to directly follow the sound of pattering, but took the turns that seemed to lead toward the rabbit's eventual destination.

The rabbit bounded across the street several feet in front of them and a tired, panting Damien trailed behind it.

Eryx frowned. "I think the guardian is trying to wear us out."

Atalanta grunted. "Damien is going to make himself useless if he keeps trying to run the rabbit down. Surely he realizes he's being toyed with."

"He may not. I think he feels guilty that he was too slow to assist in the capture of the ram," Eryx said, turning down the street the rabbit and Damien had taken.

"Fool. We have to do this four times. He'll have his chance."

They ran on in silence for a bit before Atalanta asked, "Should we just head to the plaza and wait for it there?"

"No," Eryx panted. "I don't think he'll try to reach it in a direct manner this time. It would make it too easy to capture him if he did the same thing."

They continued trying to close the distance and get ahead of the rabbit. Every few streets they drew closer to the plaza, but seemed to almost be circling around it from one side to the other. They turned a corner as the rabbit darted around another a few paces beyond. It slid to a stop and blinked at them, ears twitching. It turned back just as Damien dove from the street it had exited and wrapped his arms around the startled animal.

As soon as his hands touched the rabbit's fur, it began to change. It grew and lengthened, the soft fur becoming longer, thicker, and coarser. A pungent scent filled the air and a shaggy ox-like creature tried to shake Damien off. He coughed and wrapped his hands in the creature's hair. The ox shrank down so quickly Damien's knees slammed into the ground. A large rodent with a striped tail, dark eyes, and tiny hands scratched and clawed at his face.

He shouted and held the rodent away from him. Atalanta and Eryx ran toward him. Before they could get close enough to help, it changed again. It turned into a donkey and it kicked back, slamming its hooves into Damien's chest. He flew back and crashed into the side of a building, the sound of cracking bone reverberating through the air. Eryx dove toward the donkey but it changed into a dove and fluttered up to rest on an exposed post of a nearby building.

Atalanta ran to Damien's side and pressed a hand against his shoulder when he tried to sit up. Half of his ribs didn't rise properly along with the rest of his chest as he breathed. His breath hissed out when she gently probed the extent of the injury.

"You did not win this round."

Atalanta looked up and glared at Nereus. He appeared as a middle aged man with a close clipped beard and a longer robe. "Are you trying to kill us?" she demanded.

"There is always risk involved with such a game," he said. He took two steps to reach Damien's side and turned his staff point side down. Damien cried out when Nereus drove the crystal into his skin. Blood seeped around its edges as red light flared.

"What are you doing?" Atalanta shouted. She wrapped her hands around the staff to try and pull it out. Agony exploded along her arms and she realized she was laying flat on her back when it stopped.

Eryx crouched over her, his face a grim mask. She rolled her head to the side to look at Damien. His eyes were closed, but his chest rose and fell all in one piece. She groaned and struggled to sit up.

"There are two more rounds to play," Nereus said. He tapped his staff twice and everyone reappeared back beneath the balcony.

Hazina gasped when she saw Atalanta and Damien on the ground. "What happened?"`

"A donkey kicked him in the chest," Eryx answered. "Though he appears to be better now."

"This is an awful game," Atalanta grumbled as she pushed herself to her feet.

Nereus shrugged. "It is a new form of an old game. Many heroes have played over the long years."

"And how many survived?"

"A few. It is not meant to be easy, Daughter of the Sea. It is meant to test the worth of those wishing to gain something. Those with even more to lose."

Hazina crossed her arms and frowned at Nereus. "Are you attempting to kill us?"

"I would be saddened if any of you died, but I cannot make the game any easier," he said. "You should feel honoured. Heracles himself wrestled with me to receive information vital to the completion of his labours."

Damien climbed to his feet with a stifled moan. "Only two more challenges. Let's get this over with."

Nereus nodded once and changed into a slender antelope-like creature with curling horns that tapered to fine points. It was only two feet high at the shoulder, but it bounded away with effortless ease.

Eryx nodded at Hazina. "Come on. We'll let the injured make their way to the plaza in case we cannot catch up with him this time."

She nodded, hiked up her skirts, and ran down the street after Eryx and the guardian. They quickly disappeared around a corner and then even the sounds of their footsteps faded.

Atalanta studied Damien's stiff movements as he shuffled forward. She fell into step beside him and offered an arm. He shoved it away and continued his slow pace onward. Her lips pursed but she didn't say anything. When they had reached the intersection with the fountain again she stopped him. "You're going to fall flat on your face if you keep going."

"I'm fine," he snapped.

"Damien...I've been healed by Nereus. It wasn't pleasant. And that was a flesh wound rather than broken ribs. Asking for, or accepting, help doesn't make you any less of a hero."

He grumbled under his breath but slung an arm across her shoulders. She wrapped an arm around his waist and they continued on. It was hard to tell if they went faster or slower while leaning on one another.

The sounds of Nereus's flight and Eryx and Hazina's pursuit bounced around the buildings, growing distant and coming closer in turns. They never saw any of them, though there were a few times it sounded as if the chase were just around a corner. By the time Atalanta and Damien reached the plaza, her legs ached. Damien had leaned more and more of his weight on her and she wasn't sure how much further she could support him.

They were almost halfway across the plaza when the antelope-like creature bounded into the open space. Neither Eryx nor Hazina were anywhere in sight. It paused and glanced at Atalanta and Damien, it's short tail swishing side-to-side. It tossed its head and raced toward the landing.

Atalanta dropped Damien's arm and ran to intercept the creature. It bounced past her, only to slow as it scrambled up the stairs. She shrieked and launched herself forward, hands grasping the rear legs. Her fingers didn't fully close and the creature leapt to the side. She crashed heavily against the stone steps. It ran the last few steps to the landing before she could push herself back up.

A deep, rolling bell rang over the city. The form melted away to reveal Nereus with grey streaked through his hair and beard so long it brushed against the top of his chest. He stared down at her with sad eyes.

"You failed this round," he said. "There is one more round to complete. Then the debts will be due."

He offered Atalanta a hand up and she took it after a slight hesitation. She saw Eryx and Hazina leaning against buildings, panting and slumped. He led her down to the others before tapping his staff against the ground twice. Once more they were transported back beneath the balcony.

Damien and Hazina both swayed on their feet and leaned against one another for support. Eryx clicked his tongue and shook his head. "I have no idea how we're supposed to win this final round."

Atalanta grimaced. "If we can at least catch him—even if it's only for a short time—we'll be fine." She pushed aside the worry that regardless of how well they did during the final chase, one of them would still have to die.

"I can only allow a brief respite," Nereus warned. "No more than a few minutes."

Hazina searched through her bag and withdrew withered looking twigs. "Chew these as quickly as you can. Only swallow the juices and spit the rest out—hopefully that will help keep any sickness at bay," she instructed.

Atalanta was too tired to even wrinkle her nose at the odd twig she was handed. Its bitter juices coated her tongue and she grimaced. It took two tries to swallow any of it. A burning sensation slid down her throat and set her stomach on fire. Warmth spread through her body and pushed aside all her aches and pains—except for her stomach which heaved in protest.

"Your time is up. We will begin now," Nereus declared. He turned into a feline as high at the shoulder as the antelope-like creature had been, with black tufts of fur on its ears and a short tail. Its stub tail swished at them before it took off down the road.

"Hazina and Damien together?" Eryx asked, bouncing from foot-to-foot.

"Aye," Damien nodded, his eyes wide and dilated.

All four companions started off down the street together, but quickly separated. The cat's footfalls were much quieter than any of the other animal forms they had chased through the abandoned city. Eryx pointed down a side street and Atalanta nodded. She pressed a hand to her stomach and gritted her teeth as they ran.

They crossed three intersections and turned at a fourth before pausing. The faint padding of the cat's paws were hard to pinpoint, but the sound of Damien and Hazina running down distant streets was much easier to keep track of. Eryx closed his eyes and turned his head one way than the other. After a moment, his eyes snapped open with surprise and he took two steps back to the intersection they had just turned at.

The cat plowed into him with a yowl of surprise.

Eryx buried his fingers in the animal's fur and rolled so he lay across it. They hadn't even come to a complete stop before the cat shrank down. Its fur disappeared into slimy skin and it became a salamander. His fingers slid across the shrinking skin, but he closed a fist around the small creature. It had barely finished changing when it started to grow.

It still looked like a salamander, but its skin blackened and cracked. Flames licked between the cracks as it grew to the size of a small dog. Eryx wrapped his arms around the creature's neck, twisting to hold it from behind. The creature paused before its entire body was engulfed in flames.

Eryx shrieked. Flames licked his skin, leaving blackness and blisters in its wake. Atalanta pulled a flask of water from her bag and dumped the contents over the creature and Eryx. Steam hissed up and the flames disappeared while the salamander writhed into an odd creature with a fox-like face, long neck, and wings sprouting from its back. Its fur and wings were pure white.

It spread its wings and a blast of cold washed over Eryx and Atalanta. The steam hanging in the air froze and fell to the ground, the tiny ice crystals shattering upon impact.

"What the hell is that?" Atalanta asked, gaping as icicles crawled up Eryx's arms.

"Sn-snow sp-sp-spirit," he said, his teeth chattering. "Fr-from up n-north."

She slammed a fist into the back of the creature's head.

It swiveled its long neck to glare at her. Its eyes remained locked on hers as it changed into a sleek panther. Atalanta stumbled back, narrowly avoiding its claws. It hardly waited a moment before turning and raking claws across Eryx's face and chest. She could clearly see muscle, and even bone in some places, through the wounds.

Eryx swayed and his eyes rolled back in his head.

Atalanta scrambled forward and threw herself on the panther's back as Eryx crumbled to the ground in a growing puddle of blood. The cat snarled and twisted to scratch her. But she had learnt her lesson from the bear. Every time the cat tried to rake its claws down her skin, she shifted away.

A shudder rippled through its body and the fur flowed into feathers as it grew larger and larger. Atalanta's hands scrabbled for purchase on the back of the giant eagle. The feathers were slick beneath her hands, sliding out of her grasp. She hit the ground with a heavy thump and the eagle shrieked its triumph.

Its wings beat down heavily, lifting it into the air. Atalanta tried to push herself up to her feet, but her stomach chose that moment to forcefully expel everything from it. She retched onto the street, tears stinging her eyes as the bitter taste of the herb filled her mouth and nose.

A hand gripped her shoulder and then she felt something sharp slide into her back. Heat seared through her body. She could almost feel it burning away the bitter herb coursing through her system. When the heat and pain stopped she sat back and coughed. Her throat felt raw and she wondered if she'd screamed.

Nereus took a step back and lowered the tip of his staff to the torn and bloody body of Eryx. Blood still seeped from him, but it was much slower. Nereus placed the tip of the staff over Eryx's heart and pushed it into his flesh.

Eryx's body spasmed and thrashed as red light flashed and flickered. Muscles knit across the bones visible through the wounds, then pink flesh flowed across the muscles. Eryx collapsed back to the ground and the pink slowly lightened until it looked no different than the rest of his skin. Nereus withdrew the staff, leaving no mark behind.

He turned back to Atalanta and shook his head. His hair was pure white and face wrinkled. The robe he wore was a rich blue with white embroidered waves and sea life decorating almost every inch of the fabric. "You were unable to hold the final form," he said.

"I noticed," Atalanta responded.

"It is time for debts to be settled." He tapped his staff on the ground three times and suddenly everyone stood in the plaza in front of the stairs. Hazina and Damien blinked in surprise while Atalanta helped a groggy Eryx to his feet.

"Are you ready to pay your debts?" Nereus asked, his gaze sweeping across all of them.

"What exactly do we owe?" Damien asked, wiping the back of his hand across his mouth. The sickly-sweet smell of sick clung to him as much as it clung to Atalanta.

"One form was captured and held. You earned four questions or minor boons for such a feat. Two forms were captured, but not held. Between them, you earned five questions or minor boons, but owe twenty years. Finally, one form was not captured at all. For that, one life is owed," Nereus explained. "Who will pay what?"

Damien glanced at Eryx. Even with Atalanta's help, he couldn't stand straight. Atalanta glowered at Damien. "We are not going to sentence any of us to death," she said. "There has to be another way. How many years is a life worth?"

"Who can say? You could die tomorrow, or a hundred years from now," Hazina pointed out.

"Surely it couldn't be more than a hundred years. If we add that to the twenty years we already owe and divide evenly…That's what? Twenty-five years each?"

Atalanta shook her head. "It's thirty. And you're assuming we'll be allowed to split the debt amongst the four of us."

Everyone turned toward Nereus. He stepped down off the stairs, his staff tapping gently against the ground with each step. "Years may be divided as desired, but a life cannot be exchanged for any number of years. Nor can an immortal pay without first giving up their immortality."

"You can't ask us to choose which of our friends is to die," Atalanta shouted at him.

Nereus shrugged. "You may choose, or one my volunteer. There are many reasons why one life is worth more than another. But it is not my place to decide whose life shall be forfeit."

"That's—"

"It is all right, Atalanta," Hazina cut in. "He is right. Not all lives are worth the same."

"What are you talking about?"

Hazina sighed and brushed her hands down her skirts. She shook her head and met first Atalanta's and then Damien's eyes. "You two are destined for great things. Not because it has been foretold, or because you have divine blood. I can feel it in my heart that you will change the world, and I know the world would be worse without you. Both of you."

"Don't—"

Hazina held up a hand to forestall Damien's protest. She turned her gaze to Eryx and gave him a sad smile. "And you, Eryx, are immortal. Or so long-lived that our grandchildren's grandchildren will be dust before you might die. There is so much potential there. For good and for ill, true, but already you have brought a little more light to the world."

"But what about you, Hazina?" Atalanta asked, dashing a hand across her eyes to banish the tears collecting there. "You are a true friend with a strong heart. You've saved us multiple times and have at least as much potential to change the world as any of us."

"Perhaps, but there is no place for me in the world. And even if I could find somewhere to call home again, I have know violence for too long. My days are already numbered," she said.

"That's not guaranteed," Damien countered. "Atalanta and I have known violence our entire lives too. There is still so much for you to see and do and experience. Don't give up now."

Hazina barked out a bitter laugh. "I am tired, Damien. My heart aches for the home I can never return to. On this journey I have learnt many things I believed are little more than nursery fables, and that there are things darker and more powerful than I had ever imagined. The world is more cruel than I thought, and I can control less than I am happy with."

"Those are reasons to fall into a bottle of alcohol, or perhaps shut yourself up for a few years," Eryx argued. "Not reasons to be a sacrifice."

"Am I being sacrificed?" Hazina mused. "It is a sacrifice of my life and whatever potential I might hold, I agree, but if it is something I willingly embrace, then I do not feel I, myself, am being sacrificed."

"We still need you," Atalanta said, grabbing Hazina's hand in both of hers. "We can't do this without you."

"You will do fine. You, all three of you, are very resourceful. I have faith you will succeed."

Damien glowered. "What if I won't let you?"

"Many wish to know the day and time of their passing. To be able to choose? It is an unimaginable gift. And if this is how I choose, would you deny me that freedom?" she challenged.

Damien's gaze dropped and he shifted uneasily. Atalanta threw her arms around Hazina's neck and pulled her into a tight embrace. "I don't want you to die," she whispered.

Hazina hugged her back. "I am not afraid."

"I am," Atalanta replied.

Hazina pulled back and smiled. "It will be all right. We will see each other again, someday. I am sure of it."

Nereus cleared his throat. "Has a decision been made?"

"Yes," Hazina gave a single short nod and turned to face him with her shoulders thrown back and chin up.

"Who will pay the years, and who will pay the life?"

Atalanta glanced at Damien and Eryx in panic. She had been so caught up in Hazina's decision she forgot there were two debts owed. From the chagrined expression of Eryx's face and the horrified look on Damien's, she doubted they had remembered either.

"I will pay both," Hazina answered.

"Both?" Nereus's eyebrows climbed his forehead.

"Yes. I will pay the twenty years, and then my life will be forfeit."

A ghost of a smile traced Nereus's lips and he nodded. "Clever girl."

He touched the crystal tip of his staff to the top of Hazina's head. It flared once, an unsettling not-quite-purple light pulsing over them all. He drew it away and wisps of coloured smoke trailed after it. Red, blue, orange, white, and green. All fluttering as they slipped from her and coiled around the tip of the staff. He tapped the staff on the ground once and the tip flared with a blinding white light. The colourful wisps of smoke burned away and when the light receded Hazina stood there with faint wrinkles creasing her face and grey creeping through her hair.

She gave a shaky laugh and stared at the back of her hands where the skin had begun to sag. "That was not so bad."

Nereus brought the tip of the staff down, slicing through her with such force that it sparked against the ground when it hit. For a moment

Hazina stood there, frozen with a look of disbelief on her face, before her body vanished in a puff of smoke, as if she had never existed at all.

Atalanta bit her lip to muffle her cry, and Damien wiped a quick hand across his eyes. Nereus gave them a sympathetic smile before gesturing for them to follow him up the stairs and to the Hall of Light. Atalanta trailed behind him. Damien and Eryx fell into step behind her. She tucked her grief away and nurtured a burning anger. She would mourn her friend after she'd avenged her. Whomever was to blame for all their hardships would pay ten times over for Hazina's death.

Chapter Twelve

Red and gold light flickered and rippled through the Hall of Light. Though there were no shadows, the light made everything seem unearthly and dangerous. Damien couldn't shake the feeling that everything was bathed in blood. Hazina's blood. Atalanta gave him a weary smile. It seemed predatory and cruel in that strange light, though he knew that wasn't her intention.

Nereus led them past clusters of dust-covered furniture. Three groups of chairs and couches, a wide bed and dresser, and even a large copper tub next to an empty brazier. What purpose there could be for the ignored items, Damien wasn't sure. They weren't stacked, or covered with cloth, as one would expect if they were being kept in storage. It was almost as if they were meant to be rooms with no walls. Rooms no one had set foot in for a hundred years.

Nereus stopped in front of a collection of chairs in good repair. A low table held a platter full of strange looking fruit, and a stone hearth held a blue fire. He gave them a low bow and gestured for them to take a seat.

Atalanta flopped onto a small couch and kicked her feet up, uncaring about the dust, mud, and blood she smeared on the plush fabric. Eryx sank into a high backed chair and wiggled down, letting the chair back support his head. Damien hesitated a moment before choosing a chaise. He couldn't stop a small sigh from escaping as the soft cushions cradled his weary body.

"Rest and eat," Nereus instructed. "When you are ready, you have nine questions or boons you may ask of me. Though there are certain constraints on the answers and help I may give, I will do my best to aid you."

"Can we discuss our questions before asking?" Eryx wondered.

Nereus cocked his head. "Is that your first question?"

"No!" Atalanta said sharply. "Give us some time and we'll call you when we're ready to ask anything."

He inclined his head to her, tapped his staff on the ground, and disappeared.

"Sorry," Eryx mumbled, running a hand over his face.

Damien scratched at his chin. A thin scruff already covered his jaw, though Eryx was as clean-shaven as they day they met him. "No harm done," he said. "And it was a good thing to be concerned about."

"Still...it almost cost us a boon."

Atalanta leaned over to grab a pink, pear-shaped fruit. She tossed it at Eryx. "We've said it's fine. Stop feeling sorry for yourself because you almost made a mistake. If any of us are going to feel guilty about anything, it should be me for letting one of the forms make it to the steps."

Damien frowned. "None of us let it—"

"I didn't try hard enough," Atalanta cut him off. "And now Hazina is dead."

"She accepted it, we—" Eryx started to point out.

"Of course she said she accepted it. What else can someone do in the face of death? I should have argued harder. She shouldn't have had to pay the price for my failure."

"She made her choice, and now we need to make ours. What questions or boons are we going to ask for?" Damien said, leaning forward to catch Atalanta's eye. She flinched back, though not before he saw the raw ache consuming her.

He had never seen her in such pain. Not when she was beaten and bruised. Not when Calista was kidnapped while they were rescuing him. It was the look of a child losing its mother. It echoed the guilt, bewilderment, and agony of when his mother left.

Damien swore beneath his breath. Atalanta had lost every woman she was ever close to. Her mother, aunts, and grandmother. And now, Hazina. He silently pledged to not only avenge Hazina's sacrifice, but the pain it caused Atalanta.

"Nine questions or boons...Any idea what to ask?" Eryx said, pulling Damien out of his introspection.

"We already know it isn't Poseidon causing these problems," Atalanta said. She snagged a blue apple-like fruit and bit into it. Juices dribbled down her chin and she used her sleeve to wipe them away.

"We need to know who we're up against and how to fight them," Eryx reasoned.

Damien grunted. "It would be nice to have a guide as well. The abandoned city was enough of a maze for me."

The three companions discussed and argued back and forth until they had a set of questions. Almost all of the fruit was eaten by the time they came to an agreement. Though the fruits were sweet and filling, they all tasted like watered-down honey.

Atalanta cleared her throat and called out, "Nerues, we're ready to claim the debt owed to us."

Nereus reappeared in the spot he had disappeared from. "Then ask."

"We request a guide to lead us wherever we need to go to complete our quest," Damien said.

"It will be done."

"Who is using Poseidon's power?" he asked.

Nereus grimaced. "It is forbidden to use the thief's name in any way which suggests she is not the rightful ruler of the seas. Those who oppose her rule simply call her the Usurper."

Damien exchanged a look with Atalanta. They hadn't expected to actually get a name—Nereus warned there were conditions on what answers he could provide—but none of the possibilities they speculated about during the discussion had been women.

He cleared his throat and continued. "How do we stop them? The Usurper."

"You must take Poseidon's power from them."

Damien blinked. That wasn't an answer they'd planned for.

"How do we take back Poseidon's power?" Eryx asked.

"If you kill the Usurper using Poseidon's trident, the power would revert back to him," Nereus said. Though his face remained neutral, his eyes sparkled, encouraging them.

"Would that wake Poseidon?" Atalanta blurted out.

"It might, though it is doubtful."

Damien frowned at her. That wasn't a question they'd planned for, and it didn't give them anything useful. He mentally ran through their planned questions before asking, "Where do we find the trident?"

"Your guide will show you the way."

"What protection, or obstacles, will we have to overcome to complete our quest?"

A grin flitted across Nereus's face. "You must pass Oceanus, the great serpent, and living shadows."

"Wha—" Atalanta started, but Damien cut her off with a sharp hiss. She dropped her head and mumbled an apology.

Damien sighed. "Where do we find the Usurper?"

"In the deepest recess of Poseidon's domain, in the heart of his palace," Nereus said. After a moment's pause, he added, "Your guide will show you the way."

They were down to their final question and there were still three they had planned for that Damien thought could be helpful. He wanted to snap at Atalanta for wasting one of their questions, and almost doing so a second time, but they still wouldn't have been able to ask everything. He grunted and asked, "What do we need to be wary of, when we reach the Usurper?"

"There are many possibilities," Nereus said, frowning briefly. "The things you are most likely to encounter are nereids, sirens, ensorcelled sailors, and the brutish guards loyal to her."

"Thank you for your help," Damien said.

Nereus nodded. "When you are ready, simply step into the hearth. You will be taken to where your guide awaits you." He gave them a small bow, wished them luck, and then disappeared.

"Do we need to rest, or should we press on?" Eryx asked, running his hands over the arms of his chair.

"I'm...surprisingly not tired anymore. I feel as if we've rested for a week," Atalanta admitted.

Damien realized he didn't feel any fatigue either. He eyed the strange fruits left on the platter. "I wonder if these are why."

"We should take them with, just in case," Eryx suggested. "Eating a fruit and feeling refreshed could be useful."

Atalanta nodded and placed the remaining fruits in her bag.

Damien rose and moved to the hearth. The blue flames emitted no heat. In fact, they almost seemed to give off a chill. He hesitated a moment, then shoved a hand into the middle of the fire. Flames flared up around him, licking at his skin and he heard Eryx shout. But there was still no heat. He turned to tell them it was fine, but the flames wrapped around him and he felt like a rope around his waist yanked him backward.

The fire disappeared and he stood in a small room hacked into rock. The rough walls were set with the glowing shells, and glistened with damp. A lilting voice said, "I was expecting more than one."

Damien spun to see a young woman with bronze skin and brown hair streaked with gold. She was as tall as he was, and lean. The only curves over her body were the swell and dip of muscle. Her hair hung to her waist in an intricate braid and she wore a brilliant white blouse beneath a crimson vest, and dark leather pants. Her feet were bare and she carried an old fashioned shield and spear.

"Are you the guide Nereus said would help us?" he asked.

She nodded. "I am Paraskeve. My uncle sent me to help you overthrow the Usurper. Where are your companions?"

"Coming," Damien said. A silent 'I hope' hung in the air.

A moment later there was the crackle of flame and Atalanta stood beside him. A second crackle heralded the arrival of Eryx.

"Good. We must move quickly," Paraskeve said. She turned and touched her spear against one of the rough walls. It melted away to reveal a long tunnel.

"Who are you?" Atalanta asked.

"Paraskeve," she replied. "Come. The longer we tarry, the more likely the Usurper will realize we are coming for her."

Chapter Thirteen

Atalanta watched the swaying braid of their guide as they walked through a winding tunnel. No matter how hard she tried, she couldn't shake the feeling they were being watched. She'd tried to ask Paraskeve about it, but the woman had snorted derisively and ignored the question.

So they walked. On and on. They passed through archways which simply separated tunnel from more tunnel, and crossed over three bridges that spanned only darkness. Paraskeve never hesitated when they came to intersections. There were no signs Atalanta could see to tell the tunnels apart, but Paraskeve always chose their path with a confidence bordering on arrogance.

It was impossible to tell time in the shell-light, and nothing about the tunnels ever seemed to change. Archways, bridges, and intersections not withstanding. Atalanta's aching feet were her only indication of how long they had been walking. Neither Damien, nor Eryx, gave any indication of feeling tired, so she gritted her teeth and followed in silence.

After an eternity, Paraskeve stopped at a dead-end tunnel. She bent and ran her hands across the floor. A stone ring popped up with a tiny puff of dust. She grabbed it and pulled a thick slab of stone up to reveal a dark hole.

"Take the ladder down and move along the ledge until you come to the cliff," she instructed.

"Wha—" Atalanta started to ask, but Damien started down the hole before she could finish.

She couldn't understand why he trusted their guide so completely. She didn't doubt Nereus would provide someone, but how hard would it be for the Usurper to stop Nereus's guide and replace them with one of her own? Damien disappeared from sight and she bit her lip to keep from saying anything before she descended into the hole as well.

The ladder was carved into the stone and felt gritty beneath her hands. Her foot jarred against the bottom quicker than she expected. Looking up she could see a bit of light, though much of it was obscured by Eryx starting his descent.

Atalanta stretched out her hands and felt walls on three sides. The fourth side led out to a narrow lip of rock. Some distant light allowed for her to see the two-foot wide path and nothingness over the edge. There was a sound, so faint and faraway it was little more than a rumble whispering past her ears.

She pressed her back against the wall and slid along the ledge. Rocks skittered down into the nothingness below as she moved. It would be so easy for a misstep, or an assailant, to send them tumbling to their death.

Before her heart could beat its way out of her ribs, she came to a landing. Damien stood next to a broken railing guarding half of the edge. The faint sound now rumbled and surged all around them.

Atalanta moved up next to Damien and stared down at a wide river. It raged and frothed, tearing at the rocky walls confining it. Bursts of spray were frequently flung high enough to splatter them with water. She was sure the thrumming sound of the river should have deafened them, but it was simply loud.

Paraskeve stepped up beside her, a pained expression on her face. "ὃς περικυμαίνει γαίης περιτέρμονα κύκλον," she mumbled.

"What now?" Damien asked. "I hope we don't have to jump into the river."

Paraskeve bit out a bitter bark of laughter. "No. Only a true child of Poseidon could hope to survive in the waters of Oceanus."

Atalanta frowned. "Then what—"

Paraskeve backed up several steps and then took off at a dead run, leaping up and over the river to land on a ledge of rock on the far side. She was hard to see through the dim light and distance, but she gave them an impatient wave and backed away from the edge.

"Guess we jump," Eryx said, his voice soft and uncertain.

"Does anyone else feel like this guide of ours is going to kill us?" Atalanta asked.

Damien shook his head. "Don't you know who she is?"

"No. You do?"

He gave her a skeptical look. "Paraskeve, the daughter of Pallas, and granddaughter of Poseidon. I've never heard any myths specifically about her, but she's a goddess. Or, at least, the daughter of gods."

"Technically, we're both children of the gods too," Atalanta pointed out.

"Do you know anything else about her?" Eryx asked. "Was she known to be particularly honourable?"

Damien ran a hand through his hair. "I'm not sure. Her mother was a close companion of Athena's until there was an accident. It's why she's called Pallas Athena now."

"I'm not sure if that's a point for, or against, her," Atalanta grumbled.

"Well, I suppose there's nothing for it, but to jump," Eryx said after a moment of silence.

He backed up and took a run at the ledge. He cleared the gap easily, landing almost a foot beyond the edge. A large spray of water erupted, almost as if the river knew it had been denied blood. Eryx turned back to them, grinned, and waved. "It is not as difficult as it looks," he shouted.

Damien took a deep breath and backed up for his run. His foot hit the edge of the ledge, launching him up over the river. Stone crumbled and dropped into seething water. He landed on the other side, stumbling forward a few steps before he regained his balance.

Atalanta tugged at her tunic and backed up until stone pressed against her back. She closed her eyes and took a deep breath, blowing it out slowly. The others had all made it with no difficulty. She gave herself a shake and set out at a run. She leapt from the edge, the stone crumbling beneath her foot stealing some of her momentum. "Sard it," she snarled.

She wasn't going to make it.

Hands darted forward, grabbing her outstretched arms and yanking her away from certain death. She was pressed against a broad chest and spun away from the edge. Atalanta rested her head against them, trying to calm the panicked beat of her heart. Her knees felt weak and she wasn't sure she could have stood on her own at that moment.

"Come on," Damien snapped. He shoved past and Atalanta looked up to see Eryx holding her.

"Thank you," she said softly, pulling out of his arms.

Eryx nodded, his eyes worried as she moved to follow Damien and Paraskeve away from the river. She didn't want to address the mix of disappointment and relief she felt, and she certainly didn't want to deal with Damien's jealousy. She railed against the unwanted affection he felt toward her. Perhaps she should kiss Eryx. Or Paraskeve. Anyone, really, to make him give up his foolish desires. She knew she wouldn't though. It would hurt him, and, despite her frustration, she didn't want to hurt him.

Her turbulent thoughts were interrupted by Paraskeve stopping abruptly and holding up a hand. She pressed a finger to her lips and crouched low, creeping through a rough archway. The three companions crouched and followed her into a massive cavern.

The sides sloped steeply down to form a bowl-like depression. A spring gurgled and splashed in the middle, its water flowing over and around a silver trident speared down into the rock. The metal didn't glisten though. It glinted like the edge of a blade in sunlight.

Wrapped around the spring and trident was a massive, sleeping beast. It was serpentine, with a frill of spines behind its head creating a sweeping cone over its neck. More webbed spines ran down its back, fluttering with every breath. Its tail flicked, the wicked looking point gouging the stone.

"That is...what is that?" Damien asked softly.

"A leviathan," Paraskeve whispered.

"Any chance you can control it?" Atalanta asked.

She shot her a withering glare. "Only Poseidon himself can control it. You must either sneak past it, or kill it, to claim the trident. Many would-be-heroes have tried. None have ever succeeded."

"Wonderful," Atalanta muttered.

Eryx eyed Damien in consideration. "Your cloak is magical, isn't it? Could you use it to sneak past?"

"I could try," Damien replied.

Paraskeve snorted. "It would have to be powerful magic to fool the beast."

Atalanta glowered at her. "For wanting to dethrone the Usurper, you don't help much."

"*I* will be the one to dethrone her," she said, her glare so hate-filled Atalanta was surprised she didn't have a knife in her ribs yet.

"Then why are you here?" Atalanta shot back.

"Nereus called upon me to be your guide. I am not a true god, so I cannot deny his commands," Paraskeve admitted, bitterness dripping off her voice.

"What makes you think you're the one to overthrow the Usurper?" Eryx asked.

"There was a prophecy, given by one of the Usurper's sisters, that a child of Poseidon would take his power back. I am the last true descendant."

"Atalanta—" Eryx started, but she cut him off.

"Doesn't care what some stupid prophecy says. The Usurper can't be defeated without claiming Poseidon's trident, so that's what we're going to do."

"Suit yourself. I will not mourn your deaths."

Damien grimaced. "With that pleasant thought, we should get started."

He crept away from them. When he was at the last edge of cover between the cave entrance and the creature, he wrapped his cloak around himself and disappeared from view. Paraskeve's eyes widened and her jaw dropped. Atalanta gave her a smug smile and crept to the spot where Damien had disappeared.

She couldn't see where he was, and she was relieved she couldn't hear him either. The leviathan's breathing hitched and she sucked in a breath. Could it hear him approaching?

The beast's eyes snapped open and it let out a screech that shook the cavern. It's head rose until it almost brushed the ceiling, weaving side-to-side as it tried to spot Damien. A hiss slid past its teeth and saliva dripped to the stone below, sizzling and burying into the rock.

"Oi! Fish-breath!" Eryx shouted, standing and waving his arms.

The leviathan's gaze locked on him and its slithering hiss sounded unsettlingly like laughter. It moved toward him, the coils of its body undulating. Eryx darted off to the side, in the opposite direction Damien would have taken to reach the trident.

The leviathan darted forward, snapping at Eryx. He jumped and tumbled, hitting the ground with a loud smack. The beast's teeth buried into the stone wall. It snapped its jaw shut, tearing out a chunk of the rock as if it were freshly baked bread.

"Sard it all," Atalanta snarled. She stood up and ran toward the monster. She imagined she could hear all of her ancestors shouting a collective 'no' at her choice. Her daggers seemed pitiful next to the shear size of the creature, but she drew them and slashed at it.

Her blades skittered off its scales.

It still noticed her.

It lashed its tail at her, missing by a thumb's width, and left a deep gouge in the stone. It twisted and pulled its tail out, sending her flying as the ground heaved and shattered.

The leviathan's head whipped around, eyes darting. Atalanta groaned and picked herself up, spotting Eryx doing the same on the other side of the beast. It ignored them and struck at a spot between them and the trident. It bit into the floor and tore out a chunk, shaking its head to scatter the rocky debris in its mouth.

"Damien!" Atalanta bolted to her feet, an unfamiliar mix of rage and fear coursing through her body. She ran at the monster and dug her knives between its scales. They didn't sink very far, but they gave her purchase. Scale over scale, she climbed up its neck.

"Hades, Atalanta, I'm still alive," Damien shouted from somewhere on the ground.

The relief only took the edge off the fear and anger. She gritted her teeth and climbed higher.

The leviathan shrieked and shook its head. She flopped against its neck, biting her tongue to keep from screaming. Blood filled her mouth. Her arms felt weak and her entire body bruised. Still she climbed.

"What in Hades is she doing?" Damien demanded.

"Distracting it, you fool. Grab the trident," Eryx returned.

Atalanta only half heard their conversation. He was wrong—she meant to kill the leviathan. That moment, brief as it had been, where she believed Damien killed had broken something inside her. Hazina was already dead. She couldn't lose anyone else. Especially not him.

Her daggers slashed through the frill crowning the monster and it screamed, thrashing around harder. The dagger she'd cut the soft flesh with fell from her hand, clattering as it tumbled down the beast's body.

She clenched both hands around the remaining dagger and stared at the last bit of scale she needed to climb. It was only a couple of feet, but it might as well have been a hundred with only one dagger to give her purchase.

This was the moment she should pray for help from any god willing to listen. They'd never responded before, though that hadn't stopped her from praying in moments of desperation. But she had been through too much on this quest to be able to believe they weren't listening. They listened, they watched, and they meddled. If they wanted to help, then they could get off their divine butts and help. She wasn't going to beg ever again. Not to them.

The only other person with power she knew, and trusted, couldn't do much to help in this particular situation, but it didn't stop her from whispering, "Eudora, help me."

A rock slammed into the scales next to her and she risked a look down. Eryx's hands were full of rubble and he threw pieces at the leviathan. One slammed next to its eye, cracking a small scale. The beast roared and lashed toward him. The sudden movement flipped Atalanta over.

She yanked her dagger out and let gravity throw her past the monster's frill. The leviathan jerked to a stop as she slid down its nose. Its eyes crossed, pupils adjusting to bring her into focus. At least its head was level now.

"Gods, I hope this works," she said.

Atalanta ripped her scarf off. Her snakes writhed and rose. They snapped at the air, their eyes glowing red. The beast stiffened, but no grey stone crept over its flesh. She concentrated, willing the leviathan to stone. Her snakes' eyes flashed again and a keening whine pierced through the air. It took a moment to realize the sound came from her. She gritted her teeth together and ignored the searing pain spreading through her.

"Turn. To. Stone," she ground out.

This time, grey covered the leviathan.

Atalanta slumped against the now-stone beast's nose. Her limbs trembled and her head spun. She knew she was in pain, but it was a distant thing as her mind seemed to float three feet above her body. She could hear voices, but it took her a minute to sort them out from the thrumming in her ears.

"Atalanta, are you all right?"

Who was shouting at her? Damien or Eryx? Maybe it was Paraskeve. A giggle escaped her. Her snakes would disappear before that woman gave half a damn about her.

"Did...did she just *giggle*?" That had to be Damien. Only he could sound so horrified at something she did.

"Well, at least we know she's alive."

Atalanta's pain-induced euphoria faded into simple agony and she groaned, pulling herself to the edge of the beast's nose so she could look down. Eryx and Damien stared up at her. It was hard to read their expressions at such a distance, but she thought they looked worried.

"Are you hurt?" Eryx called.

"Not in any normal sense," she replied.

"Can you climb down?" Damien asked.

Atalanta squinted at the beast's neck. The scales were as clearly defined as before, but she wasn't sure if her dagger could give her proper purchase on the stone. And she only had one dagger left. "I...can try."

"Why do you not simply jump?" Paraskeve asked, leaning against a large chunk of rock the leviathan had ripped up and thrown.

Eryx turned and glared at her. "It has to be almost thirty feet! There is no way she could survive such a jump without serious injury."

Paraskeve shrugged. "I do not care. But now that we have bested the beast, we should take the trident and go. The longer we wait, the more prepared the Usurper will be."

"Just...give me a couple minutes," Atalanta said.

She crawled up the leviathan's head and used the frills to balance as she swung her legs over. A shiver of fear ran through her. She had been so angry when she climbed up that she hadn't given any thought to how high it was. Now, she was very aware of the amount of air between her and the ground.

There was nothing for it, but to slide down the neck. Her fingers and toes dug in to the cracks between scales. The dagger was next to useless this time, so she slid it into its sheath and focused on clinging to the rock. Bit by little bit, she descended. The stone scraped up her hands and wrists. Streaks of blood marked her passage.

Atalanta flinched when hands grabbed her waist, then relaxed and let them catch her. Damien and Eryx cradled her between them while Paraskeve watched with bored annoyance written across her face.

"Do you need a moment?" Damien asked.

Atalanta nodded.

Eryx and Damien carried her to a bit of chair-sized rubble and set her down. She couldn't stop shaking and tears pricked at her eyes. The men exchanged a confused look.

"Are you hurt?" Eryx asked, crouching in front of her.

She shook her head.

"What's wrong, Atalanta?" he asked.

She bit her lip and shook her head again. She didn't know how to explain herself. Yes, there was pain. Her whole body felt bruised, and her fingers were scraped raw, but none of that hurt as much as her heart. They'd survived and the trident was theirs for the taking. She should be happy. Relieved. Not terrified.

Damien ran a hand through his hair and stared down at her as if he were afraid she might break. "Should we just press on?"

Eryx's nostrils flared and his gaze turned sympathetic. "Give us a moment," he told Damien before wrapping his arms around Atalanta.

She stiffened and started to pull away. Eryx gently ran a hand over her hair, over and over, while he whispered a soft litany of "You will be fine, everything will be fine, it will be all right."

Atalanta relaxed into the hug, burying her face against his shoulder and letting herself cry. She still didn't know how to explain how she felt, but as her tears soaked his shirt, she felt some of the weight of it lift. She sniffled and pulled away. Eryx held her shoulders and studied her face intently.

"Thank you," she said softly, wiping a hand across her eyes.

"Can we stop wasting time?" Paraskeve asked.

Eryx and Damien both glowered at her.

Atalanta stood up and gave her a cool look. "I'm a little surprised you didn't just take the trident and run off."

"As tempting as that is, I wouldn't be able to pull it out of the stone."

"I thought you were a true child of Poseidon," Atalanta said, her voice dripping with honey.

Paraskeve snarled. "Only the one who bested the leviathan can free the trident."

Atalanta gave her a painfully sweet smile before turning and marching over to the trident. She wrapped her hand around the shaft, surprised at how warm it felt. The water bubbling around the weapon splashed against her and she felt her aches fading. A quick tug freed the tines from the stone. She held the trident up and it glinted in the unnatural light that seemed to be everywhere in the strange underground world.

"Time to dethrone the Usurper," Atalanta said, turning back to the others.

Paraskeve glowered, but nodded. "We have a long journey to the palace ahead of us. Gather your things and follow me."

Chapter Fourteen

Paraskeve led Atalanta, Eryx, and Damien back to the cliff edge. Rather than leaping across, they followed it. The path was monotonous. Nothing about the stone, cliff, or raging river seemed to change. Damien couldn't shake the feeling they were being followed, but nothing was ever there when he turned to look.

They walked for hours before there was any change in their surroundings. The cliff sloped down toward the river and a dense patch of some dark, tangled plants were suddenly in front of them. Though the cliff didn't lower all the way to the river, the plants trailed over the edge, fluttering just above the water's surface.

"What are those things?" Eryx asked, rubbing his arms.

"Living shadows," Paraskeve said. "As long as we stick to the path, they will not harm us."

"What path?" Atalanta asked, planting the butt of the trident and leaning on it like it were a walking staff.

Paraskeve pointed, her face contemptuous. "There."

"I don't see anything," Atalanta said flatly.

Paraskeve scoffed, turned, and gasped. "The path has been overrun!"

"What does that mean?" Damien asked.

"It means we have no way through," she said through gritted teeth, spreading a glare across them as if they were responsible for the missing path.

"Can we...cut our way through?" Eryx wondered.

She snorted. "Do you have magic weapons?"

"We have the trident," Atalanta pointed out.

"Do you know how to use it?" Paraskeve asked.

"I know how to fight with it," she replied.

"But you do not know how to use its powers."

Atalanta glowered. "Do you?"

Paraskeve tossed her head and huffed. "Only Poseidon can use the trident fully."

"Then why did you even ask?" Atalanta shouted. "You're just bitter that we're going to do what you haven't been able to do for half a century."

"You impetuous mongrel," Paraskeve said with a snarl. "You think a little bit of sea in the blood, and the favour of Athena, makes you special, but it does not. You are not a true child of Poseidon, and you will never be."

Atalanta's jaw clenched and she griped the trident so hard her knuckles turned white. Damien stepped between the two women and held up his hands. "We are going to have to work together to get through this. We can't afford to fight each other."

"Is there any other way to reach Poseidon's palace?" Eryx asked.

"Not unless you care to swim in Oceanus," Paraskeve said, jerking her thumb toward the raging river. A spray of water burst over the edge to punctuate her words.

"So we go through the shadows," Damien said. "What happens if they touch us?"

"Living shadows drain the life of anyone they touch. I have been told it is an unpleasant experience."

Atalanta sighed. "Right, so what hurts them? Would torches keep them back? How much magic would a weapon need to be effective?"

"What are you thinking of?" Eryx asked. She waved his question off and waited expectantly for Paraskeve's answer.

She tugged her braid in agitation. "They dislike fire, but it would not be enough to keep them all at bay. I do not know how much magic is needed, but I have seen glowing weapons cut through them."

Atalanta turned to Eryx. "Could you—"

He cut her off with a shake of his head. "I have very little magic, and certainly not anything like what you're thinking."

"We need Hazina," Damien said, a stab of guilt and pain piercing his heart.

Paraskeve shrugged. "Perhaps you had the wrong woman pay your debt."

Damien could hear faint hissing coming from the scarf Atalanta had retied around her hair. He kept his eyes locked on Paraskeve. "The closer we get to the palace, the angrier you become. Isn't overthrowing the Usurper what you want?"

"It's supposed to be *my* destiny," she shouted. "Not some unrecognized bastard's."

"And what have you done to reach your destiny?" he asked, his voice gentle.

"Destiny is preordained," Paraskeve said derisively.

"Destiny must also be seized with both hands and fought for."

Eryx nodded. "Death is the only fate that can be passively awaited."

"Maybe you never learnt what hard work means, being the daughter of gods and all that, but you can't have honestly thought the trident would fall into your lap right before the Usurper threw themselves on the tines and died?" Atalanta asked, her tone as sharp and sarcastic as Paraskeve's.

"You filthy little bawd!"

Paraskeve side-stepped around Damien and dove toward Atalanta. One hand grabbed at the trident and the other fist slammed into her ribs. Atalanta gasped from the blow and pulled the trident up so she held it between them, a hand on either side of Paraskeve's. She pulled it toward her chest and then snapped it at Paraskeve's face.

Paraskeve jerked back. She avoided being hit, but lost her grip on the trident. Atalanta swung the butt of the waepon forward. It clipped along her collarbone. Paraskeve ducked low and tackled Atalanta around the waist. They fell to the ground, wrestling in almost perfect silence.

"Stop it! We need to work together," Damien shouted at them. Neither woman paid him any attention. With the trident being fought over, he didn't want to join the tussle unless he had to. There was just too much of a chance he'd get stabbed before he could do anything.

"Give…me…the trident," Paraskeve ground out, holding Atalanta's shoulders down with one hand and trying to wrest the weapon away with the other.

"Go get...your own," Atalanta returned. She twisted and threw her hips, flipping Paraskeve over her head. The breath rushed out of her from the impact and Atalanta yanked the trident away.

"Come on now," Eryx cajoled. "We can all kill the Usurper. Together. No need to fight each other."

Both women snarled and jumped to their feet, spinning to face each other. Paraskeve narrowed her eyes and circled Atalanta. Damien wasn't sure when it had happened, but Atalanta's lip was split. Her tongue flicked out to test the cut and she winced. He jumped between them again and shouted, "That is enough!"

Atalanta dipped her head in what might have been acquiescence, but Paraskeve threw a fist at his head. He barely dodged back in time, feeling her knuckles graze his cheek.

"You brazen-faced—"

"I said, enough!" Damien cut Atalanta off. He gave her a quick, disapproving frown before turning back to Paraskeve. "You are both acting like gutter children."

Eryx stepped forward and grabbed Paraskeve's arms so she couldn't take another swing. By the murder in her face, she desperately wanted to.

"You will give me my birthright, or I will take it from you," Paraskeve said.

"I defeated the leviathan, I claimed the trident, I received Poseidon's blessing...and you think this is *your* birthright?" Atalanta asked.

Damien turned to stare at her. This was the first she'd said anything about receiving her forefather's blessing. He wasn't sure why it bothered him that she hadn't told him. Though it was a reminder that there was much they didn't know about one another.

Paraskeve spat. "Use the trident's powers then, O Chosen One."

Atalanta glowered.

"You can't, because it is not meant for the likes of you."

Atalanta squeezed her eyes shut, gripping the trident in both hand so tightly it looked like her knuckles might break through her skin. Paraskeve laughed, but she ignored her. Her lips moved in some silent prayer. Damien wanted to say something, to assure her it didn't matter whether she could make the trident do anything magical, but he never got the chance.

A flash of white light surrounded them. It was blindingly bright, though thankfully only lasted a moment. Damien blinked the stars from his vision to see Atalanta standing triumphantly, the trident glowing a soft white in her hands.

Paraskeve looked as if she wanted to spit acid. She turned her back to them and gestured at the writhing shadows. "Lead the way, daughter of Poseidon."

"I...do not know the way," Atalanta said, rolling her shoulders.

"Find the start of the path, and then just cut along it. There are no forks or branches. It will take you directly to the palace."

"You aren't coming with us, are you?" Eryx asked.

Paraskeve shook her head.

"You're supposed to be our guide," Atalanta accused.

"I led you to the trident, and now to the path to the palace. As long as you stay on the it, you will not get lost. You no longer need me."

"What about when we get to the palace? How are we to find the Usurper?" Damien demanded. "All Nereus told us was that she was in the 'deepest recess of Poseidon's domain.'"

"I can give no more insight than that," she replied. "It is not as if the Usurper sits in the same room all day, every day. Even if I went with you, you would still have to search until you found her."

Atalanta grunted. "We could use your help in the coming battle," she said. It sounded as if the words hurt her to say.

Paraskeve shook her head. "I cannot. I wish you luck."

She didn't wait for anyone to say anything else before running and jumping off the cliff into the raging river. Her body was surrounded by a soft, blue glow before the water swallowed her up. Damien thought he could see a faint streak of blue light flying upstream beneath the surface, but it could have easily been a trick of the light.

He gave his head a shake and turned back toward the shadows. They seemed to pull away from the light of the trident, faint as it was. "Let's get some torches lit and carve us a path," he said.

Reclaiming the path through the shadows had seemed so easy to start. The writhing blackness pulled away from the torchlight, and fell in tatters at a touch from the trident. Eryx wasn't sure what the fuss had been about—it was a little slow, but, compared to everything else they'd faced, easy. By the time they lost sight of the cliff and raging river beyond, he knew he shouldn't have trusted the ease of their progress.

It started slowly—a brief, chilling brush against skin—but quickly became persistent. The living shadows shied away from their light, twisting and writhing until they could slip in through the shade Atalanta, Damien, and Eryx cast. Eryx swung his torch in a winding figure-eight, side-to-side, over-and-over. His arms burned, but it was better than the chill and weary ache the shadows left every time they touched him.

"How…much further?" Damien asked. His feet scuffed along the broken path and breath came in shallow pants.

Eryx eyed him with concern. His face was pinched and dark bags made his eyes look sunken. He held his sword in one hand and the torch in the other, though the sword tip dragged against the ground.

"Not much," Eryx lied. "You take the middle."

Damien nodded and shuffled in front of him. Atalanta paused and glanced back at them. Tendrils of hair floated around her face and sweat beaded on her brow. Her brow pinched and she bit her lip.

"I don't think it's safe to stop, but we could take a minute if one of you needed," she said.

Eryx was about to agree when Damien shook his head. "Keep going. We'll rest when we're out of this cursed place."

She looked like she wanted to object, but she turned forward and pressed on. Her thrusts with the trident became harder and wider. It did little to stop the seething mass from sapping their energy.

Eryx pulled Damien's sword from his hand and awkwardly slid it back in its sheath. He gritted his teeth against the stinging chill of the shadows taking advantage of his distraction. "Staying on the pirate ship is seeming more and more like what I should have done," he muttered.

"Nobody asked for your help," Damien muttered back, his words slurred.

Eryx snorted. "Nobody asks for your help, and you still give it."

"I'm a hero, you're a pirate."

"Ah, well, guess I should let you fall over your own feet so the shadows can eat you, then," he said derisively.

"I'd deserve it. I'm not a very good hero," Damien said softly.

Eryx blinked.

"I should have saved her. There must have been something I could've done," he said. "But I just watched her die."

"Hazina…She was an amazing woman, and I think she would have done great things with her life. But she made a choice…her choice. I didn't know her as well as the rest of you, but I think she would have been offended if you'd tried to stop it once she'd made up her mind," Eryx mused.

Damien chuckled softly. "Would've told me I was being foolish, or something."

They lapsed into silence as they continued on, struggling against the sapping touch of the shadows. The farther they went, the more aggressive they became. Eryx gritted his teeth and dragged Damien on.

Atalanta muttered an oath and fell to her knees. Eryx stumbled to a stop behind her and shook his torch at the roiling shadows. "Atalanta? Are you all right?"

"Just…tired," she panted.

"We can't stop," he said. "Damien's all but unconscious, and I'm too weak to carry you too."

She bobbed her head in understanding and leaned on the trident to climb back to her feet. The glow of the tines flickered. Shadows pressed closer, lapping at them.

"Atalanta…" Eryx said through gritted teeth.

"I know," she snapped. She swung the trident in a wide arc around them, clearing some space amongst the shadows. The glow flickered twice and then went out. The torches died a heartbeat later.

Cold wrapped around them in an instant. It was as if the tendrils were crawling through Eryx's veins. His joints locked painfully and he whimpered. He would never die of old age, but he could certainly die from other causes. This was not how he wanted his final moments to go.

"To Hades with gods, and shadows, and prophecies," Atalanta shouted.

A brilliant flash of light flared. Warmth rushed back into his body and he gasped. Atalanta held the trident over her head and the whole thing was lit by a pure, silvery light. A circle, ten feet across, of burnt shadows surrounded them, and those at the edge of the light pulled away. Her arms trembled and the light flickered.

Eryx pressed a hand against her back and they marched onward. The shadows sizzled away beneath the trident's brilliance, though every few steps it would dim almost to the point of going out, before Atalanta would grit her teeth and steady the shaking of her limbs. In a short time, they reached the edge of the shadow forest.

Atalanta crumpled. The trident fell from her fingers and the glow vanished. Shadows reached for them, struggling against the pale light suffusing the air outside the forest. Their chill touch licked up their backs. Neither Atalanta, nor Damien, reacted to the shadows.

He gritted his teeth so hard he felt something crack. Every muscle in his body ached. He knew if they didn't move, they would succumb completely. Though his arms shook, he tightened his grip on Damien and hooked a hand beneath Atalanta's arm. His feet shuffled against the ground, kicking the trident along in front of them, as he dragged them all away from the last reaching tendrils of shadow.

Once they were safely away, he too dropped to his knees. Tremors ran through his body. Damien lay next to him, his breaths rapid and shallow. Atalanta groaned and struggled to push herself onto her hands and knees. For several long minutes, they stayed like that, each recovering a modicum of strength. Once the tremors subsided, Eryx stumbled to his feet and offered Atalanta a hand. Her fingers were like ice against his skin, and she had to lean on him as they studied their new surroundings.

A plain of blue-grey stone stretched out before them. Dips and rises undulated across the ground, like waves frozen just before they could crest. On the other side of the plain stood a palace with hundreds of delicate spires. They stretched up and branched out so much Eryx was sure it only stood because of magic. The walls glistened with a pearlescent sheen; the windows, balconies, and doors were edged in wide swathes of gold. It was hard to judge distances with no other landmarks, but the palace wasn't so far away they couldn't make out people moving around.

"Looks like there are regular patrols"—he coughed and cleared his throat—"around the exterior."

"And either guards stationed on balconies, or people go in and out of them regularly," Atalanta added. She leaned her head against his shoulder and pressed closer to his side. Her exhaustion grated against his senses, but he wrapped an arm around her.

Their bit of shared warmth pushed away the worst of their fatigue. He glanced down at Damien, worried that he hadn't roused yet. "We need to rest before we do anything else."

She nodded. "Agreed."

They quickly set up a small camp on the bare plain. They didn't bother with a fire, and together they rolled Damien onto a mattress. Atalanta covered him with a blanket and pressed the back of her hand against his forehead. She looked up at Eryx, her concern sharp. He pushed his mattress next to Damien's and sank down onto it with a grateful sigh. She hesitated a moment before sliding hers to Damien's other side.

"In the morning we'll finish this quest and be done with this place," Eryx said, trying to infuse a note of cheerfulness into his voice.

"No. In the morning we are going to tear the palace down and make them all—Usurper, supporter, and soldier—pay," she declared.

Chapter Fifteen

The first thing Atalanta was aware of when she woke up was pain. It radiated throughout her entire body. She groaned and rolled over. The grey light was the same as always, but there was something different. Both Damien and Eryx still slept. Their breathing was soft and even. Whatever she sensed hadn't disturbed them, so she doubted it was a noise.

She stood up and frowned down at her dress. "Is this the Between?" she wondered aloud. The first time she'd fallen into it, she'd worn a fancy velvet gown. The dress she was wearing this time was much simpler. More like the one she'd worn on Ganim's ship—though a brilliant scarlet red.

"I am unsure," a familiar voice replied.

Atalanta spun and gaped at Hazina. She stood several feet away and wore a pale gown reminiscent of the ancient chitons Atalanta's ancestors tended to wear. Otherwise she looked exactly as she remembered.

Atalanta closed the distance between them and wrapped her arms around Hazina. Tears blurred her vision and she laughed softly. "I thought I would never see you again."

Hazina hugged her back, squeezing tightly. "As did I. I was very surprised to wake up after Nereus...took my payment."

"This isn't the real world, though," Atalanta said, pulling back to arm's length and studying her friend's face.

She nodded. "I realized that fairly quickly. It has taken me some time to figure out how to move about this strange place—everything is indistinct to me, as if I were viewing it all through smoked glass."

"Have you been following us, then?"

"Only since you entered the shadows," Hazina said.

Atalanta smiled. "I'm sure it will just take some time to get used to things."

"Perhaps. Nereus says there is much for me to learn."

Her eyebrows shot up in surprise. "You've spoken with Nereus since he...you know..."

Hazina nodded. "He explained much of what has happened, and what you are to face. I feel he was relieved to have someone to talk to—the magics binding what he can say to the living are powerful."

"The living? You mean you aren't—"

"Alive? I do not think so."

Atalanta fell silent. Some of her joy at seeing Hazina faded. She supposed she shouldn't have been surprised. She'd spoken with dead relatives in the Between before. It didn't ease the ache that was creeping back into her heart.

"But that is not why I have entered your dreams," Hazina said. "I have come to offer some last bit of help."

Atalanta perked up a bit. "You can tell us what Nereus told you, right?"

"No. As I said, the magics are powerful. I am somehow linked to him, and can feel the binding on me. I am not, however, bound to only help those who best me in a silly game," Hazina explained.

"Small blessings," she said with a smile.

"Indeed. When we are done talking, you must wake the other two up. It is the middle of the night and the guards do not patrol as diligently. This will be your only chance to enter the palace undetected."

"How—"

"Do not ask," Hazina cut her off. "I can feel some of your ache, and you will feel much worse when you actually wake up."

"Well, that's wonderful," Atalanta said.

Hazina smiled a little. "You each must eat one of the fruits you took from Nereus. It will refresh you."

"I think I have more than three of them in my bag," she said.

"Only eat one. You will need the rest later."

"That's ominous."

Hazina laughed. "It is. I wish I could tell you more, but this is where we must say goodbye."

Atalanta hugged her again. "I miss you. We all miss you."

"You will see me again, some day. But now it is time for you to wake up."

Atalanta sat up with a gasp. She was back in her bed, wearing her normal tunic and pants, and Hazina was gone. Tears collected on her cheeks and she roughly brushed them away.

Eryx and Damien were slow to rouse. They all moved slowly and stiffly. Atalanta pulled three of the strange fruits from her bag and distributed them. The very first bite eased her pain and filled her body with a low burst of energy. She finished the fruit quickly, licking the juices off her fingers, and wished she could eat another.

"I feel like we only slept for a few hours," Eryx said. "The fruit helped, but I think it would have been better to rest more instead."

"Hazina came to me in a dream," Atalanta explained. "She said this is our only chance to make it into the palace. I know we're all tired, but we've got to go."

Damien pressed a fist against his mouth to stifle a yawn. "What's so special about right now?"

"The guards aren't as watchful, apparently, because it's the middle of the night."

Eryx grumbled. "Can't blame them. Only fools would try to storm a castle on a few hours of sleep and magic pears."

"Good thing we're fools then," she shot back. "Pack up your things. I'm not going to miss my one chance to get in and avenge Hazina just because you wanted to sleep more."

The disappointment and sympathy on Damien's face made her want to scream, while Eryx's annoyance and anger seemed to beg her to berate him further. She pulled a deep breath in through her nose and released it slowly from her mouth. Both men had valid reasons for looking at her that way, and if she hadn't been so tired, she was sure it wouldn't have bothered her even half as much.

"Did you have extra pear-things?" Damien asked once his bedding was packed away.

"Yes, but Hazina said we'll need them later, so no more."

"How many more do you have?" Eryx asked.

Atalanta reached a hand into her bag, swishing around until she found the fruits. "There are four."

"Then let's split one. That will leave one each for whatever future event Hazina saw," he reasoned. "And even a third of one would go a long way to making it more bearable right now."

"She said one each..." Atalanta shifted uneasily. She desperately wanted to bite into another juicy fruit. The first had barely taken the edge off her weariness.

"I can't imagine we will want to be here for more than one more night," he pointed out. "What good would the fourth fruit even be, anyway?"

Atalanta turned to Damien and raised an eyebrow expectantly. He pursed his lips and thought for a moment. "I trust Hazina, and believe she has good reason for us to keep four of the fruits, but I also don't think I could sneak past the guards, even with my cloak, right now. It could be the difference between success and failure."

She nodded and pulled one of the pear-shaped fruits from her bag. A dagger made quick work of the soft flesh. The three companions hurriedly ate their portions and then turned toward the palace.

"It doesn't look any less guarded from this direction," Eryx said doubtfully.

Atalanta shrugged. "I only know what I've been told."

They packed up their small camp. Atalanta hesitated to slide the trident into her bag, but it glittered softly in the pale light. It was also too bulky to easily hide beneath a cloak, or to fight with in tight quarters. With a heavy heart, she slid her forefather's weapon into the bag. Once they were ready, they kept to the shallow valleys of the undulating plain as they approached the palace. It wasn't entirely possible to traverse the distance in the valleys, but they crouched low and crawled over the peaks. They were almost to the castle when Atalanta first noticed that the gold-rimmed doors were fake.

"What do we do now?" she whispered to Eryx and Damien after pointing it out.

"We saw people moving in and out of the balconies—those must be real," Damien said.

"It'll be a lot harder to climb to a balcony without being seen," Eryx warned.

She chewed on her lip and squinted over the rise of stone they were hiding behind. The guards patrolled in sets of three, always exchanging a pleasant greeting as they passed patrols going in the opposite direction. It was hard to say for sure, but she thought there might have only been six groups. Which left long gaps between patrols.

"How do the guards get in?" Damien wondered.

Atalanta turned back to him with a frown. "What?"

"Well, I assume they need to sleep and eat occasionally, and there are no other buildings, so they must rest inside the palace. Which means there's a way in—other than scaling a balcony."

Eryx nodded slowly. "Do you think you could use your cloak to get close enough to find the entrance?"

He nodded and wrapped his cloak around him. Atalanta strained to hear his retreating footsteps and watched the infrequent, but consistent, patrolling guards. For several minutes, the guards didn't do anything differently.

An angry shout around the side of the palace drew the guards' attention. They called out in a burbling language. A response was shouted back and they ran to join their fellow guards out of sight.

"What are the chances this is unrelated to Damien trying to find the entrance?" Eryx asked.

"Not good," Atalanta said. "Let's go."

"Wait, what?"

She gestured to the guard-free front of the palace. "This is our chance to climb up to the first balcony."

"What about Damien?"

She flinched and shook her head. "He's good, but not that good. If he was spotted, he's been captured. We can't help him if we stay out here."

Eryx sighed. "Let's go."

They ran to the palace. The walls were perfectly smooth. No cracks, grooves, or even bumps gave any purchase for them to climb. Atalanta muttered curses beneath her breath and pulled a length of rope from her bag. She quickly tied the rope around the top of the bag and then tossed it up to the balcony.

She tugged on the rope, pulling it to one side then another, until the bag snagged between the balcony railings. "Let me go first," she told Eryx. "I'm lighter, so hopefully it won't pull free. Once I'm up, I'll brace it so you can climb."

He nodded and she started up the rope as quickly as she could. Every foot she ascended, she could see the bag sliding along the smooth surface of the railings. She had just reached the bottom of the balcony when it slipped out entirely. The bag whipped past her and she jumped to grab the railings. Her hands closed on the slick surface, but she was able to keep from falling.

"You all right?" Eryx whispered up at her.

Atalanta grunted and pulled herself up so she could get an elbow between the railings. The surface was far too slick for her to be able to hand-over-hand her way up them. With an elbow on the balcony, she swung her legs up until she got a foot wedged between another set of railings. A bit of wiggling let her hook her knee around them. From there she was able to reach up for the top of the railing to pull herself up and over.

Her body shook and sweat drenched her brow. She blew out a breath and stood up. Eryx stared up at her, bag and rope in hand. Atalanta gave him a quick wave and he tossed the bag up to her. She wrapped the rope around the railing a few times and then around her waist. "Ready when you are," she told him.

The rope tried to slide against the slick surface as Eryx climbed it, but Atalanta held it firmly. He was much quicker than her, and in just a few moments, they were both standing on the balcony. She untied the rope and stuffed it back in her bag before turning to the golden doors.

There were no handles or hinges visible. Eryx gave the door a gentle push and it swung inward without a sound. Atalanta drew her daggers and slipped inside with Eryx right behind her.

A dark hallway stretched out to either side of them. The little bit of light that filtered through the cracks around the balcony door lit up a blue tiled floor and textured walls. It was so quiet their breathing seemed to thunder all around them. There was no way to tell what might be down either side.

Atalanta turned left and crept forward. They had only made it a short distance when light filled the hall. She threw an arm up and tried to blink the stars out of her eyes. Voices could be heard and she pressed close to the inside wall.

A door only a few paces in front of them had been thrown open, allowing the bright light inside to spill out into the hall. The voices of people burbled and flowed. Though she couldn't understand the words, the tones sounded friendly and jovial. She doubted they would remain that way if anyone saw her and Eryx crouched in the hallway.

She motioned for Eryx to back up. They crept away from the door. Before they could retreat into the shadows, a woman exited the room. Her skin was pale with an odd lustre to it and her incredibly long hair was silver with streaks of pale blue. She wore a simple gown; its elegance in the undulating blue and green colours of the fabric. The woman turned toward them and her eyes widened. Atalanta raised a finger to her lips and tried to will the woman to silence.

A burbled question came from inside the room. The woman burbled something back, laughed, and shut the door. Shells embedded in the walls of the hallway sprang to life, casting pale blue light over them. The woman smiled and pressed a finger to her own lips. Atalanta relaxed and straightened up from her crouch. The woman gestured for them to follow her as she headed down the hall they'd come from.

"Who are you?" Atalanta whispered.

The woman made a hushing motion, her eyes darting around the empty hallway. Whatever she saw, or didn't see, made her shoulders hunch. She hurried forward, pausing only long enough to gesture for them to keep up. By the time the woman stopped in front of a plain door, both Eryx and Atalanta were out of breath. She looked as if they'd only been for a leisurely stroll. She opened the door and gestured them through, glancing both ways down the hall before following them in and locking the door. The room was almost bare. It held a simple bed, an end table, and a small wardrobe. The woman smiled at her, eyes bright and hands clasped. "You are Poseidon's daughter."

223

Atalanta blinked. "Uh, distant daughter," she replied.

"We had begun to despair you would ever come."

Eryx cleared his throat. "I thought people believed Paraskeve was the one prophesied to end the Usurper's reign?"

The woman nodded slowly. "That was the belief, when the prophecy was first made, but…she never did anything. She hid and caused some problems for the guards, but she never directly made a move on A—" Her voice cut off and her skin flushed as if she couldn't get enough air.

"Are you all right?" Atalanta asked.

The woman nodded. "I still sometimes forget we cannot say her name in a negative way."

"Who are you?" she asked.

"I am one of the Usurper's sisters."

Atalanta's breath caught and she gripped her daggers tighter. "You're what?"

"Her sister," the woman said, as simply as if she were saying the sky was blue. "My name is Neaera. I will not lie and tell you all of our sisters oppose her, but there are some. She can be a cruel and fickle ruler. Though her ire is most often directed toward the mortals, we have borne the brunt of it from time to time."

"How can we trust you?" Eryx asked.

Neaera turned and pulled her long hair aside. The dress was cut so low her entire back was exposed. Scars covered her back so thickly it looked as if they'd been woven atop her skin. Many were the silver-white of healed flesh, but a few were still red and puckered. "I am one of the lucky ones," she said, her voice soft. "She has only cut my back. Two of my sisters have had their faces marked, and one…one was so mutilated, the Usurper had a porcelain mask made to hide the sickening extent of the damage."

Atalanta could only stare in horror. "How could someone do this to their sister?"

Neaera let her hair fall over her back and turned to face them again. "It only happens when I betray my Queen's trust."

"What could you have possibly done to justify this?" she asked, her anger clawing its way up her throat.

"I have been too slow to respond to her summons, or did not complete my task to her satisfaction," she explained, her voice flat and unaffected, as if she were simply listing the days of the week. "Once, I dropped a pitcher of wine and it shattered. She was..." Neaera paused and blinked back tears before smiling. "Our Queen's justice is swift and decisive."

"That's not justice," Eryx said, his brows low over his eyes.

"You don't have to suffer under the Usurper any more," Atalanta said, her anger over Hazina spreading to include Neaera and her sisters. "I swear we will make her pay for every drop of blood she's spilt."

Neaera frowned for a moment, and then a wide smile spread across her lips. "Of course, Atalanta. It is good to know who the prophesied daughter is."

"Wait, how do you know her name?" Eryx asked, his shoulders tense and fists curled.

A flash of panic filled her eyes, but it disappeared as she laughed. "You told me it, of course."

"No, I didn't," Atalanta said. She looked at Neaera anew and realized her grief had blinded her to the thin sheen of sweat on the woman's brow, and the hungry gleam in her eyes, and the way she'd flinched, ever so slightly, every time they said Usurper instead of Queen.

"You must have," she said, a hysterical edge to her voice.

"No, Neaera, I did not."

Eryx took a step forward. There was a dark, predatory look on his face as he glowered down at her. "You have just a single moment to tell us what is going on, before we make you."

Neaera flashed her teeth at them in a feral grin. "The true Queen of the Oceans has promised great prizes for capturing the prophesied daughter."

Before they could respond, she leapt at them with a snarl. She swiped at Eryx, leaving red scratches on his cheek. He stumbled back, his eyes wide. Her second swipe at his face was easily blocked, and she spun toward Atalanta who had already drawn back.

"You don't need to do this," Atalanta said, dancing back from her slashing nails. "We'll overthrow the Usurper, and you'll be free."

"Free? Free?!" Neaera burst into hysterical laughter. She launched herself forward, hands wrapping around Atalanta's neck.

Atalanta gasped, black spots dancing across her gaze from the force with which Neaera's hands had hit her. She brought her daggers up and buried them in her stomach. Blood washed over her hands, but the pressure didn't let up. She wrenched the daggers up until they stopped with a jerk at the ribs.

Blood dribbled from Neaera's mouth and she let out a choking laugh. "My sister...will kill you...like your friend."

Atalanta's heart seemed to stop. "Damien?" She ripped the daggers out and dropped them to the floor. She grabbed Neaera's shoulders and gave her a shake. "Has she already killed Damien? Answer me!"

"Atalanta...she's dead," Eryx said, laying a gentle hand on her shoulder.

She shook with anger. The room blurred, and it wasn't until Eryx pulled her into a hug that she realized she was crying. He didn't say anything. He simply held her while she sobbed.

Damien's head throbbed. He was glad to find himself in an almost perfectly dark room. The walls were cool and smooth, and almost far enough apart for him to stretch out. Though the door looked like a piece of art with its curling, gate-like appearance, it was indisputably a prison door. His stomach clenched and he rolled over, expelling the contents of his stomach into a corner.

"They don't clean the cells very often...or ever," a voice commented, a thread of bitter amusement running through it.

"Wha—?"

"You should aim for the piss pot next time."

Damien wiped his mouth on his sleeve and sat up. He was on a tiny stone bed with a layer of something soft and musty on top. It was too narrow and too short for him, but it kept him off the gritty floor. Though it was took dark to make out much more than the outline of things, he thought he saw a cell door across from his.

"Who are you?" he asked.

"Someone who doesn't learn," the voice replied. It was soft, with a deep, lyrical edge to it, as if the speaker was more used to signing than talking.

"That hardly seems a reason to be imprisoned," he said.

"Mm. How did you come to be here?"

Damien closed his eyes and tried to remember what happened. "I was trying to find an entrance to the palace when someone grabbed my cloak and tore it off me."

"It was foolish to try and sneak past the guards," the voice commented. "There is rarely a moment where at least one set isn't marching along each side of the palace."

"Yes, well, I had thought being invisible would help me slip past," Damien returned dryly.

The voice was silent for a moment. "You have—had—a cloak of shadows?"

"Yes."

"And someone pulled it off of you?"

Damien rolled his shoulders. "I think so. The guards hit me pretty hard and everything is a bit...fuzzy, at the moment."

"Did you see who?"

"No. Maybe. There might have been a man made of shadows," he said. "Though that sound ridiculous."

The voice laughed. "You are locked up in the former palace of Poseidon. There are sirens, kelpies, aspidochelone eggs, kidnapped mortals, and a power hungry usurper elsewhere in this damnable place. I would not be surprised to learn of shadow men, or other strange beings."

"Truthfully, I'm surprised I'm still alive."

"The guards would never dare kill someone without the Usurper's permission. If you are of no importance, I'm sure the guards will deal with you within the next day, or so."

He swallowed and slid a foot around the cell in search of the chamber pot. There didn't seem to be one. "And, uh, what if I am of some importance?"

"Then the Usurper will kill you herself."

"Why are you still alive?"

The voice laughed bitterly. "The Usurper likes to take her time. She's slowly whittling away at me, until there's nothing left to cut. Then she will kill me. If she's feeling merciful."

Damien shivered and gritted his teeth against the urge to vomit again. "I need to get out of this cell."

"What would you do if you were free? Would you run?"

He didn't even have to think about his answer. "No. I would find my companions and kill the Usurper."

"You were not alone?" the voice asked.

"I was alone when I was captured, but I'm sure they were able to succeed where I failed."

The voice pointed out, "If you couldn't make it in wearing a cloak of shadows, what hope would your companions have?"

Damien couldn't help but smile. "They are very resourceful."

"If you say so," the voice said dubiously.

He stood and had to brace himself against the cell walls while a wave of dizziness washed over him. The walls and the door were made of the same impossibly smooth material as the railing overlooking Nereus's city. He doubted he would be able to get a good enough grip to even attempt to pull the door off its hinges. By pressing himself against the door, he could see a distant light flickering at the end of a long hallway. There were no sounds or signs of movement.

A sharp click made him turn his head. His nose smashed into one of the curls of the door and he stumbled back, tears in his eyes.

"Careful," the voice chided playfully.

A second click preceded his door opening. A figure swathed in a tattered robe stood in the doorway. The hood cast their face in shadow, but they were short and thin, and the hand holding the door open was curled from crooked fingers and thick scars puckering the skin.

"Who are you?" he asked again.

The figure blew out a long breath. "I no longer have a name. I am a plaything, a torment, and a reminder."

Damien frowned. For all that the person was articulate, he suspected they were not entirely sane. "How did you open the doors?" he wondered aloud.

"I have a key."

"Why haven't you escaped then?"

The figure laughed. "There is nowhere to escape to. Across the rolling plains to the overgrown forest of shadows? No. I stay and I pray. Someday I will be free of my flesh, and then I shall escape these halls forever."

"Right…are you going to stop me from leaving?"

The figure cocked its head to the side. "Why bother? You'll either be brought back, or killed."

Damien gritted his teeth and moved to brush past the figure. They backpedaled quickly, flinching away from him. He paused and studied the figure. "Do you want to come with me?"

"No. No, no, no. I won't wear the mask again," they said shaking their head emphatically.

"Mask?" he asked, frowning back at them. "What mask?"

The figure raised shaking hands and slid the hood off their face. Damien sucked in a sharp breath and stared in horror at what had once been a woman. Scars knotted across her forehead so thickly they extruded further than her brows. Her cheeks and jaws had been cut away until there was just a thin layer of tissue between bone and air. The outline of every single tooth could be clearly seen—and half of her teeth were missing or broken. Splotches of colour further marred her skin. Damien recognized the shiny red of healed burns, but wasn't sure what would have caused the silvery or purple ones to form. One eye was missing, a withered, blackened socket all that remained. The other held a world of pain he couldn't even begin to comprehend.

"Though this is her work, it displeases her to look upon me," she said, a tremor running through her voice.

He shook his head. "What the Usurper has done to you is terrible."

She ducked her head. "If I had not spoken out, she would not have

229

have done this."

"There is no amount of blame that should rest on your shoulders," he said, lifting her chin with a gentle finger. "She is a tyrant, and a monster."

She shrank back from him and shook her head. "I won't go. I won't bow to her, but I can't be hurt again."

Damien started to say he would protect, but then sighed. He didn't have time to argue with her, and after the damage—both physical and emotional—done to the poor woman, he wasn't sure he would ever be able to entice her away from the cells. Instead, he bowed his head to her and said, "All right. Thank you for letting me out."

She nodded absently and retreated back into her cell. With the door closed, she turned a thin key in the lock until it clicked.

Damien shook his head and turned his attention to the distant light. No one had responded to his conversation with the broken woman. Whether that was because they were too far to hear, or simply not guarding the cells was impossible to tell. He felt vulnerable and exposed as he crept toward the light. The hall was empty, save for the decorative prison doors every five feet or so. He paused at the first several to check if other people were locked in them, but all the cells were empty.

It took longer than he expected to reach the light. He stared at it for a moment, unsure what to do next. It was a simple candle on an empty table, with a cupboard behind it. He wondered if the cupboard was where they kept confiscated items, but it wasn't large enough to hold his sword.

The cupboard doors didn't open when he tugged on the handle. He held the candle up to the seam between the doors, squinting to see what sort of latch held them closed. The thin bit of metal didn't seem too sturdy. He put the candle down and yanked on the doors until there was a splintering sound and one of the handles ripped out. The hole it left was big enough for him to slip a finger inside and flick the latch.

There was an odd assortment of items inside the cupboard. Several candle stubs, a dented cup, two arrows, and his quail brooch. He picked up his brooch. It was warm in his hand. Without his cloak, he simply pinned it to his tunic and continued down the hall.

He didn't know where he was going, but he followed the winding halls, took three flights of stairs down, and wandered without stop. He never hesitated when he came to a junction, choosing his path almost without thought. It wasn't until he came upon a slice of light spilling from a slightly ajar door that he paused. It was the first light since the candle and his eyes adjusted slowly. There was the faint sound of voices, and he crept to the door to peer inside.

A room filled with over-sized cushions, luscious rugs, and low chaises lay before him. Six women cradled strange looking babies, cooing and speaking softly to them. He squinted. The babies were porcelain pale, hairless, with black eyes and sharp teeth. The women, on the other hand, looked perfectly human.

One of the babies made a strange noise, halfway between a cry and a sing-song coo. The woman holding it lifted the baby, bared her breast, and stared ahead without blinking as the thing latched on. Damien could see blood trickling down the little monster's chin.

He slipped inside the room. The women didn't even seem to notice him. One of the baby-monsters let out a startled wail. All six women turned to look at him with identical frowns on their faces.

"Who are you? What are you doing here?" the woman feeding one of the monsters demanded.

"Are you the women from around Otranto?" he asked.

The women stared at him blankly.

"The women kidnapped from their homes? From their families?" he pressed.

One of the woman, her face vaguely familiar, frowned in confusion. She squeezed her eyes shut and shook her head. She opened her mouth to speak, but the creature she held wailed. The noise pierced through him, like the stab of a knife. The frowning woman gasped and cradled the creature to her chest.

Damien growled. "Let these women go."

The baby-monsters stared at him with unblinking eyes. The one feeding had stopped, its mouth ringed in red and the woman's bare breast showing the bite mark clearly. One of the creatures burbled something, and then they were all burbling.

"What the—"

"Yes, yes, I'm coming," someone called from out in the hall.

Damien quickly backed up to the wall. A woman with a mass of blue-grey hair entered the room. She wore a dress of shifting blue and white and her skin had an almost green tinge to it. A large, white sphere was cradled in her hands. It wasn't quite a foot across, but the way she held it against her body suggested it was heavy. It took him a moment to recognize the egg.

"Here we are," she said, walking up to the women and burbling babies. "Hush now, I can't understand you when you all speak at once."

The babies fell silent, their eyes still locked on Damien. The blue-haired woman set the egg down and hit the top with her fist. Cracks spiderwebbed across the surface. She peeled off part of the top and picked up a small chalice from beneath one of the chaises. She gave the chalice a shake and then dipped it into the sphere, filling it with a golden liquid.

"All right, now drink up, my little otters," she said, holding the chalice to the lips of the first baby-creature.

Damien silently moved behind the blue-grey-haired woman. The creatures burbled and gesticulated toward him, but the woman ignored them, focusing on the one slurping greedily at the liquid in the chalice. He unpinned his brooch, grabbed a fistful of her hair, and pressed the edge of the brooch against her neck.

The woman froze, her hand trembling and eyes rolling back in an attempt to see him. "Don't..."—she licked her lips—"please don't hurt me. Or the children."

"And what of the Otranto women?" he asked, pulling her head back further.

The woman whimpered.

Damien growled and shifted his gaze to the baby-like creatures. They all stared at him with wide, unblinking eyes. He couldn't tell what they might be thinking or feeling. Were they afraid, angry, or something else? They weren't burbling any more. He thought that was a good thing.

"Let the mortals go," he demanded.

"I can't!"

He pressed the edge of the brooch harder against her neck and tears welled in her eyes.

"I am only a nereid—all the mortals are ensnared by sirens," she said, her voice quivering.

"All? How many are there?"

"I don't know." She flinched when Damien gave her hair a sharp tug. "I swear—on Poseidon's beard! There are about ten women and almost twice as many men. But the sirens take the mortals away when they have been used up, and bring new ones when they're bored. No one but the sirens actually know how many mortals are in the palace."

Damien's jaw clenched. He couldn't leave the women—or any of the other imprisoned people—to the sirens' devices, but he also needed to find Atalanta and Eryx. Surely putting an end to the Usurper's reign would help the kidnapped victims. He pulled the woman to her feet by her hair and asked, "Where can I find the Usurper?"

The woman's eyes flashed and her mouth twisted. "You call her an usurper, but she is our rightful Queen. She rescued us, and has brought a golden age upon this kingdom. The mortals have forgotten their place, and she is making them remember."

"She is a murderer and a tyrant," he shot back.

The woman burbled something and the baby-creatures began shrieking. The noise was so loud and piercing it was as if nails were being driven into his eyes and ears.

Damien released the woman and pressed his hands against his ears in a futile attempt to drown out the sound. His knees buckled and he hit the floor so hard his teeth rattled. The room spun and tipped. The captured women stood, holding the wailing monsters, and surrounded him. Wave after wave of sound pounded against his senses. His stomach roiled, he vomited, and collapsed completely. The last thing he saw before the world went dark were several armed men rushing into the room.

The palace was a labyrinth. It circled endlessly, with stairs leading up or down to yet more spiraling hallways. Eryx wanted to burn the place to the ground and be done with it. Atalanta trailed listlessly behind him as they descended yet another set of stairs. She radiated an aching numbness. It made his skin itch. He said a silent prayer of gratitude that she was at least moving silently.

"We have to be below the level of the plain by now," he said softly.

Atalanta bobbed her head. He doubted she'd actually understood.

With a stifled sigh, he continued on. After their encounter with Neaera, he avoided all other denizens of the palace. Even when they passed a room with several mortals inside. He doubted they would be unguarded if they weren't on the Usurper's side. Whether their support was magically induced or not wasn't important. Killing the Usurper and getting out alive was the only thing that mattered.

Eryx paused and gestured for Atalanta to hold. She stopped, her shoulders hunched and eyes empty. He turned toward the open door several feet in front of them. A faint glow of light spilt from where the door had been left ajar. The soft murmur of voices tugged at him. Inch by inch, he crept forward, only catching a few words every now and then. His jaw ached from how tightly he clenched his teeth. It wasn't until he was directly next to the door that he could reliably make out what was being said.

"You are certainly tenacious," a woman said. Her voice was soft and lilting. It called to mind lazy mornings in bed next to a lover. "If you weren't such a thorn in my side, you would make a diverting inamorato."

"Just as well. I doubt I would enjoy your bed," a man replied. His voice was muffled and slightly slurred. Eryx frowned. It sounded familiar.

A crack of flesh hitting flesh rang out. "You will address our Queen with more respect, cur."

"Calm, my daughter," the lilting-voiced woman said. "He has been beaten enough—his words are simply false bravado."

"As you say, Mother."

Eryx leaned forward and peered through the open door. A man with dark hair and skin lay crumpled at the feet of the most beautiful woman he had ever seen. She was short and delicate, with a heart shaped face, strong nose, heavy brows, and plump lips. Her skin was an off-white with blue-green highlights and green hair cascaded almost to the floor. Three other woman stood nearby. One had identical colouring, but was taller and broader. The other two were pale-skinned and blonde.

"Now, my sirens may not be able to charm you, but my daughter will happily beat the truth out of you. Would it not be simpler to tell me what I want to know?" the beautiful woman asked.

"Go to Hades," the man said. He pushed himself up slowly and awkwardly. Eryx's breath caught.

Damien.

Blood marred Damien's face and his arms shook from the effort of rising to his knees. His lip was split and swollen. Yet he straightened and faced the women. Eryx couldn't fully see his face, but the stiffness of his shoulders said he was glaring at his captors.

The taller woman growled and flexed her fists. "Why do you toy with this mortal? Kill him and be done with it."

"He has friends here, creeping through my palace," the beautiful woman replied, her mouth tightening into the briefest of frowns before smoothing into a patient smile. "Should they make it past the guards, the sirens, my sisters, and your sisters—"

"No one can make it past them all," the taller woman protested.

The beautiful woman openly frowned at her daughter. "Desma, would you care to enlighten Ianthe on the danger of these particular mortals?"

One of the blonde women nodded. "Of course, my Queen." She shot Damien a scathing look before turning to the taller woman. "He travels with a brutish woman descended from Medusa and a snake-tailed woman. They killed one of my sisters a year ago, and hurt another's spirit so severely she can no longer sing. Then a fortnight back, they attacked one of the children, killed one of the brothers, and—"

"Yes," Ianthe interrupted. "I was there both times these failures were reported."

Desma seethed. "You might be Amphitrite's daughter, but you have never contributed to the glory of the sea."

Eryx tuned out Desma and Ianthe arguing and turned back to Atalanta. "Two things," he whispered. "It seems the Usurper is Amphitrite."

Atalanta nodded, her gaze skittering along the hall.

He sighed and continued, "And Damien is still alive."

Her eyes instantly snapped to him. "What?"

"Damien's alive. Not sure for how much longer—though if one of the sirens and Amphitrite's daughter keep arguing, it could be awhile before they get around to killing him."

Her expression didn't change beyond a flicker of her eyes, but Eryx had to take a step back as the force of her emotions slammed into his senses. There was relief, obviously, but the pure, unbridled anger pouring off of her hurt. It was like sticking his hand into a fire.

She pulled the trident out of her bag, her knuckles white from how hard she gripped it. "As much as I want to rush in and kill the bitch, we probably should make a plan," she said.

Eryx nodded and turned back to the doorway. He couldn't see the whole room without pushing the door open further, and the arguing women wouldn't provide enough of a distraction for that to go unnoticed. The room could possibly be called a throne room. There was a large chair made from what could only be the shell of an adolescent aspidochelone. A collection of velvet and tasseled cushions were strewn over the chair's wide seat. It could have been a throne, or simply an extravagant chair. There was little else in the room beyond draped strings of softly glowing shells along the ceiling. He crouched low and stuck his head as far into the room as he could manage. Off to the side, behind the sirens, was another door. He tried to mentally measure the size of the room. Would the door be accessible from the hall, or did it lead to a small, adjacent room?

He pulled back and straightened before turning to Atalanta. "There might be another door in, further down the hallway."

She nodded and set off, her feet making almost no sound despite her hurried steps. Eryx quickly followed. They paused at the first door they came to. She nodded to him and he grasped the handle. Eryx shoved the door open and ran through. They were in a sitting room of some sort. Low couches and piles of cushions filled the space. There was no one there.

Atalanta kicked a cushion so hard it flew across the room and bounced off the far wall. Before he could say anything, she turned and left, continuing down the hall.

Eryx muttered and followed her. He didn't catch up until she stopped in front of the next door. This time, he pressed his ear to the door. He didn't hear anything. He shook his head and gestured for them to continue on. They had only made it a few feet when the door opened. The two sirens exited, talking softly to each other.

Atalanta darted forward, tucking the trident into the crook of her arm like a spear and drawing a dagger with her free hand. She thrust the trident into the back of one of them, the tines starting low and angling upward. Her dagger buried between the ribs of the other one. She gave it a twist and dragged it from near the spine out to beneath the shoulder blade. Both women crumpled to the ground when she wrenched her weapons free.

She turned back to Eryx, her face still blank. Blood coated the weapons and dripped down onto the ground. Her hands were still dark from the dried blood of Neaera. Standing there, with the light spilling from the open door behind her, she looked like an avenging fury. She thrust her chin toward the open door and he grimaced. Killing the sirens hadn't muted her anger in any way. It had merely honed it. It no longer burned. Instead, it felt as if a knife edge was being dragged excruciatingly slowly over his skin.

He slipped into the room the sirens had exited from. The small space appeared to be an antechamber to the throne room, with two benches and a smattering of cushions. The sirens had left the inner door ajar and the sound of a whip hitting flesh was clear. Eryx glanced at Atalanta. Her calm expression was starting to crack, letting her anger show. Hissing surrounded her. The writhing of her snakes made her hair look as if it were rippling in a breeze. Given the force of her anger, he was surprised the snakes were only now becoming agitated.

They stepped up to the next door. Eryx took a quick look through the opening. Ianthe and Amphitrite were facing away from them. Ianthe wielded a barbed whip while Amphitrite watched. Damien's back was bloody. Strips of fabric—hopefully only fabric—fluttered every time the whip snapped against him. Damien barely jerked from each lash. If he were unconscious already, then at least he wasn't feeling each blow.

Eryx nodded to Atalanta and slowly opened the door. It took a quick hand on her arm to stop her from rushing in to the room. She glared at him, her snakes hissing louder. He mimed throwing a knife.

Atalanta blinked. Some of the tension drained from her shoulders and she nodded. Her snakes settled, their hissing inconsistent and faint. She took a moment to study the room before raising her dagger. Eryx laid a soft hand on her shoulder and gave her a small smile. She drew in a deep breath and let it out slowly. Her arm snapped forward and the dagger sliced through the air before burying itself in the armpit of Ianthe.

Ianthe screamed, the whip falling from limp fingers. Amphitrite started to turn toward them, but Eryx slammed into her. They fell to the ground in a tangle of limbs. Despite her small size, he found himself struggling to keep her pinned.

"Mother!" Ianthe shouted. Her attempt to reach them was halted by quick thrusts of the trident from Atalanta.

Ianthe snarled and fumbled a short sword from her belt. She barely got it up in time to block a savage thrust. Blood welled along her arm where the tines had sliced. She stepped inside Atalanta's reach and slammed the sword's pommel up into her jaw.

Amphitrite used Eryx's distraction to throw him off. He skid along the floor a few feet, his ribs bruised from the force with which he hit the ground. Amphitrite was up on her feet before he'd even stopped sliding. She raised her hands, wrists bent down, while Atalanta and Ianthe struggled for control of the short sword. Her wrists flipped back and fingers curled.

Eryx climbed to his feet, an electric tingling sliding along his skin. Amphitrite's hair drifted around her body. It sounded as if a fountain had suddenly started in the middle of the room, though nothing was visibly different. He reached Amphitrite a moment before water rushed down on them from the ceiling. The force of it knocked him back and he sucked in a lungful of water before he was able to get his head above the rising liquid.

Both Atalanta and Ianthe had disappeared beneath the water. Amphitrite stood in the middle of the column of water cascading into the room, her hair and clothes only drifting as if she were in a still pool. Some of the cushions bobbed and swayed on the top of the water. Nothing and no one else was visible.

He took a deep breath and dove beneath the water.

Atalanta and Ianthe were still struggling. The water around them was tinted pink from their blood, and both women were bleeding from several cuts. Atalanta kicked away from Ianthe, grabbed the trident off the floor where she had dropped it, and launched toward her. Ianthe twisted away from the attack. One of the tines sliced open her side. A plume of red in the water said it was a deep cut.

Eryx tore his eyes away from the fight. He trusted Atalanta to survive. Damien, however, was injured and unconscious. Eryx swam to where he floated near the floor. Leather straps around wrists and ankles attached him to small, iron rings set into the floor. The knots were already swollen from the water. Eryx kicked to the surface—the water was a good foot deeper already—and took another gulp of air. He dove back to Damien and pulled him as upright as the straps would allow. When he crushed Damien against his body in a sharp hug, no bubbles escaped. Eryx held Damien's jaw and pressed their lips together, breathing air into him.

He let Damien float and turned his attention to the leather straps. They were thick and solid. He planted his feet on the floor, grabbed one of the straps and pulled as hard as he could. His arms and back burned from the strain. The iron ring snapped out of the floor so suddenly he would have fallen on his back if they hadn't been floating in water. Eryx was able to get a second ring out before his vision started to darken and lungs screamed.

This time, when he surfaced, the room was more than half full of water. It took several deep breaths to settle his lungs. He breathed as deeply as he could and dove back down to Damien. He gave him another sharp hug and was pleased when a few bubbles escaped. Once more he breathed into his mouth.

Eryx turned sharply when a body cut through the water next to them. He raised his fists before realizing that the body was Ianthe. With her throat torn open she wasn't much of a threat. He peered through the water and spotted Atalanta. She was bloody, but the trident was in her hand and she was almost upon Amphitrite.

Eryx ripped the third ring from the floor, trying to keep an eye on the fight. Atalanta stabbed Amphitrite, though not fatally. Amphitrite hit Atalanta in the chest with an open hand strike. It shouldn't have been enough to do more than possibly knock her breath out, but Atalanta was thrown back several feet, bubbles escaping her the entire way.

Once the third ring came free, he grabbed the last strap and pulled.

Atalanta righted herself, but instead of shooting to the surface to get more air, she swam right back at Amphitrite. This seemed to surprise the goddess as much as it surprised Eryx. This time, when the trident struck her, the tines went all the way through.

A cloud of blood coiled from Amphitrite's mouth. She grabbed Atalanta's head with both hands and slammed their foreheads together. Atalanta reeled back, losing her grip on the trident.

The final strap came free and Eryx kicked to the surface with his arms around Damien's chest. He gulped in air and struggled to position himself and Damien so they were both floating on their backs, with Damien's head supported by Eryx's chest. His arms were like lead and his head swam from the extended exertion without air.

The rush of water stopped.

Eryx tried to see, but could only make out dark blurs where Atalanta and Amphitrite fought. A flash of white light swallowed their forms and Eryx blinked stars from his eyes. Before he could see again, the water disappeared. They crashed to the ground, half landing on the aspidochelone throne. The sharp pain radiating through his back and ribs said something was broken. He groaned and rolled his head to the side.

Atalanta stood in the middle of the room, an arm wrapped around her middle and wet clothes clinging to her body. There was no sign of Amphitrite, though Ianthe's body lay in a crumpled heap on the far side of the room.

"Where...where is she?" he asked, wincing when the breath it took made his ribs scream in agony.

Atalanta coughed a little, water dribbling down her chin. "Dead."

"...body?" he managed to say.

She shrugged, her eyes turning toward them. Her brows pinched and she stumbled forward. She had to use the trident as a walking staff to make it to them. She dropped the trident and fell to her knees beside them. "Is he...is Damien—"

"He's alive," Eryx cut her off.

Atalanta nodded and dug around in her bag for a moment. She pulled out the three remaining fruits from Nereus. One for each of them. Eryx ate his while Atalanta cut one into tiny pieces and fed them to Damien.

The fruit seemed to burn this time. It lit a fire through his body, worse where he was injured. As the burn faded, he realized that so did his pain. He was sure his ribs had been broken, and maybe a few other things as well. Yet, now, he simply felt sore. He sat up and repositioned Damien on his lap. Though an entire fruit had been fed to him, he was still unconscious. Atalanta fingered the final fruit.

"You need to eat it," Eryx told her.

"Damien needs another one," she replied.

Eryx shook his head, eying her wounds. The ones on her arms and legs were only bleeding a little, but the one on her stomach had soaked her tunic, and didn't seem about ready to stop. "You'll die if you don't eat it."

"But Damien—"

"Is alive. He'll just have to heal the rest of the way on his own."

Atalanta grunted, but ate her fruit. Eryx was glad to notice the visible cuts on her skin knitting back together. He rolled Damien over and breathed a sigh of relief. The whip marks were all closed. Still red and only half-healed, but closed. Damien's chest rose and fell evenly. He was in no immediate risk of dying. They had, somehow, survived.

Damien

The shores of Centumcellae were a welcome sight after so long on *le Droit Margerie*. Eryx, Atalanta, the refugees from Methoni, and the rescued women from Poseidon's palace, had disembarked a fortnight before. Damien wished Atalanta, and even Eryx, would have stayed longer. The ship might have been his, but the sailors were still awkward about the hippocampi and aspidochelone. He understood the desire to return home though.

He watched the sailors, his sailors, unload the cargo they had purchased in Otranto. The city might have disliked outsiders, but they had nothing against outsiders' coin. He felt he had gotten a good price for the wines and dyed wools. Whether that was true or not, could only be discovered by successfully selling the goods in Centumcellae.

The harbour was a bustling hive of activity and he limped after his sailors as they wove their way through the crowd. One of the men, Zohane, led the march to where city merchants were buying things from fishing boats, cargo ships, and everything in between. Zohane had pushed to be made *le Droit Margerie*'s Quartermaster since they first took on cargo. Damien found the scruffy man to be gregarious and cunning, but he wasn't convinced such qualities were enough for the responsibility. Still, he had agreed to allow Zohane to direct the selling of the goods in Centumcellae.

Damien's attention wandered while Zohane haggled with the merchants. His body still hurt. Ached. No amount of praying to Ptokheia sped his healing. Atalanta had been annoyed that his goddess wouldn't help him, but he knew it was because they were out of danger. Why heal him when he had the luxury of healing naturally? It was still frustrating to fight against the stiffness left by scars and damaged muscles.

His lazy perusal of all the people moving around the docks was arrested by the sight of a young woman. She had rich brown skin and her black hair was only half contained by the complicated loops and braids common to women of wealth. The way her voluminous curls fanned around her shoulders with no veil or ornamentation was both beautiful and defiant. Her gown was a rich, creamy yellow with a swirling pattern of leaves and flourishes picked out in white, the sleeves and bodice alternating lines of blue and white. A plump woman with a ruddy face walked beside her, her lips constantly moving.

The beautiful woman didn't seem to be paying her companion any attention. Her gaze fell on Damien and he felt his breath catch. She began moving through the crowd toward him, her skirts clutched in her hands. The other woman hurried after her. It didn't take long before he could hear the plump woman's voice over the crowd.

"This is foolishness, Daniella! You mustn't spurn Nichola de Bennis! Think of your father! Your brother! What of your mother?" the woman shouted.

Daniella kept walking. Damien glanced around, wondering who she was heading for. There was no one obvious nearby whom a woman of status would be interested in talking to. His stomach tightened. Was she coming to speak to him?

She stopped a short distance from him, her eyes running over him appraisingly. He was acutely aware of his patched tunic and worn boots. The other woman huffed, clutching at her stomach, and glared at him. Daniella smiled and said, "My darling Tita, this is the man I told you about."

Tita sniffed and straightened, her glare just as fierce as before. "I cannot image a man such as this could make you a legitimate offer."

Damien blinked. Made her an offer? He was sure he'd never met her before. Not even a siren could have made him forget Daniella. Before he could think of anything to say, she stepped closer to him and laid a hand on his arm. He could feel the slightest tremor in it, but there was no hint of fear or nervousness in her face.

"He is a fine gentleman," she returned. "You must forgive his appearance—he has only just returned from a long voyage."

Zohane cleared his throat. Damien, Daniella, and Tita turned to look at him. "Sir, the sale has been made. Are the men free to enter the city for the night?"

"Yes. Thank you."

Zohane dipped his head and turned back to the sailors who were staring at Damien and the two women with open curiosity.

"See, Tita? He owns a merchant's ship!" Daniella turned back to the other woman.

Tita snorted. "A scoundrel can have men help him keep up his tricks. You will come back with me and accept Nichola's proposal."

Daniella's hand tightened on Damien's arm and her jaw clenched. Damien laid a hand over hers and said, "As it seems I have made an offer first, it would be unfair to all parties involved to pressure the lovely Daniella into accepting either proposal without first allowing me to be properly introduced to her father."

Tita's cheeks reddened further. "If you try to work your tricks on Goodman Balbus, I will personally call for the guards."

"This Nichola de Bennis, is he a very wealthy merchant?" Damien asked.

Tita made a noise of strangled disbelief. Daniella shook her head. "He is a master craftsman, to be sure, but is unknown beyond Centumcellae."

"Then I see no reason why your father should not prefer me—ours would be a very advantageous match."

Daniella gave him a sharp look. "Nichola has promised my brother, Alberto, that he will only sell his wares to him, so they might both profit."

"Your brother should never have encouraged you to fall in love. It will be his ruin," Tita wailed.

Damien nodded. "I am no craftsman, but between my lands and my ship I am sure I can offer something equally valuable."

"You have land?" Daniella blurted out.

He shrugged and nodded, a smile tugging at his lips. Her subterfuge was an enticing as her beauty. "I didn't tell you before because I rather enjoyed the romance of winning your heart as a simple merchant."

Tita glared some more. "We shall see if you are who you claim to be. Come. We will let Goodman Balbus sort this out." She turned and pushed her way through the crowd, stopping after a few feet to make sure they were following.

"Thank you, and I am very sorry to have made you lie," Daniella whispered.

Damien grinned. "What lie do you think I've told?"

She looked up at him, a small frown creasing her brow. "You've claimed to be gentry. I am confidant I can use the deception to get out of this preposterous marriage my father wants for me, so I am not mad, but you could get in trouble for it."

"You needn't worry. My family has owned land nearby for many generations."

Her steps faltered and she would have fallen if Damien didn't snake a quick arm around her waist. "I...I never would have inconvenienced you if I'd known. I just saw you with those sailors and I thought you might be a merchant, and—"

"It is my pleasure to help a fair maiden in need of assistance," he cut her off.

She shot him a shy smile. "Thank you, again. My father will be unable to insist on Nichola now. We need only pretend for a short time, and then we can think of a benign scandal to end the deception. Nothing that would ruin my family, but enough that other men will think twice before pressuring my father to give them my hand."

Damien's heart skipped a beat. "Why do you wish to avoid marriage?"

Daniella laughed. It was a rich sound, full of life, and ended in a small snort that enthralled him. She shook her head. "I am a poor merchant's daughter. One who is obviously not the dutiful daughter I am supposed to be. I would not be a dutiful wife—my brother says I do not know how to keep my thoughts to myself. There is no reason why someone would want to marry someone like me, except as a ploy to increase their wealth."

He smiled. "And what about love?"

She looked up at him and he felt he could have drowned in her eyes. "I would happily marry for love, but I'm not convinced it is real."

"Why not?"

"Please don't misunderstand me, sir," she said, untangling her gaze from his. "I love my family, and they love me. I have just never seen a couple whom married for anything other than practical reasons. Money, status, avoiding a scandal, or forming an alliance."

Damien scratched his chin and silently berated himself for not having shaved the scruff before they reached Centumcellae. "I suppose those factors would be at play in any marriage, but that doesn't mean there isn't love there. After all, love can grow in the strangest of places."

She chuckled. "True enough, sir."

"If we are to be engaged, for however long that might be, you should probably call me by my given name—Damien," he said.

She glanced up at him in surprise, then bit her lip and quickly looked away. "Very well...Damien."

He leaned down so he could whisper in her ear, "You might come to regret picking me for this subterfuge, Daniella. I'm not the sort to do anything by half measures."

Her breath hitched and he grinned. However things played out, he would enjoy every moment he got to spend next to her. Especially when he could fluster her like that.

Atalanta

Atalanta's feet ached by the time she could see the roofs of Tudela on the horizon. "There it is," she told Eryx. "Home."

"Do you really believe your friend will be able to offer me employment?" he asked for the hundredth time since leaving Damien's ship.

"Of course. Hector is a dear friend. He would do it as a favour to me, even if you weren't fit for it," she reassured him.

Eryx gave her a look, one she'd come to be familiar with during their long journey from Otranto. It was the same one he gave her whenever she spoke of home and Hector. Somewhere between amusement and puzzlement. He never said anything though, and she didn't have the energy to disabuse him of whatever odd notions he held. They continued on in silence.

The thought of her home—a tiny wattle-and-daub structure—spurred her to walk faster. It wasn't much. A main room with an open hearth, raised pallet, and an odd assortment of stools clustered around a battered table. The second room was barely large enough to stand beside an old washtub, but it afforded an amazing sense of privacy when she used it to bathe, rather than it's usual purpose of cleaning her clothes. It was the first place she had ever truly considered 'home.' She could picture it, with a fire burning in the hearth, and perhaps even a pot of water set to boil. The image of Hector waiting for her was a little surprising, but it mostly filled her with a disappointed longing. If there were a way to let him know how close she was, she had no doubt he would go and tend the hearth so it would be just as she pictured when she got there.

"There's no need to rush," Eryx grumbled. "It isn't as if there will be a warm meal waiting for us."

She flushed. Had she spoken her wishful thoughts aloud? She gave herself a shake and laughed ruefully. "I know, but we're so close. I don't want to spend another night sleeping beside the road."

He smiled. "Is that really the reason?"

"Of course. What other reason could there be?"

"I've found it's usually a person, and not a place, that makes someone anxious to get home."

She didn't know what to say to that, so she ignored him. His knowing chuckle made her flush all over again. Thankfully, he didn't push the issue further. It didn't take much longer before they reached the ebb-and-flow of people whose lives revolved around Tudela without taking place within the city itself. It was only a little farther to reach the narrow street lined by the cramped homes of small families, elderly couples, retired whores, and her. Their journey was halted when someone called out to her. She turned to see a woman with pinched cheeks and broad hands waving at her. Though the woman's hair was still pure black, her face was creased by more wrinkles than there were patches on her clothes.

"Still wearing men's clothes, I see," she said, the only thing to suggest her disapproving tone wasn't in full earnest was the smile that lit her eyes.

"Aye, Goodwoman Colmenares," she replied. "Eryx, this is Goodwoman Colmenares, an old busy-body who lives near me."

Goodwoman Colmenares chortled. "A pleasure to meet Atalanta's brother at long last."

Atalanta and Eryx exchanged a puzzled look. "Eryx isn't my brother."

"Oh?" Her eyebrows rose to an alarming height as she looked between the two of them. "Does Hector know you've left him for someone else?"

"What are you talking about?" Atalanta asked, her weariness making it hard to keep from snapping.

Goodwoman Colmenares frowned. "I try to be understanding about you working—Heaven knows young women shouldn't be protected by brutish men—but I cannot be silent if you're cavorting about with other men. Especially not now, that Hector has made you a proposal."

Atalanta gaped at her, the words somehow having lost all meaning.

Goodwoman Colmenares bit her lip and fluttered her hands. "Oh, dear. Was I not supposed to know? Hector didn't actually tell me. I put it together when he said you had gone to see your brother."

Eryx gave her a smile that she dubiously returned. "It was supposed to be kept private, Goodwoman...Colmenares, was it?" At her nod, he continued. "I am Atalanta's cousin. Her brother was unable to leave Italy at the moment, so I've come in his stead, to see our dear girl married at last. I would appreciate it greatly, if you wouldn't mention the engagement to anyone else. At least, not until the banns are announced."

Atalanta felt as if her mind were wrapped in ice. She couldn't follow the brief conversation between Eryx and Goodwoman Colmenares. She wasn't even sure how they found their way to her house. But the next thing she knew, he was gently pushing her inside. Despite the lack of fire or boiling water, it was exactly as she'd pictured it. Some of the tension drained from her. As tiny and simple as it was, her home was her refuge. She took the few steps across the room to sit heavily on the edge of her bed.

Eryx eyed her warily. "Stay right here, I'll be back in a little."

She nodded absently, not really registering that he was leaving. Her thoughts were too busy tangling up upon themselves. She didn't want to get married. Hector was one of her dearest friends. His lover would not be happy. Tudela wouldn't have so easily become 'home' if it weren't for him. As much as she might wish otherwise, she was never able to make a permanent home anywhere. Her curse and lifestyle always meant she'd either have to leave, or be driven out. People were much more willing to overlook a married woman's eccentricities than a single woman's. She wouldn't make a good wife. Not for Hector. Not for anyone. But she loved him.

"Atalanta?"

She gave a start and stared into Hector's eyes. "Where did you come from?"

"Your friend fetched me," he said, gesturing to Eryx who stood a few paces away, watching her anxiously.

Her muddled thoughts straightened enough for her to realize she was angry. Angry at Goodwoman Colmenares for sticking her nose into other people's business. Angry that society viewed an unmarried woman as a problem. Angry that Hector hadn't done anything to nip the rumour in the bud. And angry that she would never be able to enjoy the normalcy of marriage.

She pushed off the bed and stood up, giving Hector a little shove so he stumbled away from her. "What were you thinking?"

"I was trying to protect you," he protested.

"From what? Rumours? Do you think people will be suddenly more understanding when we don't get married? Do you think I'll actually be able to stay here, now?"

"Atalanta—"

"No, Hector. I can't believe you told *Goodwoman Colmenares* I was going to see my brother!" she shouted. "You know what she's like. She only needs a wisp of cloud to decide there's a fire."

He straightened and frowned at her. "Did I lie? You told me yourself that Damien is like a brother," he returned. "Haven't you just come back from seeing him?"

She blinked, some of her fire dimming. He had a point. But he also hadn't stopped the rumour. "And what does Lucas think of all this? I can't imagine he likes the idea of me replacing him in your bed."

Hector paled and he squeezed his eyes shut for a moment, drawing a long breath in. "Lucas left shortly after you did."

Atalanta's heart seemed to stop. She took a small step toward him. "I'm sorry. I knew how much he meant to you."

He shook his head. "I'm only grateful he didn't start a rumour about that, before he took off."

"Was it that bad of a split?"

Hector hesitated a moment before nodding. Atalanta felt her heart break for him. She closed the slight distance between them, and pulled him into a hug. His arms slid around her waist and crushed her against him while his shoulders shook with silent sobs.

"Shh," she soothed, rubbing his back. "It'll be okay. You still have me."

He sniffed and pulled away, somewhat reluctantly. "Do I?"

She wiped a tear off his cheek. "Of course. We'll figure things out."

Eryx cleared his throat and they both turned toward him in surprise. He'd been so quiet they'd forgotten he was there. "If I may make a suggestion?"

"Who is your attractive friend?" Hector mock whispered.

Atalanta couldn't help but giggle. "Hector, this is Eryx. Eryx, this is Hector."

"Does he"—Hector raised an eyebrow and gave her a wink—"know about us?"

Eryx smiled. "I know you two are in love with each other, despite there being no sexual attraction. It's beautiful."

Hector blinked. "What?"

Atalanta patted his cheek. "Eryx isn't mortal. He can sense things, like emotions, and my ancient heritage."

Hector blew out a breath. "I didn't believe you when you first told me about the old gods, and even after I helped you get rid of that petrified brigand, I didn't think I would ever meet one."

"To be fair, you still haven't," Eryx put in.

He let out an exasperated chuckle and pressed a brief kiss on her forehead. "Life would never be boring with you as my wife."

"What?"

He dropped his arms from around her waist and captured her hands. "Atalanta Arrephori, you accept me for who I am, and, though I know there are still secrets in your heart, I would be honoured to make you my wife."

She gaped at him, her heart pounding in her chest. "I—"

"As her cousin, I approve," Eryx cut in.

She rolled her eyes. "You're not my cousin."

He grinned. "Close enough. Now, say yes."

Atalanta and Hector laughed. Though she never actually said the word, the smile she gave him was confirmation enough. The three of them spent the night laughing and talking about the future. It felt warm and comfortable, sitting between Hector and Eryx, daydreaming about the house they would all live in together. She wasn't sure at what point it had been decided Eryx would live with them, but it felt right. As right as it did to think of Hector as her fiancé. Her heart swelled, and she couldn't remember why she'd argued with Hazina, all those long days ago, about never wanting to get married.

Calista

A breeze slipped through crooked shutters and played with the frayed curtain hung along a wall before tangling in Calista's black curls. She barely even noticed. Her attention was focused on the symbols painted on her only table. Similar symbols covered ever surface in the one-room house—even on the blankets left in a heap on the bed.

The wall behind the curtain was the only place where the symbols had any semblance of order. Lines connected the symbols there, creating a web across the rough wood which half-hid the marks of hundreds of symbols being painted and then scraped off. Calista's fingers were stained from the paints, and splatters marred her gown and face. It had been several weeks since she cared.

"You need to look after yourself," a voice interrupted her concentration.

She looked up and stared blankly at Hazina for a moment before a smile broke across her face. Hazina's hair was in its usual bun atop her head, but she wore a loose chiton and shawl of rich purple, trimmed in gold. "Being dead suits you."

Hazina's mouth pinched. "I would be more comfortable in my own clothes, but Nereus insists."

"How long has it been?" Calista asked.

"Since when?"

"Since you died? Since Atalanta married? Since they defeated the *daemon*?"

Hazina shook her head. "You have spent too long in your visions, my friend. It has only been a little more than a fortnight since my death. Those other events have not happened yet."

Calista rubbed her forehead and sighed. "There are so many threads to follow...I can't see how they can survive it all."

"Survival may not be the best outcome," she pointed out. "I do not have your gift, and neither does Nereus, but I can see some of the paths before us. And all roads lead to Hades."

Calista shoved away from the table and trudged over to a bucket of water. A chipped cup floated on the surface and she scooped it up, swallowing a mouthful of the stale liquid before dropping the cup back in the bucket. She spun to Hazina and fluttered her hands helplessly. "When the mantle passed to me, I was so hopeful. The old gods will sleep or die, and the natural balance of this world will be restored. Such an ending should be happy."

"Will it not be?"

"Not if they both die!"

Hazina nodded a little, plucking absently at the fabric of her dress. "You are not worried about a good ending, but one that makes you happy."

"That's not true. I—"

"Would rather watch the world burn?"

Calista dropped her eyes from Hazina's gaze. She knew she was being selfish. She knew, far better than Hazina did, what the cost would be if they walked away at the end. And yet she still went days without rest, searching the future possibilities for a way to save as many of her friends as she could.

"You have a role to play," Hazina said, her voice soft and sympathetic. "You must take care of yourself so you will be able to do what needs to be done."

"I won't stop looking."

"I never asked you to."

Calista nodded and lifted her gaze back to Hazina. The early evening light spilt through the cracks in the shutters. Beams of light passed through her body, picking up a faint purple hue as they did. Even as she watched, she could see Hazina fading away. "Do you have to go so soon?"

Hazina smiled ruefully. "It is tiring to appear this way."

"You could come to me in my dreams instead."

She laughed. "I would, if you ever slept."

Calista chuckled and ran a hand through her curls, wincing when her fingers snagged in the tangles. "Well, I will see you soon enough, I suppose. It has been a very long time since I entered the Between."

"Nereus told me of the *daemon*...I am sorry—"

Calista waved the concern away. "I always knew I would have to face him again. My only regret is that he'll harm our friends."

Hazina gave a final nod, her form so faint it was barely an outline against the symbol-covered walls of the room. "Be well, my friend. We will meet again soon."

Appendix

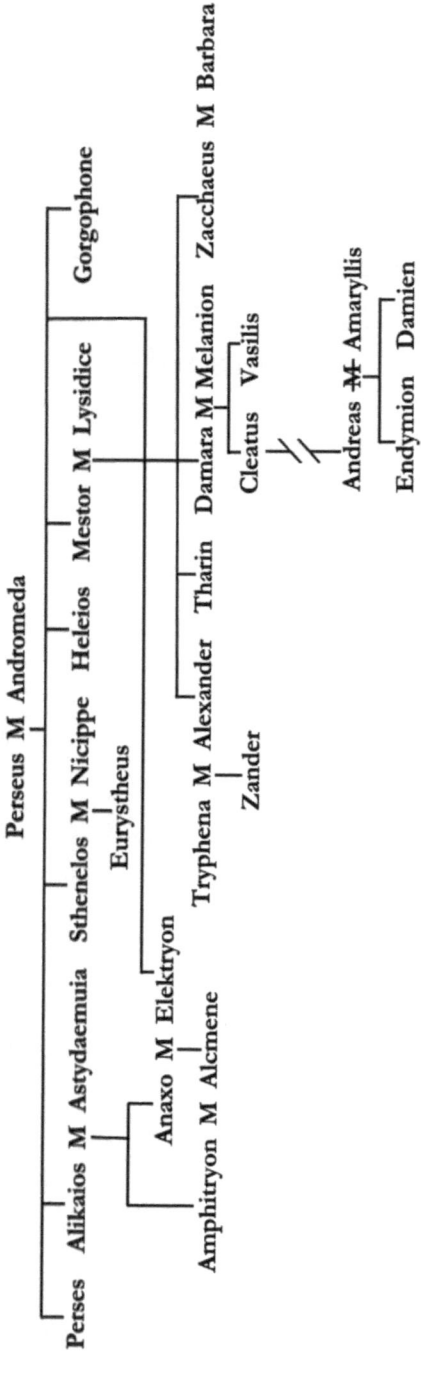

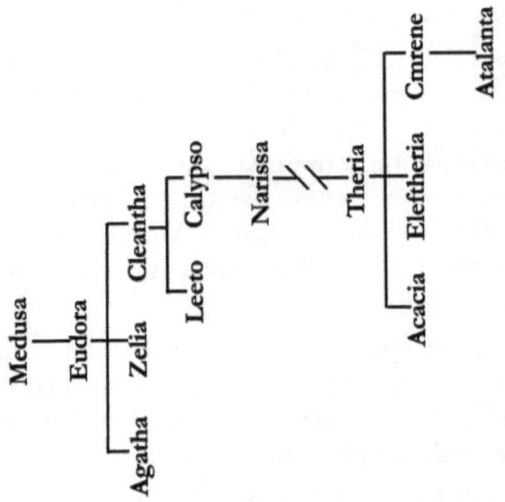

A Note on History and Fantasy Elements

The Legend's Legacy series is historical fantasy, and, as such, it aims to be historically accurate whenever possible. Much time and effort was put into researching places, customs, and the people who lived between 1488 and 1500. Any errors are my own, and not a reflection of the people or sources used to create these works.

This is the world my characters live in, but due to their fantastical heritages, they are not quite part of it. As such, there are many details about the tensions between countries, religious factions, and even individual cities that has been omitted or glossed over. It was a period of great change across the entire world. I highly recommend *The Mediterranean in History*, edited by David Abulafia to the curious. It is a good place to start, though there was much of interest happening elsewhere as well.

From historical accuracy, I'd like to turn to the biggest aspect of fantasy in the series—the nature of the gods and magic. There is some discussion in the books themselves in regards to these elements, though it may leave some readers with more questions.

In the reality inhabited by Atalanta, Damien, and their companions, the gods are extraplanar beings who crossed through the World Between Worlds (the Between) when their native world(s) began to die. Gods rely on human belief to exist. This 'feeding' on belief does not harm humans. There are also extraplanar beings, like Eryx, who feed on emotions. This doesn't harm humans, either. There are some, however, who feed on 'life force.' This is harmful. While some of the extraplanar beings who feed on these other human-generated forms of energy are considered gods, when I use the term, I am referring to the species of beings who feed on belief.

Human belief systems initially developed independent of the gods (or other extraplanar beings). The gods took advantage of the early pantheons, taking on the roles most suited to their personalities, temperament, and natural talents. Gods are able to use the power of belief to aid their followers and, in some instances, grant the devout special abilities. Through this direct involvement in human life, they shaped how these belief systems evolved.

It is important to note that not all divine figures across all religions are gods (or other extraplanar beings). And that in geographically similar locations, a single god may have different names among different groups—or even multiple names within a single group. For example, Mars and Ares are the same god despite their differences. Similarly, Apollo and Helios are the same god.

The differences are partly due to cultural differences among worshippers, and partly affected by the changing attitudes of the gods themselves.

In regards to semi-divine figures (such as demi-gods, powerful spirits, and personified forces of nature), some are gods or other extraplanar beings, some are "half breeds" (born to a god/extraplanar being and a human woman), or one of the few supernatural creatures native to Earth.

Extraplanar beings, gods included, have no physical form. They can 'posses' a human, or expend a small bit of power to create a form. It requires more energy to create a form that can interact with the physical world. Most extraplanar beings settle on a single form and do not change it in any significant way for centuries. Those who are comfortable changing forms are often trickster gods/figures in myth.

Gods, and some extraplanar beings, are able to grant their followers special abilities and powers. These may be abilities that the god possesses, or ones gained from human belief. Abilities gained through belief may or may not be ones the god can directly use. For example, Apollo personally has very limited prophetic ability, but he can grant the ability to his chosen followers with great accuracy/strength.

Powers/abilities granted by an extraplanar being have no easy explanation for the mechanics of how they work.

Magic, on the other hand, is natural. It has concrete rules and limitations. The innate level of magic in a human has very little to do with the types of magic they can perform. All magic users require years of study and practice. There is never any risk of accidental magic use, or of an untrained magic user losing control of their magic. A partially trained magic user could, conceivably lose control of their magic, but in 99% of the cases, this only harms the magic user.

Magic traditions vary around the world. They are based on how a culture perceives magic. Where magic is seen as asking spirits for help, that is how the magic users are trained to manifest their powers. While this type of visualization is less effective then direct use of magic, it is easier to learn. Learning one 'type' of magic does not preclude a person from learning a different 'type' later on.

A trained magic user is only limited by their senses, imagination, and personal energy.

The combination of human magic and godly powers is very potent. Gods often encouraged their priests/shamans/practitioners to find those with magical aptitude among the faithful to become initiates, so that in the event that a god required the combined force of magic and power, they would have individuals dedicated to them who could facilitate. Often this is done through a willing possession of the faithful.

Though the combination of magic and power is strong, it has not been able to help the gods combat the so-called "eternal sleep" that has claimed many of them. This is an affliction that the gods first saw in 1500 BCE. At that time, it was believed to be a side-effect of dwindling followers/belief to feed upon. The gods have since discovered that while a large number of followers offers some protection, it is not a significant amount. Those remaining have almost all chosen to remain on Earth, rather than the Between, to conserve energy.

When a god succumbs to the eternal sleep there are distinct effects on their followers and the world in general. First, any powers they granted will remain, but will slowly fade over time. Second, prayers, sacrifices, requests, and tributes to the god will go unanswered—this is very obvious to those who used to receive a response to such rituals. Finally, the god's area(s) of effect will no longer be able to be controlled by godly intercession. Other gods (especially those in geographically distant locations) who had access to the sphere of influence prior to the god succumbing to the eternal sleep will still be able to use their powers as normal (such as the many gods seen as presiding over the seas/oceans). This is of great concern to the gods, as a god who dies or gives up control does not prevent another god from taking on that sphere of influence.

Some gods, sensing that they are soon to fall to the eternal sleep, choose to pass their powers to another god, so that it isn't lost.

Religions that once had gods filling the roles of their deity/deities may or may not suffer as a consequence of the god(s) succumbing to the eternal sleep. In some cases, this marks the start of the religion falling out of favour, or of mass conversions, but not always. Some religions do better without the involvement of a god. By modern day, no extraplanar beings (gods or otherwise) fill such roles, so it should not be assumed that an active god is a requirement for a belief system to thrive. It should be remembered that humans developed belief systems before the first extraplanar being crossed through the Between and settled on Earth, and that gods are not required for humans to have a fulfilling spiritual life. Unfortunately, the gods who most need to hear such a reminder are unlikely to listen to the words of a mere human.

Liked this novel?
Subscribe to find out as soon as the sequel,
Demons in Between, is available

Subscribe for email alerts at www.agwitow.ca/subscribe

Check out my other published work by going to www.agwitow.ca/books

Thank you for reading this novel. Please take a moment to leave an honest review for Poseidon's Wrath on Goodreads.com

Other Books by Amanda Witow

The following list was accurate at the time of publication, but new books and short stories are coming out all the time.
Find out as soon as anything is released by going to www.agwitow.ca and subscribing for email alerts.

Legends: Arrephori
Legends: Son of Zeus
Legend's Legacy

Amanda is a nerd, a book lover, a wife, and a ninja.

No seriously. She's a ninja.

She lives with her husband and two cats in windy/sunny/snowy/sweltering Saskatchewan. Despite temperamental weather, she loves it there. In 2012, she graduated with a BA in psychology and classical studies, and has had a love affair with myths and fairy tales since she was a young girl. She is a frequent participant in NaNoWriMo and Camp NaNo, and has "won" many times.

You can sign up for email alerts, or even a selection of awesome newsletters at: www.agwitow.ca/subscribe

Connect with Amanda at:

> www.agwitow.ca
>
> twitter.com/agwitow
>
> agwitow.tumblr.com
>
> www.facebook.com/agwitowbooks
>
> www.instagram.com/agwitow/
>
> Goodreads: goo.gl/jl7Mc2

Katherine doesn't believe in ghosts, but her house is undeniably haunted. As she gets to know her ethereal house-mate, she learns that having a haunted house doesn't have to be all jump scares and property damage. Just as she and Eloise are settling into a comfortable daily rhythm, the young ghost goes missing.

With the help of a medium, Katherine will risk it all to bring Eloise home.

Here is a short preview of Eloise.

In a sleepy little Nova Scotian town, swallowed by the expanding sprawl of Halifax, was a cluster of homes inhabited by young families and students. Despite being newer builds to replace older ones, the houses were all rather shabby. In fact, there was an air of neglect to the entire neighbourhood. No matter how often the residents repainted their fences, tended their gardens, or straightened the eavestroughs, the houses always looked just this side of decrepit. Which was probably why Katherine was able to afford the narrow three-storey home.

Well, that, and the fact that it was haunted.

"Morning, Mrs. Viens," Katherine waved to her elderly next-door-neighbour.

"Ghost still hasn't driven you out yet?" Mrs. Viens cackled. Her grey hair was wrapped up in oversized foam rollers, she wore a faded old sweater beneath bright polka dot overalls, and she cradled a sickly looking potted plant in her arms.

"It's been two months, and I still don't believe in ghosts," she replied.

"Don't say I didn't warn you!"

It was a familiar conversation, and Katherine supposed it would become annoying eventually, but she found the eccentric and energetic old woman endearing. It was nice to have someone care about her when she so far from her own family. And none of the other neighbours liked to socialize much because of the whole 'haunted house' thing.

She waved goodbye and headed out to the main streets to catch a bus to the hole-in-a-wall restaurant she worked at six days a week. It was a soul-crushing job in the way most low-level service industry jobs were, but the owner was a pleasant man and the other servers were all university students like her. It helped her power through when dealing with shitty customers.

The bus was crowded with business people and students whose day started at 8am. She wedged herself between a seat and one of the support bars, pulled out a textbook, and tried to get a bit of studying in.

Halfway through her ride there were enough seats were open that she was able to take an actual seat. It made reading significantly easier.

Quick enough, she pulled the cord for her stop, was off the bus, and moving with the flow of people down the sidewalk. The garish, neon sign of Millie's Diner flashed over the crowd. Katherine ducked down an alley and around to the back of the restaurant. One of the cooks stood outside, sucking back on a cigarette as if it were his last chance at life.

"Morning, Sassy," the cook grunted.

"Already finishing off your first pack of the day, I see," she replied.

The cook laughed and she slipped past him into the kitchen. She knew she'd been told his name, but she couldn't remember what it was and everyone just always called him Hatter. After working there for two years, it was a little late to ask.

Narciso Gallo, the owner, was busy prepping things for the day and he only gave her a brief nod as she continued through the kitchen and out to the restaurant itself. Getting ready to open was a matter of habit by this point, and in what seemed like no time at all, Katherine unlocked the doors.

A few people shuffled in, most of them regulars, and she fell into the usual routine of waiting on tables. A couple hours later, another waiter joined her as the tables filled up and the lunch rush began. By the time it ended, she'd burnt her hand, had a customer shove a plate of 'too crispy bacon' at her with no warning so the plate had fallen and shattered, and been called several sexist slurs.

"God, I hate customers sometimes," Katherine grumbled to Bruce, the other waiter.

He chuckled and put away glasses behind the mini counter that served as the restaurant's bar area. "At least the old men tip 'cause you're pretty. The old women just pinch my ass and expect that to be compensation enough for putting up with their BS."

"I wish Narciso would try and get a younger crowd in," she said.

"Eh, there's jerks in every generation," Bruce said with a shrug. "At least the seniors know it'd be creepy to actually ask us out. Wouldn't have that protection with people our own age."

"Speaking of,"—Katherine nodded her chin toward the door where a pair of young men had just entered—"looks like there's some potential creeps now."

Bruce looked up and then continued to put away glasses. "Oh, nooo… I would take the table, but I'm just soooo busy."

She laughed and stuck her tongue out at him before heading toward the new customers. "Welcome to Millie's Diner, table for two?"

"There's a third who'll be joining us, and we'll need a round of whatever you've got on tap," one of the men said.

Her smile stayed firmly in place as she led them to an empty table, handed them menus, and left to get their drinks. She wasn't hopeful about the manners of people who drank at 2:30pm and ordered their drinks before they'd even sat down. Two plates of dry rib appetizers later, their third friend joined them and ordered a second round of beer for the table.

"What kind of beer do you like to drink, sweetheart?" the new man asked.

"I'm a rum-and-coke kind of girl, I'm afraid," she said, struggling to keep her smile strong. It wasn't that the three men weren't good looking—the latecomer was actually very handsome—but there was something about customers hitting on service workers, regardless of everything else, that made her skin crawl.

"We could be persuaded to switch to the hard stuff, if you'd join us for a drink," one of the others said with a wink.

Katherine forced a laugh. "Would if I could, but it's actually illegal for a server to drink while their on the clock, and my boss is a stickler about that sort of thing."

"Really?" the latecomer asked, his eyebrows shooting up. "I've never heard of that before."

She nodded. "Yeah, I know. A lot of places are willing to look the other way, so not even all servers realize."

"Huh…"

"So, a round of beer for you three?"

They nodded and she slipped away, thankful they hadn't pressed her further about her lie. It was a long hour and a half before the trio finished and were ready to pay their bill. She endured a few more crude come-ons with an increasingly brittle smile before everything was squared. "Thank you," she told them. "Enjoy your day."

"You too, sweetheart," the latecomer said with a smile that would've been charming if she wasn't his server. "If you'd like to go out sometime, give me a call."

He slid a business card across the till counter and she picked it up more out of surprise than any real desire to have his number. It was an off-white that couldn't quite claim to be cream-coloured, with black curling script. Nathan Thomas, paranormal investigator.

"Paranormal investigator?" she blurted, her cheeks burning as she looked up from the card to meet his gaze.

"I investigate claims of hauntings, possessions, and that sort of thing. And when I find them, I get rid of them," he explained.

She blinked, unsure if he was joking or not. "I...see..."

"Call me, sweetheart, and I'll show you all the best haunted places in Halifax."

Katherine watched him leave with a mix of disbelief and revulsion.

Bruce stepped up beside her with an incredulous look on his face. "Did he actually just say he was a ghost hunter?"

"Yes."

He whistled. "You really do get the weird ones, don't'cha?"

She just groaned.

"Didn't you tell me your house was haunted, though? Maybe it's Fate."

Katherine laughed. "My neighbour thinks it's haunted. I think the cupboards just need to be fixed."

"Too bad he wasn't a carpenter then, huh?"

"...in fields and by the roads, I saw on all sides men and animals—like statues—turned to flinty stone at sight of dread Medusa's visage..."

Medusa has been vilified in myth and legend throughout history. A monster justly slain by the heroic Perseus. But there is more to her story than what the myths said.

Medusa joined the temple of Athena, eager to serve, only to be turned out when she was most in need of help. Cursed and hunted, she fled Athens and everything she had ever known. This is her full story.

Here is a short preview of Legends: Arrephori

Sweet child,
beautiful girl,
sleep now, my love.

Come my beautiful girls, let me tell you of your grandmother. The memory of men has already marred her reputation beyond repair, but we, her descendants, will remember the truth. We will always remember who Medusa really was.

Many years ago, your grandmother lived in a small city. She came from a family of warriors and merchants. Although Athens was just beginning to rise in importance among the city-states of Hellas, it saw much trade and much war. This brought wealth and prosperity to Medusa's family, and she grew up among luxuries. Yet, she was the youngest daughter and so was to be sent to a temple.

Even at seven years old, Medusa was already lovely. Her skin was pale and hair a deep auburn that burned gold in the sun. Neighbours said a child as lovely as she must surely be given to Aphrodite, but her parents owed their fortune to the patron goddess of the city. So Medusa was sent to join the young maidens, the Arrephoroi, in service to the goddess.

"Bring the baskets, girl," a priestess instructed.

"Yes, priestess," Medusa answered. She lifted a heavy basket above her head, straining to keep it steady. Once it was balanced, she asked, "Why do we bring gifts from the temple to Poseidon's spring?"

"Do you remember the story of how Athena became the patron goddess of our city?" the priestess asked.

Medusa nodded and then struggled to keep the basket from spilling. "Poseidon offered our forefathers a salt spring while Athena offered an olive tree."

"Yes, that is right. Every year, two young maidens carry secret gifts down to the spring to honour Poseidon. That is what you are carrying," the priestess explained.

Medusa thought on what she had been told, but yearned to know more. "Why must we honour Poseidon when we are in service to Athena?"

The priestess chuckled. "You are the most curious Arrephori I have ever met. We honour Poseidon as thanks for his gift—even if our forefathers chose Athena's instead."

With her questions answered, Medusa followed the priestess's instructions without protest. Thus did her service to the goddess begin.

Legends: Son of Zeus

a Legend's Legacy short story

Amanda Witow

"...valiant Perseus, pray tell the story of the deed, that all may know, and what the arts and power prevailed, when you struck off the serpent-covered head..."

Years after Perseus slayed the monstrous Medusa, he calls his family together and reveals the shame he has carried ever since that fateful quest--he slew Medusa, but not her daughter. Now the task must pass to some of his youngest descendants, but it is a decision that will have consequences Perseus could never have foreseen.

Here is a short preview of Legends: Son of Zeus

The throne room was cold.

No fire burned in the hearth.

Damp sea air whispered through the windows—a not-so-gentle reminder of the changing season. Red and gold sunlight filled the long room, dancing across the crowd gathered there.

Perseus regarded his children and their children. Almost all of them had come when he called for them. From his eldest son, down to the two eight-year-old boys born to the children of his fifth son. Only the babes and nursing women were missing.

He studied the young boys as his family waited with varying degrees of patience. The boys were so similar they might have been twins. They returned his scrutiny with solemn eyes.

Eyes that were echoes of Andromeda's.

Perseus pushed aside the ache he still felt three years after she had passed on to Hades.

Every face in the room held some reminder of her. Some small legacy of her beauty and strength.

Yet many of them had started legacies of their own. In fifty years—even in twenty—her legacy would fade from memory. As would his own, unless his family would carry it forward.

"Thank you for coming. I'm sure you are all curious why I sent for you." He paused and regarded the faces before him. *Will they do as I ask?* "I wish to discuss the gorgon."

One of his sons' sons scoffed.

Loudly.

The man had vibrant red hair constrained by a beaten gold crown. His skin was the colour of faded leather and his square jaw had a stubborn cast. But his shoulders were curled and hands soft. A name danced just beyond reach. *Amphitryon. Alikaios's only son.*

"We all know the story of how you slew the monstrous Medusa, forefather." Amphitryon gestured at the numerous tapestries around the room. Each depicted a different stage of Perseus's heroic adventure when he was a boy of sixteen.

"I have a kingdom and worries of my own," Amphitryon continued. "I do not have time to listen to an old man muse about his glory days."

Alikaios clicked his tongue. "Be civil, Amphitryon. What would your mother think?"

"Nothing. She has been dead for several years."

"Have a care how you speak of the dead, brother," Anaxo warned. She did not look much like her brother or father, and Perseus would not have been able to put a name to her face if she hadn't spoken. "The gods may take offence to such disrespect."

Amphitryon snorted. "The gods have been no friend to me."

"They have laid the foundation for this family's success, and protected us over the years. I will hear no disrespect of them in my hall," Perseus thundered.

Amphitryon's brow furrowed and he opened his mouth to speak. He closed it with a sharp click and spread a glower around the room before he turned on his heel and stormed out.

A heavy silence replaced him.

The two boys broke the quiet with their soft whispers. One was dark, and the other light, but they both had Andromeda's eyes.

"Come here, boys," Perseus ordered.

"Forefather, they're still young," a pregnant woman interjected.

"I know"—he paused until he could recall her name—"Damara. I wish them to join me, not to chastize them."

She pressed a light kiss on her son's head before sending both boys up the dais. Her skin was almost as dark as Andromeda's had been, but her hair and eyes were too different for her to be a living ghost. Perseus's heart was both saddened and relieved.

The boys stopped in front of his throne and waited with their hands clasped behind their backs. He could tell they were trying not to fidget—they weren't entirely successful.

Perseus smiled at them. "What are your names, my boys?"

"I'm Zander," the pale one said.

"Cleatus," the dark one said.

Perseus gestured for them to come closer. They shuffled forward.

"Come now, don't be frightened," he said. He lifted Zander to sit on a wide arm of the throne. Cleatus was quick to climb up on the other arm.

"I'm not frightened of anything," Zander informed him.

"Is that so?" Perseus chuckled. "And what about you, Cleatus? Are you unafraid?"

Cleatus bit his lip and shook his head.

"Come now, speak up," Persues cajoled.

"Sorry, forefather," Cleatus said softly. "There are many things that frighten me. Father says I will never be a hero if I am always frightened."

For Want of a Breath

Amanda Witow

A water spirit responds to the tears of a young, abused girl. Their friendship isn't conventional, but it is strong and lasting. As the girl grows into a young woman, the friendship becomes something more.

Trigger Warning: abuse

Here is a short preview of For Want of a Breath.

Far from the watchful eyes of man, beneath the wind-kissed waves of the sea, there are mysterious creatures. Born of the sea, and capable of great magic, they are to be feared and respected. Few men have ever caught more than a distant glimpse of them, and even fewer have lived to tell the tale. Yet stories are spread far and wide of these sea-dwelling beings.

Some say they look almost human, if it weren't for the scales and long tail in place of their legs. Others claim they more closely resemble the dolphins that frolick in the wake of ships. I can tell you that neither is truly accurate. Nor can my simple words convey the feeling of seeing one for the first time.

I was young, still a girl, when I met Selyna. Her words to me are a treasure I will always carry in my heart.

"Why do you cry, *kapuros?*"

My heart thudded in my throat and I looked up to see her staring at me. Her eyes were dark with flecks of silver, like the bottom of a well reflecting the stars on a cloudless night, and her skin a deep blue-grey. Even without her odd colouring, I would have known she wasn't human by the way she fit together. Her neck was slightly too long, her arms a little short, hands webbed with elongated fingers, and her torso was narrower at the top.

"Please do not hurt me, water spirit," I begged.

She stared at me for what felt like an eternity before asking, "Why would I hurt you? Have you forgotten to pour out an offering to the sea before leaving on a long voyage? Have you harmed a creature of the sea for reasons other than food or survival? Or worst of all, have you broken trust with one of my kin?"

"None of those, water spirit," I replied, brushing away my tears. "But all my life I have heard stories about you. About how your kind can bring great gifts, or great sorrow. And that there is nothing we humans can do."

The water spirit threw her head back and laughed. The sound was like bells in a fog, distant and muffled, but clear and beautiful all the same. When her laughter subsided she gave me a grin. It was full of dangerously sharp teeth, and yet, my fear melted beneath its warmth.

"I will never tire of the stories the *kapuros* tell of us."

"What is the truth, then?" I asked.

"Truth is a fickle thing to give. Mine may not be the same as yours, and yours may not be the same as anyone else. I can tell you that I have never harmed someone that was innocent in the eyes of the sea," she said.

I nodded. I understood well what she meant. My mother always said I was a lazy, selfish, ungrateful child. It was the reason she hit me so often. But no matter how hard I worked, or how little I asked for, or even how often I thanked her, she never saw me as anything else. Her truth and mine were very different things.

"Will you tell me now, why you were crying?" she asked.

"I did not fetch water from the well quick enough."

Her head tilted and she frowned, a crease forming between her brows. "Did you stop to play in the midst of your task?"

I shook my head. "I hurried as quickly as I could, but it wasn't fast enough."

"You will become faster as you grow older and stronger. It is no reason to cry, little *kapuros*." She reached for my hand and gave it a gentle squeeze. Her skin was rough, like burlap, and surprisingly warm.

"My mother does not believe I will ever become faster. She says I am a lazy child and hits me to teach me to be better," I explained. "I wouldn't normally cry at my punishment, but today she hit me harder than she ever has before."

The water spirit's eyes narrowed and her lip curled back. "Your mother should not hit you."

I shrugged. "She is my mother, and is trying to teach me to be a better child. I do try my best, but it never seems to be enough. Some day I will make her proud."

"If I could leave the sea, I would tear your mother apart," she snarled.

"No! She is my mother! I love her!"

She jerked back from me as if I'd struck her, and fear filled me so completely that I couldn't move. I was sure she was offended and would lash out at me. Part of me wanted her to drag me beneath the waves. The cold water would wash away my pain, and I would never have to face my mother's anger again.

Guilt brought fresh tears to my eyes.

"Hush, little one," she said, running her rough hands over my hair and down my back. "I will not hurt her, if you do not wish me to. And I will never harm you."

I hiccuped and scrubbed my eyes with the heels of my hands. "I am a bad child. My mother is right to hit me."

"No, little one," she said, pulling me against her. "A mother should never hurt her children. A mother should protect her children from harm."

I let myself cry against her shoulder until I was exhausted, and she simply held me and hummed a tune I have no name for. When I was finished, she kissed the top of my head and let me go.

"There now. Do you feel better?"

I nodded and she smiled. She brushed a tear off my cheek and I hardly noticed the roughness of her hand.

"Let us make a deal," she offered.

I bit my lip. The stories said making deals with water spirits was a dangerous thing to do. She had been nothing but kind to me, but it was hard to quiet the fear the fishermen's tales bred. She must have known what I was thinking, for she assured me once more that she would never harm me. Finally, I agreed.

"Every time you are hurt, by your mother or someone else, you can come to the shore and call for me. I will come to you and ease your pain," she explained.

"What would I owe you for such kindness?" I asked.

She drummed her fingers against the stoney shore as she thought. "You must bring me a stone with a hole in the centre of it every time you call for me."

I thought about her offer. I desperately wanted to see her again, though I couldn't shake the guilt I felt for wanting to cry on her shoulder. Her cost was simple. All the girls in the village would spend their free time hunting for such stones to make bracelets out of. Not that I had ever been allowed to engage in such a frivolous pastime.

"I'll bring the stones. How do I call you?"

"Simply come to the shore, any shore, and say my name. Selyna. I will hear, and I will come to you."

And with that, she slipped back into the sea. I sat on the shore for some time after, wondering if I had imagined meeting her, but my heart said she was real. I had met a water spirit and lived to tell of it.

Keep an eye out for these exciting titles,
slated for release in 2019

An anthology of stories originally shared on agwitow.tumblr.com in a wide variety of genres and styles. Each story has been lovingly revised and expanded, and several brand-new, never-seen-before, short stories are mixed amongst classics like *The Last Student of Eva Yllamorel*, *The Wayward Soul*, and *Herbs for Brown-Thumbed Witches*.

Familiar's Mark
A Fantasy Short Story

Amanda Witow

Following a devastating accident, an amnesiac cat must rely on the kindness of a strange woman to find his mage...and fix the mage's mistake before it's too late.

MODDERS
A SCI FI SHORT STORY
Amanda Witow

Kyle is a six-year-old boy from a small community mostly made up of Pures. It's all he's ever known.

He knows that Augs and Modders live in the cities, and Modders—with their metal limbs, and wires in their skin—are dangerous. But a trip to the city with his father will change everything.